"The plot delivers just the right amount of emotional punch and happily ever after."

—*Publishers Weekly* on *Lone Star Christmas*

"Clear off space on your keeper shelf, Fossen has arrived."
—*New York Times* bestselling author Lori Wilde

"A marvelous Christmas romance novel, a fantastic family saga, and a deliciously desirous addition to the beloved series!"

—*Books and Spoons* on *Lone Star Christmas*

"An amazing, breathtaking and vastly entertaining family saga, filled with twists and unexpected turns. Cowboy fiction at its best."

—*Books and Spoons* on *The Last Rodeo*

"Fossen certainly knows how to write a hot cowboy, and when she turns her focus to Dylan Granger…crank up the air conditioning!"

—*RT Book Reviews* on *Lone Star Blues*

"Overall, this romance is a little sweet and a little salty—and a lot sexy!"

—*RT Book Reviews* on *Texas-Sized Trouble*

"This is much more than a romance."
—*RT Book Reviews* on *Branded as Trouble*

"Nicky and Garrett have sizzling chemistry!"
—*RT Book Reviews* on *No Getting Over a Cowboy*

"Delores Fossen takes you on a wild Texas ride with a hot cowboy."

—*New York Times* bestselling author B.J. Daniels

Also available from Delores Fossen and HQN Books

Coldwater Texas

Lone Star Christmas
Lone Star Midnight (ebook novella)
Hot Texas Sunrise
Texas at Dusk (ebook novella)
Sweet Summer Sunset
A Coldwater Christmas

Wrangler's Creek

Lone Star Cowboy (ebook novella)
Those Texas Nights
One Good Cowboy (ebook novella)
No Getting Over a Cowboy
Just Like a Cowboy (ebook novella)
Branded as Trouble
Cowboy Dreaming (ebook novella)
Texas-Sized Trouble
Cowboy Heartbreaker (ebook novella)
Lone Star Blues
Cowboy Blues (ebook novella)
The Last Rodeo

The McCord Brothers

What Happens on the Ranch (ebook novella)
Texas on My Mind
Cowboy Trouble (ebook novella)
Lone Star Nights
Cowboy Underneath It All (ebook novella)
Blame It on the Cowboy

To see the complete list of titles available from Delores Fossen, please visit www.deloresfossen.com.

DELORES FOSSEN

A COLDWATER
Christmas

HQN™

HQN™

ISBN-13: 978-1-335-50496-8

A Coldwater Christmas

Copyright © 2019 by Delores Fossen

Recycling programs
for this product may
not exist in your area.

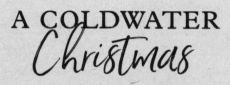

A COLDWATER
Christmas

CHAPTER ONE

WATCHING FROM THE window of the police station, Sheriff Kace Laramie wasn't sure if he should deal first with the senior citizen flasher, the traffic violation or the whizzing longhorn.

As a cop in a small ranching town like Cold water, Texas, Kace didn't usually have to pick between wrongdoings and disturbances, but apparently today they were experiencing a sort of crime wave.

When he saw the flasher, Gopher Tate, reach to unbutton his ratty raincoat, Kace moved him up to the number one spot of which situation should get his attention. There wasn't anyone around Gopher, and the man never flashed a full monty, especially in winter, but Kace didn't want anyone shocked or complaining if they got a glimpse of Gopher's tighty-whities covering his wrinkled junk.

"Liberty," Kace called out to Deputy Liberty Cassaine as he pulled on his jacket and hat and then headed out the door of the police station. "Go after that idiot who just blew through the red light. Red Porsche, Oklahoma plates."

No need for Kace to specify which light, since there was only one, and it was on Main Street, right in front of the police station. It was also next to the clearly marked sign with the posted speed limit of 30 mph. By Kace's estimate, the guy wasn't exactly speeding, but the light had been red.

Liberty leaped up from her desk in the squad room, crammed the rest of a goo-loaded sticky bun into her mouth and hurried out to the cruiser in the parking lot next to the building. Kace went across the street to deal with Gopher.

As Kace walked, he gave the pissing longhorn a glance. Like the rest of Coldwater, it was a familiar sight. It belonged to the librarian, Esther Benton, who affectionately called the bull Petunia.

Petunia had a fondness for breaking fence, wandering onto Main Street and disrupting traffic. Today though, the bull wasn't in the street but rather had taken to the sidewalk, working its way through the dancing Santas, glittering candy canes, and other assorted decorations that the town and business owners had set out for Christmas. Those particular items had only been in place for a couple of hours and had replaced the gobbling turkeys and cardboard cornucopias from Thanksgiving. In a month—specifically December 26—the Christmas decor would be boxed up, and the New Year's stuff would be set out.

Coldwater had no shortage of overly done spangles, adornments of questionable taste and downright tacky holiday plastic.

Kace gave Petunia another glance to make sure the longhorn hadn't moved. It hadn't. It was now underneath the awning of the taxidermist's shop, Much

Ado about Stuffing, and it had pissed a puddle deep enough to drown an alley cat.

Apparently, hydration wasn't an issue for Petunia.

Once Kace had finished with Gopher, he'd need to get the longhorn moving, call Esther and tell the woman she'd need to pay for another cleanup. Ironically, Gopher often did janitorial services for the town so Kace would be tapping the man for the job if he didn't have to arrest him first.

Gopher still had hold of the sides of his raincoat, but his grip dropped away when he spotted Kace. "You gonna arrest me?" Gopher asked, making it sound as much a challenge as a question.

"Depends. You got a good explanation as to why you're on Main Street wearing a raincoat when there's not a chance of rain in the forecast?"

Gopher's forehead bunched up as if giving that some thought, and he glanced up at the cloudless blue sky. "I like to be ready in case there's a change in the weather."

Well, it was an explanation all right, but it wasn't an especially good one. "You've got two choices, Gopher. Come with me to the jail or button up that raincoat and clean up after Petunia."

Gopher contemplated that, too. "But I got a different color bow on today, and nobody's had a chance to see it."

Since that bow, whatever color it was, would be tied around Gopher's junk, Kace didn't intend to give the man an audience. "Choose wisely," Kace advised him. "Cleanup or lockup."

"Cleanup," Gopher finally grumbled, and he continued to grumble while he got busy buttoning the raincoat.

With that task ticked off his to-do list, Kace turned toward Petunia. He took off his cowboy hat to smack the bull on the butt, but he stopped in mid-whack when Gopher spoke again.

"Say, ain't that your wife over yonder?" Gopher asked.

That got Kace's complete attention, and he followed Gopher's gaze across the street. Specifically, to the parking lot of the police station, where he spotted the tall blonde getting out of a silver SUV. Not easily getting out, either. She was taking a wriggling, fussing baby from the infant seat in the back, and the kid wasn't cooperating.

But, yeah, it was January Parker all right. *Jana.*

"My ex-wife," Kace corrected.

And because Jana had been his ex for fifteen years, that correction just slid right off his tongue. Of course, Kace had seen her more than a time or two since then, whenever she'd visited her mother, Eileen, who still lived in Coldwater. Jana, however, lived about an hour away on a ranch near Blanco.

"Didn't know she had a kid," Gopher remarked.

Kace knew. Gossip about Jana just seemed to stick in his mind even when he would have preferred that it didn't. Last he'd heard, Jana had had a daughter, and judging from the blond curls haloing the baby's face, this was her child. Kace guessed she was about a year and a half old. Also, last he'd heard, Jana was divorced or in the process of divorcing husband number two.

"Jana always did fill out a pair of jeans," Gopher commented. "A little more of her to fill them out these days, but the years have settled just fine on her."

Kace scowled at the man, but there was no way he could deny such an observation even if it had come from Gopher. Jana did indeed have an ass that got noticed, and apparently childbirth hadn't affected that part of her anatomy. Kace could see that firsthand because of the way Jana was leaning into the back seat. The maneuver caused her jeans-clad butt to be aimed in their direction, and the short waist jacket she was wearing did nothing to conceal it.

Jana finally managed to hoist the toddler out of the infant seat and onto her hip. The kid didn't care much for that, either, because she kicked her legs, threw back her head and let out a wail loud enough to start a stampede. Jana ignored that and started walking. She didn't glance across the street at Gopher and him but rather kept her attention pinned to the police station.

"It appears Jana's about to pay you a visit," Gopher added.

Gopher was a wellspring of information today. Jana was indeed headed for the police station. Maybe not specifically to see him, though. She could be going inside to file some kind of complaint or report a crime. That didn't help the knot that was already forming in Kace's stomach.

Kace silently cursed. He'd been divorced from Jana plenty long enough not to feel the punch of attraction whenever he looked at her. Thankfully, the lust was tempered with the memories of their godawful marriage. Of course, plenty would say it was a marriage that should have never happened in the first place. Jana's mom definitely felt that way, and Eileen had made it her mission in life to see that their wedded "bliss" ended as fast as she could manage it.

Fourteen months and three days.

That's how long it'd taken Jana to cave into Eileen's demands that she divorce her "cowboy husband" and find someone more suitable for their tax bracket and social standing. Eileen might have been a local, but she had always set herself apart from the rest of Coldwater, what with her sprawling house, fancy cars and snobbish ways.

Unlike Eileen though, Jana wasn't into fancy. Those great-fitting jeans weren't a fashion statement. Neither were the cowboy boots. From everything he'd heard, Jana raised horses and did a lot of the hands-on work herself. Apparently, Eileen hadn't been able to pressure her into giving that up and becoming a socialite.

"I'd best go see what she wants," Kace muttered when Jana finally made it inside the police station, but he shot Gopher one last warning glare. "Keep the raincoat closed and get started on cleaning up after the longhorn." Whether Gopher would actually do that was anyone's guess so Kace would have to keep an eye on him.

Kace's phone rang just as he started across the street, and he answered it when he saw Liberty's name on the screen.

"Uh, Kace," Liberty said right away. "This guy I pulled over for blowing through the red light says he knows you."

Absently, Kace considered the license plates that'd been on the Porsche. He knew plenty of people from Oklahoma, but he hadn't recognized the car. Nor had he gotten a look at the driver.

"That's not going to get him out of a ticket," Kace insisted.

"He's not trying to get out of that," Liberty explained, and then she paused. Paused long enough that Kace had time to get to the police station. "Uh, he says he's your father."

Kace stopped, and his hand froze in midreach for the door. He already had the knot in his stomach from seeing Jana, but what he felt now was like being showered with knots.

"Kace?" Liberty said. "You still there?"

"Yeah," Kace managed, though he wasn't sure where he got the air to speak. His lungs and throat had clamped shut. Too bad there wasn't a lock on the hellish memories from his past.

A past that his so-called father had created.

"According to his driver's license," Liberty went on, "his name is Peter Laramie."

Liberty didn't ask if that was really his father's name. Kace's late mother had called him Petey. Well, she had done that when she hadn't been calling him a sonofabitch and other assorted obscenities.

"He's fifty-four and from Lawton, Oklahoma," Liberty added.

Despite the tornado going on in his head, Kace did the math. His father had been just nineteen when Kace was born. Young. But not so young that he hadn't gotten married and fathered three more sons. Of course, it hadn't taken more than a signature on a license and some sperm to accomplish those things.

"Kace, you okay?" Liberty asked.

"Fine." And he gathered as much breath as he could manage. "Write him the ticket," Kace instructed, and he hit the end call button.

If his father was in town to see him and his three younger brothers, then he'd find them soon enough. Anyone in Coldwater knew where to locate Judd, Callen, Nico and him.

Kace put his phone in the pocket of his jeans, dragged in another breath and went inside to face Jana. He didn't have to look for her. Kace just followed the fussy sounds of the baby. Sounds that led him straight to his office.

Apparently, Jana had indeed come to see him. This was going to be his day for not only a small-town crime wave but also for surprises that weren't of the good variety. So far, Jana was running second in the surprise department, though. Nothing was going to beat Peter Laramie cruising into town.

Ginger Monroe, the receptionist/dispatcher, was at her desk, and she had one of her unnaturally red eyebrows raised to a questioning arch while she volleyed glances between Jana and him. Kace was always a little perplexed when Ginger made that expression or any other one for that matter because she wore her makeup so thick that it coated her face like a mask. Still, she managed to convey not only some amazement but also intense curiosity.

Kace had some intense curiosity of his own.

"You got a visitor," Ginger said in the same tone she would have informed him of a persistent fungus in the bathroom.

Ginger's reaction was what he'd expected. After the divorce, the town had taken sides, and most folks had sided with Kace. Of course, Ginger did work for him so that might have played into her decision-making process. As for the rest of the town, Kace figured that folks thought he'd been screwed over by Eileen and also by her daughter, who hadn't had the gumption to stand up to her mother.

"Jana didn't say what she wanted," Ginger added, using more of that fungal tone.

Well, Kace would soon find out. Pushing aside the rest of his childhood memories and memories of the divorce, he went in to find out why Jana was here. The odds were that their conversation wouldn't be private. Heck, it might not even be heard because of the baby's loud cries, but even if Jana and he managed a whispered chat, the content would soon get around. Kace suspected that Ginger and maybe some of his deputies had taken up lipreading.

Kace took off his cowboy hat and coat and put

them on the wall pegs when he went into his office. "Jana," he greeted.

Thankfully, he managed to keep his voice in check. Hard to do though now that he was face-to-face with her.

As usual, the front side of her looked as good as the back even though her ponytail was a little mussed, and her expression was frazzled and weary. Kace figured the squirming kid was responsible for most of that, but this visit was likely part of it as well. Unless it was for a social visit, and this clearly wouldn't be, most people got stressed being in a police station.

The little girl yanked off her pink jingle bell cap as if it were the thing that'd pissed her off. She let out another loud wail and reached for him. Kace didn't reach back, but that didn't stop the kid from practically lunging out of Jana's grip. The motion unbalanced Jana, and if Kace hadn't caught onto the baby, both of them would have likely landed against him. The baby took advantage of the near mishap and vised her little arms around Kace's neck. She also hushed.

Suddenly, it was quiet enough that even a whisper could have been heard, but it didn't last. The moment Kace tried to hand the little girl back to Jana, the kid started to squeal again. This time, Kace got smacked in the face with that pink hat, and he took some blows from her little kicking feet. For someone whose tiny boots were four inches long, tops, she packed the wallop of an angry mule.

"No! No! No!" she shrieked, and the moment Jana quit trying to tug her from Kace, the kid hushed again. Complete silence that had both Jana and him checking her. Kace could feel her still breathing, but that was the only sound she was making.

Jana gave a weary sigh and pushed some stray strands of her hair from her face. "Marley's teething, and she missed her nap."

Well, that explained the crappy mood, but it didn't address why she'd quieted down in Kace's arms. Or why the kid settled her head against his shoulder as if she belonged there. Of course, none of that hit the number one spot of Kace's questions about this situation.

Why the heck was Jana here?

"Could you please just hold her while we talk?" Jana asked.

She certainly wasn't looking at him. That's because she was fishing around in the huge diaper bag that she'd set on his desk, and she pulled out a bottle of water. Jana guzzled some as if she'd been crawling through the Mojave for days, and then she sank down into one of the chairs.

Kace didn't especially want to hold the kid. He didn't have much experience doing that sort of thing and wasn't sure he was doing it right. Plus, Ginger would no doubt spread some kind of gossip about this that would get back to Belinda Darlington, the woman he sometimes dated. Belinda seemed to live on the eternal hope that Kace would change his mind about marriage and fatherhood and would make those changes with her.

He wouldn't.

Ever.

But if Belinda got wind of his holding Jana's daughter, then that might fuel some jealousy and hope that Kace didn't want Belinda to have. Still, if he handed Marley back to Jana, then the crying might start up again. Jana looked as if she clearly needed a break from that, and it would help speed things along.

Marley must have been resigned to the current situation, too, because she cuddled the hat against her like a blanket, stuck her thumb in her mouth and started sucking. Kace could practically feel the kid's muscles go slack.

"Thank you," Jana muttered. After drinking more water, she looked up at him with her intense blue eyes.

Eyes that could apparently still do a number on him.

Like her butt, those baby blues gave him a few tugs on the heartstrings. So did her mouth, but it tugged at a different part of him. That mouth had always been a hot spot for him. Kace silently cursed himself for recalling that and shoved that notion aside.

"Marley's always cranky when she gets back from visits with her dad," Jana went on.

Visits, as in a custody thing, and even though he tried to stop his attention from going to her left hand, he looked anyway. No wedding ring. That must mean the divorce was final.

"Since I doubt you brought your daughter in so I could arrest her for extreme crankiness, care to explain why you're here?" he prompted, making sure he sounded and looked like a cop.

Of course, his stern demeanor was somewhat diminished by the fact he was holding a thumb-sucking baby wearing pink overalls and tasseled cowboy boots. Plus, Marley's wispy curls kept landing on his mouth, and he had to blow them away since they were tickling him.

Jana nodded and gave another sigh, but she didn't say anything until she'd stood and met him eye to eye. "Kace, we have to stop this wedding."

He was sure he blinked twice, and Kace searched back through his memory to see if he'd missed something. "Are you talking about my brother?"

Because that was the only wedding Kace knew anything about. His brother Judd and his fiancée, Cleo, would be having a small private ceremony once they set an actual date, but there was no reason for Kace or anyone else to stop it. Judd and Cleo had been in love since they were teenagers so nobody would question why they were taking the "I do" plunge.

Jana pulled back her shoulders, shook her head. "You haven't heard?"

Well, hell. That gave him a new jolt of concern. "Heard what?"

She stared at him. Really stared. And she mouthed

some profanity. "I just assumed your father had told you."

Now, that wasn't just a jolt. It was more like an avalanche. "Told me what," Kace snarled.

Jana's hands went onto her hips. "Your father asked my mother to marry him, and she said yes. They're making plans for a wedding, Kace." Her eyes narrowed to fiery slits. "Plans that you and I are going to stop."

CHAPTER TWO

JANA HADN'T BEEN SURE how Kace would react to her visit, but she hadn't expected this stunned silence layered with a hefty dose of skepticism. She'd thought he had known about their parents' *relationship*.

Apparently not, though.

And that meant she was going to have to fill him in.

By the time she was done, Kace would likely be as riled as she was. Well, maybe he would be. Kace had never cared much for her mother, and unless something drastic had changed, he'd cared even less for his father. Still, if there was anyone who would be on her side for stopping this wedding, it would be Kace. He of all people knew what his father was.

With Marley still in his arms, Kace just stared at her, obviously waiting for her to explain the bombshell she'd just delivered. She briefly considered taking Marley from him before she launched into the talk, but this was the first time in the past half hour that her daughter hadn't been crying or fussing. Marley looked perfectly at peace with her cheek squished against Kace's shoulder, and she was actually falling asleep. Even if it was, well, unsettling to see Kace holding her, Jana decided to take unsettling over the disruption.

"Your father hasn't been in touch with you?" Jana asked.

"No." And since Kace had practically growled that answer through clenched teeth, it let Jana know that he felt the same way about Peter Laramie as he had years ago when Kace and she had been together. Of course, some of the venom in his tone was likely for her. He still carried a lot of resentment over their divorce.

Welcome to the club.

She had resentment, too, but Jana aimed most of that particular feeling at herself. *Most.* The rest was for her mother.

"I haven't spoken a word to my father since he walked out on his family when I was about ten years old," Kace added.

So, no contact for a very long time, considering that Kace was now thirty-five. That no contact surprised her because Jana had assumed that Peter had visited her mother here in Coldwater. Even if he had, it was possible no one had noticed him because her mother's house was so far out of town.

"I just assumed you'd kept tabs on him or something," she commented.

"No need. He lost any importance to me when he left." He added a shrug that she suspected was meant to convince her that he didn't care about this one way or the other. And maybe that was partly true. But there was importance because of the mark the man had left on his children.

"Your father's here in Coldwater right now," Jana told him.

Kace nodded. "Deputy Cassaine just informed me of that when she wrote him a traffic ticket. But I haven't seen him. Nor do I have any intentions of seeing or talking to him."

Jana groaned. *Not good.* She needed Kace on her side about this. This upcoming marriage had disaster written all over it.

Kace glanced down at Marley, who was sleeping now. That seemed to be his cue to hand her back to Jana, and thank goodness the baby remained sleeping while he did.

Without the "baby shield" and the commotion of Marley's fussing, Jana got her first good look at Kace. A look she hadn't gotten in a couple of years, and even then it had been a glimpse from a distance as she'd driven through town and spotted him.

It was no glimpse today, though.

He was right there in front of her, only inches away, and Jana had no trouble seeing those ice-gray eyes. Cop's eyes that could make you feel as if you'd committed a felony or two. Once though, they had made her feel something totally different.

The curl of heat flickered inside her. It always did when it came to Kace. Which was totally reasonable. He was tall, dark and hot with that black hair and warrior's face. Well, a *pretty* warrior's face anyway. Kace would hate to know that he could have been mistaken for a model in those snug Wranglers and great-fitting dark gray shirt. He would equally hate that some of the women in town had dubbed him Deputy Tight-Buns when he'd first pinned on a badge.

He cleared his throat, just a quick brusque sound to remind her that she was staring at him and he was still waiting for her to get on with her explanation. Jana decided to summarize things for him.

"I believe your father is a gold-digging SOB with a slime streak several miles long."

Kace lifted his shoulder. "And your point would be?" he asked, clearly not disagreeing with her.

Jana gently rocked Marley so that she wouldn't wake up while she got to the *point*. "A couple of months ago, Peter met my mother at a party given by their mutual friends in San Antonio. They've basically carried on since then. Yesterday, he asked her to marry him, and she said yes."

Jana had tried to explain what was going on without adding any emotion to it. Hard to do though when it riled her to the core.

"Eileen knows that he's my father?" Kace asked.

Jana nodded. "I ran a background check on him and gave her everything I learned. She knows that he abandoned his family. Abandoned *you*," she emphasized. "She knows that his leaving eventually led to your mother's overdose on drugs, which then led to you and your brothers being placed in foster care."

Hellish foster care in some instances. Kace's younger brothers, Callen and Nico, had nearly been killed at the hands of a monster who'd been their foster mother's boyfriend.

And Jana knew that Kace blamed himself for it.

It wasn't logical for him to do that, but he was the oldest and therefore had put that on his shoulders. Thankfully, Kace and his brothers had eventually ended up here in Coldwater, where they'd gotten a prizewinning foster father, Buck McCall. Buck had given the boys love and stability. A home. But Jana knew all of them carried the emotional scars from their past.

A past that Peter Laramie had set into motion by leaving.

Kace huffed and put his hands on his hips. "You believe Peter committed some kind of crime, maybe even blackmailed your mother into becoming engaged to him?"

"No, but I believe he *will* commit a crime," Jana blurted out but then stopped. "I believe he's capable of committing a crime," she amended, "and I'm sure you feel the same way."

He tapped his badge. "I tend to need some kind of evidence before I arrest a person. The law's just funny that way."

The frustration quickly replaced that coil of attraction. "His past is all the evidence you need. He spent time in jail."

Judging from Kace's slight shift in posture, he hadn't known about that, and it prompted her to reach into the diaper bag and take out the two-page background report that Jana had hired a PI to do on the man. Kace kept his eyes connected with hers for several long moments before he took it.

"He served six months for drug possession," Jana pointed out though there was no way Kace could miss it. She'd literally highlighted it.

"Twenty-four years ago," Kace said as he read through the report. "That was about a year after he left my mother."

Jana heard the judgment in his tone. Twenty-four years was a lifetime ago, and he hadn't had a repeat offense. That still didn't make him a good guy. Jana could feel his sliminess all the way down to the marrow of her bones. And she didn't think she felt that way about him solely because he'd ditched his family and spurred the problems Kace and his brothers had gone through.

"He lists his occupation as an artist, and he owns a shop called What-Knots," Kace added, still reading.

"A junk store with a so-called art gallery attached," she corrected. "And *artist* is a very subjective term. Anyone with a paintbrush could call themselves that."

Kace made a sound that could have meant anything, but she didn't think it was one of agreement. He continued to scan through the rest of the report that included the man's divorce from Kace's mother along with his previous residences in Texas and Oklahoma. What it didn't include was a single instance where he'd ever attempted to contact any of his sons. That only added to his sleazeball label as far as Jana was concerned.

"He doesn't seem like the sort of man Eileen would marry," Kace commented, his attention still on the report. "He's got the money, but he doesn't travel in her social circles."

"Exactly!" Jana agreed.

Though some would see that as a plus for Peter. Jana loved her mother—most of the time anyway—but no one could ever accuse Eileen of having a common touch. Not until recently anyway. Her mother was going through, well, changes, and while some of those weren't all bad, this marriage was.

"But opposites can and do attract," Kace said. This time, he looked up at her, their gazes colliding, and she knew he was talking about them now.

Yes, they had been opposites, but when compared to her mother and Peter, Kace and she had practically been birds of a feather. They'd wanted the same kind of life on a ranch. They'd wanted kids. Jana had anyway. And that gave her a hard pinch of a reminder. The truth was, if it hadn't been for the kid factor, Kace and she might have never married.

But this wasn't about them, Jana quickly reminded herself. Kace and she were finished. However, she couldn't say the same for her mother and Peter. And yes, they were the king and queen of opposites.

Eileen was old money and worth millions. Eileen's father had been as rich as his father and grandfather before him. They weren't exactly Texas royalty, but her mother belonged to enough snooty clubs to run in elite social circles. Much to Eileen's dismay, that sort of thing didn't appeal to Jana. She just wanted to raise her daughter, run her horse ranch, put her divorces behind her and make sure her mother wasn't making the biggest mistake of her life.

"Did your father get drugs for your mother?" Jana came out and asked, but she didn't wait for the answer. "Because if he did, he contributed to her death."

"That's a stretch. She didn't overdose until a couple of years after he left."

Well, there went that theory. "Still, she wouldn't have used drugs in the first place if he hadn't made her life miserable. Maybe he even abused her in some way."

"Not that I ever saw." He stayed quiet a moment, and she worried that maybe she'd triggered some really bad memories for him.

Of course, she had.

This situation was likely bringing it all back for him. Jana had woken Kace from enough nightmares to know that things had stayed with him long after he'd gotten out of the tangled mess of his childhood.

On a heavy sigh, Kace handed her back the report. "What exactly do you think I can do about any of this?"

"You can stop the wedding," she said without hesitation. "They're already planning it for Valentine's Day at my mom's house. That's less than three months away. Between now and then, you and I can convince her what kind of man Peter Laramie really is."

Kace shook his head. "If that report didn't convince her, then I don't know what good I can do."

"You can remind her of what he did to you and your brothers." Jana's voice was a little louder than planned, and it caused Marley to squirm against her. "You can use your badge to intimidate Peter into leaving town," she added.

This time, her voice wasn't too loud, but there was plenty of emotion in it. She was on the verge of begging.

"You know I can't do that," Kace said. No shout or whisper for him. No emotion, either. It was his flat cop's voice that coordinated well with his flat cop's eyes. "This isn't my rodeo, not my clowns."

Jana wanted to curse, and she wished she had a stronger argument to convince him to help her. She couldn't very well ask him to do it as a favor for old time's sake, since their old times hadn't been that good.

Well, parts of them hadn't.

The divorce had been a serious dark spot, but the beginning of their marriage had been like their courtship. Scalding hot. Jana didn't think it was an exaggeration that Kace and she had had sex more times in those two years than she had in the fifteen years that'd followed. Scalding hot, incredible, memorable sex—that she was trying hard not to remember now. She didn't need thoughts like that in her head when she obviously had to come up with a way to get him on board with this marriage battle.

"I've already talked to my mother's friends,"

Jana went on, "and they've had no luck convincing her to give this relationship more time, not to jump into marriage with a man she hardly knows. A man who's seventeen years younger than she is, I'd like to point out."

"He's fifty-four," Kace commented. "Yeah, that's a big age difference all right."

It was indeed a big gap since her mother hadn't had her until she was thirty-six, and Kace's father had had him when he was still a teenager.

"But Eileen's not exactly robbing the cradle," Kace added.

"No, but I think her turning seventy-one has made her desperate. She mentioned that life was passing her by, and shortly thereafter she got involved with your father. I think he's playing on her emotions and trying to make her feel as if he can help her turn back the clock or something." Jana looked at him. Paused. "I don't have anyone else I can go to for help."

"How about your husband?" Again, Kace's voice was flat enough, but his gray eyes turned a little stormy.

"*Ex*-husband," she corrected, and she continued before Kace could remind her that he, too, had that same label. "Dominick doesn't want to get involved."

Kace didn't say "wise man," but he managed to convey just that with a simple grunt.

"Understandably, there's some animosity between Dominick and my mother since the divorce," Jana felt the need to add. What she wouldn't admit was that Dominick downright hated Eileen and probably secretly hoped that his ex-mother-in-law was marrying someone who'd give her a few emotional sucker punches.

"*Understandably*," Kace repeated, "there's still some animosity between your mother and me. Approaching her about this would likely just cause her to tell me to mind my own business. It's not illegal for your mother to get engaged to my father."

Jana made an *aha* sound. "But what if it is? My own father could be out there, alive and well. Yes, he left when I was a teenager." That'd been one of the things that Kace and she had in common. "And yes, my mother believes he's dead, but what if he isn't? And she didn't do any paperwork to officially declare him dead, either. Then, my mother would be committing bigamy by marrying Peter, and that's a crime."

She didn't feel as if she was grasping at straws, but Kace must have thought that because he gave another grunt. This one had a weariness to it.

"I know that over the years both you and your mother hired PIs to find your father. And just because he wasn't officially declared dead, it doesn't mean the state doesn't accept that he is." He paused. "Do you have any proof whatsoever he's alive?" he asked.

"No, but that doesn't mean he's dead."

Kace stared at her a long time. "The Galveston cops believe he drowned when he was sailing on his boat in the Gulf of Mexico."

"He could have faked his death," she quickly reminded him. It was possible.

"Your father's been gone for twenty years," Kace calmly pointed out. "Even if he's still alive, your mother wouldn't be prosecuted for bigamy because she believes she's a widow."

Jana hadn't actually thought the bigamy angle would work with Kace. It certainly hadn't caused her mother to budge. But Jana thought she might have something else in her arsenal to get Kace's help.

"Please," Jana said, and she hoped he realized that was the first time she'd ever begged.

Much to her relief, Kace didn't seem to dismiss that. In fact, his grunt turned to a sigh. "Is this about money?" Kace asked. "Are you worried Peter will take her for everything she owns?"

Jana dragged in a long breath because she doubted Kace would understand this. "Yes. My mother isn't the sort who can live without funds. And no, it's not just because she's high-maintenance. Her whole self-worth is tied to her money. It would crush her to lose everything."

"Then, the solution is simple. Your mother can do a prenup. If this is really a case of true love, then the groom won't mind—"

"She won't ask him to sign one," Jana interrupted.

That had been the third-round argument to try to talk her mom out of this. The first had been about having the *lovebirds* wait until they knew each other better before saying I do.

Her mother had nixed that.

The second argument had been for Eileen to look deeper into Peter's past, to go to Oklahoma and talk to people who knew him so that she could find out if there were any red flags.

Her mother had nixed that, too.

The third argument had been the prenup. The fourth, another search for Jana's father. The fifth—the one that Jana was working on now—was for Eileen to talk to Kace and his brothers to try to learn about Peter's character flaws. Jana was certain the man had plenty of them if he could turn his back on his four sons.

"Eileen's my mother, and I don't want her hurt," Jana threw out there, and in her mind that was the biggest reason of all to stop the wedding.

And Eileen would be crushed if this marriage didn't work out. She wouldn't be able to survive a divorce or being abandoned again by another husband. Her ego was just that fragile.

After yet another long pause, Kace finally nodded. "All right, I'll talk to Eileen."

The relief washed through her. Jana forgot all about a sleeping Marley in her arms and tried to hug Kace, but she only managed more like a body bump. Just enough contact of her hip against his that he noticed. Her body noticed as well, and as if on cue, she got another tug of attraction.

He was hands-off, of course. But the tug gave her an even harder yank until she got a flash of a memory. A really good one of Kace naked and in her bed.

It was a bad time for it to happen, but their gazes collided again. And held. She couldn't be sure, but

Jana thought that maybe he was getting some flashes of memories, too.

Stupid, stupid, stupid.

She shouldn't mentally be playing with fire. Especially with the ink not yet dry on her second divorce. She'd failed not once but twice at this whole relationship thing, and she had put Kace through too much to even consider them going for another round.

Yes, she still clearly saw him naked.

The image vanished in a flash though when she caught movement in the doorway. Kace must have caught it, too, because he automatically stepped in front of her. And that put him face-to-face with their visitor.

Peter Laramie.

"Son," Peter said, smiling and extending his hand in greeting. "It's good to see you."

CHAPTER THREE

EVERYTHING INSIDE KACE went still when he saw his father's face. The feeling didn't last. Nope. Because a fierce storm slammed in right behind that stillness.

Way too many memories and the raw emotions that went along with them.

The images came, clipped and fast like rounds from his service weapon. Kace had been nearly ten the day his father had left, and despite all the time that'd passed, he could still remember it in perfect detail. The packed suitcase—a scuffed brown one with a broken left wheel. The loud argument that'd gone on between his parents. The slamming of the door as his father had stormed out. Kace had stood there for a long time, waiting for him to come back.

He hadn't.

His father hadn't exactly been a prize, and in fact he'd made an art form of ignoring his sons while he was either drunk or worked on his so-called paintings. But being ignored had been a damn sight better than being abused, and that abuse had started not long after the slam of the door.

At least the man's clothes didn't bring back any bad memories. Peter wasn't dressed like an out-of-

work bum with four kids but rather what Kace figured was an outfit more suited for a trendy artist. A
black leather jacket over a white T-shirt and black
skinny pants. Yep, skinny. His hair—also black—
was practically to his shoulders and mussed in such
a way that looked careless, but Kace figured a lot
of care and money had gone into it to get that style.

Kace didn't take his father's hand that he was
still holding out for a shake, and he put his own now
fisted hands back on his hips. He was pretty sure he
was scowling, and Kace didn't try to make his expression even remotely friendly.

"If you're here to challenge the traffic ticket,
you'll need to speak to the receptionist," Kace said,
his voice thankfully void of any emotion. He didn't
want to show this piece of shit anything that was
going on in his head.

His father eased back his hand, but unlike Kace,
he managed a friendly smile. "No. I'm not challenging it. I didn't see the red light, but if your deputy
says I ran it, I'm sure I did. I was distracted when I
drove into town."

"Then, there's nothing you and I need to discuss,"
Kace calmly informed him.

Kace took his cowboy hat and jacket from the
pegs on the wall, slipped them on and turned back
to Jana. Kace opened his mouth but realized that he
didn't have a clue what to say to her. Seeing Jana had
caused nearly as much of a firestorm of emotions
as seeing his father, and that was Kace's cue to get

moving. Without waiting for anyone's reaction, he walked straight to the front door and outside.

Kace hadn't realized he'd been holding his breath until he dragged in some much needed air. Cold air at that. For once, the forty-degree temps actually felt good to him. He kept dragging in his breaths, kept walking, and he headed just up the street toward the building where two of his brothers had offices.

Callen actually owned the place, and he ran his cattle broker business on the second floor. Nico rented space from him and had his office for Laramie's Bucking Bulls on the bottom floor. With some luck, they should both be in since it was early afternoon of a normal workweek.

While Kace walked, he texted his other brother, Judd, who was one of the deputies, and asked him to come ASAP for a family meeting. Judd wouldn't like that because it was his day off, but Kace didn't care. He didn't want any of his siblings running into their father on the street. It'd been a bad enough shock for Kace, and he needed to give them a heads-up along with filling them in on the *wedding* plans.

Hell.

He hated that his father still had this kind of hold over him, and Kace wasn't going to stand for it. So what if the man married Jana's mother? So what if Peter ended up living in Coldwater? This was Kace's home. His brothers' home, too. And their sonofabitch of a father wasn't going to throw any monkey wrenches into that.

Kace hoped so anyway.

However, it was possible that Jana was right to have some concerns about her mother and this marriage. Kace didn't know the man that his father had become, but unless there'd been some significant improvements, then Eileen could be facing big trouble. Trouble that wasn't his, Kace quickly reminded himself. If his father committed some kind of crime, then Kace would arrest him. Barring that though, there wasn't a whole lot he could do.

Even if it was obvious that Jana expected something from him.

But Jana was yet someone else he needed to push to the back burner until he dealt with the issue of his father.

Kace threw open the door to the building, already heading toward Callen's office, but he came to a stop when he saw not only Callen but also Nico in the reception area. No receptionist or assistant today, and Kace was thankful for it since he wanted this conversation to be private.

"You're here about our worthless shit of a father showing up," Callen said right off the bat.

Okay, so Kace wasn't going to have to drop a bombshell after all. It had already been dropped. "Let me guess. Liberty called Shelby?" Kace asked.

Callen nodded. Shelby was Callen's wife and also friends with Liberty, and Kace should have known his deputy wouldn't have kept something like this to herself.

"Does Judd know yet?" Kace added.

Callen gave another nod. "He's on the way here, and FYI, he's in a pisser of a mood."

Not a surprise. Judd wasn't usually a rose-colored glasses kind of guy, and in many ways their trek through the bad parts of foster care had affected him the most. Ditto for their father leaving. Judd had been eight at the time and closer to the man than the rest of them had been. Callen, who'd been seven, and Nico, who'd been barely five, just hadn't blipped too often on their dad's radar.

"Our *father* came to the police station—" Kace started.

"With Jana?" Nico immediately asked.

Kace frowned. Of course, someone had blabbed about Jana's visit, too. "No. She came by first, to tell me about her mother marrying Peter." He decided to stick with calling the man by his given name. It didn't clog up his throat the way saying "our father" did.

"I'm betting Jana's upset about this," Callen concluded. "She asked you to try to stop the wedding."

Even though Jana and he had been divorced for well over a decade, clearly his brothers still knew her well. "She did, but I told her that other than having a chat with Eileen that I couldn't help. That's when Peter came in."

"And what did he want?" Callen pressed when Kace didn't add anything else.

Kace had to shrug. "I didn't wait around to find out. As far as I'm concerned, he's got nothing to say that I want to hear."

His brothers mumbled what sounded to be agreement, but no one had time to voice anything else before the door flew open. *Flew* being the operative word, and it would have smacked Kace in the shoulder if he hadn't darted to the side.

And Judd stormed in.

In the pecking order, Judd was the next to oldest of them, but he was the biggest. He'd not only gotten an extra couple of inches in height from their shared gene pool, he'd gotten wide shoulders and the seemingly permanent expression of someone about to throw some punches.

"It's true?" Judd immediately asked. "Did the douche bag really come to Coldwater?"

Kace suspected that over the next couple of hours Peter would get called other vile things—many of them from Judd.

"He's here," Nico verified.

Unlike the rest of them, Nico's voice wasn't dripping with anger and concern. It was just his nature. He was way too laid-back in most instances, but Kace was glad to have a cooler head in the room. It would maybe balance out the one serious hothead who was in the process of unpinning his badge from his shirt. The moment Judd finished doing that, he thrust it out for Kace to take.

"I'm going to kick the douche bag's ass," Judd announced, "and I don't want to be wearing a badge while I'm doing it."

Just as Kace hadn't obliged Peter with a handshake, he didn't take Judd's badge, either. "Put that back on," Kace growled, and it was an order from not only Judd's boss but also his big brother. "Kicking his ass will only give him more importance than he deserves. I want all of you to just ignore him."

That got the expected results. Glares from Judd and Callen. A halfhearted lift-of-his-shoulder agreement from Nico.

"You think it's wise to ignore a rattlesnake?" Judd snarled.

"There's no proof of his recent snakelike behavior," Kace pointed out, trying to be the voice of reason.

Callen huffed. "You think he's marrying Eileen for her beauty and charming personality?"

"No." He didn't think that, because Eileen didn't have either of those attributes. "But the woman's got a right to marry a snake, former or otherwise."

Again, the door flew open, and again Kace had to do some dodging to keep from being hit. This time, Shelby rushed in, and she went straight to Callen. "Are you okay?" She caught his face in her hands and studied him with very concerned eyes.

"I'm fine," Callen assured her, easing her hands away so he could pull her into a hug.

"I saw him," Shelby said. "He was coming out of the police station."

Kace didn't ask how she knew it was Peter. For one thing, there weren't many visitors to the police station so he could have been easy to peg. Easier, too, because of the resemblance. Kace had seen plenty of himself and his brothers in Peter's face.

"What are you going to do?" Shelby asked.

"Kick his ass," Judd answered, and he would have gone out the door if his fiancée, Cleo Delaney, hadn't come in. This time, the door did hit Kace, but he didn't mind. Cleo was the one person in Texas who could reason with Judd when he was in this mood.

"Good," Cleo concluded. "I can help you kick his ass."

Kace groaned and stepped in front of them. So much for Cleo's reasoning abilities. "There'll be no ass kicking. Do you think I want to have to arrest all of you? And besides, you're half Peter's size," he reminded Cleo.

"I could cheer Judd on while he punches the scum's lights out," Cleo reminded him right back.

"No punching, either," Kace snarled, and he made sure he sounded mean and pissed off. That mood came a little easier when the door nearly smacked into him again.

This time, it was Nico's girlfriend, Eden Joslin, who came rushing in. Since there was now a crowd in the room, she glanced around, and the moment she spotted Nico, she hurried to him.

"Are you all right?" Eden asked, echoing Shelby's earlier concern.

"Fine and dandy." Nico flashed her a smile—his specialty—but it didn't quite make it to his eyes. This had shaken all of them.

"Are you going to beat up your sperm-donor father?" Eden pressed.

Nico smiled again, this time a little more genuinely. "Kace says we can't, that we should just ignore him."

"Well, screw that," Eden concluded, and she turned to the rest of them to plead her case. "You should at least give him a piece of your mind, complete with some choice curse words to let him know what a sack of crap he is for running out on his kids." She got an agreement from everyone in the room but Kace.

Kace looked up at the ceiling for a second, hoping for some kind of divine intervention. He really didn't want to arrest his entire family and their significant others. Intervention came, thank goodness, but it wasn't divine.

Their foster father, Buck McCall, walked in.

Clearly, word of Peter's return was traveling like wildfire because there was no way Buck's arrival was a coincidence. When they'd been kids, Kace and his brothers had had several foster placements, but none had been better than Buck. Maybe that's why Peter's return was fueling Kace's anger as much as the rest—because Buck was their real father in every way that mattered.

"You boys okay?" Buck immediately asked.

No one answered. In Callen's and Judd's cases, it was probably because they didn't want to admit to Buck that they were in an ass-kicking state of mind and get a lecture from him. In Nico's case, he was probably still trying to decide how he felt about all of this. Just because he was the baby of the family, that didn't mean he didn't have the memories that went along with this shitstorm.

"We were just discussing what we should do about it," Nico volunteered.

One by one, Buck gave them each a glance. No doubt using his paternal radar to suss out what was going on in their heads. That might have been slightly easier for him to do in Shelby's case because she was his biological daughter.

"You know I never did abide by someone using their fists unless there was no other choice," Buck said. He paused. "Any of you feel like you don't have a choice?" His gaze settled on Judd.

Judd didn't get a chance to answer because there was a loud baby's wail just as Jana opened the door. This time, Kace and Buck both got hit because there was no wiggle room for them to get out of the way.

The reception area was already jammed so Jana stood there in the doorway, giving them all a once-over as Buck had done.

"Uh, I guess this is a bad time," Jana concluded. At least that's what Kace thought she'd said. It was hard to hear what with Marley's crying. Obviously, the little girl hadn't stayed asleep to finish out her nap.

"A bad time," Kace confirmed, but he was apparently the only one who felt that way.

Buck smiled at her, and Shelby pushed through the others to give Jana a hug. Shelby even tried to take Marley, but the little girl would have no part of that. She batted away Shelby's reaching hands, and her irked toddler's gaze zoomed right in on Kace. Just as she'd done in his office, she reached for him. And just as he'd done in his office, he didn't want to take her, but the kid practically launched herself at him. This time, it was Jana who collided with Shelby, and Kace scooped up the kid.

Marley instantly hushed.

The kid's lack of wailing definitely got everyone's attention. They all turned to Kace as if they expected some kind of explanation, but he didn't have one.

"Kace, the baby whisperer," Nico joked.

Kace gave him a look that could have frozen hell.

"Tace," the little girl attempted, causing some "isn't that cute" *awww*s from Cleo, Shelby and Eden.

But it wasn't cute. It was downright disturbing. There was nothing welcoming about his expression and body language—something that Jana obviously picked up on. However, his brothers and Buck were looking at him in that puzzled WTF kind of way. They probably thought that he'd been secretly seeing Jana and that's why her daughter had taken to him like this. No secret meetings, though. Best he could figure out, the kid was just a lousy judge of character.

"I'm sorry," Jana muttered, her apology apparently aimed at all of them. She maneuvered herself inside and shut the door. "It's been a long rough day."

She went to Kace and pulled Marley out of his arms. Of course, Marley began to fuss, but Jana fished around in the diaper bag on her shoulder and came up with what appeared to be some kind of hard cookie. Marley started to gnaw on it, but she kept her eyes firmly on Kace.

"A rough day for you, too," Nico said, going to Jana. He kissed her cheek, then did the same to Marley. "I was sorry to hear about your divorce," he added to Jana. "Are you all right?"

Obviously, Nico had kept up with Kace's ex-wife, but Kace didn't think his *all right* query was limited to only Jana's marital woes. Peter had caused some chaos in her world, too.

"Things might be looking up," Jana said, moving her attention to Kace. "I just got a text from my mom, and she said she's having second thoughts about the wedding."

Kace hadn't expected to get yet another surprise today, but it was darn good news. For Jana anyway. With all the doubts she had about Peter, this might ease her mind a little. But it didn't seem to be doing that.

"I tried to call her, but she didn't answer," Jana went on after she blew out a long breath. "She's probably upset, maybe with me for pushing this so hard, but I honestly believe she needed to put this marriage on hold until she got to know the man better. Then, I figured after getting to know him, she'd send him packing."

Marley gnawed on the cookie and then thrust it at Kace, clearly offering him a bite. He shook his head, and that caused Marley to grin at him.

For some stupid reason, he grinned back.

Thankfully, not for long, though. That's because

the door opened again, and to make room, it sent all of them scattering. Jana ended up against him. Marley, too. And the little girl used the opportunity to offer him the cookie again. It didn't land on his mouth but rather his ear. It was wet, mushy and smelled like bananas. It felt like wet, mushy bananas as well and had him choking back what would have been a very unmanly sounding *ewww* and some profanity.

Liberty stepped in, and her eyes went a little wide when she saw all ten of them gathered into the small space. "Family meeting," Liberty concluded in a mumble as her gaze skirted over them. Her eyes finally connected with Kace. "Boss, we need to talk." She tipped her head to outside, but then the deputy motioned to his ear. "You've got something smeared there." And Liberty did make an *ewww*, both the sound and with her expression.

Kace wiped away the gunk, dug out a handkerchief and continued to clean up while he stepped outside with Liberty. He had no doubts, none, that everyone inside was watching them. Everyone from across the street, too. Heck, it was possible that every adult in Coldwater was trying to get a glimpse of what was going on.

"Please tell me that Peter Laramie isn't still waiting in my office," Kace snarled.

"He's not," Liberty quickly confirmed. "That's because he's on the way to the hospital."

Well, that was yet one more surprise of the day. "What happened?"

Judging from the way Liberty was dodging his gaze, she knew this answer wasn't going to please him any more than it did her. "Your father claims someone sabotaged his car and that he's the victim of foul play."

CHAPTER FOUR

FOUL WAS THE operative word.

The moment he approached Peter's car, Kace got a whiff of the god-awful scent, a mix of rotten eggs, farts and puke. He didn't think the car itself was responsible for the stench, but it was hard to tell since it was now smashed into the light pole outside the diner on Main Street.

Normally, a sight like that would have drawn a crowd, but everyone was pretty much keeping their distance. Kace saw a lot of hands being waved in front of the faces of those milling around outside the diner and in the parking lot. Even baby Marley screwed up her little face and attempted to say "stinky."

"Stay back," Kace said to no one in particular, but his entire family entourage and Jana had followed him to the crash site. Since it had been just up the street, they'd all walked. As he'd instructed, they did stay back, all but Liberty and Judd, who had pinned his deputy's badge back on.

Kace did a quick assessment of the vehicle. The front end was indeed bashed in and the air bag had been deployed, but it didn't look too serious. No broken glass. No blood. Just the stench, and he soon spotted the source of that.

A stink bomb.

The remnants of one anyway, and it appeared to have been set on a timer. It was tucked in the narrow space behind the passenger's seat. Kace gave a heavy sigh. He was betting Peter hadn't been the one to stink up his own car, but he'd need to question the man to make sure.

"I can talk to him," Judd volunteered.

Kace could practically see the anger still vibrating off his brother. While Judd was a darn good deputy, having him question their good-for-nothing father when he was in this state of mind wasn't a wise idea.

"I'll do it," Kace insisted, and he glanced back at Jana and the others. "Why don't you try to wrap up the family meeting?" he added to Judd.

Clearly, Judd would have preferred confrontation duty, but Kace thought Judd needed a little more cooling-off time before he came face-to-face with the man who'd fathered him.

"Peter's at the hospital?" Kace asked Liberty.

She nodded. "He called nine-one-one and reported the accident when Ginger answered. He told her where he was and that he was going to walk up the street to the hospital. That's when he said it was foul play."

So if the man could walk, his injuries weren't that serious. Kace hoped. He didn't want Peter to have any reason to hang around Coldwater. Of course, if he was marrying Eileen, that would likely involve plenty of hanging around. Maybe even moving there. That reason alone made Kace want to rethink his reluctance to help Jana put a stop to the wedding.

While Liberty and he went up the street, Kace checked again for any signs of blood and didn't see any. However, the audience he'd had at the diner continued to follow them. Not his family or Jana. Judd had obviously convinced them to let Kace handle this, but others—including Petunia, the longhorn—were moseying along behind Liberty and him. Even Gopher had ditched his cleaning duties to try to get a whiff of what was going on.

When Kace reached the hospital doors, he shot them all a warning glance to stay put, and Liberty and he went in. Ruby Myerson, the receptionist who was seated at her desk, immediately got to her feet.

"Your daddy's in the ER," Ruby informed him.

So apparently everyone in the hospital knew who Peter was. Of course, Kace hadn't thought he would be able to keep that kind of news to himself. Ditto for the stink bomb and the car crash.

"Why don't you go back to the car and get started with that," Kace told Liberty. "Get some eyewitness accounts." And he was certain there'd be plenty of those.

Liberty didn't jump to hurry back out. "I can question Mr. Laramie if you're not up to it."

While he didn't relish the notion of spending even another second with Peter, Kace wouldn't dump this on her. He went in the direction of the emergency room while Liberty headed back out.

Like everything else in Coldwater, the hospital wasn't that large so it didn't take Kace long to walk through the waiting area and to the ER. As soon as he was in the treatment area, he spotted Peter.

Much to Kace's surprise, there wasn't anyone else around. Peter wasn't behind one of the two curtained-off areas but rather sitting on an exam table. His clothes were covered with the white talcum powder from the air bag, and there were some mild abrasions on his face—also probably from the air bag.

Peter took one look at Kace and eased off the table to stand. "I figured you'd send one of your deputies to talk to me," he said.

Kace skipped right over that. He had to do his job, but that didn't mean making small talk or needlessly verifying that this meeting was damn uncomfortable. "Tell me what happened."

Peter nodded and dragged in a deep breath as if resigned to Kace's brusque tone. Kace wanted to snarl that he could get a whole lot more brusque than this, but Peter started his explanation.

"As I was driving from the parking lot of the police station and heading back to Eileen's, something exploded in my car. If you got a whiff of it, you know it was a stink bomb."

Kace made a sound to indicate he had indeed gotten the whiff and made a circular motion with his index finger to indicate he wanted the man to continue.

"It made a loud popping sound," Peter went on, "and it stank to high heaven. I looked behind the seat to see what it was, and that's when I lost control of my car. I hit the light pole. I couldn't get the car started so I walked over here."

"*Walked*?" Kace repeated.

"No one jumped to offer me a ride," Peter muttered.

No. It was like taking sides when he and Jana divorced. Still, someone would have helped had his injuries been serious.

Before Peter could add anything else, a nurse came moseying into the room. Kace knew her, of course, and he groaned softly. It was Annabelle Mason. She was eighty if she was a day and as slow as a sloth unless it came to gossip. She excelled in that particular area, which meant she would likely repeat anything and everything she heard here. That's why Kace didn't say anything. He just stepped back and waited to see what she wanted.

"I got the eye drops," Annabelle announced. She stopped midway between them and gave them both long glances. "Did I interrupt something?"

"No," Kace said.

Apparently, Annabelle wanted a tad more info than that, but Kace didn't give it to her. He just waited until she'd taken her moseying pace the rest of the way toward Peter. Waited some more for Peter to sit so she could administer the drops at a snail-crawling pace.

"The powder from the air bag irritates the eyes," she said. "Doc Adams said your dad would be right as rain once he had these."

Kace doubted that. Peter didn't look in a "right as rain" kind of mood. He seemed annoyed, put out and about as comfortable as a freshly branded steer's rump. Kace figured he could apply all of those emotions to himself as well.

"All righty then?" Annabelle asked Peter after the drops were in his eyes.

The man blinked, nodded and wiped the excess drops from his cheeks. He thanked her and nodded again when Annabelle didn't budge. The woman just stood there as if she expected to be privy to the conversation that was about to follow.

"I can leave now?" Peter asked her.

"Oh sure. Just stop by the front desk and pick up your paperwork." Still no budging and since Kace was tired of waiting, he motioned for Peter to follow him.

There weren't going to be a lot of private places for them to have a conversation in the hospital, but Kace didn't need to clear up a lot right at this moment.

"You'll need to come into the police station and give Deputy Cassaine a statement," Kace informed him.

"You won't be doing that?" Peter asked. Kace couldn't tell if he was disappointed or just confused.

"The deputy can handle the official interview." He would ask Peter just a handful of questions to get things started, and then go about putting this—whatever the hell *this* was—behind him.

"Is Eileen coming to pick you up?" Kace asked.

Because there wasn't anyone by the vending machines, where Kace stopped.

Peter shook his head. "I didn't want to tell her about the wreck over the phone. Best to do that in person."

Kace figured that ship had already sailed. "I suspect someone's called her."

"Someone's probably tried to do that." Peter checked his watch. "She wouldn't have answered her phone, though. This is her yoga and meditation time." He paused. "But I should get out to her house soon. She'll be worried if she catches wind of what happened."

Maybe. But if Jana was right about that text, her mother was having doubts about this marriage. That still wasn't Kace's concern though, especially since he did have a problem standing right in front of him.

"What exactly do you think happened? How do you believe that stink bomb got into your car?" Kace asked.

"Someone obviously planted it there," Peter answered without hesitation. "A person who wanted to get back at me, maybe even hurt me."

Kace couldn't completely dismiss that last part. Hurting might have been what the culprit had in mind, but if so, it was a stupid weapon of choice.

"Planted," Kace repeated. "How'd the person get into your vehicle?"

Peter sighed. "I forgot to lock it. I noticed that when I left the police station and got back to my car. I forget to lock my car a lot," he added.

Which meant the stink bomb might not have been put there recently.

"I saw a timer," Peter went on. "That means the person didn't want to be around when the bomb went off, but I think it's pretty obvious who would do something like this."

Hell. The father of the year was about to sling some slime at Kace or one of his brothers. "My brothers were with me when you wrecked," Kace pointed out. "Before that, Judd wasn't even in town. He was out at the McCall Ranch where he lives. Callen and Nico were at their offices."

Of course, none of those were really solid alibis—which only proved their innocence in Kace's mind. If one of them was going to do something like this, they would have made sure they could account for their whereabouts.

Peter blinked as if doing a double take. "I didn't think you or your brothers would pull a stunt like this."

Oh. Well, that was something at least. Kace wasn't going to have to drag them into the investigation.

"I think we both know who's responsible," Peter went on. He looked Kace directly in the eyes. "Jana did this, and I can prove it."

JANA HAD NEVER thought to use a stink bomb as a bargaining/wake-up tool, but she thought she could get this particular angle to work with her mother.

Since bargaining with Eileen often involved arguing, Jana left a sleeping Marley with Bessie

Tarver, the woman who'd once been Jana's nanny and was now Eileen's household manager. Marley would be in very good hands with Bessie, and since Bessie's quarters were at the back of the house, the baby wouldn't be in hearing distance of any possible shouting.

Jana steeled herself up and marched into her mother's office. Actually, it was much more than that, what with a large sitting area complete with a massive fireplace, floor-to-ceiling bookshelves and artwork jammed along every single inch of wall space.

Bad artwork.

Her mother had always had a notion of finding the next Picasso, Dalí or Pollock, but what she ended up buying was bad stuff that a monkey could have painted. And in one case that was literally true. The splattered and smeared painting over the fireplace— titled *Primitive Urges*—had been done by Charles, the Capuchin Monkey.

In addition to bad art, her mom also had a penchant for *experimental* furniture. There was the tiger print couch, complete with roaring tiger heads for sofa arms. Odd-shaped yellow-and-green leather accent chairs that looked like blobs of melting butter or the remnants of a bad cold. But the worst were the naked butt coffee and accent tables. All four in the room were the bottom half of torsos, bare round butts extended, and topped with clear glass. Someone had obviously convinced her mother that nudes were signs of good taste.

Unfortunately, those *good taste* choices extended to the rest of the house as well. Definitely no home and hearth vibe when it came to Eileen and her domain. Even the Christmas tree in the living room was decorated top to bottom with expensive blown glass ornaments that fell and shattered so often that it made going near the tree a hazard.

Her mother was at the large bay window, looking out at her pristine gardens that were now decorated with Christmas lights and animated elves and reindeer. This year's over-the-top addition was an actual gingerbread house. It was six feet high and dripping with icing and huge gumdrops on the roof. Jana suspected it would be a feast for the critters, and there wouldn't be much of it left by Christmas.

Eileen was still wearing her yoga clothes, or rather her interpretation of them. She had on a blinding pink bodysuit, complete with earrings, a bracelet and two engagement rings. Yes, two. Eileen had the one Jana's father had given her on her right hand and the new one from Peter on her left. Eileen was also sipping some kind of smoothie that was the color of cheese mold.

One look at her mother, and Jana knew that she hadn't heard about Peter's car wreck. Too calm, and she wasn't flitting around as if the world was on the verge of imploding.

Despite having just worked out, there wasn't a strand of her mother's blond hair out of place, and she was still wearing her usual shade of red lipstick. Of course, her tall and willowy body was perfect.

If it hadn't been, Eileen would have fixed that. Jana wasn't sure if it was vanity or control, but no way would Eileen let age, wrinkles or cellulite get the upper hand.

"Where's Marley?" Eileen asked but didn't wait for Jana to answer. "I told you that I wanted to have a tea party with her."

So she had, and Jana had seen the party all set up in the dining room. An antique porcelain pot and tiny antique plates with tiny cookies. Marley could end up breaking something, but she'd love the cookies. Better yet, Eileen would enjoy it. Despite everything, Jana had no doubts that her mother loved her granddaughter.

"When you look at your phone messages," Jana began, "you'll see there's been a problem."

Eileen's forehead likely would have creased had she had creasing abilities. The frequent Botox injections had given her that frozen look, but she hurried— no, she flitted—to her desk and looked at her phone, which she had likely silenced.

"What's happened?" Eileen blurted out. Obviously, there were many more missed calls and texts than she normally would have had after a one-hour yoga workout and meditation session.

"Peter was in a car accident. He walked away from it," Jana quickly added. "He's fine."

As expected, her mother didn't take her word for it. She practically threw the smoothie onto her desk, sending some of the liquid splattering, and she phoned Peter. Jana didn't have to guess about that because Eileen put the call on speaker, and several moments later, Jana heard the man's voice.

"I'm all right," Peter immediately said.

"My God. You were actually in a wreck?"

"Yes, a minor one. I'm okay."

Her mother likely hadn't heard a word after the "yes" because she started to rattle off more of those *My God*s while she raced around in a circle.

"Where are you? I want to see you. I'll come and get you— Ouch!" her mother yelped when her leg connected with one of the snarling teeth of her tiger couch.

"Are you all right?" Peter asked. "What happened?"

"I'm fine. But you're not. A car wreck. My God." Her mother's words were rushed together, and it ate away at Jana to see the genuine concern in her eyes. It also ate away at her that her mother could end up getting crushed by this relationship.

Something that Jana knew loads about.

"I'm about to leave the hospital. I got checked out as a precaution," he said, interrupting Eileen's gasp. "My car's going to the shop for repairs, but Deputy Cassaine's giving me a ride to your place. I'll be there in about fifteen minutes. Just stay put and I'll see you soon. I love you, Eileen."

"Oh, I love you, too," her mother all but purred. When Peter ended the call, her mother just stood there and pressed her phone to her chest. Or rather to her heart.

Jana wasn't immune to that symbolic gesture, either. Maybe Eileen did love the man. Or rather she loved the man she thought he was.

"Someone put a stink bomb in Peter's car," Jana explained. Best to get into the bargaining/wake-up she needed to do. She gave her mother a chance to let that sink in, but Eileen only gave her a blank look. "The stink bomb went off and caused the accident."

That erased the blankness, and Eileen's eyes widened as much as her nearly frozen face would allow. She moved her phone, no doubt to call Peter again, but Jana took hold of her hand to stop her.

"Someone obviously doesn't like Peter," Jana went on. "In fact, someone might hate him so much that they want to do him harm."

Eileen frantically shook her head. Then, she huffed. "Are you trying *again* to make me think badly about him?"

Jana couldn't exactly deny that. "You texted me and said you were having second thoughts about marrying him," she reminded Eileen.

"Second thoughts about having the wedding *here*." Eileen huffed again. "I considered maybe having the ceremony in the church instead."

So, not the right second thoughts. That meant Jana had to spell this out for her mother. "Someone wants to harm Peter," she repeated.

"Do you mean one of his former girlfriends, the ones you keep telling me about?"

Jana had indeed told her mother about Peter's previous relationships, including one with an exotic dancer and with Kace's mother. Ditto for telling Eileen about his failed business ventures and spelling out in the nth detail about him running out on his family. None of that had put a damper on Eileen's feelings, but maybe this would.

"If someone's trying to harm him," Jana went on, "then you could be hurt, too. You could become this person's target. That's why I'm asking you to put the wedding on hold until we can figure out what's going on with him."

Eileen stared at her a very long moment, and then when she huffed, Jana made a huff of her own. Her mother definitely wasn't buying this.

"Honestly, Jana, when will you give up this witch hunt about Peter?" Eileen asked, and she managed a frown.

"When I'm convinced that he's the good and decent man you believe he is. He abandoned his family," Jana pointed out for the umpteenth time.

Another long stare from her mother. "That's really what this is about. Kace and his brothers. But specifically Kace. I swear if I didn't know better, I'd think you still had feelings for your first ex-husband."

Jana hadn't missed the condemning tone that went with *first* and *ex*. Eileen abhorred divorce as much as she did wrinkles and gray hairs. But Jana had to admit—privately—that she still got a punch of lust whenever she was around Kace. That definitely didn't happen with ex number two, Dominick. However, that probably had something to do with the hurt and betrayal still being so fresh with him.

At least Jana hoped that's all there was to it.

While she was hoping, she added that she wished the images of a naked Kace would quit popping up like a jack-in-the-box into her head. Images of them kissing, too. And yes, of them in bed.

"Peter's first marriage was a long time ago," her mother went on. "They didn't divorce, and now that she's dead, that makes him widowed, just like me."

"No," Jana argued. "He and his wife were separated for years before she died. You and dad were together right up until the time he disappeared."

"Died," Eileen corrected. "Your father is dead. When are you just going to accept that?"

Jana refrained from her usual response of *when pigs fly*. That was always a trigger for more arguing.

"I can accept a lot of things." Jana chose her words carefully. "But I'm surprised you can accept falling in love with Kace's father. You certainly didn't accept my marriage to Kace." Okay, that obviously wasn't the way to go about this because it caused her mother to give her a frosty look.

"Kace is not his father." The frost made its way into her words, but then Eileen's expression softened. "We might not see eye to eye on this, but Peter's a good person. A successful businessman who's overcome his past."

If she substituted *lawman* for *businessman*, then her mother could be talking about Kace. Of course, that wouldn't make a difference because Eileen would never see Kace as a success.

"Can you at least consider the possibility that it could be dangerous for you to be under the same roof as Peter?" Jana asked, forcing her mind to get back on the right track.

Her mother's chin came up. "We're not under the same roof. He'll be staying in the guesthouse until the wedding."

Now it was Jana's turn to frown. "I was going to stay in the guesthouse with Marley."

No frown this time. Nope. Her mother got that dismissive this-is-a-done-deal look. "Sorry, but I've promised it to him, and besides, it wouldn't be proper for Peter and me to share a house before we're married. I don't want to give the gossips anything to talk about."

Jana wondered if her mother had even heard what she'd just said. "Just you being with Peter is gossip fodder. Mom, people know what he did, and his being here in Coldwater is like rubbing salt into his sons' wounds."

As she'd done every other time that Jana had brought that up, Eileen dismissed it with a wave of her perfectly manicured hand. "That was years ago, and Peter's now a respected businessman."

The jury was still out on that, but Jana heard the footsteps heading their way that let her know this conversation was about to end. Once again, she'd failed to convince her mother to be wary of the man making those footsteps.

"Peter," Eileen greeted when he stepped inside her office. She hurried to him and pulled him into her arms.

Peter brushed a kiss on Eileen's cheek, but his

gaze went straight to Jana. He smiled at her, a kind of I-know-something-you-don't-know smile.

"I'll be staying at my grandmother's house for a while," Jana remarked, heading for the door.

That got her mother's arms off Peter. "Of course, you won't. You'll be staying here. I've already had your and Marley's things taken to your old room."

Then, Jana would just have to move them. "We've been through this," Jana reminded her. "We don't do well under the same roof, either."

Though they still wouldn't be that far apart. Her late grandmother had left the place to Jana, but the house was on the grounds. It didn't have internet—that was the reason Jana had intended on staying in the guesthouse—but her grandmother's house would have to do.

Jana stepped around Peter and her mother and headed out of the office and toward Bessie's quarters. However, she hadn't made it far when she heard Peter's voice.

"Wait up, Jana," he called out to her.

Jana looked back, expecting her mother to be with him, but Peter was alone.

"I'm not staying here in the house," Jana insisted. "And I'm sorry my mother sent you to try to convince me to do that."

"She did send me," he readily admitted, "but that's not why I wanted to talk to you." He glanced back over his shoulder as if to make certain they were alone. "This is about the stink bomb."

Jana had been about to keep walking, but that got

her attention. "What about it? You know who put it in your car?"

His eyebrow rose, and he stared at her—as if he expected her to blurt out some kind of confession.

"Are you accusing *me* of doing that?" she demanded.

"Yes." He didn't hesitate, either. Peter took out his phone, hit a play button on a recorder, and Jana heard her own voice.

"I don't know what you want from my mother, but I won't stand by and let you hurt her or take her for a ride. If I find out you aren't who you're claiming to be, then you'll be very sorry."

Jana had indeed said that. However, she hadn't known he'd been recording it. And hearing it now gave her a very uneasy feeling.

"FYI," Peter continued. "I've let Kace listen to this so he knows what's going on."

Oh mercy. Kace thought she had planted that stink bomb? *Great. Just great.* "Did you put that stink bomb in your own car to set me up?" she demanded.

"Peter?" her mother said, making her way toward them. "Did you convince Jana to stay here?"

"No," Peter answered, his voice sweet. It wasn't so sweet though when he whispered to Jana. "I want you to back off and accept the inevitable—that I will be marrying your mother. If you don't, then I'm sorry. I'll be forced to press charges against you."

CHAPTER FIVE

KACE READ THROUGH the report he'd just gotten from the crime lab, and he frowned. Hell. He'd hoped to get a break on what folks were now calling stink-bomb-gate, but this was the opposite of a break.

He stood, ready to go out to Eileen's place, but he'd just reached for his hat when Judd came in. "DeeDee Merriweather," Judd said, reading through his own report. "She's Peter's business partner, and she's got a sheet."

Kace didn't have to ask why Judd was running such info. After the stink bomb/car wreck two days earlier, he'd asked Judd to dig into Peter's background, and an association with someone with a criminal record could be a red flag.

Kace took the report, but his "red flag" notion fizzled when he saw that it was a reckless driving charge and a shoplifting arrest when she'd been nineteen—over twenty years ago. Hardly enough concern for some people to exclude doing business with her.

"Yeah," Judd said after looking at Kace's expression. "Not exactly on the FBI's Top Ten Most Wanted list."

Kace made a sound of agreement. DeeDee's record definitely wasn't worth mentioning to Eileen or Jana. "Anything else on the woman?"

"It's hard to pick through financials without probable cause or a warrant, but it appears that DeeDee ponied up the money for What-Knots. Peter helps run the business and is listed as co-owner."

Interesting, and having a chat with the woman might shed some light on things. "Why don't you give DeeDee a call?" Kace said. "Just tell her that someone tampered with Peter's car and that we're investigating. See if she volunteers anything useful."

Judd nodded, then tipped his head to the hat that Kace had just put on. "Going somewhere?" he asked.

"Yeah, to Eileen's to have a chat with Peter and her." Kace handed Judd a copy of the report from the crime lab.

Judd read through it, and his gaze came back to Kace's. "Jana's staying there at her grandmother's house."

"I heard." And Kace left it at that.

Judd, however, didn't leave it. He huffed. "I have very clear memories of you after your breakup with Jana. Lots of booze and a really bad attitude. *Bad*," he emphasized. "Just remember that before you start things up with her again."

Kace pulled back his shoulders and didn't have to muster up looking offended. He was. "I'm not starting up anything with Jana."

Well, nothing more than the stuff he didn't want to feel, but there wasn't anything he could do about that other than use the willpower he knew he had.

Along with relying on those memories Judd had touched on. There'd been booze. There'd been attitude. There'd been hurt. Kace really didn't want another dose of that.

"Besides," Kace went on, "the ink's barely dry on Jana's latest divorce, and she's got her hands full with the baby and her mother. I doubt she wants to go for a second chance at screwing up with me."

Judd stared at Kace as if his nose had had a sudden growth spurt. "Just don't do anything with Jana that you wouldn't do in front of her mother."

Well, that seriously limited activities since he didn't especially want to do anything in front of Eileen. Still, Kace didn't have any trouble nodding in agreement because he was going with the no-touching rule when it came to Jana. If he kept his hands and mouth off her, then nothing else could happen.

Judd was still giving his cautionary warning glances when Kace headed out. His trek to Eileen's didn't get any better though because the moment he stepped outside, he practically ran right into Belinda.

"Kace," she said on a rise of breath. "I was just dropping by to see you."

That was obvious, not only because her hand was literally reaching for the door to the police station but also because she was dressed to the nines. Black jeans, high-heeled shoes and a green sweater that was almost the same color as her eyes. She was wearing makeup, and her dark brown hair tumbled over her shoulders.

It immediately occurred to him that this was how

she usually dressed for a date. With him. She worked at the bank and normally wore business clothes.

"Sorry, I was on my way out," he told her.

Her smile wavered a little, and he wanted to curse because suddenly he knew what this visit was about. Jana. With his ex-wife back in town, Belinda had likely wanted him to clarify where she stood with him. That was probably why she'd sent him three "thinking of you" and smiley face texts over the last two days. The timing wasn't a coincidence since that had been when Jana had arrived.

"I won't keep you," Belinda said. Her voice was polite, the smile was still in place, and she took hold of his hand. Her fingers dallied over his. "I was hoping that I could fix you dinner tonight."

Dinner with a side dish of sex. That's the way their relationship had worked for years. Never too frequently though, because Kace hadn't wanted Belinda to think that there was more between them than there actually was. In fact, he just realized that it'd been a couple of months since their last *dinner*.

Kace didn't have to think hard to know that he didn't want to be with Belinda tonight, and it didn't have anything to do with Jana. Belinda rarely pushed for their relationship to be something more, but she was pushing now. And he doubted she would let it go as long as Jana was around. He could just wait that out, wait for things to go back to normal, but that would only end up hurting Belinda more in the long run.

"I'm sorry, but I can't," Kace said, and he made

sure he had direct eye contact with her. He dragged in a long breath, ready to do what he should have done ages ago—end things with her. "Belinda, this isn't working out—"

"It's okay," she blurted out before he could finish. "I have to go. We'll have dinner some other time." She ran off as if her pants were on fire. Considering those heels she was wearing, she got away from him fast.

Hell.

Kace debated going after her and finishing this, but Main Street wasn't the best place to do that. However, he would drop by Belinda's soon and tell her that he was ending their friends with benefits relationship. He'd been a fool to believe that he could have something casual with Belinda. It did make him wonder though why he hadn't realized that sooner.

He froze for a moment, repeated his mental *hell*, and really hoped this sudden clear sight had nothing to do with Jana. He'd meant all those things he'd said to Judd about not jumping back into bed with her.

Kace went to his truck and drove out to Eileen's. Because the estate was out of town and not on the main road, he hadn't been here recently. In fact, he hadn't been out this way since his divorce.

He probably didn't have reason to come here today, either.

What he had to tell Peter was something that could be done over the phone. Clearly though, this was his day for confronting things. Of course, the confrontation with Belinda had failed, but maybe he'd fare better with getting Peter to back off on accusing Jana of trying to intimidate him into running.

He pulled to a stop in front of the grand house and wasn't surprised to see that it was already decorated to the nines for Christmas. And it wasn't solely for Marley's benefit. Eileen always decked out the place. That included a waving, ho-ho-ho-ing Santa on the roof.

Weaving around Santa's waiting sleigh and reindeer, Kace went to the front door and rang the bell. A maid answered, a woman he didn't recognize, which meant she wasn't from Coldwater.

"I'm here to see Peter Laramie," Kace said, tapping his badge.

She gave a nervous nod and hurried off, no doubt to find the man, and Kace stepped inside the foyer to look around. It was as weird as it had been years ago.

Apparently, Eileen was going through a circus art theme, complete with a seven-foot-tall juggling clown mannequin for a coatrack and a trapeze light fixture complete with dangling crystal acrobat figures. A fake elephant rug with a massive head was on the floor.

He wondered how many times people had tripped over that.

In the corner was a massive Christmas tree, every inch of every branch covered with glass ornaments that somehow managed not to look out of place with the other junk in the room.

Kace had never felt at ease here in this place, and it wasn't just because of the tacky decor. Eileen had always helped with that unease by looking down her nose at him. Something that she obviously intended to continue doing, because that's exactly what she did when she came into the foyer. Peter was right next to her, his arm around her waist.

Eileen hadn't continued the circus theme with her clothes but rather had on what she'd always called her signature color. Pink. In this case, it was a skirt and a top that looked like indigestion medicine.

Peter had gone with his black outfit but wore a dark red shirt instead of the white tee that he'd had on when he'd first shown up in Kace's office. He looked every one of those seventeen years younger than Eileen. In fact, he looked young enough to be her son. Something that Eileen wouldn't want anyone pointing out.

"This is Peter's work," Eileen said when she noticed Kace eyeing the rug that he was stepping around. "Isn't he talented?"

That wasn't the word Kace would have used. *Weird* fit better. And probably Eileen had paid a bundle for this weird shit. "I thought you were a painter," Kace pointed out.

Peter shrugged and smiled when he looked at the dangling acrobats. "I work in many mediums and like to do collections. This is part of what I call *The Greatest Show*."

Not very original. Not very good, either, but then Kace had to admit he didn't know squat about art.

"I hope you've caught the person who played that

horrible prank on Peter," Eileen said when Kace's attention went back to her.

Her comment told Kace a couple of things. Peter hadn't passed on his suspicions about Jana to her mother, and the man had soft-pedaled the situation. *Prank* would likely worry Eileen less than Peter's earlier assessment of *foul play*, and he might not have wanted to stir up an argument between Eileen and Jana. Getting between a mother and her child could blow up in his face. Kace certainly hadn't fared so well when he'd tried to get Eileen to back off from interfering in his marriage to Jana.

And therein lay the problem of Kace's being here.

Every little thing brought him circling back to things—feelings, emotions, memories—that he should be keeping at arm's length.

Hoping to put a quick end to this conversation, Kace ignored Eileen's remark and turned to Peter. "I sent what was left of the stink bomb and the timer to the crime lab."

Kace wouldn't mention that he'd called in some favors from a friend to put a rush on things. If he hadn't, it would have taken months to get back the results, since this wasn't classified as a priority investigation.

"The brand of the stink bomb is Smelly Bobs," Kace went on, "and it's sold online and in a few novelty shops. There were no prints or any kind of trace evidence on it."

"Well, that's not acceptable," Eileen said on a huff. "You need to find and arrest the person."

Again, Kace ignored her and kept his attention on Peter. "I checked around town, and no one bought the equipment needed to put the timer on the Smelly Bob. No one saw anyone lurking around your car, either. The next step is to look into the possibility that someone in Oklahoma planted it before you made the trip here. Do you know of anyone who would have done that?"

Eileen made a sound that could have only been disapproval. "Of course, you'd want to believe it was someone there. Then, you won't have to investigate your own brothers. Or yourself."

There were few things that could have gotten Kace to purposely turn to Eileen, but that did it. "I'm going to pretend that I didn't just hear you say that I'm obstructing justice, especially when I know you don't have anything to back it up." Ignoring her indignant huff, he turned back to Peter. "My brothers and I learned you were in town less than a half hour before the stink bomb. That wasn't enough time to put together something like that."

Peter nodded. However, he followed it with a look that Kace had no trouble interpreting. The Laramie brothers couldn't have done this, but it still didn't let Jana off the hook.

"Back to my question," Kace continued. "Do you know anyone in Oklahoma who could have planted the Smelly Bob?"

"No." Peter scrubbed his hand over his face. "And trust me, I've given that some thought."

"No problems with your business partner, DeeDee Merriweather?" Kace pressed.

"No." But Peter hesitated just enough that it caused Kace to make a mental note to do more checking on the woman.

He stared at Peter, waiting for him to add more, but when he didn't, Kace turned to leave.

"This won't stop the wedding," Eileen called out to him.

"Not my rodeo, not my clowns," Kace muttered. "Seventy-one is plenty old enough to decide who you'll be marrying."

"I'm sixty-seven," Eileen corrected, and then Kace heard her proceed to tell Peter that the *sheriff* had obviously been mistaken about her age.

So Eileen hadn't been honest with her hubby-to-be. Still, it was none of his business, and he just kept walking back to his truck.

Kace had convinced himself to drive back to town, but then he saw Jana's SUV parked on the side of her grandmother's house. The place didn't have a garage, and Jana had left the vehicle beneath a cluster of trees. While it wasn't necessary for him to tell her about the lab report, he found himself walking in that direction when he heard some sounds.

Squeals, maybe?

Unlike the main house, there was nothing grand about this place. It was a simple, two-story, white Victorian house that had been built by Eileen's ancestors around the same time they'd first settled in Coldwater. In fact, that was the reason it was likely still standing—it had landed on a historic registry. If not for that and the fact that Jana's grandmother had left the place to her, Eileen would have likely bull-dozed what she would consider an eyesore.

Kace heard more squealing as he got closer, but it didn't seem to be someone in distress. Just the opposite. It appeared someone was having fun, and that fun was in the back of the house. However, what he saw on the front porch had him rethinking that notion.

There was a broken phone on the steps. Not just broken though—smashed to bits. There was also some torn-up paper, and the front door was wide open. All that put together wasn't necessarily a sign of trouble, but it got Kace moving faster. He didn't go through the house but rather around through the yard and to the back.

And he came to a dead stop.

Jana was in the glass sunroom, and she was prac-tically naked, wearing only her bra and panties. He didn't have to guess the reason for her near nudity. There was a kiddie pool in the sunroom, and with Marley wearing only a diaper and toddling along behind her, they were running around in it, splash-ing water.

His breath stalled in his lungs.

Not because of Jana being nearly naked with her wet underwear plastered to her body but because of her smile. It lit up her whole face, and for just a bad couple of seconds, Kace didn't remember the argu-ments, the breakup or the pain that'd followed. He got strong flashes of how damn happy they'd been before things had gone to hell.

Still smiling and all lit up, Jana kicked up some water again. So did Marley, and the little girl giggled like a loon. After all the earlier fussing and crying, that was good to hear as well. But it didn't last.

Jana froze when her attention landed on him, and Marley, whose balance and running skills weren't nearly as good as her mom's, smacked into Jana. That dropped Marley on her butt in the pool, and while she didn't cry, the giggling stopped.

"Kace," Jana said, automatically scooping up the child. "I didn't hear you drive up."

He tipped his head toward Eileen's and went into the sunroom. The room was warm, thanks to the sun blazing through the glass and a portable heater in the corner, but it certainly wasn't hot enough to be cooling off in a kiddie pool. "I'm parked at your mom's. I, uh, had to talk to Peter."

Well, Jana certainly wasn't lit up now, and she was starting to shiver as she walked toward him. The door that led to the kitchen opened, and someone familiar came out. Bessie Tarver, Jana's former nanny. She greeted Kace with a warm smile. A genuine one. Eileen might have been chilly to Kace, but he'd never gotten that from Bessie.

Bessie had gray hair, and her step was a little slow, but she made it to Jana, pulling Marley into her arms and cocooning her in a towel. Bessie handed another towel to Jana.

"No, no, no," Marley protested, and she waggled her hands at the pool. "Back."

"Maybe later. Now it's time for a cookie and some milk," Bessie told her, and those seemed to be the magic words because Marley's smile returned, and she no longer seemed interested in water games.

"You want some cookies?" Bessie asked him.

Kace shook his head. "No, thanks. I just need to speak with Jana and then be on my way."

Bessie didn't waste any time taking the toddler inside, and Jana did some fast moves to wrap the towel around her body. The peep show was over, but unfortunately, Kace was going to have some trouble forgetting the image of her nipples pressed against her wet bra.

"Sorry about this," Jana said, going closer to the heater, "but Marley saw the pool my grandmother had left back here, and she wanted me to fill it. Not exactly winter fun, I know, but Bessie and I heated the water and added some bubble bath. We thought this would be a fun way for Marley to take a bath."

Kace was still trying to figure out what to say when Jana followed his gaze to her towel. "My swimsuit's at my other house," she explained, "and I didn't think anyone would come back here to see me."

Seeing her in a swimsuit likely would have given him the same reaction. Heck, just seeing her probably would have.

"You're here about the investigation?" she asked.

He nodded and moved slightly to the side in case Jana wanted to go in and put on her clothes, but she stayed put. "There were no prints on the stink bomb. Nothing that can be traced to anyone specific. It's called a Smelly Bob, and a person can buy it in plenty of places."

Her gaze stayed on him. "I didn't do this."

"I know."

Surprised, she blinked. What she didn't do was look relieved. "You're giving me the benefit of the doubt because of our past."

"No. I know that you sucked at chemistry and anything mechanical. I recall you having trouble putting a key on a split–key ring."

Now there was relief, and he wondered if Jana knew that she'd been holding her breath. She released her breath now, and the weariness crept back into her expression.

"Plus, this isn't your style," he went on. "You'll use any dirt you find on Peter, but you wouldn't sneak around with a teething toddler on your hip and put that thing in his car. Too risky in case it went off while you were still holding Marley."

Jana stayed quiet a long moment as if gathering her composure. "Thanks for that."

He shrugged. "I believe you're innocent, but Peter doesn't. He thinks you're the one who put the Smelly Bob in his car."

She muttered some profanity under her breath. "Yes, I figured as much. He's been giving me a lot of stink eye over the last couple of days. I thought maybe it's because I was stink-eyeing him, but I knew he had to be considering who'd done something like that to him."

Yep, there were enough bad vibes coming off Jana that Peter would have picked up on it.

"Are you settling in here all right?" Kace asked, knowing it would be a lead-in to his next question.

"More or less."

Judging from her tone, he was guessing *less*. Since that could have something to do with the other thing he needed to ask her, Kace went ahead and hitched his thumb in the direction of her front porch. "What's with the broken phone and the torn-up papers?"

She opened her mouth, closed it, and while dodging his gaze, Jana reached down, picked up her jeans and shimmied them on over her wet panties. He got another glimpse of nipples when she did the same with her shirt.

"Jana?" he prompted, and he hoped like the devil that whatever had gone on didn't have anything to do with Peter and the Smelly Bob.

She nodded, acknowledging that he was waiting for an answer, and Jana finally lifted her head.

Shit.

There were tears in her eyes.

"Kace," she said, though it was all breath and no sound. "I'm so screwed." On a hoarse sob, the tears started flowing and she stepped right into his arms.

CHAPTER SIX

JANA CERTAINLY HADN'T counted on doing this. Dang it. Waterworks weren't normally her go-to response unless she was alone where no one could see. But she definitely wasn't alone, and Kace wasn't an audience she wanted for this.

"I'm sorry," she muttered, wiping away the tears. Much to her disgust, more came sliding down her cheeks.

She had to hand it to Kace. Even though he'd rarely seen her like this, he didn't react with shock or demand to know what this was all about. He just stood there, letting her boo-hoo on his shoulder.

Oh, and he put his arm around her, too.

That surprised Jana almost as much as her own tears. She knew that Kace wanted nothing more to do with her, and yet here he was offering her comfort.

As good as it felt to be in his arms again—and it did feel amazing—it also made this even worse than it already was. This was a pity hug, maybe something he even saw as his duty, to calm down a person who was connected to his investigation. It probably didn't matter to him that once he'd held her in a different kind of way, that he'd had her in his bed.

And plenty of other places.

No, that didn't matter. This was about getting her calm so he could repeat his question about the broken phone and the papers. In hindsight, she should have cleaned up that mess instead of looking for a quick fix to her rotten mood. Instead of clearing away the evidence of her mood and temper, she'd taken Marley to the sunroom for the play bath. It had worked, too. For some glorious minutes Jana had forgotten her troubles and just enjoyed being with her precious little girl. But the glory moments were over.

She pulled back from Kace and frowned when she saw that she'd wet the front of his shirt. Realized, too, that the outline of her water-soaked bra, and her nipples, were highly visible. *Great.* Now she'd added nipples to this already awkward mix, and she didn't have to guess that he'd seen them because he reached down, picked up the towel that she'd dropped, and handed it to her. Jana positioned it in front of her like a shield.

The corner of Kace's mouth lifted in a quick, short-lasting smile. "Bad day?" he asked.

The burst of laughter left her mouth before she could stop it. Even though she appreciated his attempt to make light of this and put her at ease, it didn't help. Jana was well aware that she'd cried and laughed all in the same minute. And she'd started this whole encounter wearing nothing but wet underwear.

Kace didn't say anything about what he'd obviously seen on the front porch. No needling questions or cop's stares to spur her to a confession. He just stood there in that easy way of his and waited her out.

Jana took a moment to try to find the right way to tell him this. "My ex-husband Dominick is a dickhead."

All right. Not her best effort, but she often found herself resorting to name-calling when it came to Dominick.

Kace lifted an eyebrow. "He broke the phone and tore up the paper?" he asked.

"No, I did that, but it was because of what he did."

Jana considered just leaving it at that since whatever she would add to the explanation would also add to her humiliation, but stuff like this didn't stay secret for long. Kace and everyone else in Coldwater—heck, the whole state—would know soon enough.

"FYI, I'd rather you not say *wed in haste, repent in leisure* when I'm done telling you this," Jana said. "I've already gotten enough snark and judgment from my mother."

More pity came to his eyes, and Jana hated seeing it there so much that she considered doing something else rash and stupid. Like kissing him. Of course, that was probably fueled by that hug of comfort he'd given her. Best not to add the temptation of his mouth after her body was all stirred up from that.

"Dominick cheated on me," she started, since that was the easiest way to start all of what she had to say. Yes, that cut her to the bone and had made her feel like a fool, but it had only been the beginning of what Jana was now calling Dominick's levels of hell.

"I'm sorry," Kace said, and that was washed in pity, too. Oh well. That was better than some other emotions he could have aimed at her. Like—why should I give a rat's ass about your relationship with your second ex?

"In addition to the cheating," she went on, "Dominick had a bad habit of tapping into my bank account and investment funds. Some I knew about. Others I didn't find out about until he'd drained them." Here was the hard part, and she needed a long deep breath to continue. "Since his name was on the accounts, technically he didn't steal from me, but that's what he did. Now I'm going to lose my ranch."

She didn't look at Kace but figured he was thinking she was an idiot to have let this happen. Owning her own ranch had been her dream, and she'd used nearly every penny of her savings and trust fund to make it happen.

"The ranch is a profitable business," she went on, "but I had to buy out Dominick's half. I didn't have a prenup," Jana added in a mumble.

Still no verbal condemnation from Kace, but she figured it was there on his face. That's why she didn't look at him.

"I couldn't prove Dominick's adultery," Jana explained, "so I had no choice but to split the assets. Then, today he called to say he'd sent me papers, saying that he wants to see Marley more than just one day every other week." That required another long breath, and she had to tamp down the anger—no, the rage—so she could continue. "He doesn't actually want to spend more time with her, but he figures I'll pay him off to stop it from happening."

Now it was Kace who dragged in a long breath. "Yeah, he's a dickhead." She jolted when she felt his fingers on her chin, but he only lifted it to force eye contact. "I take it you called him after you tore up the papers, and that's when you smashed your phone?"

"Yes. Stupid, I know. Now I'll just have to buy a new phone and clean up the mess I made on the porch." In the grand scheme of things, those things were minor, but now she was without a phone for a while.

"Do you want me to intimidate Dominick or something?" Kace asked. "Show the badge, threaten him?"

Sadly, she actually considered it for a couple of seconds, but Jana shook her head, pushed her wet hair from her face. "No. But you can maybe see how all of this has played into my mother's relationship with Peter. It's hard for me not to think that he might be hosing her the way that Dominick did me."

Kace made a sound of agreement. Paused. "You'll really lose your ranch?"

"I already have." She shook her head, cutting off what she thought he might ask next. "And no, I won't ask my mother for a loan. It's not a matter of pride. It has more to do with me not wanting her to rub this in for the next couple of decades."

Kace made a sound of agreement. Apparently, her brain and mouth took that as a signal to keep on blathering.

"I've put my place in Blanco up for sale and will stay here for a while until I can find a smaller ranch. Maybe do something like Shelby."

No need for her to spell out that last part. His sister-in-law owned pastureland where she raised, trained and boarded horses. Something like that wouldn't generate as much income as her Blanco ranch, but it would get her back on her financial feet.

If only the rest of her problems could be worked out so easily.

"And you could possibly have to give in to Dominick's demand to see Marley more often?" Kace pressed.

She didn't trust her voice to answer with words. Her throat automatically clogged up with emotion, so Jana just nodded and took a moment to collect herself. "That's another reason I had to sell my ranch. I'll need money to hire the lawyers to fight Dominick. No way am I giving him that much time with our daughter."

"I don't blame you. Eileen would help with something like that, though," Kace quickly pointed out.

"Yes, she would. She loves Marley, and she's come to understand what kind of person Dominick really is. Ironic, since my mom's the one who pushed me to start dating him. He has the right social pedigree," she spat out.

This time the sound Kace made was one of understanding with a tinge of sarcasm. According to Eileen, he definitely hadn't had the right pedigree.

"Being here under my mom's thumb isn't ideal," Jana went on, "but this way I can keep an eye on Peter."

And maybe if she got lucky she could find out if he was up to anything before the wedding. That was on her to-do list along with reinventing her life and fighting her dickhead ex-husband.

The silence came, and it was an uncomfortable one. Jana soon realized that might have something to do with the towel. It had slipped down, and she was showing the wet T-shirt nipple thing again.

"Sorry," she muttered, and she started walking toward the front porch. "I'll pick up my mess and then go in and change. Thanks for letting me cry on your shoulder and vent a thousand vents."

Kace fell in step alongside her as she went to the door. "Seems to me you have reason to vent. Look, if there's anything…"

But he waved the rest of that off, and Jana knew why. Kace was already more involved with her than he wanted to be, and he was probably getting tons of internal signals and reminders that he should just back off and not try to fix her toxic life.

Even though she probably should have gone to her room to change first, Jana went through the house and to the front porch, where she started picking up the debris and shoving it into the pockets of her wet jeans. Kace helped, gathering up the shattered bits of the phone case that had landed on the steps, and he handed them to her.

"Got to get back to work," he said, heading to the main house, where he'd left his truck.

Jana couldn't help but watch him walk away, and because she was watching, she saw him stop when he reached her SUV. But he didn't just stop. He looked in the front passenger's window, putting his face right up next to the glass. After, Kace didn't say anything, but the way he stared at her let her know that he'd seen something that he hadn't liked.

Shoving the rest of the debris in her pockets, Jana hurried off the porch and went to him. "What's wrong?"

But there was no need for Kace to answer since she saw what had garnered his attention on the passenger's seat of her SUV.

A cardboard box.

Jana shook her head. "What the heck is that? I moved some things from my ranch, but I didn't use boxes like that."

She glanced around as if she expected to see whoever had left it. Kace did the same, even looking down at the ground. Maybe for tracks.

"You didn't put that in there?" he asked, sounding like a cop, and he definitely wasn't doing any nipple peeking now. He was still looking inside the SUV. Or more specifically, inside the box.

Jana shook her head and moved in to have a closer look. And on a garbled gasp, she staggered back.

That's because the box was filled to the brim with unopened Smelly Bobs stink bombs.

KACE SAT BACK in his chair at the Gray Mare Saloon and read while he waited. Not fun reading, either. This was the job.

He had been a cop for over a dozen years, and during that time he could count on one hand how many lab reports he'd needed for an investigation. Heck, he could count on one hand how many actual investigations he'd had as a small-town lawman. But here he was again for the second time in a week reading a report—this one from the box he had taken from Jana's SUV.

No prints. Not even Jana's.

That was a red flag because it meant the person who'd put it there had worn gloves. Jana would have hardly done that, only to leave a smoking gun—or in this case a box of Smelly Bobs—in plain sight where anyone could have seen it.

And that meant someone was setting her up.

Going with the obvious, it could be Peter. After all, he was right there on the grounds of the estate, and maybe he wanted to smear some mud on Jana to ensure that she didn't convince her mother not to marry him.

That theory was a stretch though because the bottom line was that Peter could have gotten hurt in the car wreck. Still, he could have risked it. Too bad Peter hadn't shown any odd behavior when Kace had told him about what had been in Jana's SUV. Peter had seemed to dread the prospect of the culprit being Jana. He'd gotten enough of a pained look on his face to be believable, and he hadn't pressed Kace to arrest Jana.

Or tell Eileen.

In fact, Peter had said that he wouldn't mention anything to Eileen until Kace had gotten back the lab report or uncovered any other evidence. Even then the man hadn't thought Eileen should know unless there was another instance. Maybe he was doing that to give Jana the benefit of the doubt, or he could be worrying that his bride-to-be would call off the wedding if he accused her daughter of stock-piling Smelly Bobs.

Kace would keep Peter on the suspect list and try not to wince that he actually had such a list. For him being a small-town cop was smoothing out the bumps that happened in a community, keeping everyone safe and making Coldwater a decent place to live. Suspect lists seemed something more suited for a place where folks didn't know their neighbors.

Or their neighbors' business.

He'd keep his ear to the ground and try to pick up any gossip about the person who could have done this. If it was someone from out of town, then somebody would have likely seen him or her.

Kace was still contemplating who would have done something like that when the front door of the Gray Mare opened, and his brothers came in. They were right on time, and Kace had chosen this table all the way in the back of the saloon so they could have a somewhat private chat along with a pitcher of beer. Kace had already ordered the beer and Judd's usual

Coke. Of course, there'd been no trouble with the service since Judd's soon-to-be wife owned the place.

Cleo was doing paperwork in a small office behind the bar, but she likely wouldn't join them for this conversation. Even though Kace hadn't spelled it out for her, she knew this was sort of a wellness check he needed to do as the big brother.

Nico, Callen and Judd took their seats, each of them giving Kace the once-over. Apparently, he was being subjected to a wellness check, too. Kace wanted to assure them that he was fine, and for the most part, he was. Except for the dreams. He'd wrestled with them for years and had won—until Peter's return. Now he was back to the nightmares that snowballed, not only because of Peter's abandonment but the shit times in foster care.

Kace figured his brothers were battling the same damn thing.

To get business out of the way first, Kace handed Judd the lab report, and he read through it while Callen and Nico poured themselves beer.

"Someone's setting up Jana," Judd concluded, and he passed the paper to Callen. Several moments later, Callen made a sound of agreement, and then he gave the report to Nico.

"Peter came to see me," Nico said as he read. That got Kace's, Callen's and Judd's attention. He didn't say anything else until he'd finished with the report. "Yeah, a setup. I'll bet she's pissed about that."

Despite the other thing—*Peter came to see me*—that Nico had tossed out there, Kace couldn't help but think about Jana. She had indeed been pissed but not just about the setup. Also about her slimy second ex.

Kace also thought about *her.*

Specifically, his body's reaction to her. But there was no time for him to relive that now. Correction— no time to relive that *ever.*

"What the hell did that dickwad want when he came to see you?" Judd asked Nico.

Nico lifted his shoulder. "To tell me he was sorry for what he did. I got the feeling that he thought I'd be the easiest of the bunch to sway."

That was a wise move on Peter's part. Nico was the youngest and the least likely of them to judge.

"I told him to go to hell," Nico added.

So, his kid brother had judged after all. *Good.* Nico was a nice guy, and Kace didn't want Peter trying to get into his good graces until they'd figured out if the man had any *graces* that qualified as good.

"I got the feeling that he's worried," Nico went on, and he looked at Kace from across the table. "Worried that Jana will convince you to do something to turn Eileen against him."

Well, Jana had wanted him to try to stop the wedding, but that clearly hadn't worked. However, she had said that she was still working with a PI to locate her father. Kace considered that well past the long shot stage. Though, if he'd been in Jana's shoes, he might have done the same thing.

"I told Peter to back off Jana," Nico went on, "that she had enough troubles in her life without him slinging accusations at her. I mean, she's lost just about everything because of her divorce."

Nico had obviously been keeping up with Jana, but Kace couldn't say the same for Callen and Judd because they both looked at him. And scowled.

"Not her divorce from me," Kace clarified. "Her latest divorce."

"The guy took her to the cleaners," Nico verified. "After she's sold her ranch in Blanco, she wants to buy my place here in Coldwater."

Clearly, Kace hadn't been paying enough attention to gossip. Unlike Judd and Callen, who nodded in agreement over what Nico had said. "Jana wants to buy your place?" Kace asked, and he sounded dumbfounded enough to get stares from all three of his brothers.

"She does. Eden and I want a bigger place so it could work out for all of us," Nico explained.

Kace did know about Nico and his significant other wanting a bigger place so he could expand his rodeo bull business, but this was the first he was hearing about Jana possibly being in on this.

"But your ranch is right next to mine," Kace pointed out. "We share not only the creek but plenty of fence." He cursed the tone of his own voice when he heard it. It sounded whiny.

"I remember catching Jana and you bouncing in the hayloft in Buck's barn," Callen pointed out. "Sharing a fence line and creek water won't require you to get bare-assed naked with her."

And judging from Nico's snicker and Judd's "good

one" knuckle bump, they thought this was a joke. It wasn't. He didn't want to live next to Jana. Hell, if he was thinking about her this much when she was out of sight, he didn't want to know how much worse it'd be if they became neighbors.

"I was just wondering why she didn't mention anything about this to me," Kace grumbled. He'd just seen her a couple of days ago, and they'd talked about plenty of things. She could have worked this into the conversation since she'd had no trouble spilling everything else.

Kace's phone rang and he cursed when he saw Eileen's name on the screen. He considered letting it go to voice mail, but he got a bad thought. Maybe something had happened to Jana or Marley.

"Kace, you need to get out here to my place right now," Eileen blurted out before Kace could say a word. "It's horrible. Just horrible." She made a hoarse sob, then coughed. "Stink bombs are going off everywhere."

CHAPTER SEVEN

EILEEN HADN'T EXAGGERATED the *everywhere*.

The moment Kace stepped from his truck, he realized that. There were clumps of debris in the yard, by the bottom step of the front porch, under trees and even chunks of something on the plastic Rudolph and several of the other reindeer.

Kace had left the Gray Mare seconds after getting Eileen's call, and during the ten minutes or so it'd taken him to get to her house, the stench hadn't completely dissipated. The place smelled like a hog pen.

"Do you see what they've done?" Eileen said, rushing out the door to Kace.

She had a dainty lace handkerchief pressed to her nose, and Peter was right behind her. No handkerchief for him, but his mouth was twisted up, and Kace didn't think the man was only reacting to the stench. He seemed to be scowling at Kace.

"*They*?" Kace immediately asked, hoping that Eileen had seen who'd orchestrated this.

"They," she repeated, sounding snooty and hysterical at the same time. Peter tried to comfort her by pulling her into his arms. "Whoever did this. It had to be more than one to set so many," Eileen insisted.

Not necessarily. Kace spotted a timer in the one by the verbena. The stink bombs and timers weren't that large, so a person working alone could have hidden them the night before and been long gone before the timers went off.

"Did you have any visitors or see anyone unusual on the grounds?" Kace asked. "Maybe someone new on your gardening crew?"

"No. Nothing like that," Eileen snapped as if annoyed by the questions he had to ask. "No one's worked here for several days."

"We weren't here," Peter volunteered. "We had dinner in San Antonio and ended up staying the night."

So, plenty of opportunity for someone to come in and plant them. Of course, it would have still been a risk since Jana or Bessie could have seen the person. Other than Eileen, they were the only other two people who lived on the property, though Eileen had plenty of day help to tend her horse, grounds and even the house.

"I'll want a list of anyone who works for you or has worked for you in the past year," Kace told her. "That includes any caterers or decorators you've hired."

Then, he could talk to each one. God knew how long that would take, but he had to rule out a pissed-off employee. Considering Eileen's personality, there had to be plenty of those.

Eileen swished the handkerchief like a fan in front of her face. "You have to quit pussyfooting around and make an arrest. This has to stop. I'm trying to plan for a wedding, and I don't have time to deal with this sort of vandalism and destruction."

Kace was pretty sure that was the first time he'd been accused of pussyfooting, but it wasn't unusual for Eileen to make unreasonable requests. "I need the person responsible before I can arrest someone."

He didn't think it was his imagination that Peter's scowl deepened. Kace just scowled back at him. "Jana didn't do this," Kace told him.

That got Eileen untangled from Peter's arms, and she looked at Kace before turning her puzzled gaze to Peter. Kace decided to let the man do his own answering on this.

Peter certainly didn't jump right into an explanation, and he even cleared his throat first. "Kace found more stink bombs in Jana's SUV, and I thought maybe she was upset enough to have put one in my car. Maybe upset enough to have done this." He tipped his head to one of the debris patches.

It was a good thing that Eileen wasn't a poker player because her expression hid nothing. Her mouth dropped open so wide that there was a risk of a bug flying into it, and she volleyed round eyes at Kace and her fiancé.

"Kace believes someone set up Jana," Peter went on when Kace stayed quiet.

"Well, of course, someone did," Eileen blurted out. "Jana wouldn't have done something—" She stopped, obviously rethinking what she'd been about to say. "I'll talk to Jana."

"*I'll* talk to her," Kace insisted. "You just come up with that list I asked for, and while you're at it, include any of your friends who might object to this marriage."

"No one objects," Eileen snapped.

Kace gave her a "suit yourself" shrug, and he looked at Peter. "I want a list from you, too. Include customers you might have riled, former girlfriends, anyone you might have crossed paths with who just doesn't like you."

Kace figured, if Peter was being honest, he and his brothers could land on a list like that.

"I'll go see Jana." Kace didn't wait for Eileen to object. He headed in that direction, making a quick stop by her SUV. No box of Smelly Bobs today, and he noticed that she'd parked it directly in front of the house, maybe so she could keep a better eye on it.

Just as it had happened at Eileen's, Kace hadn't even made it to the porch when the front door opened, and Jana came out. She was carrying Marley on her hip while shoving her phone into her jeans pocket.

"Mom just called and told me what happened," Jana blurted out. "I didn't do this."

Kace nodded, and he went up the porch steps. Marley wasn't fussing today. In fact, she gave him a big smile, causing dimples to flash in her cheeks as she reached for him. Kace hadn't intended to reach back, but the kid ended up in his arms again. Not only that, she smacked a sticky kiss on his cheek.

"Sorry," Jana said, wiping his face with her wrist. "Marley just had applesauce."

The little girl babbled something that might have been her attempt to say "applesauce," and she paired it with an *mmm* sound before she dropped her head on his shoulder. Kace tried to hand her back to Jana, but the kid coiled her arms around him and held on.

"Maybe I look like her dad?" he asked, trying to figure out why Marley always seemed to want to cling to him.

A burst of air, loaded with dry humor, left Jana's mouth. "Not in the least."

Kace wasn't sure if he'd just been insulted or not, and he didn't want to take the time to find out. Going with that promise he'd made to himself to keep his hands and mind off Jana, he needed to talk to her and get the heck out of there.

"Your prints weren't on the box of Smelly Bobs," he told her. "That's the good news. The bad news is someone is trying to frame you. Did you see any-one who might have put those stink bombs in your mom's yard?"

She shook her head. "I was in Blanco and then meeting with the Realtor most of yesterday. I got a cash offer on my ranch. It's a solid one that I ac-cepted, and the buyers want a quick closing."

There definitely wasn't much enthusiasm in her voice about that, and she motioned for him to come inside. He did, but since he didn't plan on staying that long, he didn't shut the door behind him. Kace also didn't take the seat she offered when she tipped her head to the sofa in the living room just off the foyer.

It had been years since he had been in this house,

and a few things had changed. There were baby toys amid the dark Victorian furniture and rugs, and the old lady smell was gone. Marley could be responsible for that, since everything was being filtered through the applesauce scent that was wafting around her.

"Does this mean you'll be buying Nico's place now that you've sold your ranch?" he asked.

"Yes, that's what I want to do." She eyed him with some caution. "How would you feel about that?"

Kace probably should have played it down so as not to make a bigger deal about this than necessary, but he didn't want Jana to believe everything was hunky-dory. "You really want to be my neighbor?" he countered.

"The property is a good place for my horses, and I could move in by Christmas," she countered right back. "But if you say no, I won't buy it."

Well, hell. That meant Nico might not get another buyer for a long time. Property in Coldwater wasn't usually a hot commodity, and he didn't want his brother putting his plans on hold hoping for someone else like Jana to come along. Besides, there'd be about six acres between his house and the one Jana would buy. That was enough distance.

Probably.

"You do what's best for Nico and you," Kace told her.

Jana cocked her head to the side, and Kace didn't think it was his imagination that she wasn't accepting his comment as his true feelings. However, she didn't get a chance to voice her opinion because his phone rang. The sound caused Marley to whimper, and that's when Kace realized she'd fallen asleep on his shoulder. Jana quickly took the baby from him and went into the living room while Kace glanced at his phone screen.

Judd.

"Please tell me there wasn't another stink bomb incident," Kace said when he answered. He also stepped back into the still-open doorway in case he needed some privacy for this conversation.

"There were reports of one, but it turned out to be Petunia," Judd told him. "Yeah, the longhorn got out again, and it seems to have some kind of intestinal problem."

"Sorry I missed that," Kace grumbled, the sarcasm dripping from his voice. "Is Gopher around to clean it up?"

"He's already working on it. But that's not why I called. Anything on who left the latest round of stink bombs at Eileen's?"

"Nothing. What about you? Did you get something new?"

"Maybe. After you left to go out to Eileen's, I called the shop in Oklahoma to nail down DeeDee's whereabouts. Just to make sure she didn't have some part in this. According to the office assistant, DeeDee hasn't been in for four days now. It seems as if this is very rare, that she hardly ever misses work and especially not this time of year because they get a lot of Christmas shoppers."

Interesting. "Did the office assistant know why DeeDee was out?"

"That's the thing. DeeDee didn't tell the assistant anything other than she wouldn't be in. I tried calling DeeDee, but she didn't answer." Judd paused. "I'm finding it hard to believe that she skipped town right around the time our sperm-donor dickhead showed up."

Yeah, it was indeed suspicious. "Keep trying to track her down. I want to talk to her." Kace lowered his voice to add the rest. "Do a run on Jana's ex, too. Dominick Farris."

Judd didn't question why. He just assured Kace that he'd get right on it, and he ended the call.

Kace put his phone back in his pocket and headed toward the living room to let Jana know that he was leaving. But he practically smacked right into her. Kace had to step to the side, and he ended up ramming his shoulder into the wall. Jana's own sidestep sent her knee into a table that must have been made of lead because it didn't budge, and the crack of her kneecap practically echoed through the house.

No baby in her arms, thank goodness, or Marley might have gotten jostled. Or heard the profanity that both Jana and he growled out. But Kace soon spotted the little girl asleep in a playpen in the living room.

Wincing and rubbing her knee, Jana motioned for Kace to follow her. He did—while rubbing his shoulder.

"I need to tell you I'm sorry," she said the moment they reached the front door, "and don't wave that off until you hear what I have to say." He had indeed been about to wave that off, but Jana just rolled over him and kept talking. "Since I've come back to Coldwater, I've thrown your life into chaos, and I want you to know that I'll fix that."

"Chaos?" he repeated. That seemed to put way too much importance on her return. "I'm just doing my job," Kace said, opening the door.

Since she frowned and huffed, that obviously wasn't the response she wanted. "I'm talking about the whole package. You having to see me because of the Smelly Bobs and Peter. You having to see my mother. And now me being your neighbor. But I swear once things settle down, I'll do my best to stay out of your way. I won't even come into town unless it's necessary."

Hell. It made him feel crappy that she would have to rearrange her life. Especially with a baby. After all, there'd be times when she needed stuff for Marley, and he didn't want her postponing her errands just because she was worried about running into him.

"It's okay," he assured her. The cold air was starting to seep in, a reminder that he should finish this conversation and head out. "What happened between us was a long time ago. We've both moved on with our lives, and it won't bother me to run into you."

Kace was proud of himself. That actually sounded good. A "water under the bridge" outlook.

"Oh," she muttered.

That put a halt to his heading out plan. For such a little word, it seemed to mean a whole lot. But what?

Kace was trying to figure that out when Jana took a deep breath. One of those soft, silky sounds that took him back to another time, another place. When there was no bridge over the water.

Kace made the mistake of looking at her face, and their gazes practically collided. This time, he was the one who took a deep breath when her attention lowered to his mouth.

His attention lowered to hers, too.

He couldn't have told anyone how it happened, but suddenly there was no space between Jana and him. One or both of them had closed the distance, and Kace found his hand on the back of her neck. All in all, it wasn't a bad place for his hand to be because he used it to haul Jana to him. And then he broke every rule in the frickin' book.

Kace kissed her.

JANA HAD SEEN the kiss coming, and she did absolutely nothing to stop it. In fact, she was pretty sure, of the two of them, that she had moved faster than Kace to get her mouth on his.

The relief washed over her. Yes, relief. Like a starving woman who'd just been given something delicious to satisfy her hunger. Of course, in the back of her mind, she knew this was one morsel she shouldn't be tasting, but the front of her mind was calling the shots here. That and the parts of her body that Kace's mouth had sent zinging.

Oh, that taste. She remembered it so well. Remembered just how clever his mouth could be, and it vaulted her back to another time. When they'd been together. When they'd been lovers. In those days, all it had taken was one kiss—or in some cases, one look—and she'd wanted to drag him off to bed.

Jana did a different kind of dragging for now. She put her arms around him and maneuvered him closer so that their bodies were pressed together. Kace was a good six inches taller than she was, but they had always lined up just right when it came to making out. That hadn't changed. Nothing had. Well, except for all her extra emotional baggage and the fact that Kace now seemed to be even better at kissing than he had been way back when.

The front of his jeans brushed against hers, and she felt the tight muscles of his chest on her breasts. She slid her hand down his back, feeling him respond to her. Feeling herself respond to him. And she thought that maybe her response was similar to a pressure cooker that had been set too high.

Even with all the jockeying for position for her to get closer to him, the kiss thankfully didn't stop. It raged on, and he deepened it, keeping it long, slow and hot. It was perfect except the problem with long, slow and hot was that it made her want more.

More that she couldn't have.

That reminder jetted to the front of her mind, and she regained just a sliver of common sense when she heard the rustling sound. Here she was in her foyer with Kace kissing the daylights out of her, and that sound could be Marley already waking up.

But it wasn't.

The moment that Jana tore her mouth from Kace's, she caught the movement from the corner of her eye. Movement not coming from the living room, where she'd left Marley but from the porch. She whirled around and came face-to-face with someone she definitely hadn't wanted to see.

Dominick.

Crap. What the heck was he doing here? Dominick grinned in that cocky way that she supposed she had once found appealing, but these days the only thing appealing about him was, well, nothing.

"Interrupting anything?" Dominick asked, sliding his cat-green eyes from her to Kace.

Kace let go of her, and as if it were instinctual, he stepped protectively in front of her. "Yeah, you are," Kace snapped, and he sounded ready to launch into a "mind your own business" lecture.

"This is Dominick," Jana told him, hoping to stave off that lecture. She glared at Dominick. "And I wasn't expecting him today."

Dominick kept up the smile and outstretched his arms. "I just dropped by to check on my baby girl."

"It's not a good time for that," Jana said through clenched teeth, and she upped her glare to make sure Dominick knew that he'd better not have meant that "baby girl" term of affection for her.

"Thought I'd just pop by," Dominick countered as if that explained everything. He hardly spared Jana a glance and certainly didn't look around for Marley. He kept his attention fixed on Kace, and Dominick extended his hand in greeting. "I'm guessing you're Kace Laramie. *Sheriff* Laramie," he emphasized when his attention dropped to Kace's badge.

Kace shook the offered hand, but he also pinned his gaze to Dominick. Jana didn't have to guess that they were sizing each other up. Comparing ex to ex.

"Marley just went down for her nap," Jana blurted out. "It'll be an hour or more before she wakes up."

Dominick shifted toward her as if waiting for her to ask him to come in. Jana didn't. The man had robbed her blind, and while she had to be civil to him in front of Marley, civility didn't apply now.

"There's a diner in town if you want to wait there," Jana added.

Dominick continued smiling. "Actually, I'd intended to go into town anyway and speak to the sheriff. Good timing on my part that he's already here. Though I got to say, I'm a little surprised you two are so…chummy."

Jana groaned, ready to risk civility standards and tell Dominick to take a hike, but Kace answered before she could. "What'd you want to speak to me about?"

"Our mutual ex-wife," Dominick answered without hesitation. He looked at Jana again. "And Marley."

"You were going to talk to Kace about Marley and me?" Jana folded her arms over her chest.

Dominick finally dropped the smile, but Jana got a bad tingling feeling about his new expression. It was as if he was trying to look serious while he was smirking beneath the surface.

"I got a call from someone who blocked their number," Dominick said, and he took out his phone to show Kace the record. It did indeed say Unknown Caller on the screen. "The person told me that Jana might be in trouble. Something to do with planting a device that caused bodily harm."

Because Jana was still working out what that tingle meant, it took several seconds for that to sink in. Apparently, Kace got it sooner than she did.

"Who called you?" Kace demanded.

Dominick lifted his shoulder. "He wouldn't say, but it was definitely a man."

Peter. Who else? And she was going to have a chat with her mother's fiancé about making accusations.

"I didn't put that Smelly Bob in his car," Jana snarled.

Dominick bunched up his forehead, maybe not realizing that was the name of the brand of stink bombs. "The caller was upset," he went on. "He said it was important for me to know that you're not yourself right now. He hinted that you might not be mentally stable."

Her first instinct was to howl out a denial. Yes, howl. But Jana fought to hold on to her composure because an outburst might indeed make her seem unstable.

"Of course, I'm not myself," she agreed once she got her teeth unclenched. There was no hope for relaxing her hands. They were now in tight fists. "You've drained my accounts and nearly put me into bankruptcy." She was so mad that she sputtered out a few more sounds before she continued. "You're an emotional leech, you go through money like water and you belch like a gutted squeaky toy."

Obviously, that last part wasn't something she'd intended to say.

"It's an annoying wheezing sound," she added to Kace. "And he's got a lot of digestion issues so he does it often."

Kace didn't actually seem sympathetic that she'd had to endure that, but he hadn't heard the irritating sound.

"All right." Dominick's tone sounded as if he were speaking to someone who was mentally defective. "Maybe now that you've got that out of your system, we can finish this conversation like adults."

"There's no conversation to finish," she snapped. "I didn't set off those Smelly Bobs, and everything I said about you was true."

Dominick made a sound that let her know he wasn't convinced of any of that. "Anyway, as a parent I have to take the accusations seriously. If you're really going around endangering your mother's fiancé, then I need to rethink things." He handed her the envelope that Jana hadn't even noticed he was holding.

"What is this?" Jana demanded, opening it.

"My lawyer is scheduling a meeting with your lawyer," Dominick answered without hesitation. "We're going to talk about me petitioning for shared custody of Marley. I want as much time with our daughter as you're getting. That means I'll get her two weeks out of every month. Holidays, too. Including this Christmas." He paused. "Jana, you've had too much time with Marley, and I'm going to fix that."

CHAPTER EIGHT

KACE PUSHED THE GELDING, taking his usual morning ride to check some fences and the other horses. He was riding at a full gallop—hardly leisurely—but there was a lot of restless energy bubbling up inside him, and he thought this would help.

It didn't.

But neither had any of the other things he'd tried over the past week. Having a beer with his brothers. Working for fourteen straight hours. Christmas shopping, for Pete's sake—something he hated. All of that to try to push aside the memory of kissing Jana. Nope. Didn't work at all. He still remembered her taste, the feel of her in his arms. But most of all he remembered that it was a huge mistake.

Kace doubted that the kiss had added to Dominick's obvious need to strike out at Jana by threatening to get more time with Marley, but seeing Jana in a lip-lock with her first ex couldn't have helped. He had no idea if Dominick was going to push that threat, and Kace was doing his best not to think of it.

Not my rodeo.

But it sure felt as if it was. And no, it didn't have anything to do with Marley wanting him to hold her whenever he was around. Nothing to do with kissing Jana. It was the fact that Dominick was a pissant who'd stomped on Jana's life, and now the man wanted to do more damage. Kace highly suspected that Jana was right, that Dominick didn't actually want shared custody of his daughter but that this was another ploy to get more cash from Jana.

Kace finished up the ride, cursing that not only had it not cleared his mind but had cluttered it even more. He was still thinking about Jana, and it wasn't just limited to the kiss. He felt sorry for her. Hell, he wanted to help her, and if that wasn't a big-assed red flag, he didn't know what was.

He tended to the gelding, finished his chores in the barn and headed back to his house so he could clean up before going into work. It was his day off, but there was always paperwork to do. It was a sad day in a man's life when he started lying to himself, but this time the distraction might actually do the trick.

Before Kace even made it to his porch, his phone dinged with a text message from Judd.

Just a heads-up, Silla stepped in cow shit outside the Much Ado and is threatening to sue. She's mad enough that she might head out to your place.

Apparently, his morning might have some variety after all. Not good variety, though. The cow shit had likely come from Petunia, the escaping longhorn, and Silla was Silla Sweeny, who was rich, snooty and mean. Much Ado was Much Ado about Stuffing, a taxidermy shop owned by Buck's wife, Rosy. Rosy likely had insurance, and Silla probably wouldn't actually sue, but she'd want to cause a ruckus if Petunia's dung had stunk up her pricey shoes.

And speaking of rich, snooty, mean and pricey shoes, all of that was waiting for him on his front porch.

Eileen was there, pacing and looking completely out of place in her pink dress, matching coat and heels that were probably more suited for a swanky party than a visit to a ranch. There was a cloud of perfume coming off her in waves—a heavy floral and musk scent chosen by someone with no sense of smell.

"I've been waiting for you," Eileen snapped as if they had an appointment for which he was late.

He held up his phone that he'd yet to put away. "Most folks call before they pay me a visit at home."

Her narrowed eyes conveyed the message that she wasn't most people. The gesture also caused her eyelashes to stick together because of the thick layer of mascara she was wearing. "We need to talk."

It was petty of him, but Kace didn't invite her inside, where the central heating would have been a lot more comfortable than standing outside. He might have been more hospitable if she hadn't wrinkled her nose at him.

"You smell like a horse," she complained.

Yeah, he probably did. "You smell like a funeral

parlor." He wanted to curse at the snarky comeback, but Eileen just brought out the worst in him.

She sniffed at herself, frowned but didn't dispute the funeral jab. It seemed to take her a moment to gather her snooty composure. "My wedding will go on as planned. Despite all this with the stink bombs, it won't stop me from marrying your father."

"Peter," he automatically corrected. "If I have the need to call anyone Father, it's Buck. And personally, I don't give a rat's ass who you marry."

Eileen practically snapped to attention like a soldier. Unfortunately, the whip of her body flung another gust of that perfume his way. Also unfortunately, what he'd said wasn't actually true. He did care. Not for himself but because of Jana. Kace wouldn't exactly be jumping with joy at the prospect of seeing Peter if the man moved to Coldwater, but Jana was worried to the bone about Peter hosing her mother.

"All right then," Eileen said. Her voice was both indignant and conveyed that they'd accomplished something.

They hadn't.

"Why are you here?" Kace came out and asked.

"I wanted you to know that I'm doing your job for you. I've put security cameras all around my home and the vehicles. Including Peter's. If someone else tries to set another of those horrible bombs, you'll have proof to make an arrest."

"Good." And because that's all he could think to

say on the matter, Kace stepped around her, intending to get on with his morning.

"There's more," Eileen said, stopping him.

Kace waited, but she didn't add anything else. He groaned and didn't bother to put on a cordial expression when he turned back to face her.

"It's about that PI Jana hired." Eileen picked at some nonexistent lint on her top.

He hadn't expected that subject to come up. However, Kace had thought Eileen might bring up what Dominick was trying to do to her daughter.

"I'm sure Jana told you that she hired someone to look for her father," Eileen added, still lint picking. "I don't think it's good for her to cling to the notion that her father will come back. He's dead. Anyway, I was hoping you could convince her to drop the matter."

Kace just stared at her. "And why would you think I could or would do that?"

A flustered sound left Eileen's mouth. "Because I know about you kissing her. Dominick told me that he'd seen Jana and you carrying on in public and Jana had fallen back under your spell. Dominick believes you're the reason Jana's acting so irrationally."

There were so many things wrong with what she'd just said that Kace didn't know where to start. Truth mixed with bullshit. "Did Dominick also tell you that he threatened to get shared custody of Marley? He wants her two weeks out of the month and holidays, including this Christmas."

Judging from Eileen's wide eyes, Dominick hadn't mentioned that, and Kace finally saw an emotion he'd wanted to see. Serious concern. *Good.* Because Eileen should be worried about her daughter and granddaughter.

"Jana and I weren't kissing in public," he clarified. But he didn't get into the details of what they'd been doing in front of that opened door when Dominick had seen them. "And I've never had the ability to put anyone under my spell. Jana was upset because of Peter's accusations and Dominick's screwing her over, and she ended up crying on my shoulder."

He didn't berate himself for giving his own version of truth and lies. Jana had indeed done some shoulder crying, but it hadn't happened on the day he'd kissed her. That last one had been born of pure lust.

"You should be helping Jana," Kace spelled out for her. "She's already lost her ranch, a place she loved, and now she's got to deal with her worries about Dominick and you."

"Me?" Eileen challenged.

"You," he verified. "She's worried you're making a mistake marrying Peter. It doesn't matter if she's right or wrong about that—she's worried."

Eileen stayed quiet for several long moments. "You really think Dominick might try to get shared custody of Marley?"

"Yes." And Kace didn't hesitate. "I think he'd do pretty much anything if he thought it could drain the rest of Jana's bank account. I also believe he might be the one setting the Smelly Bobs so that he can try to set up Jana."

During her next pause, Eileen's jaw tightened. "I could see him doing that. See him using Marley, too. I doubt he'd let Jana or me see her when it's his weeks to have her."

Kace figured the chances of that were sky-high. Dominick would use this as a bargaining tool to get Jana to cave to his demands.

"Oh God," Eileen muttered under her breath. "I'll see what I can do about Dominick."

Good. Kace knew firsthand just how effective Eileen's interference could be in a relationship. The woman might have awful taste in fashion, decor and men, but she badgered and wheedled enough to get what she wanted.

"I'm still marrying Peter," she added several seconds later, and there was some defiance in her voice.

"Have at it," Kace told her, and he went inside, shutting the door in case Eileen thought this conversation should continue.

He headed straight for the bathroom, where he intended to grab a quick shower. That didn't happen. The moment the hot spray of water hit him, it was as if his mind opened, and the worries came. He didn't have a vested interest in Marley, but he knew how much Jana had always wanted a child.

Their child.

And it had nearly happened, too. Or at least Kace and she had thought it had happened. In fact, that's what had spurred his marriage proposal.

The memories shoved his worries aside, but the memories weren't easy to relive. Well, in some ways they weren't. He could still see Jana coming into the barn at Buck's where Kace had been mucking out the stalls. She'd had a terrified look on her face, and with tears in her eyes, she'd told him that her period was late, that she might be pregnant.

Even now, Kace could feel the gut punch of emotion that had caused. He'd been scared spitless, but that hadn't stopped him from pulling Jana into his arms—yeah, muck and all—and asking her to marry him. Clearly, it wasn't a romantic proposal, not with the stench in the barn and the fear radiating off them in waves. But still she'd said yes.

They hadn't bothered with a pregnancy test but instead had gotten married right away, only to learn a few days later that the pregnancy scare had been just that. A scare. Jana had gotten her period, and there'd been no baby.

Despite his fears and concerns, that had felt like another gut punch for Kace, but it had been worse for Jana. Much worse. It'd been a crushing blow. Heck, she had already picked out baby names. Had mentally built their future and happiness on having a child. That's why they'd never used birth control after that.

Maybe Jana and he had wanted a baby too much, and when it hadn't happened, Kace figured their disappointment had gotten all coiled together with Eileen's interference. Jana started to question whether or not he would have even married her had it not been for his believing she was pregnant. And it had added some fuel to the divorce. A divorce that had eventually led her to marry Dominick and have the baby she desperately wanted.

And now she could lose what was most important to her—Marley.

That brought on fresh anger over what Dominick was trying to pull. It brought on sympathy, too, and he knew from experience that was a bad mix. He should probably avoid Jana for at least a couple of days until all of this settled down. That was the thought he had on his mind when he stepped from the shower and immediately heard the knock at the door.

Hell. He hoped Eileen hadn't been out there this whole time.

Still wet, he dragged on his jeans, went to the door and threw it open. Not Eileen. Belinda. And right next to her was Jana. Not with Marley, either. Jana was standing there looking stunned and embarrassed. Belinda was standing there in a red sweater dress and sex-against-the-wall high heels. Definitely not morning wear. Nor did the dress cover enough to keep warm in the winter air.

Kace couldn't think of any scenario where this was going to end well.

"Uh, when I drove up Jana was on your porch," Belinda said.

Jana had to stop chewing on her lip before she could respond to that. "I knocked, but you didn't answer."

Of course, neither of those comments explained why they were there, and they were doing more gawking than talking. Belinda's hungry gaze was sliding down his bare chest as fast as the water from his shower still was. Jana was eyeing his porch light with intense fascination, which meant she was trying not to look at him.

"I, uh, should be going," Jana finally said. "I just found out my mom had visited you and figured I owed you an apology."

"And I came over to bring you this." Belinda lifted a bag from Patty Cake's Bakery. "Fresh cinnamon rolls. I thought we could chow down and catch up over coffee since you don't have work today."

"I do have work," he quickly assured her. "I was just getting dressed to go in." Kace caught onto Jana's arm when she started to walk away. "But I do need to talk to you about Eileen's visit."

That was the second lie he'd told today. He didn't especially need to rehash that conversation with Jana, but it seemed the better alternative than the not-so-subtle sex offering that Belinda was making. There were strings a mile long on those cinnamon rolls. Plus, nibbling on them would give Belinda hope that he'd soon be nibbling on her.

"I need to have a word with Jana," Kace added to Belinda when the woman didn't budge.

"About the investigation?" Belinda concluded, and she sounded hopeful.

Now, here's where a third lie would have saved Belinda some hurt feelings, but it would have also given her some encouragement to come right back in those heels and with her pastry foreplay.

"In part," Kace admitted, "but Eileen and I talked about other things. Things that Jana needs to know."

"Oh." Belinda blinked. "Okay. Maybe I should bring these to your office then, and we can have them on your break." She lifted the bag again as if he'd gotten sudden memory loss and forgotten it was there.

If there was a picture of *awkward* in the dictionary, this would be it. "Come inside and wait," he told Jana. He pulled on his coat over his bare chest, and took hold of Belinda's arm to get her moving off the porch and back to her car.

Judging from the way it was parked, it looked as if she'd skidded to a stop on the gravel driveway. Maybe because she'd been in a hurry to get to the door before Jana. Those same bits of gravel dug into his feet, reminding Kace that he was barefoot and barely dressed.

"You don't have to say it," Belinda muttered when they were out of earshot of Jana. "I know I'm acting like a desperate jealous lover."

No way would he have actually spelled that out, but it was a nail-on-the-head description.

"And I know you want to remind me that we don't have that kind of relationship," Belinda went on. "We've always kept things casual. Friends with benefits." She paused, shook her head. "God, I hate that expression."

There were worse ones. *Fuck buddies.* But sadly they were accurate labels for what had gone on between Belinda and him.

"I'm well aware that you've seen other women over the years," Belinda went on, clutching the bakery bag to her chest. "I've seen other men. We've always gotten together whenever it suited us. And don't apologize for that," she quickly added.

Since that's what he'd been about to do, Kace stayed quiet.

Belinda's eyes came to his. "I think the reason this bothers me is because Jana's your ex-wife, and I know how much the divorce threw you for a loop."

It had indeed, and even though Kace had never discussed that with Belinda, or anyone else for that matter, maybe he'd worn his broken heart on his sleeve.

"I'm just worried about you, that you'll get hurt all over again," Belinda added.

Her concern didn't give him as much comfort as it should have. That's because it meant Belinda cared about him. Cared too much.

"No need to worry," he assured her. He could have explained that Jana and he knew they weren't right for each other. Their divorce proved that. But there was no way he could say that to Belinda and not give her hope of their own possible relationship.

"But?" Belinda questioned when he didn't continue.

Kace nodded. There was a *but* all right, and it was best if he made a clean break. "You deserve a guy who'll jump at the invitation to share those cinnamon rolls with you. I can't give you that, Belinda. I can't ever give you *me*."

Of course, he'd told her similar things before, but this time it seemed to sink in. At least he hoped it would.

Kace cursed when he saw that Belinda was blinking hard as if trying to fight back tears. *Hell.* He hoped she didn't cry. But Belinda seemed to steel herself up. She brushed a quick kiss on his cheek, got in her car and drove off. Fast. While kicking up more of that gravel. Seeing her quick exit caused Kace to kick up some feelings as well.

He felt like a dick.

And now he was going to have to deal with Jana. There might be a round of tears with her visit, too.

"I'm sorry," Jana said the moment he came in the front door. She hadn't gone far. She was still in the small foyer. "If I'd known Belinda was going to be here, I wouldn't have come."

Belinda had likely felt the same way about Jana. "It's okay," he said, putting his jacket back on the wall peg.

"No, it's not. I didn't want to cause trouble between you two."

He lifted his shoulder, remembering again that he wasn't wearing a shirt and wondering if he should just finish this talk with Jana and then get dressed or prolong the visit by going inside to grab some clothes. Kace decided to go with just finishing it.

"Belinda and I aren't together anymore," he explained, giving Jana the condensed version.

"Oh." She sounded surprised. "Oh," she repeated, and this time she sounded as if it had sunk in.

Kace figured she was about to ask if the not being together had something to do with her so he cut Jana off at the pass with a question of his own. "Where's Marley?" He tipped his head to her SUV.

"At the house with the sitter. I hired Piper Drake."

Kace wasn't surprised about that. Piper was Nico's foster sister. Well, sort of. Piper and Nico had had the same foster mother anyway, and even though Nico and Piper had never actually lived under the same roof, they still thought of themselves as siblings. After the foster mom had passed away, Piper had moved to Coldwater with her own biological mother. Piper was also a teenager and pregnant.

"Piper doesn't have morning classes so she agreed to help out some," Jana added. "But I need to get back soon since this is her first time with Marley."

Kace supposed that someone had mentioned to Jana that Piper was a good kid who'd been looking to make some extra money. Money that she technically didn't need since Nico and her mother would cover her expenses. Still, Piper had wanted to earn some cash to put in savings for the baby.

"Your mom came by to tell me that she installed security cameras," Kace explained. "She also wanted me to talk you out of pushing the PI to continue to look for your father."

The breath she released was part sigh, part huff. "I won't do that, and I'm sorry she tried to involve you." A muscle flickered in her jaw. "What else did she want?"

"Eileen didn't know about Dominick wanting to

have Marley more often. She seemed upset about the possibility of that happening."

This time her breath was mostly a groan. "That means she'll interfere. Not in a good way, either. You know how she can be when she's sticking her nose into other people's business."

"Yeah. I've got some firsthand knowledge of that. But maybe it's not so bad if she interferes with Dominick."

The surprise practically danced across her eyes. "You're defending my mother?"

"I wouldn't go that far, but it might not hurt for you to have some backing on this. The stakes are pretty high."

She made a quiet sound of agreement, and this time there was no surprise-dance in her eyes but weariness. Jana pushed her hand through her hair. "I made such a big mistake marrying him, but if I hadn't, I wouldn't have gotten Marley."

Kace didn't have to be a parent to understand that. Jana loved the little girl. Still, she'd have to deal with Dominick and his antics for at least a while. If he truly was a gold-digging leach, then he would likely move on to someone else.

"We both know what it's like to deal with problem fathers," she grumbled.

Kace was still dealing with his, and heaven knew if and when that would end. Maybe not for years if Peter did marry Eileen and move to Coldwater.

"Uh, I should go," Jana added.

When he heard the change in her tone, Kace

looked at her. He wished he hadn't, though. That's because her tone change and sudden need to go didn't have anything to do with their topic of discussion. This was about his half-naked body. He knew this because Jana was looking at anything but him.

"I should apologize for that kiss, too," she said.

Oh yeah. This was about his body, and Kace wished that it was one-sided. For reasons he didn't want to explore, her reaction to him was causing him to react. To her.

And she was fully dressed.

That kiss had really screwed up things between them, which was a very good argument for why it shouldn't happen again. That, and more kissing would just complicate the heck out of an already complicated situation.

Jana cursed, her gaze practically colliding with his. "We're going to end up having sex again, aren't we?" she snapped.

Now Kace was the one who was surprised. Floored, actually. He couldn't get his mouth to form words.

"Sex," Jana repeated as if it were a particularly nasty flu strain. Then, she groaned. "I don't see a way around it."

Oh, he wanted to disagree with that. There were plenty of ways around it. Ways that included his staying away from her. But Kace didn't believe that was going to happen.

Nope.

As much as he wanted to fight it, he doubted he'd

be able to occupy the same air space with his ex-wife and not have it lead to sex. Of course, it'd be wrong, but it might have one huge side effect of burning off enough of this lust he was feeling so he could think straight. Then, he might be able to come up with something better than just standing there while the horny hormones assaulted both of them.

"I need to get back and check on the sitter," Jana said, fluttering her fingers to her SUV.

For one scalding hot moment, Kace thought she might lean in and kiss him. If she did, it'd all be over. He'd have to take her right then, right there. But he got a reprieve when his phone rang. That was enough to cause Jana to issue a quick goodbye, and she practically ran out of the house and to her SUV.

Kace frowned at her speedy exit. Frowned, too, at the Unknown Caller that popped up on his phone screen. This might be the only time in his life he felt relief over a telemarketer. He didn't say anything when he hit the answer button, but it wasn't long before he heard the caller's voice.

"Sheriff Laramie?" the woman greeted. "I'm DeeDee Merriweather, and I understand you've been trying to get in touch with me for the past couple of days."

"Yes," he verified. "I wanted to ask you about your business partner." And find out if she'd had any part in setting those Smelly Bobs. "I'm guessing you know that he's here in Coldwater?"

"Yes, I know," she said. Kace couldn't quite put

his finger on her tone, but he thought he detected some anger there. "Is he in some kind of trouble?"

An interesting question. Of course, both Kace and Judd had tried to call DeeDee so the woman had to know something was up. "Someone vandalized his property," Kace settled for saying. "I wanted to find out if maybe it was someone with a grudge against him and wondered if you'd be willing to answer some questions."

"A grudge?" It sounded as if she chuckled. "Yes, that's a possibility."

"Would you be the one holding a grudge?" Kace came out and asked.

"Absolutely," DeeDee quickly confirmed, "but I haven't vandalized anything. Why, did he say that I did?"

"No." In fact, Peter had said very little about his business partner. Everything Kace and Judd had learned about her had been through a background check. "But I'd still like to talk to you."

"All right." Again, no hesitation. "I'd be more than happy to sit down and talk to you about Peter," she went on. "From the messages you left, I understand you're in Coldwater, Texas. I can come there day after tomorrow if that suits you."

"It does, but we could possibly just take care of this over the phone."

"I don't mind making the trip." Now DeeDee paused. "I'm guessing it's not a coincidence that Peter and you have the same last name?"

"No. He's my birth father." And Kace left it at that.

"Well, Sheriff Laramie, I'm betting there are plenty of things you don't know about your dear ol' dad. I'll see you day after tomorrow and can fill you in."

CHAPTER NINE

Sex.

Specifically, sex with Kace.

Jana figured there were plenty of things she should be thinking about, and that wasn't one of them. Still, she just hadn't been able to get him off her mind since the day before when she visited him at his place.

Her plate was full with other things to think about, what with taking care of her baby, dealing with Dominick, selling her ranch, buying another place and worrying about the huge mistake her mother might be making. A mistake that could put Eileen financially in Jana's shoes.

Even though it wasn't easy, Jana knew she could adjust to having less, but she wasn't sure her mom could cope. And that's why she had to take another stab at convincing her mother to take some precautions. Maybe do a prenup, or better yet delay the wedding until she knew Peter a little longer.

Jana's hopes got dashed on the last possibility when she walked into her mother's house and spotted the decorations. It was a circus.

Literally.

The tacky circus decor was no longer just in the foyer but instead had spilled into the parlor and great room. The furniture had been moved out and replaced with things normally seen under the big tent. Trapezes, large sculptures of upright bears, tigers and even an elephant. The Christmas tree was tucked into the corner as if it were an afterthought.

"Phant," Marley attempted, and she also squirmed and wiggled to get out of Jana's arms. Jana held on. She didn't want one of those critters toppling over on the baby.

"Don't you just love it?" her mother asked.

Jana wished she'd heard some of her mom's usual sarcasm, but there was none. It wasn't in her eyes, either, when Jana turned back to look at her mother, who was making her way toward her.

"It's for the wedding," her mom added. "All of it is Peter's work."

Her mother hadn't needed to clarify that since Jana already knew the man had done the pieces in the foyer. They weren't her taste, but it hadn't been so bad when there'd only been a couple of them.

"We toyed with a jungle theme," Eileen went on, and she scooped Marley into her arms to give her a kiss and a hug. "How's my little princess this morning?"

"Phant," Marley attempted again, waggling her fingers in the direction of the elephant.

"Sorry, sweetie, but they're not toys." Eileen gave the baby a mock pout. "But let's go to your place and see what's in there."

Jana didn't have to guess what would be in there. Toys and lots of them. She didn't mind her mother going overboard for Marley, but it always gave Jana a small jolt. Eileen certainly hadn't been this generous or playful with Jana herself. Instead, Eileen had focused on her social gatherings and committees. Jana recalled lots and lots of parties that she'd watched from the second-floor balcony.

"Where's Peter?" Jana asked when she didn't see the man. He always seemed glued to Eileen's hip whenever Marley and she visited.

"In the guesthouse. He's working on an art project today. Something special, he said. I think it might be a wedding gift for me."

And Eileen did something that squeezed at Jana's stomach. Her mom giggled. Yes, giggled. Clearly, her mother was happy, and while on the surface that was a good thing, Jana knew the happier you were, the harder you fell.

She followed her mom down a back hall to what Eileen had dubbed Marley's place. Not a nursery. That was upstairs. Not a bedroom. That was upstairs as well. This was a gigantic sunroom that Eileen had converted into part playroom, part park in an over-the-top kind of way.

There was a toddler swing set, reading area, a six-foot-tall dollhouse, kiddy computer station and hundreds of toys. No exaggeration. There were over a dozen toy chests filled to the brim. Today, there were new things added to the mix—smaller scale versions of stuffed circus animals. Clearly that pleased Marley because the moment Eileen stood her on the floor, the little girl toddled straight toward the elephant.

"You didn't bring her over yesterday," Eileen pointed out, and she made her way to a sitting area so they could watch Marley dart from one new plaything to another. "Honestly, Jana, our differences shouldn't stop me from seeing my granddaughter."

"That had nothing to do with our *differences*. I had to go to Blanco to finish the arrangements for having my things packed there." Jana pushed aside the ache that caused in her heart. What's done was done, and it was time to move on.

"And you didn't tell me about buying Nico's place," her mother added. Eileen was definitely doing some sulking.

"Nothing's final on that." Though, if all went well, it should be final in a day or two. "I can't go to closing on Nico's ranch until I've completed the sale on the Blanco place. I need the cash from the first to pay for the second. And no, don't offer me a loan," Jana said before her mother could do just that.

A loan coupled with plenty of maternal disdain for the decisions that Jana had made to bring her to this point in her life.

"Certainly you don't object to me buying Nico's ranch," Jana went on, "because it'll mean you'll get to see Marley more often."

The silence came between them, and it wasn't a happy variety like the delighted squeals from Marley, who was now having a "conversation" with and hugging what appeared to be a stuffed orangutan. And Jana knew full well the reason for the silence. It was because her mom was concerned about this shared custody battle brewing between Dominick and her.

"I want to pay off Dominick," her mother said.

Jana groaned even though she'd known that would be her mom's first response to this situation. "No. Dominick's already gotten enough money from me, and he won't stop even if you offer him a payment. He'll just keep coming back for more."

"I could get him to sign some kind of agreement." Eileen suggested that so quickly that it meant she'd already given it some thought.

"He won't sign an agreement because it would be admitting to blackmail or extortion."

Her mother's nod—which had also been quick—told Jana that Eileen had considered that as well.

"The best thing to do is wait him out," Jana went on. "Dominick has nothing he can use against me. If he presses and tries to take this back to the judge, I'm sure Kace would vouch for me. He knows I didn't plant those stink bombs."

Her mother's deep blue eyes, which were a genetic copy of her own, shifted to Jana for a long look. One that seemed to question whether or not Jana was truly innocent. It went on for a while, like a cop's stare, but Jana wasn't the one who broke. Her mother finally huffed and put her attention back on Marley, who was now trying to drag the elephant closer to a giraffe, maybe to create her own menagerie.

"I feel guilty, you know," Eileen said a moment later. "I'm the one who pressured you to marry Dominick. Obviously, that backfired on me, and now you're thrown together with Kace again because of Dominick's accusation." She paused. "Did you really kiss Kace the way that Dominick said?"

Jana didn't know exactly how Dominick had described the kiss, but even if he'd embellished it, it had still happened. "Yes."

"And you think that's wise?" her mother asked.

The answer was no. It wasn't wise. Jana had no doubt about that. But that didn't mean it wouldn't happen again. Of course, when it did, she'd have to put reins on her heart to keep it from galloping off again.

Rather than get into a discussion about Kace, Jana moved on to the next point she wanted to make. "Dominick isn't the only one accusing me. Peter thinks I had some part in planting the bombs, too."

"I've talked to him about that, and he thinks it best if there's a truce between the two of you. He'll forget all about the stink bombs if you'll stop trying to push him out of my life. Honestly, Jana, you have to see how happy the two of us are together."

"I was happy with Dominick when we were dating and first married." But Jana waved that off. Snarky reminders weren't going to work here. "Peter's just not the man I thought you'd marry. He's not in any of your clubs—"

"He's an artist, and I've always been interested in art." She paused. "He's good in bed. I mean, really good. First time in my life I've had multiples, you know."

Jana figured her loud groan would have happened a whole lot sooner if her jaw hadn't frozen for a few seconds. There wasn't a word of this she wanted to hear, and it should be classified as a form of child abuse. Still, it made her wonder if her mom was under some kind of sex spell. It could happen. Jana had firsthand experience of that with Kace. Once they'd hooked up in high school, it was as if she'd developed romance tunnel vision. Kace had been it for her. Too bad that in her case, sex spells didn't last.

Or could reappear at the oddest times.

Like now, for instance. She heard Kace's voice, and thoughts of kissing him came at her like a giant pile of rocks tumbling down a hill. The romance tunnel vision came, her gaze zooming right to him as Estelle Mason, the maid, ushered him in.

"Tace," Marley called out, and she began to toddle her way over to him as if they were old friends.

Jana tried to get ahead of her daughter, failed, and Marley ended up giving Kace's leg a strangling hug. Because Jana knew his face so well, she saw the moment of surprised discomfort before he scooped the little girl up in his arms. Marley showed her approval by hugging him and then babbling off descriptions of her new toys as she pointed to each one.

As expected, Kace didn't seem especially comfortable with that, and in between the acknowledging glances at Marley's toys, he gave Jana and her mother quick looks to let them know that this wasn't a social visit.

Crap.

Jana hoped someone hadn't set off another Smelly Bob.

With Eileen trailing right along behind her, Jana

went to Kace and took Marley from him. Of course, her daughter protested. Apparently, Jana wasn't the only one who had some kind of tunnel vision for Kace.

"Peter has some visitors," Kace said, looking at Eileen. "They're out front, but it's best if Marley doesn't see them," he added to Jana.

Well, that got Jana's attention. Exactly what visitors could Peter have that would warrant shielding Marley? She intended to find out.

"Could you watch Marley for a few minutes?" Jana asked Estelle, and as expected, the woman gave her a quick agreement. Also as expected, Marley went to her, and Jana suspected the maid had given her little girl enough sweets that Marley knew this would be a good arrangement for her.

"Is Peter here?" Kace asked Eileen once Estelle had taken Marley in the direction of the kitchen.

"Yes, he's in the guesthouse. What's this about? Who are his visitors?"

"Could you please just get him and bring him to the front driveway?" Kace said, obviously dodging her questions.

Eileen gave a shaky nod, and she hurried out the back door. Jana followed Kace when he headed toward the front.

"Who are the visitors?" Jana asked.

"Strippers," he said.

Of all the answers she expected, that hadn't been one of them. Maybe loan sharks, out-of-town cops there to arrest him, jealous former lovers, etc. But she was still processing the notion of strippers as Kace opened the front door, and Jana saw the white van with the logo on the side.

Tit for Tat.

There were painted balloons dancing around the logo. No, she amended as she got a better look. They were pink pasties. They coordinated with the silver ones that the tall, busty brunette was wearing while she leaned against the passenger's side door. Her long tumbling hair covered up much more than the rest of her outfit, which consisted of the pasties, a mink-like bolero, tight leggings and silver stilettos.

The woman looked bored and put out until her gaze landed on Kace, and then she flashed him a *very* welcoming smile. Since Jana had flashed him similar smiles in the past, she knew it was an invitation for sex.

No wonder Kace hadn't wanted Marley to see this.

"Well?" the brunette said. "Got it all worked out with Peter Peter Woman Eater?" She said the stupid nickname with affection and lust, which were likely as fake as her 32DDs.

"Soon," Kace answered her as other women began to get out of the van. A curvy blonde wearing nylon jogging pants and a long-sleeved cropped boob-hugging tee that was meant to simulate workout clothes. The redhead wearing a short toga, thong and a sparkly garland coiled around her hair. All three were shivering in the cold.

Kace motioned for the women to stay put, and he turned to Jana. "They showed up at the police station, asking for directions. Juicy—that's the blonde—said that Peter had hired them for his own personal bachelor party. According to Jezebel, the redhead, they were supposed to meet him at a room he booked at the inn."

Well, now. Peter Peter Woman Eater had been a naughty perv. Maybe naughty enough to cause her mom to end the engagement. And while Jana would have liked to hang on to that joyful possibility for a while, this didn't make sense.

"If they had a room at the inn, why'd they go to the police station?" The inn was just up the street, and they would have had to pass it to get to Kace.

"Good question," Kace said. "I don't think anyone here is going to like the answer."

No. Jana was suddenly sure of that.

"Cricket, the brunette, told me they got lost," Kace went on, "but when I looked in the van, I saw the address for the police station. The way the three of them jiggled in, clamoring for Peter, I got the feeling this was some kind of weird setup, one meant to get the wrong kind of attention."

Yes, and proof of that were the other vehicles she noticed at the end of the driveway. Several men were out of their trucks and using binoculars to ogle the strippers. Jana scowled at them and pointed to the bare spot on her finger where she knew these men had wedding rings. Maybe that would spur them to go about their business.

"What is this?" Peter asked when he stepped onto the porch with them. As expected, Eileen was right by his side, and she did some stripper ogling of her own. Definitely no lusty interest but rather stunned horror.

"Peter Peter Woman Eater," Cricket called out. "Come out here and warm us up." She waggled her crooked finger at him, motioning for him to come to her.

But Kace did his own motioning, along with grumbling. "Stay where you are until I can get this sorted out."

"Why would you bring these women here?" Eileen demanded from Kace.

Kace handed Peter a piece of paper with Tit for Tat emblazoned across the top of the letterhead. It was a contract for three strippers, and Peter's signature was at the bottom. Or rather Peter's signed name was there.

"I didn't do this," Peter insisted as his eyes skirted over the contract. "I didn't do this," he repeated like a plea to Eileen.

Her mother's mouth was in a firm disapproving line, but Jana noticed that it wasn't aimed at Peter or the strippers. It was on Kace.

"Obviously, this is some kind of prank," Eileen concluded. "Why haven't you caught the person doing this to Peter?"

Jana had her own look at the contract. A prank, maybe, but if so it was an expensive one. Coupled with the cost of the suite at the inn, this would be about fifteen hundred dollars.

Kace didn't roll his eyes or blow out a weary

breath, but he had to be tired of hearing her mother harp on about him not doing his job when it came to her beloved fiancé.

"According to the contract, this has been paid in full," Kace pointed out. "I called Tit for Tat on the way over, and they said the person claiming to be you used cash."

"They're either lying or they got duped by someone pretending to be me," Peter snapped, but it seemed as if his fit of temper went as quickly as it came. "I'll go to this place and straighten things out."

"I can make arrangements for one of my deputies to do that," Kace offered.

Peter waved that off, but before he could say anything else, they heard another vehicle pulling into the driveway. At first, Jana thought it was one of the gawkers coming closer for a better look, but it was another van. This one had Jeb's Party Favors emblazoned on the side.

"Is this something for the wedding?" Jana asked.

Both Peter and her mother shook their heads.

A man stepped out, gave them a perky wave and threw open the back doors of the van. After some maneuvering around, he emerged carrying a huge Mylar balloon bouquet.

Of smiling penises.

There was no mistaking them, and they were even complete with balls. They jutted up into the air like erections and made slapping sounds when the wind whipped them against each other. The strippers hooted and cheered.

Eileen gasped and pressed her hand to her chest as if it were the most horrifying sight she'd ever seen. If her mother hadn't been reacting that way, Jana might have laughed. Well, for a few seconds anyway. But then she was sure she would have gotten around to feeling bad because someone was trying to shed a very bad light on the man her mom was marrying.

"Peter Laramie?" the delivery guy who was still all grins called out. His grin widened when Peter lifted his hand in acknowledgment. "Here's your order," he happily announced.

"Who sent these?" Peter demanded.

Finally, the guy's grin faded. Probably because with the exception of the strippers, he was seeing a lot of scowls from those on the porch. "Uh, according to the order, you did. One dozen pink cock-and-ball Mylars. What should I do with them?"

Jana was betting that Peter wanted to mutter a suggestion that wasn't anatomically possible. Instead he said, "I don't care. Just get them out of here."

Her mother's shock/horror/embarrassment had now progressed to the point where she'd buried her red face against Peter's chest. Of course, Jana felt for her. She loved her mother and hated to see her like this. But what was worse was that these stupid pranks were causing Jana to feel some sympathy for Peter, too.

Which may have been his intention all along.

Kace and she exchanged a long glance, and he seemed to be asking silently if she was okay. Jana nodded, felt the unspoken conversation happen between them. Felt that inevitable slide of heat, too. He was like a big ice-cream sundae to a dieting woman. Delicious and very much wanted.

"I'll make sure the balloon guy and the strippers leave," Kace said. "Let me know if you want me to deal with finding out who sent them here."

Peter nodded and took her mother back inside, but Jana followed Kace out to the vans. "He really doesn't care what happens to the balloons?" Cricket asked.

"No, he just wants them gone," Kace told her.

"Well, that's a boatload of awesomeness. We'll take them." And despite teetering on ice pick heels, she hurried to gather up the Mylar penises.

Jana watched as the three women batted and slapped the balloons into their own van. It was very pornographic in a juvenile humor sort of way.

Kace and Jana didn't say anything, not until the strippers and the balloon guy were back in their vehicles and were driving away. Jezebel gave Kace a wink and the call-me sign.

"Yes," Kace said.

Since he wasn't looking at her, it took Jana a moment to realize that he'd spoken to her and not to the stripper. "Yes?" she questioned.

"To sex." Now he looked at her, and there was some weariness mixed with the heat. "But just sex," he emphasized. "I don't think either of us are up for anything more than that."

Not trusting her voice, Jana made a soft sound of agreement, but inside she felt giddy. Like happy liquid gold. Yes, yes, yes! She was going to get another taste of Kace after all.

CHAPTER TEN

KACE WOULD HAVE eaten a field of cacti before he admitted that touching a dead stuffed thing gave him the creeps. He didn't want anyone to know that he got goose bumps and shivered—yeah, actually shivered—when he clamped his hand over the taxidermy armadillo.

It felt scaly and very much dead.

Still, he got a good hold on it from its place on the shelf and while balancing on the stepladder, he passed it down to Rosy.

"Thank you," Rosy gushed, lovingly putting the armadillo like a baby in the crook of her arm. "Now, I need Miss Fluffy."

Kace felt another round of goose bumps and shivers. The stuffed cat was even creepier than the armadillo. Of course, it was all about degrees of creepy when it came to the contents of Rosy's taxidermy shop. Kace would have felt more at ease walking through a cemetery at midnight on Friday the thirteenth than he did here.

Still, he'd do pretty much anything for Rosy. Not only was she his foster father's wife, Rosy had been a stand-in mom for him too many times to count.

That's why he'd come right away when she'd called and asked him to get some things from the high shelf.

"Thank you," Rosy gushed again when she had Miss Fluffy in her arms.

"Anything else?" Kace asked, and he hoped like the devil she wouldn't ask him to take down Mr. Rat, the ferret. With its glassy bead eyes and grinning fanged mouth, it would win the creep award.

"No, that's it," Rosy answered. "I just wanted to create a new holiday display for the window and these guys will do just fine. They'll really draw a crowd once they have on some Christmas finery."

Not likely, but Rosy did a nice part-time business with hunting and fishing trophies along with those who wanted to preserve their beloved fur babies. Kace just didn't get the appeal, but apparently enough did to keep Rosy busy.

Kace came down from the ladder, put it away and checked his phone to make sure he hadn't missed a text from Ginger. Nothing. But Ginger should be contacting him any minute now to let him know when DeeDee arrived. Well, unless DeeDee had changed her mind about coming in. The woman hadn't answered Kace's latest text when he tried to confirm their meeting.

He wasn't dreading seeing DeeDee as much as he had touching Miss Fluffy, but it had potential to turn out bad. If DeeDee dished some dirt on Peter, Kace would have to let Eileen and Peter know, and they wouldn't welcome the news with open arms. Jana might, though.

Jana.

He hadn't actually needed to have her name come to mind to think about her. Lately, Kace hadn't been able to go more than five minutes without the image of her slamming right to the front of his thoughts. Not especially convenient images of her, either. These were more of the dirty sex variety, and they were especially clear because the two of them had had their share of dirty sex. Now there was a high probability of more of it in their near future.

But just sex. I don't think either of us are up for anything more than that.

Yeah, he had indeed said that. As if it would have made it better somehow. Sex would still be sex, and it would still be a complication no matter how many ways he qualified it. Knowing that full well hadn't stopped him from asking Jana to come to his place on Friday night. He'd cook her dinner, and if it didn't happen before or during the meal, they'd land in bed after. Or likely on the floor since it'd be closer.

His body was burning for her, and despite the insanity of it all, Kace knew he wouldn't even try to muster up the willpower to resist her. If he'd wanted to do that, he wouldn't have invited her over in the first place.

Of course, there was the possibility that Jana wouldn't be able to get a sitter or that she would come to her senses and cancel the sex date with him. But Kace figured Jana was just as weak as he was right now.

"There's another one," Rosy said, snagging Kace's attention.

Hell. He hoped he didn't have to handle Mr. Rat after all, but Rosy's attention was on the window, not her stash of critters. Kace went closer and saw the Mylar penis jutting across the sky. It was the fourth one he'd seen since the strippers had taken the balloons the day before. Obviously, they'd let them go, maybe as a joke, but Kace knew Peter and Eileen weren't ha-ha-ing over this. Neither were any of the parents who were having to explain to their kids what was floating through their airspace.

"Maybe you can shoot them down," Rosy suggested.

Kace had considered it, but from what he'd read, the balloons would be deflating soon and would fall out of the sky. The trick would be to make sure they didn't get tangled with any power lines. If that happened, he'd be sending a bill to Tit for Tat for the stupid prank.

"Eileen's gotta be red-faced with embarrassment over this," Rosy remarked.

"She is."

And Eileen was also mad. No surprise there. Her anger had only revved up when Peter hadn't managed to get any answers when he'd paid personal visits to Tit for Tat and Jeb's Party Favors. Both managers had told him that a man had come in and paid cash for the items and services. A man who didn't especially look like Peter but had still used his name. Since neither manager nor any of their staff could give them the real identity of the customer, that was a dead end.

Kace watched as the Mylar penis whirled around, dangling for a few seconds and then floating away.

"Are you getting ready for Christmas?" Rosy asked while she coiled some gold tinsel around Miss Fluffy's neck.

It wasn't exactly small talk. Rosy knew from experience that Kace tended to put off his holiday shopping. And he hadn't finished this year's yet. It was a reminder that in between sex fantasies about Jana he needed to get online and order some things for his brothers, their significant others, Rosy and Buck. Maybe he'd get something for Marley, too. Or not. That might feel like, well, some kind of commitment to Jana, and it was obvious neither one of them was looking for that.

"I'll have the presents wrapped and ready," he assured her.

Rosy didn't say anything for a long time, and she didn't make eye contact with him until she'd finished arranging a tiny strand of twinkling lights around the stuffed armadillo. "And how are you dealing with your dad being around?"

"Well, I won't be getting him a present." It wasn't a comfortable topic even without the embarrassing balloon, but it was a question he'd been getting a lot. "It's causing a few flashbacks," Kace admitted.

Rosy plopped the "adorned" stuffed critters in the display window and slid her arm around him. "For

Judd, too. I suspect it's bothering Callen and Nico as well, but they're not saying much."

No, they weren't talking about it, which was Kace's reminder that he needed to check on them. Since they both should be at work, he might have time to see them before DeeDee's arrival. Kace was about to do just that, but Rosy spoke before he could say his goodbye.

"Are you seeing Jana on Friday?" she asked.

Kace wondered why he even bothered to feel the need to groan. Nothing stayed secret in this town for long.

"Piper mentioned she was babysitting for Marley on Friday," Rosy added, "and I think folks just filled in the blanks that Jana would be seeing you."

That was some big-assed blanks-filling, but maybe not much of a stretch, since Kace thought some folks in Coldwater might have ESP.

"Oh well," Rosy went on, "you don't have to talk about that if you don't want." However, that didn't stop Rosy from proceeding. "Word is that Belinda is still pining away over you so I'm guessing she won't be happy about you seeing Jana. Just something for you to consider if you run into her."

He'd run into Belinda all right, and he would definitely take into consideration her pining away for him. Kace would have liked to dismiss that, but he'd seen that look in Belinda's eyes when she'd come to his house.

Hurt.

The one thing he'd been trying to avoid with her

when he'd started their loosey-goosey relationship. Even though he'd spelled that out for her, Belinda obviously hadn't felt either loosey or goosey when it came to him.

"For what it's worth, Belinda didn't seem so down when I saw her about a week ago," Rosy went on. "She was picking up a big box at the post office. Some party favors. So I'm guessing she bought some things to cheer her up."

Everything inside Kace went still. "Party favors?" he asked.

Rosy nodded but was no longer looking at him. That's because the Mylar balloon or maybe one of its fellow penises zipped across the sky again. "The box was from some party supply company."

"Jeb's?" Kace pressed.

Rosy shrugged. "Maybe. I only got a glimpse of it before Belinda hurried out. You should probably talk to Inez Peterson."

The postal clerk. Kace would do just that, but he already had an uneasy knot forming in his stomach. Did Belinda have something to do with the stupid stunts that had been aimed at Peter? And if so, why? Kace didn't have time to dwell on that because his phone dinged with a text from Ginger.

Miss Thunder Tits just arrived.

Kace was hoping that Ginger meant DeeDee and not that one of the strippers had returned.

"Gotta go," Kace told Rosy, and he brushed a kiss on her cheek before he headed out.

There were people on Main Street, but no one spared him a glance. That's because all had their attention focused on the sky and the reemergence of the floating cock. This time it was pointing down as if about to piss all over them.

Kace hoped the interest in the inappropriate party favor choices would wane before the balloons did.

When Kace went into the police station, he had no trouble spotting DeeDee. It seemed she had an entire mountain of red hair coiled around her head. It was only a few shades brighter than the sweater she was wearing over skinny jeans. And then there were the boobs. For once Ginger hadn't exaggerated on that particular description. Kace wasn't sure how the tiny woman could stay upright with breasts that large. In fact, the boobs probably weighed more than the rest of her did.

Kace knew from DMV records that DeeDee was fifty-nine, but she definitely didn't look it. He suspected lots of cosmetic surgery and treatments had gone into giving her a wrinkle-free face without so much as a speck of a freckle. She was attractive in an overly done stripper kind of way.

"Say, did you know there are giant dicks floating over your town?" DeeDee immediately asked.

He sighed, nodded. Not a good impression for visitors, but then he doubted DeeDee would linger in town after this interview.

"I'm Sheriff Laramie," he greeted, and shook her

hand when she offered it to him. Of course, it was tiny, too, except for the long bloodred nails.

"DeeDee Merriweather," she reciprocated, and then she tipped her head to the door. "May we close that while we chat?"

All right. Probably not a good sign of things to come, but then neither was this personal visit. The initial interview could have been done over the phone, and Kace could have brought her in only if there'd been red flags.

Kace obliged her by shutting the door and then hitching his thumb to the small watercooler in case she wanted something to drink. DeeDee shook her head, took the seat next to his desk and crossed her legs.

"Peter Laramie's as much of a dick as the ones flying over your town," DeeDee volunteered. "He's not the man he's pretending to be. I know that might not be something you want to hear about your father."

There were plenty of things Kace could have said in response. *I don't consider Peter my father. Tell me more. Are you trash-talking with good intentions, or do you have some kind of ax to grind?* Instead, he just waited for the woman to continue, and he didn't have to wait long.

"Full disclosure here, I've known Peter for about three years now, and we were once lovers," she said. "He's really attractive and has some talent so I helped him buy What-Knots so that he'd have a place to show his work. It makes some money, but Peter spends it as fast as it comes in."

"*Lovers*?" Kace settled for asking because once he knew the backstory of that relationship, he might suss out just how many grains of salt he should take with what she was saying. He didn't especially want to give Peter the benefit of the doubt, but he also wanted the truth as to who was behind the pranks.

DeeDee nodded. "We ended things about seven months ago, and that's when I quit pumping money into the business. That's also about the time he started trolling for another sugar mama, and I think he found one in Eileen Parker."

"You know her?" Kace asked.

"Of course. Everyone in our old social circle has at least heard of her and her charity to support the arts. Peter scoped out Eileen and made sure he was at that party so he could meet her."

For the second time today, Kace felt that clench in his gut. Not because he believed this woman. He wasn't sure about that yet. But the clench was because what she was saying could possibly be true. If so, this could come back to bite Eileen and therefore Jana and Marley.

"You sound pretty pissed off at Peter," he remarked.

"I am," DeeDee said with punctuated anger in her voice. "I ponied up a lot of money because I thought he was in love with me. Obviously, he was just in love with my bank account. Well, no more. He doesn't get another penny from me, and I'm drawing up papers to force him to either buy me out or sell What-Knots so I can try to recoup some of my investment."

"Was your investment part of a trust fund or inheritance?" he asked, playing on a hunch.

DeeDee's chin came up, and he knew indignation when he saw it. "No. If you must know, it was from my divorce settlement."

That didn't surprise him. Judd had run a quick background check on the woman, and she'd been divorced three times. Of course, that didn't mean she'd gotten good settlements from those, but if the shop wasn't turning a big profit, she'd gotten her money from somewhere.

"Just how pissed off are you at Peter?" he pressed.

"Very." The indignation gave way to some more fire in her gold-brown eyes.

"Pissed off enough to try to get back at him?" Kace countered to prompt her to add more.

Now she blinked and lowered her chin. "What do you mean?"

"I mean someone put a stink bomb in Peter's car and then set more around the property where he's staying. Do you know anything about it?"

"No." Her answer was fast enough that he didn't really think she was lying. "Did he say I did that?"

Kace didn't deny it. "You're sure you didn't try to get a little comeuppance by playing pranks on him?"

No quick answer this time, and she eyed him with suspicion. "I didn't come here to be wrongfully accused of anything," she snapped. "And if someone's been *pranking* him, then I suggest you look at Peter."

Kace jumped right on that. "You think he did these things to himself?" he asked.

"Very likely. I'd imagine that Eileen's friends and family are trying to talk her out of a hasty marriage to Peter. What better way to get sympathy than by becoming the victim?"

Since Kace had considered that very thing, he didn't dismiss it. "Has Peter done that sort of thing before?"

"I'm not sure. Possibly. He didn't have to do that with me because my friends all thought he was a fine catch." DeeDee paused and then studied him. "You favor Peter. A lot."

So, it was gut clench number three for the day. Yes, Kace knew there was a strong resemblance and wasn't pleased about it, but he'd had no say whatsoever in his gene pool.

"Let me make sure I'm understanding what you're saying," he told her so they could get this conversation back on track. "You and Peter had a relationship, broke up, and you're upset. Maybe rightfully so," he added when he saw a new flare of anger on her face. "But you don't actually have any proof that he's done something wrong or is only after Eileen Parker's money?"

DeeDee smiled, and it wasn't pretty. It reminded him of Mr. Rat, the ferret. She took a paper from her massive handbag and gave it to him. "I think this should do it. There's all the proof you'll need to run Peter out of town."

CHAPTER ELEVEN

JANA STOOD IN her front window and looked up at the sky. What the heck? There were more pink smiling penises, about a dozen of them, all floating around. Too many to be left over from the original batch of Mylars. Plus, there were now also boob balloons. Those definitely hadn't been part of the original bouquet that had come from Jeb's.

So, someone had released more. Someone with some spare cash, too much time on their hands and a nasty grudge against Peter.

Well, maybe against Peter.

This was possibly meant to embarrass her mom as well. Which it had done. Eileen had basically shut herself in her house and was looking into hiring someone to shoot down the balloons. Jana didn't care much for that solution, but if the prankster kept this up, there might not be another choice.

"Teet," Marley attempted, pointing up at the balloons. She meant *tweet* as in *bird*, and Jana didn't correct her. Thankfully, her little girl was too young to understand what she was seeing, but the same couldn't be said for the older kids who lived in or near Coldwater.

"Teet," Marley repeated in midyawn. She rubbed her eyes, a clear sign that she needed a nap, but she seemed to perk up when the truck came to a stop. "Tace," she babbled when Kace stepped out.

Jana intended to go to the door and greet him, but first she had to deal with the flush of heat that started at her head and oozed all the way to the tips of her toenails. He was so long and lean, and mercy, did he fill out those jeans just right. He wasn't wearing a coat today, thanks to the milder temps. He had on a long-sleeved shirt, and that meant she got to see the outline of his incredible chest as well.

Just seeing him was foreplay, and she immediately wondered if he'd decided not to wait until their "date" on Friday.

"Tace," Marley said, reaching for him the moment Jana opened the door.

Kace took the baby as she babbled out more of her greeting. "Good to know," Kace told her at the end of it, though there was no way he could have known what she'd told him.

"Why do you think she's so…comfortable with me?" Kace asked Jana.

She had to shrug as they went inside to the foyer. "Marley definitely has her likes and dislikes." And maybe she was picking up on her mom's accelerated heartbeat and too-fast breathing. If so, Marley might think of Kace as a fun party of sorts.

"Teets," Marley told him as she pointed to the sky. Kace's eyebrow rose.

"Not *t-i-t-s*," Jana spelled out. "*Tweets* for birds. Any idea who's responsible for these new ones?"

Kace shook his head. "I've already called Jeb's Party Favors. They didn't do these. Of course, there are several places on the internet that sell them, but I won't be able to get a search warrant. Not for something like this."

No. The risqué balloons weren't an actual danger though they could create one. "My mom wants to shoot them down," she let him know. "In fact, Peter or she might have already done that. I wasn't here, but Bessie said she heard a couple of shots yesterday."

He nodded, sighed. "I'll try to convince Eileen not to do balloon target practice. Wouldn't want someone shooting a power line. Plus, I'd likely get complaints about the noise from the Sweenys."

That was also true. The Sweenys were her mom's closest neighbors and had just as much money and snootiness as Eileen. They often made a fuss during hunting season even when the shots were far off from their property.

Kace glanced down at Marley, who was still babbling away at him. "I need to talk to you."

Jana knew he didn't mean Marley, and that ooze of heat cooled a little. *Crud.* Had Kace come here to cancel their date and tell her that he was going to keep his hands off her forever and ever?

Probably.

Of the two of them, Kace had far more willpower

about this sort of thing, and he'd likely decided that being with her was more trouble than it was worth.

"Sure." Jana tried not to let her doom and gloom show, and she motioned for him to follow her into the house. "Bessie's in the kitchen so I can have her watch Marley for a little while." No way did Jana want her baby there while she was trying to steel herself up for rejection.

Jana took the baby from him, and as expected, Marley protested. It was a little louder and grumpier than it should have been because she was so tired. In fact, Marley was already starting to doze off by the time Jana made it to the kitchen, where Bessie was putting away dishes. Something that Jana had told her not to do. She didn't expect Bessie to do any cleaning for her at all, but she'd had zero luck convincing the woman of that.

After Jana had settled Marley with Bessie, she went back to the front of the house and found Kace in the living room. He was by the fireplace and looking at some of the pictures she'd put on the mantel. Some would have called it a waste of time since she'd soon be packing them up and moving them, but Jana enjoyed seeing them there. Photos of Marley as an infant. Of her first birthday. Even one of Eileen holding her shortly after Marley had been born.

Kace turned to her, and she again saw the troubled look in his eyes. Jana repeated her mental *crud* and was about to blabber something about knowing why he was there. Along with a demand for him just to give her the bad news fast and get it over with.

Then, she could lick her wounds and rationalize why it was a good thing that he wasn't going to be with her after all. However, Kace spoke before she could manage to get her mouth working.

"I just got through interviewing Peter's business partner, DeeDee Merriweather," he said.

Okay. She hadn't seen that coming though it made sense that Kace would want to talk to the woman. Judging from Kace's expression, the meeting hadn't gone that well.

"You found out something about Peter," she concluded.

"Maybe." Kace took a folded-up piece of paper from his pocket and handed it to her.

When Jana unfolded it, she saw a list of names. *Women's* names. There were four of them with their contact info, but she didn't recognize any of them.

"According to DeeDee, these are women Peter's scammed over the years. Women older than him who, again according to DeeDee, he seduced and coaxed into giving him lots and lots of money. DeeDee claims he did the same to her."

Jana released the breath she'd been holding.

"You look, uh, relieved," Kace said.

Probably because she was. "I thought you were going to tell me you didn't want to see me." And she quickly tried to wave that off. Obviously, this was far more important, and it smacked of a big *I told you so* Jana wouldn't actually say aloud.

"Is there any proof that Peter did what DeeDee claims?" Jana asked.

Kace stared at her, probably debating if he was going to address her confession about why she thought he was there. "I called all the names on the list," he finally said. "Two hung up on me, one didn't answer and the fourth told me to relay a message to Peter that he's an anus wart. I pressed her to give me some info on why she felt that way about him, but she hung up on me."

Well, not exactly a guilty verdict, but it was certainly suspicious. "If you show that list to my mother, she isn't going to believe it. She'll insist that DeeDee is lying."

Kace nodded so quickly that it was obvious he'd already come to the same conclusion. "I'll keep trying to find out more of what happened with these *relationships*, and I'll need to talk to Peter about it. Maybe he'll tell Eileen, maybe not, but I wanted you to know in case this causes her to melt down."

It would do that. Eileen would basically have a hissy fit. Maybe it wouldn't last long, and even if it did, it wouldn't cause Eileen to call off the wedding. Her mom was in a Peter-and-her-against-the-world kind of mind-set that didn't allow for the possibility that she was marrying an anus wart.

But her mom wouldn't be the only casualty in this latest wave. Nope. Eileen would somehow blame Kace for it. A kill-the-messenger sort of thing. And it would also mean Kace would have to be with his father again. A salt-in-the-wound sort of thing.

Damn Peter.

Damn this blasted engagement.

Jana could see the toll this was taking on Kace, and she went to him to pull him into her arms for a hug of comfort. She got the hug part right, gathering him up against her, but things went south in a hurry. All she'd meant to do was murmur some words of understanding. She certainly hadn't meant to kiss him.

But that's exactly what she did. And more.

Jana Frenched him.

It was off-the-scale amazing, of course. The taste of him so familiar and yet new and exciting. Kace had always been able to pull that off, making it seem as if everything was the first time.

She slid against him with Kace's help. He hooked his arm around her waist, dragging her even closer. Cursing her, too. Or maybe the profanity was aimed at himself, but he was definitely grumbling some bad words whenever they broke for air. Clearly, he wasn't a fan of what they were doing, but that didn't stop him. Nope. It was hard to deepen an already French kiss, but Kace managed it.

Like all really great kisses, this one did its job of firing her up and making her want more. Jana didn't actually time it, but she thought she could fit it into the race car category. Zero heat to scalding hot in just a matter of seconds. And like all really great scalding hot feelings, it made everything seem urgent and necessary.

Touching him, for instance.

Her hands were on his back. Oh, the tight and toned muscles that stirred there. In fact, plenty of the rest of him stirred, too, because she felt the flex of his arms when he aligned their bodies just so. Then, she felt a similar flex and hardening behind the zipper of his jeans. That sent her soaring from the scalding hot to the molten lava stage, and her body was already preparing itself for the delicious delights that she knew Kace could give her.

Except he couldn't.

They were in her living room that had no doors to close it off. Bessie was with Marley, but that didn't mean the woman couldn't come walking in once she put the baby down for a nap. So, there'd be no sex.

Not here anyway. And certainly not now.

But that didn't mean the kissing and touching could just continue. If Bessie walked in on them, it wouldn't be the first time that she'd caught Kace and her in a lip-lock. The woman had witnessed them making out on multiple occasions when they'd been in high school. Still, Jana preferred not to have anyone witness a display of sex-starved hormones.

Despite the little pep talk/back off decision she'd just had with herself, the kissing didn't stop. She melted into a puddle when Kace caught onto her butt and pressed her against his erection. It was just like old times. Clothed foreplay that still managed to seem as if they were naked. For something with bad timing, it could well lead to an orgasm.

When Jana heard the ringing sound, she thought maybe it was her own ears reacting to the rising temp in her body. But Kace tore his mouth from hers. "Your phone," he said.

She wouldn't have gotten that answer right even

with a multiple choice. That's because Kace had fried some of her brain cells along with doling out heat to the rest of her.

Thankful that answering a call didn't require a lot of mental power or especially steady hands, Jana took her phone from her jeans pocket and saw the name on the screen.

Frank Ballard.

Okay, that did require some brain power for her to remember exactly who he was. The PI she'd hired to look into her father's disappearance.

"I need to answer this," Jana muttered.

And despite the fact that the call could be important, she'd debated that. Maybe though, once she was done talking to him, Kace and she could pick up where they'd left off. Jana figured Kace wouldn't have any trouble zooming her into the hot zone again.

"Mr. Ballard," she said when she hit the answer button.

"I might have some news about your father," he told her in lieu of a greeting.

That got her attention in a way that little else could. When her lungs started to ache, Jana realized that she was holding her breath. "Is my father really dead?" she managed to ask.

That got Kace's attention, too, and it instantly cooled the heat in his eyes.

"I'm still not sure," the PI said, "but I found something interesting. There's an Arnie Parker living in Hawaii, and judging from the info I found, he's the right age to be your father."

Even though that was only two sentences of information, it took Jana several long moments to process it, and then she shook her head. "My father's name is Arnold, and he never went by a nickname."

"Maybe not, but he could have started using the name if he didn't want to be easily found."

That gave Jana another kick of surprise. And dread. When she'd thought of finding her father, she'd had to consider the reasons he might have left. The reasons he would have essentially faked his death. Her top answer was amnesia. She could accept that maybe he'd gotten injured in a boating accident and couldn't remember who he was. She could even buy into that he didn't want to have further contact with Eileen. But if he'd been "hiding" all this time, her father had been hiding from her, too.

"I tried to contact him by phone," the PI continued, "but he didn't answer. The call went straight to voice mail, and when I tried a second time, he'd blocked me."

"You left him a message the first time you called?" she asked.

"A vague one. I didn't want to scare him off by telling him I was a PI so I told him I'd found something of his, and I wanted to return it."

Jana supposed it was reasonable for someone to block the number of a caller they didn't know. Maybe a caller they thought was trying to scam them. Of course, a man who didn't want to be found could block it, too.

"I'm going to keep trying to contact him," the

PI explained, "but if I can't get him on the phone, do you want me to go to Hawaii and pay him a personal visit?"

Jana thought of the cost of something like that, but no amount of money would outweigh learning the truth. A truth that could stop her mother from making a huge mistake by marrying Peter.

"Yes," Jana answered. "Do what's necessary."

Because if that was indeed her father, she had to know.

CHAPTER TWELVE

THERE WAS A deflated Mylar penis on Eileen's front lawn.

If Kace wasn't mistaken, it had multiple bullet holes in it. Even though it was just a balloon, it made him wince a little because it looked as if someone had taken out their frustration on the balloon man part.

Of course, he was doing more thinking about his man part than he should—thanks to that kissing storm he'd had with Jana. Since he stood no chance of convincing himself that the kisses had been the wrong thing to do, Kace just rolled with it. It'd been a while since he'd made a string of mistakes, and apparently he was going to use them all up on Jana.

Unfortunately though, the making out with her had left him feeling edgy. Not in a good way, either. In an unfulfilled needy way that made him want to go back over to her house and finish what they'd started. But the timing sucked what with Marley being there and Jana learning what the PI had found. Plus, Kace actually had a job to do. He had to see Peter and talk to him about DeeDee's accusations.

Definitely not as much fun as kissing Jana.

Of course, Jana likely wasn't having much fun, either, right now since she was probably brooding about her father. If Arnold Parker had really been hiding out from his family all this time, there'd be hell to pay. Hell followed by a whole bunch of chaos. Jana would get caught up in the middle of that. Too bad. Because she was already shouldering way too much.

Kace stepped around the penis and went to the front door where he rang the bell. He wasn't sure if he could consider it good luck or not that Peter answered, but it would give Kace a chance to talk to the man in private.

"Eileen's doing yoga," Peter said. "Should I go and get her?"

"No. I'm here to see you." He'd get to the part about DeeDee, but for now Kace hitched his thumb to the downed balloon. "Who shot it?"

Peter didn't even glance in the balloon's direction. "Eileen. She used her daddy's rifle. Don't worry. I talked her out of shooting down others."

Good. Well, it was good if Eileen would actually refrain from firing off bullets.

"I interviewed DeeDee Merriweather," Kace told him. "I came here to talk to you about that."

Because Kace was watching the man, he saw the flash of pleasant surprise turn to dread. Peter had already guessed that this wasn't a personal call. As far as Kace was concerned, there'd never be one of those because there was nothing personal he had to say to the man who'd fathered him.

Peter stepped out onto the porch, motioning for Kace to follow him, and they went around the side yard to the guesthouse. A location that didn't exactly please Kace. It seemed too cozy, but then it was entirely possible that Peter didn't want Eileen to hear any part of a conversation that involved DeeDee.

Kace had been in the guesthouse many times before when Jana and he had sneaked in here to have sex. That was another reason the place didn't please him. Too many memories of her. Of them together. And coming on the heels of that kiss, it wasn't a good thing. Best not to have lust on his mind when he was discussing an investigation with Peter.

They stepped inside the guesthouse, the warm air from the heating spilling over them, and Kace saw that the place hadn't changed a bit over the past decade. It had an open living, dining and kitchen area, a bedroom and bath. No strange art or circus decor here.

Since Kace wanted to keep this visit short, he immediately took out the paper that DeeDee had given him and handed it to Peter. The man didn't ask any questions, but he did take a long slow look, followed by a long slow sigh.

"I'm assuming DeeDee told you that I'd been involved with these women," Peter said.

"She did, and she made some accusations."

Peter laughed, but it wasn't from humor. "I'll just bet she did." With the paper still in his hand, he sank down onto the sofa and looked up at Kace. "You probably gathered that DeeDee and I were once lovers, and now that it's over, she's bitter."

"Oh yeah. Got that. Does she have a right to be bitter?"

"Yes," Peter answered.

Kace hadn't been expecting a direct response. Especially one that could possibly confirm Jana's and DeeDee's gold-digging theory.

Peter made another sigh before he continued. "DeeDee did invest heavily in the shop and the art studio. What she probably didn't tell you was that she also profited."

No, she hadn't mentioned that. "She said you drained a lot of her funds."

"For the shop and studio, yes, but after I became involved with Eileen, DeeDee also sold a lot of my artwork, and she kept all the money from that. Thousands of dollars of artwork that she sold without my permission," he emphasized. "I didn't ask for a cut of that since she'd put up the majority of the money for our business."

Kace thought he'd be able to verify that. And it didn't surprise him that DeeDee hadn't mentioned it. Clearly, she'd wanted to show Peter in the worst possible light. Maybe because she was a woman scorned. Maybe because she had a legitimate beef about him having taken her for a ride.

"I ended my relationship with DeeDee months before I met Eileen," Peter went on. "DeeDee was upset, but she got a lot more upset when she realized

I was going to remarry and that my bride wouldn't be her."

Again, that could be the way things were, but there was still the problem of the other women.

Kace tipped his head to the paper. "What about them? Did they give you money, too?"

"The first two did." Again, it was a fast admission. "I thought of the money as investments in my career. So did they, at the time. But after the relationships ended, there was some bitterness."

"And the other two?" Kace prompted when he didn't continue.

"No money. No investments. Just attraction and sex. The breakup with the last one was especially... venomous."

That's the one who'd called Peter an anus wart, so Kace had already figured that out.

Peter groaned and squeezed his eyes shut for a couple of seconds. "I know how bad this looks, but I didn't steal money from these women. Nor did I lead them on. I had sex with them. Consensual sex that they knew up front had no strings attached. I insisted on that." He paused. "After your mother, I just didn't want to get that tangled up again."

Kace hated that he could understand that. And had firsthand experience of what led to that thought process. Of course, in his case, it was because Jana had crushed him when she'd filed for divorce. But in Peter's situation, he'd been the one to leave.

Peter looked up at him, their eyes connecting. "I was only nineteen when I married your mother, and she was already pregnant with you. That's not why I married her, though. I loved her in that crazy, mindless way that only young lovers can."

That sounded a little too poetic—and personal— for Kace, but he didn't stop Peter from waxing on about it.

"I was an artist even then," Peter said. "I hadn't sold a painting yet, but I worked on honing my craft as much as I could considering I also had a job to support your mother, your brothers and you." He paused, and it seemed as if he got lost in the memories for a couple of moments. "It wasn't all bad, you know."

"Didn't figure it was since you knocked her up four times," Kace grumbled. He probably should scowl at himself for saying it like that, but he didn't owe this man anything. Well, nothing that wasn't related to the badge and this investigation.

Peter gave a wry smile. "I would say I was irresponsible, but that won't sound right, either, considering how close you are to your brothers."

"Irresponsibility can have some good side effects. Sometimes," Kace qualified, and they were straying too far off the subject.

"I didn't know how to deal with your mother," Peter continued before Kace could stop the subject-straying. "So, I took the chickenshit way out and just left." His gaze came to Kace's again. "I don't expect you and your brothers to ever forgive me for that."

"Good," Kace snapped. "Because it's not going to happen."

This time, Kace did scowl at himself. He sounded like a kid. The same kid that this piece of chickenshit had crushed to dust when he'd walked out. But he wasn't that kid now.

And Kace didn't want to wallow in the past any longer.

"Look, we're never going to be father and son," Kace told him. "I had some really bad foster parents but a really good one, too, in Buck McCall. He's my father in every way that matters."

"You don't need me," Peter concluded, and there wasn't any animosity in his voice or expression. "I get that. But I hope that one day you can look at me and not want to punch me in the face."

"Judd's the one who wants to punch you." It was the truth, and since Kace had just opened a wide-assed door, he kept on opening it. "Callen will bury you if you do anything else to cause us trouble or pain. Nico, well, he's Nico. Normally, he's very easy-going until he's pissed."

"And I've pissed him off," Peter said with a nod. "What do you want to do to me?" he came out and asked.

"To end this conversation and see you as little as possible."

Kace's words didn't have the bite and sting to them that they could have had. He definitely didn't want to dwell on his feelings for Peter because that would mean tapping into the god-awful memories of the past. It just wasn't worth it to churn up that kind of bile.

"Back to DeeDee," Kace continued. "She obviously hates you, and I'm wondering just how far she'd take that hate if she wanted to get back at you." He paused, giving Peter some time to let that sink in.

"You think she could have planted the stink bombs and sent the strippers and those balloons?" Peter asked.

Kace shrugged. "You know her a lot better than I do. Is her bad-mouthing you just talk, or would she do something malicious?"

Though some would have considered the penis balloons more of a funny prank. Not Kace. He knew this was an embarrassment for Eileen and could therefore be a way to get back at Peter. Maybe even cause some trouble with his upcoming marriage.

"Possibly," Peter answered. "Probably," he amended after he groaned and shook his head. "Did she say anything about doing that?"

"No. It's just something I'm considering. Don't contact her," Kace quickly added when Peter took his phone from his pocket. "I'll have one of my deputies ask around town to find out if anyone has seen her. If she set off those Smelly Bobs or released this second batch of balloons, she might have come to town to do that herself."

Of course, it was just as possible that she'd hired someone to do it. After all, it was a man who'd ordered the strippers and the original balloons. There were possible male suspects on Kace's list. Dominick and Peter, to start. So, if it wasn't one of them or someone else that Kace hadn't flagged, then the man could have been hired.

"I'd like to do something else," Kace went on as he took the paper with the names from Peter. "I'd like for word to get around that you've taken down the security cameras. You could come up with an excuse if you want to elaborate. Maybe say that the wildlife keeps triggering them. Or that they're making you or Eileen uncomfortable."

"But we'll leave the cameras up in the hopes that whoever is doing this will return for another prank?" Peter supplied.

"That's right. You'd have to do a better job of hiding the cameras. Right now, they're out in the open. Put them in trees or up in the eaves."

He could tell from the way Peter was nodding that he approved of the idea. *Good.* Now maybe it would work, and they could soon put an end to this nonsense. Then, he wouldn't have to constantly be seeing Peter.

"Let me know once you've moved the cameras," Kace went on, "and I can help you spread the word that they're down."

Maybe if the culprit was DeeDee, it wouldn't take her long to hear about it, and she'd make a fast move that they could then catch on the security cam. Kace wasn't sure exactly what charges there'd be for that, but at a minimum he could hit her with trespassing and reckless endangerment for the stink bomb that had caused Peter's car wreck. After he gave it some thought, he figured there'd be other charges.

"After everything that DeeDee told you, you probably won't believe this, but I love Eileen," Peter said when Kace turned to leave.

Kace shrugged. "Not my rodeo, not my clowns."

"That's not entirely true." Peter's tone was quiet, almost subdued. "You and Jana have a past, and I think you care for her. That means you care what happens to Eileen."

Kace wanted to say something snarky about Peter assuming there was still some "caring" between Jana and him, but Kace could hardly deny it when he still had the taste of her in his mouth. Yeah, he cared, and he didn't want Eileen hurt because, in turn, it would hurt Jana. However, that didn't mean Kace thought that Peter hit the hunky-dory mark for Jana's mom.

"I hope you really do love Eileen," Kace said. "I don't want her to be another name on this list."

Kace turned to walk out just as the door opened and in came the woman herself. Eileen. Since her face was dewy with sweat, and she was wearing a disturbingly tight pink bodysuit, Kace surmised that she'd just finished her workout.

"You're here about those balloons," Eileen greeted. She glanced at the paper he was holding, but since Kace wanted to leave the explanation about it to Peter, he refolded it and put it back in his pocket.

"Yes." In part, that was the reason for his visit anyway. "I'll let Peter fill you in on what should be done."

Kace expected Eileen to pepper him with questions. Or insults about him not doing his job. But she just stood there, her gaze connecting with his while blocking the doorway.

"I need you to tell Jana to back off," Eileen finally said.

In case this was about Jana's and his upcoming date, Kace decided to stay quiet and see where this demand was going.

"She shouldn't have hired that PI," Eileen added a moment later. Kace couldn't tell if she was pissed off, worried or both.

"Jana told you about that?" Kace wanted to clarify that Eileen hadn't gotten the info through snooping.

"Yes. A few minutes ago. She called me to give me a heads-up." Her mouth tightened. "She said this PI found a man with a similar name to her father's. It won't be Arnold, and that's why you have to tell Jana to stop this nonsense."

"Even if I wanted to do that, I wouldn't. Hiring that PI was all Jana's doing," Kace reminded her.

"I know that, and I know it was wrong. This is just going to get her hopes up again, and she'll be hurt." She paused long enough to drag in a breath. "I never thought much of you as a son-in-law, but Jana seems to listen to you. Reason with her. Tell her not to go through with this."

Kace looked her straight in the eyes. "No. Whatever the PI finds out, you'll just have to deal with it. And FYI, I never thought much of you as a mother-in-law."

He knew that comment wouldn't hurt Eileen's feelings. Kace also knew it was true as true could

be. But he hated that he'd stooped to her level of unnecessary snark.

Kace stepped around Eileen and walked out. No
way would he help Eileen bully Jana to stop this, but
Kace knew this might not all turn out rosy. Eileen
was right about one thing.

Jana could be hurt.

With everything else she had going on, something
like this might be the final straw, and he didn't want
to see her crushed.

Well, hell.

Apparently, this was his damn rodeo after all.

CHAPTER THIRTEEN

JANA STOOD BY her SUV and just looked at the place that she would soon own. Nico's ranch. It wasn't her first trip here. She'd already done an initial check and then a walk-through, but she'd wanted another one before closing on the sale so she could make some notes about what she planned to change or keep.

She took in the small Craftsman-style house. It was a keeper with its white porch and stone-gray exterior. The corral, however, wouldn't do. She would need to add another one along with stables or else expand the barn. Obviously, Nico hadn't needed a lot of barn space since he raised rodeo bulls.

Beyond the house and barn was the pasture. Not completely flat, and it was dotted with massive oaks. There were ten acres, she knew. Small, too, when compared to her ranch.

Her *former* ranch, she amended.

That sale was a done deal what with the buyers pushing for a quick closing. Especially considering how close to Christmas it was—less than a month away—that was a good thing, and Jana hoped if she repeated it enough that she would soon believe it. She'd had a lot of good memories there, including having Marley, but with Dominick's antics, there were also plenty of bad memories. Enough to make her want to put that all behind her and start fresh.

The front door opened, and when Nico stepped out onto the porch, he grinned at her. "Right on time."

"Barely." She returned the smile, and it got even wider when Nico's significant other, Eden, joined him. "It took me a while to get Marley settled. She was cranky when she got up this morning."

Normally, she would have just brought the baby with her, but Jana had made arrangements with Nico to take out one of his horses so she could check out the back of the property. She hadn't wanted to take Marley along for that so had left her with Bessie.

Jana went to the porch and gave them both hugs. When she stepped inside, Jana did the same mental assessment of the interior as she had the rest of the place. No changes here, either, except for some painting, and she thought it would soon feel like home once she got their things moved in. She wanted that to happen, too, before Christmas so she could get a tree. Marley was old enough now to notice such things, and she didn't want her little girl missing out on opening Christmas presents.

"You want something to drink?" Nico asked. "Coffee? Coke? Multiple shots of hard liquor?"

Jana appreciated that Nico wasn't going to pretend all was well. "No, thanks. Maybe after the ride, though."

"Are you doing okay?" Eden gave her hand a squeeze.

Of course, everyone knew about her divorce. Probably about the crappy way Dominick had treated her, too. Then, there was the stress about her mother's wedding. Jana doubted folks knew about what the PI might or might not have found, but that would soon get out as well. Her mom wasn't exactly one to babble about the sordid parts of her personal life, but her household staff would almost certainly overhear her talking about it to Peter. Ditto for talking about DeeDee's list.

"I'm fine," Jana answered. "And you?"

Eden slid her arm around Nico's waist. "Great. Guess you know that I was one of Coldwater's favorite topics of gossip."

Jana nodded. "Because of the blog you write." *Naughty Cowgirl Talks Sex.* Apparently, it was a successful one that Eden had secretly written for years. Now it was all out in the open, along with Eden and Nico's relationship.

"You've done us a favor by taking some of the spotlight off Eden," Nico commented, and he chuckled when Jana made a face. "Don't worry. They'll move on to something else soon. Well, they will if Kace and you don't give them any fodder. But I'm guessing that some fodder's about to happen."

Jana wondered if lust created an invisible sign. Maybe like an aura. A sultry red one that pulsed with *I'm in need of an orgasm with Kace Laramie.*

"I suppose you know about our date tomorrow night?" Jana asked.

"Oh yes," Eden and Nico said in unison. "There's a pool."

Jana blinked. "Excuse me?"

"A betting pool," Eden clarified. "Some believe you'll cancel because you're too riled at your mom and your ex to start up again with Kace. Others guess Kace will cancel to save you both from another breakup. Clearly, folks aren't optimistic about the two of you," she added, tongue-in-cheek.

Actually, Jana wasn't especially optimistic except when it came to sex. That would be somewhere on the flippin' fantastic scale, but Kace and she had enough baggage to sink multiple ships.

"Gossips," Jana muttered while she shrugged. "You'd think the stink bombs, balloons and strippers would have gotten more airtime than Kace and me."

"Naw." Nico dismissed that with the wave of his hand. "Dick balloons don't hold a candle to talk about the town sheriff." He paused, and his expression got serious. "Has Kace talked to you about Peter?"

"Some." Jana wasn't sure if this was topic specific or if Nico was just trying to get a general feel for things. "Because of the investigation, I think he's had to see Peter a lot more than he'd like."

Nico nodded. "Peter said something about that when he called me."

That got Jana's attention. "You talked to Peter?"

Before Nico could even answer, her concern for him surfaced. Along with all his brothers, Nico had landed in bad foster care because of his father's abandonment, and Nico had nearly been killed from one of the beatings he'd taken. Talking to his dad had likely triggered flashbacks.

"It's okay," Nico assured her, and he repeated it to Eden, who was looking as worried as Jana. "It was just a quick phone call, and I told him I didn't want him to get in touch with me again, that it would cause too much trouble for my brothers. Especially Judd. He's past just being pissed off."

Yes, Jana had definitely picked up on that. But there was something missing in what Nico was saying. "If it didn't cause trouble for Kace, Callen and Judd, would you want to see your father?"

Nico's shoulder lift barely qualified as a shrug. "Honestly, I barely remember him so I don't have the grudges they do. Heck, I don't have the grudges they do about what happened to me in foster care."

That caused Jana to smile. She was glad Nico had been able to get past this, but Jana knew he was right about his brothers not having done the same.

"FYI, I'm concerned that Peter might be a gold digger," Jana said. Though she did like the *anus wart* description better. "If he is, he might try to wheedle some cash out of Callen."

Callen ran a hugely successful cattle broker business and was what the gossips called "richer than Davy Crockett." But he was also smart along with being as riled as Judd was. Jana couldn't actually see Callen giving Peter anything but a piece of his pissed-off mind. Still, better safe than sorry, and with that warning given, she tipped her head to the barn.

"I'd like to take that ride now," she said. "Any particular horse you want me to use?"

"Honeysuckle, the buckskin mare," Nico answered. "She's as gentle as they come, and I've already brought her into the barn for you. You're sure you don't want Eden and me to go out with you?"

"No, thanks. I just want to take my time, look around." And maybe burn off some of this restless, angry energy that was bubbling up inside her. Judd and Callen weren't the only Coldwater residents who were pissed off.

"Eden and I will be leaving for work soon, but don't hurry the ride," Nico told her. "Don't worry about locking up, either."

Ah, that was one of the joys of living in a small town, and it outweighed the gossip. Sometimes anyway.

Jana said her goodbyes to them in case they were gone when she got back, and she made her way to the barn. It was cooler than it had been the day before, but it was still in the low sixties. Not exactly winter weather by most people's standards, but that was Central Texas for you. Even this close to Christmas, they could end up with temps in the eighties. Or there could be an ice storm.

Jana glanced around the tack room and its overall size and space before she went to the mare that Nico had already saddled for her. She gave Honeysuckle several pats and a murmured greeting before she climbed into the saddle and took the horse into the pasture. The plan was to keep the ride slow so she could take in the landscape, but she found herself pushing the horse, moving Honeysuckle from a walk to a canter. She might have pushed to a gallop if Jana hadn't spotted someone just ahead. Not on the property but rather on the other side of the fence.

Kace.

Well, he'd said they would be neighbors, but Jana hadn't expected him to be out here this morning and so close to Nico's property line. Judging from his stance and equipment, he was mending the fence.

The sound of the horse must have alerted him because Kace's head whipped up, and he met her gaze from beneath the brim of his cowboy hat. She could tell from his sour expression, he wasn't in any better mood than she was.

His denim shirt was partially open, catching some of that breeze, and his jeans rode low on his hips. He looked a little sweaty.

And amazing.

Of course, Kace's looks always fell into the amazing category.

He didn't say anything to her, not even a greeting, and he kept a firm grip on the fencing pliers he was holding. Jana got off the horse and, walking Honeysuckle closer to Kace, she stopped beneath the shade of one of the massive oaks. She looped the reins over one of the fence posts so the horse wouldn't wander off.

"Bad morning?" she asked.

Kace shook his head, but there was so much frustration in the gesture that Jana was pretty sure that was a yes. "Someone put a Peter Is a Dick sign around Petunia's neck. There was an asterisk instead of an *i* in dick, but no one had any trouble figuring out that complex code of communication."

It took her a moment to realize who or what Petunia was—the longhorn that belonged to Esther Benton and was always escaping and finding its way to Main Street. The escape occurred so often that the diner had come up with a Petunia Burger special on the menu. Which was a little bent, considering the longhorn was, well, beef.

"What about you? Did you have a bad morning?" Kace asked.

She nodded but probably shouldn't tell him that her day had gotten better just by seeing him. It improved even more when the wind whipped aside his shirt and gave her an even better peek of his abs.

"There's a betting pool that favors you canceling our date," Jana told him, and yes, that was giving him an opening to do just that. But he looked so miserable, so unsettled, that she didn't want him to carry through on what could be a pity date.

"I heard."

Kace didn't add more, and he kept that intense stare on her. With his expression and the way he was standing, he reminded her of an Old West gunslinger ready to draw. Of course, a gunslinger probably didn't have pecs like that. Or that mouth.

He cursed, keeping her attention on his mouth,

and in a move that surprised her, he tossed down the pliers and his gloves, caught onto a post and hefted himself over the fence. The moment his boots hit the ground, he came toward her. Fast. This time like a knight storming the castle.

But what he *stormed* was her.

Kace slid a hand around her neck, his arm went around her waist, and in the same motion, he yanked her to him and kissed her. It was hard, hungry and exactly what she wanted. Of course, she hadn't known just how much she wanted it until the taste of him registered in her already fuzzy brain.

His kisses could do that to her. Haze things up. Make her want him. Correction, make her *need*. And the need came at her with a vengeance.

It felt so good to be in his strong arms and to have him hold her like this. His firm grip, the way his chest felt against her breasts. The way he devoured her mouth like a man starved for her. Jana quickly realized just how starved she'd been for him.

She did her own share of holding by hooking her arms around his neck and sliding her fingers into the back of his hair. His cowboy hat fell off, but neither of them did anything about that. The kiss just kept raging on, and in the back of her mind, she had one insane thought.

If folks knew what was going on, it would skew the town's betting pool.

Kace finally broke the kiss, but apparently that was only so they could drag in much-needed breaths. It lasted only a few seconds, just enough time for their bewildered gazes to meet. There was enough concern in his sizzling gray eyes that Jana thought maybe this was it, that he'd put an end to the wild-fire he was stoking and climb back over the fence.

He didn't.

However, he did belt out more curse words, and it was sort of creative the way he combined them, but he didn't say anything else. And he certainly didn't stop. He caught onto her face, going in for another kiss that was just as greedy and satisfying as the first one.

The heat inside her went up so many notches, and it just kept climbing when he pressed her back to the tree. He followed that up by pushing his front to hers. Of course, that lined everything up just right so that she could feel him hard as steel against her jeans.

Oh, that made her ache. That was the problem with having firsthand knowledge of what Kace and that steel-hard part of him could do to her. Instant third-base foreplay, and there hadn't even been any nudity or fondling involved.

Kace must have used his ESP to clue in on that fondling notion because he slid his hand between them and cupped her breast. Her breath caught and hitched when he flicked his thumb over her nipple. It hadn't been hard to find since it was puckered and pushing against the front of her bra.

"We're outside," he ground out, both a reminder and a warning that a) they shouldn't be doing this and b) they couldn't get naked.

When they were teenagers, that probably wouldn't

have stopped them. They would have just kept up the making out while hoping the cover of the tree would be enough to conceal them. But since they weren't seventeen, that meant Kace would put a stop to this.

He still didn't.

Just as Jana was about to whine—yes, whining would have been involved—about not being able to get some release from this scorching heat he'd stoked in her body, he flicked open the buttons of her shirt. Mercy, he was fast. Maybe doing all those fence repairs had given him clever fingers because he had her shirt open in no time flat. Then, he did some more heat stoking when he shoved down her bra and tongue kissed her nipple.

"You remembered," she whispered on a gasp of pleasure.

Intense pleasure speared through her and made her want to grind against him. It had been so long since they'd done this, and Jana hadn't been sure he would recall that this was one of her favorite types of foreplay. He continued toying with her favorites when he kissed her stomach.

If she hadn't been hot, wet and ready for action, it might have bothered her that Kace could be comparing her to how she looked when they were younger. She definitely no longer had the body that she did way back when.

"I need to lose five pounds," she said.

It was a mindless mumble. One that caused Kace to give her only a flicker of a glance before he moved back up to her mouth for another kiss.

Jana felt both heavy and light at the same time. Parts of her were floating on a pleasure cloud, but there was one part in particular that was letting her know it wanted a lot more attention.

Specifically, naked attention.

If Kace hadn't still been Frenching her and if she'd managed to speak, Jana might have suggested they make a mad run to his house so they could strip down and he could give her that *attention*. But any notion of a mad run stopped in its tracks when Kace unbuttoned her jeans. With the same fast moves he'd used with her shirt, he lowered her zipper and slid his hand into her panties.

Well, they weren't naked, but that no longer seemed to be an issue. At least she didn't believe it was. Then again, she couldn't actually think. However, she could feel. Oh yes, she could feel.

His fingers moved inside her, touching her. He remembered that, too. The exact location of the hottest spot on her body. These weren't gentle, slow strokes. Nope. She'd been here enough times with him to know what he was doing.

He was getting her off.

But she wasn't doing the same to him. When they were in high school, before they'd become actual full-fledged lovers, they'd done plenty of mutual hand jobs and even some bump and grinds, but there was nothing mutual about this. She was within three or four finger strokes of a climax, and she wasn't even touching him in any spot that would lead to his own orgasm.

Jana tried to remedy that. Hard to do when her body had gone all selfish and needy and was pushing her to demand *now, now, now*. But she managed to work her hand between them so she could press her palm to the front of his jeans and that impressive hard-on he was sporting.

However, Kace stopped her.

He caught onto her wrists, bracketing them in his left hand while the fingers of his right hand just kept on giving.

"I want you with me on this," she said, though she doubted her words were actually coherent enough for him to understand. Even to her own ears, it sounded like pig latin. And worse, the next words she spoke were that mantra throbbing in her head—and other parts of her. Specifically, the part of her that Kace was stroking.

Now, now, now.

Even if that, too, came out like pig latin, Kace managed to interpret it just fine. He not only gave her *now* but also the mother of all orgasms.

CHAPTER FOURTEEN

KACE WASN'T SURE if he felt more like a randy teenager or an idiot, but he was leaning more toward idiot. He hadn't gotten Jana and him naked in Nico's pasture. That was something at least. But if anyone had come riding their way, they would have seen Kace's hand in Jana's jeans.

Not exactly the actions of a town sheriff and a responsible adult.

Of course, this wasn't the first time he'd acted on impulse around Jana, but it had to be the last. Heaven knew how Dominick would use something like this against her if he found out. And since the hand job had happened out in the open, the chance of someone seeing it and that news getting back to Dominick was far greater than if Kace had just taken Jana back to his place.

That still might happen, too.

Well, it would if he couldn't talk himself out of seeing her tonight, and since he was still on the path to holding up his idiot label, he doubted he could convince himself. Her visit would lead to some great sex. Some relief for this dull ache in his groin. But it had the potential to shoot Jana in the foot.

With that dismal prediction looming over him, Kace left the police station to go across the street to Callen and Nico's office for a "family meeting" that Callen had called. Kace suspected it was going to be more of a "bash Peter" kind of dialogue, but he was hoping it would get his mind off Jana for at least a few minutes.

Cold showers damn sure hadn't worked. Neither had going over the police station budget, which normally would have put him into a mental coma. Maybe though, some profanity-laced sperm-donor bashing would do the trick.

Kace practically stopped in the middle of the street when he saw the hot pink protest sign leaning against his brothers' building. Even though the sign wasn't that big, he had no trouble recognizing the same Peter Is a D*ck message that'd been on the longhorn.

Sighing, Kace finished crossing the street, picked up the sign and stuffed it into the nearest trash can. No need taking something like that to his brothers, especially since he was sure none of them were responsible.

But who was?

He had plenty of suspects. DeeDee, Dominick, Belinda and the string of women on DeeDee's list. Heck, he still couldn't even rule out Peter himself. Kace had hoped that the person doing this would just get tired. Or get caught. But so far, neither of those things had happened. And the person hadn't made an appearance on the security cams that Peter had said he would set up.

Kace made his way up the stairs toward Callen's office where he heard his brothers chattering. Chattering that came to a dead stop the moment Kace stepped into the room. He couldn't be sure, but he thought they all looked guilty of something. Maybe they'd been concocting some kind of plan to put the screws to Peter.

"I'm not going to try to run Peter out of town," Kace said right off the bat. "And as much as I hate having him here, I won't hassle him."

Judging from their expressions, that hadn't been the topic of their discussion. Not even close. Judd's mouth was in a flat line. Not an unusual expression for him, but he seemed even more sullen than usual. Callen was frowning and rubbing the back of his neck. Also not unusual for Coldwater's "cattle king," but there was definitely tension in the room that Nico's brief smile couldn't wash away.

"You said you weren't going to screw around with Jana," Judd challenged.

Shit. Had someone really seen Jana and him in the pasture?

"This is an intervention," Nico chimed in.

"An intervention where we tell you to stop dicking around with her," Callen contributed.

Well, hell. Kace hadn't seen this coming, and maybe it wasn't a good go-to reaction, but it put his back up.

"I don't recall interfering in any of your personal

lives. Except for yours," Kace quickly added to Nico, "and that was just to tell you to give your dicking around a rest. You'd already nailed every eligible woman in town."

No way could Nico argue with that last part so he just shrugged. "We don't want you to go through all the getting-over-Jana mess again. It put Judd and me through the wringer last time."

Nico hadn't included Callen in that wringerfest since he'd been living in Dallas back then. But yes, there'd enough angst on Kace's part that it had given his brothers some concern. All right. More than just mere concern. They'd likely thought Kace was never going to get over it.

And in some ways, he hadn't.

"Not that it's any of your business, but I have no intentions of marrying Jana again," Kace said. His voice was tight and tinged with, *remember who's the big brother here*.

"It's not marrying her again that we're worried about," Callen clarified. "It's this date with her. We figured if things had progressed to a date, then you'd already nailed her."

Normally, Kace didn't object to a word like *nailed*, especially when there were much cruder ones, but he didn't like it when referring to Jana. Unfortunately, his dislike might be because he had come so close to nailing her. Yeah, he'd given her an orgasm, and while that'd been satisfying, it hadn't relieved any of his own sexual frustrations.

"Were all of you under the impression that I actually wanted relationship advice?" Kace threw back at them.

It was nowhere near his best effort, and heck, he could even see where they were coming from. He'd just mentally hit his head with a rock for complicating Jana's life with his dick issues. But he didn't need or want his brothers stating the obvious. Since that's what they'd no doubt continue to do, he turned to walk out and nearly slammed right into Peter.

"Kace," Peter said on a rise of breath. Not surprise. More like steeling himself up. Good thing, too, because he immediately got some backlash.

"What the fuck do you want?" Judd snarled.

Even a hardened criminal might have backed off after hearing Judd's tone and seeing his stony *I'll rip you to pieces* expression, but Peter held his ground. He lifted a small gift bag.

"When I went to Kace's office, his deputy told me he was over here so I thought I'd bring this by for all of you."

Judd's eyes went to slits. *Mean* slits. "We don't want any Christmas presents from you."

Peter nodded and set the bag on Callen's desk. "Not a Christmas present. It's some photos of your grandmother. My mom," he clarified. "She passed away a long time ago, before Kace was even born, so none of you got a chance to meet her. There are also several necklaces and a ring she used to wear. I know she'd want you to have them."

Callen had already reached out, probably to knock the bag into the trash, but that stopped him. However, that didn't mean they were going to gush over the "gift." It didn't seem right though to throw away something that had belonged to a woman who'd never actually wronged them.

"I was wondering if we could all sit down and talk," Peter said a moment later. "I think we all owe each other that much."

Oh shit. That was the wrong thing to say, and his brothers immediately jumped on it.

"I don't owe you dick," Judd snarled while he jabbed his index finger at Peter.

"Same here," Callen concurred. "You lost that right to tell us anything when you turned tail and ran. And I don't remember asking you to come into this building, *a building that I own*, and say a single word to any of us. Kace might have to deal with your sorry ass because of this investigation, but the rest of us don't."

After Callen had marked his territory, Nico said, "I gotta agree. I'm not holding a grudge about the past, but if you're pissing off my brothers, I stand with them."

Peter nodded again, a resigned kind of nod as if he'd expected just that. What he didn't do was leave. Judd did, though.

"Go to hell," Judd growled before he stormed out.

"Consider his leaving better than the alternative," Kace told the man. "He could have punched your lights out. That's often Judd's go-to response for people he considers assholes."

Kace nearly added an FYI to let Peter know that

all of them considered him an asshole, but there was no need to drill home that point. Peter didn't appear to be an idiot so he already knew.

Now Peter turned to leave, but he stopped when Nico spoke. "You tied my shoes," Nico said.

Kace definitely hadn't expected his kid brother to say that. Apparently, neither had Callen because he gave Nico a strange look that was part scowl, part surprise with a touch of "you, idiot" thrown in.

Nico lifted his shoulder in one of his trademark lazy shrugs. "I was about four years old, I guess," Nico went on. "I was trying to play chase in the yard with my brothers, and I kept tripping and falling. You stopped me, tied my shoes and told me not to bust my butt again."

As memories went, it wasn't an especially good one, but it was possibly the only one Nico had of Peter. It caused Peter to smile with what could only be gratitude. Gratitude that Callen didn't share because he gave the man a withering stare. With the smile still curving his mouth, Peter finally walked out.

"*You tied my damn shoes*!" Callen growled. "*You tied my damn shoes*!" His voice got louder and angrier each time he said it.

Nico didn't show any reaction whatsoever to Callen's protest. He calmly lifted his hands. "Sometimes, you just have to remember the little bit of good stuff that went along with all the bad shit."

That silenced Callen, even though he was still looking at Nico as if he'd sprouted a second nose. It silenced Kace, too, who was somewhat surprised by the words of wisdom that'd just left his kid brother's mouth. Of course, maybe Kace had been looking for wisdom just like that. Because it justified what he'd done to Jana against the oak in the pasture.

Well, it justified it if he didn't think about it too hard.

There'd been plenty of crappy times between Jana and him, but the sex had never been bad. Maybe if it had been, there'd be nothing to make him want her again.

Nico leaned over, looked in the bag and tipped the contents onto Callen's desk. That set Callen off again, causing him to curse, and he stepped back, clearly with no intention of looking at what Peter had brought them. Kace and Nico looked through the items and saw the pair of photos. One of the shots was of a pleasant-faced woman with thick black hair and high cheekbones. So this was the source of that Native American blood that Buck had always commented on.

"Maybe if she hadn't died so young, things would have been different," Nico remarked.

Callen just kept on cursing, some of it now aimed at Nico and Kace. That didn't deter them from moving on to the second photo. This one was of the grandmother and Peter, who appeared to be a teenager. It drilled home a reminder of just how young Peter had been when Kace had been born. That didn't excuse his behavior, though. If Peter had been too young to be a father, then he should have done something to prevent it.

A thought that didn't sit well with Kace, either.

As hardheaded as Judd and Callen were, Kace was still glad they were his brothers.

Just as Peter had said, there were necklaces—three of them. One was studded with turquoise, and the other two were plain silver. The ring was also silver and had some kind of small red stone.

"She was half Apache," Nico said, still studying the pictures. He put the ring on his pinkie finger and studied it. "I know because I had my DNA tested on one of those genealogy sites."

Callen stopped cursing and stared at Nico. "Why the hell would you do that?"

"It was just something I wanted to do. You know, in case I ever had kids. We never had anyone to fill in the blanks for us. I mean, we didn't even know her name." He tipped his head to the photo of their grandmother. "It's Lenna, by the way."

For reasons Kace didn't want to explore, it made Kace feel, well, closer to the woman he'd never met. Maybe that had something to do with the fact that Nico had her eyes, and Callen had the shape of her face. Kace figured he had genetic pieces of her, too, but he didn't have time to deal with thinking about that now.

"This intervention is over," Kace concluded, heading for the door.

He had no intentions of doing anything with the "trip down memory lane" goodies Peter had brought them, but it pleased Kace when Nico scooped them back up and put them in the bag. Maybe that meant he'd be keeping them. If so, that was good because if he'd left them on the desk, Callen would almost certainly have thrown them in the trash.

Kace hadn't even made it to the door when he heard the footsteps coming up the stairs, and he braced himself for round two. Peter might be returning to put them through the emotional wringer again. But it wasn't Peter.

It was Dominick.

Shit. Kace hadn't counted on having two unwanted visitors today.

Dominick hiked his thumb in the direction of the police station. "Your dispatcher said you were here. Guess you don't have a dress code for office attire," he added with some snark when he combed his gaze over Kace. Dominick had maybe been expecting him to be in a uniform. Or at least in something less casual than jeans.

"Not really. That's because we have to let just about anyone go in there so we can't be too particular," Kace answered, snarking right back. Though there could be an argument made for Ginger's often odd fashion choices.

Dominick aimed his finger at him. "Good one."

Kace skipped right over the *compliment*. "What do you want?"

Dominick glanced at Callen, then Nico. "I thought it was time for you and me to have a little chat. In private."

Kace doubted there was anything this dick could say that he wanted to hear. He didn't make introductions, nor did Kace give the man the privacy he'd suggested. However, he did step out into the hall with Dominick in case Callen wanted to use his office for work.

"I want you to give Jana a push on the new settlement," Dominick immediately said.

Kace had been about to shut Callen's office door, but that stopped him. "What new settlement?"

"Oh, Jana didn't tell you?" Judging from Dominick's shit-eating grin, he was going to enjoy spilling this news. "Well, I figure Jana owes me some alimony."

The anger came at Kace like a punch to the gut. "Alimony?" he managed to say, though his teeth were already clenched. "In addition to all the money you're getting from the sale of her ranch?"

"Apples and oranges," Dominick insisted. "The ranch is part of marital assets, but I need the alimony to live on. You know, to have the lifestyle to which I've grown accustomed. And I figured Jana would agree to it because of what I saw you and her doing."

"And what would that be?" Kace heard his own dangerous tone, knew he had a dangerous expression to go along with it, but he didn't try to rein in anything. Here Jana was struggling financially while trying to raise her daughter, and this turd was going after yet more of her money.

"You know," Dominick said with a wink. "I saw you two kissing at her granny's house. I don't think she wants a judge to know that since it'll make her look, well, like a floozy to a judge. So that's why I know she'll agree to the new settlement. If not, it could end up costing her a whole lot."

Oh, that didn't help the anger. It roared through Kace like an F5 tornado.

"Between you and me," Dominick went on, "you can have Jana. I mean, she's not nearly as special as she thinks she is."

Still no help tamping down the anger. "She was pretty special to you when she had all her money."

With his smug smile still in place, Dominick gave a noncommittal shrug, but Kace could see the verification of that all over his stupid dick face.

"What about Marley?" Kace asked, his words low and hard. "Have you thought about how draining Jana's funds would hurt her?"

Dominick dismissed that with a flap of his hand. "The kid'll be fine. Her rich granny will step up to the plate if she needs anything. Besides, it's only fair that Jana pay up. She had a lot of nice perks being married to me. Of course, you know all about that since she's giving those perks to you now." Dominick leaned in closer. "Say, does Jana ever moan out my name when you make her come?"

Kace saw red. There was no other word for it. Red that came in a hot, blinding rage. His normal logic and common sense flew straight out the window.

Just as Kace's fist flew right into Dominick's face.

CHAPTER FIFTEEN

JANA WISHED SHE had the power to teleport because she would have used it to get to the police station. As it was, she was moving at a snail's pace. Marley hadn't exactly cooperated getting into her car seat, and Bessie hadn't been around to babysit her. That had slowed Jana down considerably and then so had the school bus that she'd gotten behind on her drive into town.

She drummed her fingers impatiently on the steering wheel when the bus made yet another stop, and she tried to stave off the worries that were flying through her head. Before she panicked, she needed the whole picture, and Jana was far from having that. So far, all she knew had come from a brief conversation and a text. The conversation had been with her mom, who'd told her that there was a rumor buzzing that Kace had punched Dominick.

Yes, punched him.

Jana just couldn't see the unflappable Kace doing something like that, so she had practically dismissed it even when Kace hadn't responded to her Are you okay? text. However, when she tried reaching out to Judd and asked Is Kace okay?, he'd replied with No.

Jana hadn't asked for more details. This was something best sorted out in person.

The bus finally pulled off the main road so that Jana could get around it and drive the rest of the way as fast as she safely could. There were more cars than usual in the small parking lot. More gawkers, too, on Main Street, and the gaggle of people definitely had their attention on the police station.

Thankfully, Marley had finished fussing and was now babbling cheerfully as Jana hauled her from her car seat and into the building. One step inside and she knew there was no sign of cheerfulness here. Even Ginger was looking somber and concerned.

"He's already left," Ginger said right off. "Your second ex-husband," the woman clarified. "He came over here to file charges."

While there was some snark in Ginger's tone, Jana couldn't fault her for that. She often found herself using a similar tone when Dominick was concerned.

Jana didn't ask Ginger for any other details. Instead, she walked past the dispatch desk and made a beeline for Kace's office. She could see him in there, seated at his desk, while Callen, Nico and Judd loomed around him. Jana hurried in, feeling relief when she didn't see any signs of injury, but the relief was short-lived when she noted his expression.

Well, crap.

"Yeah, I punched Dominick when I was at Callen's office," Kace readily admitted.

Kace's clearly sour mood didn't deter Marley. "Tace!" the baby called out, and she reached for him.

Since his brothers were in the way, Marley just clung onto Callen, then Nico, then Judd, leapfrogging to get to Kace. Kace stood, took her, and Marley greeted him with a cheek kiss—which was probably sticky since she'd been eating a banana when Jana had whisked her from her high chair and to the SUV.

Marley continued with her cheery tone and babbled out something to Kace, followed by "O-tay?"

No one, including Jana, had a clue what Marley had said before her "Okay," but Kace smiled at the little girl and said, "Sounds good to me."

Despite this being a crisis, that just melted Jana's heart, and in that blink of an eye, she saw it. This was the family Kace and she should have had. Too bad Jana had gone and ruined things. And now she'd ruined things again, because if it weren't for her, her second ex wouldn't have been in Coldwater.

"What did Dominick do or say to make you punch him?" Jana asked, but then she quickly waved that off. "I'm guessing there'll be some adult words used in this explanation so let me see if Liberty can watch Marley for a few moments."

Marley batted away Jana's hands when she tried to take her from Kace, but her daughter accepted Nico holding her. Marley even gave him a cheek kiss, too.

"I'll take her outside for a walk," Nico offered, confirming Jana's theory about the probable use of adult words.

"Dominick was being a dick," Callen told her the moment Nico and Marley were out of earshot. "He said—"

"It doesn't matter what he said," Kace interrupted. "I lost my temper and punched him. He filed charges, of course, and he left for San Antonio so he could talk to his lawyer."

Oh God.

Jana groaned and because her legs had gone all spongy, she sank down on the edge of Kace's desk.

"I'm sorry," Kace told her.

"Screw that," Judd growled. "The asshole deserved it. I just wish I'd been the one to punch him."

"Same here," Callen concurred. "The dick deserved it."

Jana didn't doubt that for one second. Kace certainly wasn't the type to resort to a fistfight, but it left her with one burning question. A question that Kace had already cut off.

"What'd Dominick say to you?" she repeated.

Kace didn't answer. But Callen did. *"Does Jana ever moan out my name when you make her come? That's what the asshole said."*

All right. So Jana suddenly wanted to punch Dominick. Calling him a dick or an asshole was far too kind, and it was obvious he'd been trying to goad Kace.

And it had worked.

"I'm so sorry," she told Kace, and then Jana repeated that apology to Callen and Judd. "Dominick wouldn't have done this had it not been for me. He wants me to sign a settlement to give him alimony. This despite him already legally robbing me blind. I had to sell my ranch because of him, and I've drained my bank accounts."

That brought on more cursing from Callen and Judd, and while Jana appreciated their profane support, it wouldn't help this situation.

"Dominick wants money from you?" she asked Kace.

Kace nodded. Then, shrugged. "From the town, too. He said he's going to sue me and the Coldwater town council. Me, because I punched him, and the town council because they're my employer. Dominick thinks the council should be responsible for anything I do while wearing a badge."

Yes, she could see Dominick doing that. Could also see Kace's brothers trying to fix this. Especially Callen. From all accounts, he was loaded.

"You won't pay him off," she said to Callen, shifting her gaze to Judd and Kace to let them know that was meant for them as well.

"Neither will you," Kace snapped. "I'm not going to have you deal with my mess."

She sighed, touched his arm and rubbed gently. "Dominick is my mess. In fact, I figure he went to you to prod you into convincing me to sign that new settlement."

Kace didn't jump to disagree with that so she knew she was right.

"When you didn't bite," she continued, "Dominick baited you. Both of you witnessed it?" she added to Callen and Judd.

"Nico and I did," Callen verified. "He definitely baited Kace."

"And I was stupid enough to fall for it," Kace grumbled.

"Not stupid. Dominick has a way of making people want to smother him in his sleep," Jana explained.

What she wouldn't mention was that Kace's reaction was, well, flattering. He'd defended her honor and apparently hadn't said anything snarky about having recent firsthand knowledge about name-moaning when he'd brought her to orgasm.

"What happens now?" she asked Kace.

Kace dragged in a long weary breath before he answered. "The mayor's looking over Dominick's complaint. And I'll talk to Roy Eccleston."

Jana knew Roy. He was the town's sole attorney and probably didn't have a lot of experience dealing with situations like this. Of course, neither did her lawyer, but it wouldn't hurt to contact her and see if she could help.

The next question Jana wanted to ask was the hardest. Still, she had to know. "Could you lose your badge over this?"

Kace didn't jump to answer, and his hesitation lasted until it was interrupted. All four of them looked in the front of the building when they heard the familiar voices.

Peter and Eileen.

Great. This would no doubt be a good example of fanning some flames. Even if her mom was there to verbally bash Dominick, it wouldn't help, and Peter's mere presence would downright hurt.

Her mother was looking perfectly groomed and frazzled at the same time. Peter was past the frazzled point—possibly because of the box he had tucked under his arm. A cardboard box that was making noises. Whatever was inside it was rattling and bumping against the sides and top of the box.

"Someone left this for me at the end of the road on Eileen's property," Peter said.

"Snakes?" Kace immediately asked.

Jana didn't wait for the answer to that, and even though it was cowardly of her, she dropped back behind Kace's desk. If that was indeed a box of snakes, she didn't want them near her. Or Marley. Jana glanced around the squad room to make sure her little girl wasn't there, but she was obviously still outside with Nico.

"Not snakes." Peter set the box on Kace's desk. "Vibrators."

Clearly, that stunned them all to silence. Not the box, though. It continued to make noise, and when Kace opened the lid, Jana saw the pink rubber vibrators. Huge ones. All of them buzzing and vibrating. There was also a typed note on top of them.

To Peter. Here are some dicks for a dick.

Okay. So obviously this was another prank meant to humiliate and harass the man, but Jana had a hard time not laughing. Whoever was doing this certainly had a weird sense of payback—or whatever the heck this was. The person also had money. Jana hadn't actually priced vibrators, but the dozen or so in that box wouldn't have been cheap.

"They were turned on like that when you found them?" Kace asked him.

Peter nodded. "The lid was open so I could see what was inside."

Callen leaned in for a look. "Either they weren't on the road too long or those are damn good batteries."

Judd, Kace and Jana made sounds of agreement. Her mother only huffed.

"You've got to stop this nonsense," Eileen told Kace. "I know you're having your own troubles with Dominick, but things can't go on like this."

Kace didn't even acknowledge her but instead kept his attention on Peter. "Did you see anyone suspicious near Eileen's place?"

Peter shook his head. "No, but I've had a lot of deliveries. Art supplies needed for the rest of the wedding decorations. But I signed for all that I ordered. I didn't order these," he emphasized. "Obviously, I touched the box but nothing inside. Not even to turn them off. So, I'm hoping you can check for fingerprints."

Kace took another of those long breaths. "Sure." He shifted to Judd. "Can you get the paperwork started on that?"

Jana had to hand it to Kace. He kept a completely straight, professional face, but he had to be considering how a small county lab would react to getting a box of vibrators.

"Thank you," Peter said, glancing at both Kace and Judd before his gaze settled on Kace. "I'm sorry about what happened with Dominick. Is there anything I can do to help?"

"No," Callen and Judd said in unison. Judd repeated it and added a scowl before he hauled the box out of the room.

Callen was scowling, too. "I thought we made it clear earlier at my office that we want nothing you have to offer."

Jana hadn't known about another Laramie confrontation, but it didn't surprise her. There was still a lot of ill will and old baggage. Still, the timing sucked since it was likely that confrontation had happened around the same time as the one Kace had with Dominick.

"Dominick called me," Peter went on. "He was on his way to see a lawyer, and he suggested I might try to convince Jana to sign the settlement with him. He didn't come out and say it, but he made it sound as if he'd lay off of you if Jana did *the right thing*."

There was another wave of profanity, and since Marley wasn't there, Jana contributed some curse words. And an apology.

"Kace, I'm so sorry," she repeated. Or rather what she tried to say, but Kace cut her off.

"Don't. This isn't your fault." Kace groaned and scrubbed his hand over his face. "It's mine. I shouldn't have punched him. That gave him leverage over you and me."

"You wouldn't have had to punch him if he hadn't gotten in your face about me," she pointed out just as quickly.

"Kace was defending you?" Eileen asked before Kace could say anything else. "What did Dominick get in his face about?"

No way would Jana repeat what Callen had told her so she jumped in with an explanation that she hoped would suffice. "Dominick just wanted to get a rise out of Kace. In fact, Dominick likely planned for this to happen. A sort of insurance to make sure he got more money for being the rat that he is."

Jana doubted her mother knew how much careful wording it'd taken to tell her that without cursing or saying anything crude.

"You were defending Jana," her mother concluded, and her voice was quieter now. She paused a long time. "Thank you for that, Kace."

Jana was surprised that lightning bolts and hellfire hadn't rained down on them. Her mother showing any kind of gratitude to Kace was certainly a first. Of course, it didn't last.

"This doesn't mean I approve of your and Jana's date tonight," Eileen went on. "I mean, really, what are you two thinking?"

Her mother wouldn't want to know, but Jana had no trouble identifying her thoughts. She wanted Kace's hands back on her. Specifically, his hands back in her jeans, and maybe this time, it would be a satisfying experience for both of them.

Best not to mention that.

"You two have a date?" Peter asked.

Apparently, he was the only person in Coldwater who hadn't heard about it. Also apparently, Eileen wasn't going to let them dwell on the subject.

"Something has to be done about these pranks on Peter and about Dominick," her mother went on. She was back to her old self again. Snooty tone and all. "It's time for me to hire a private detective to deal with both of them."

Jana wasn't sure what a PI could do when it came to Dominick. Also, Kace might not like outside interference in a police investigation. However, he didn't have a chance to voice any disapproval because they got another visitor.

Mayor Bubba Green was walking toward Kace's office. And yes, Bubba was indeed his real name. Apparently, his folks hadn't considered that might not be a wise choice for their baby boy. A boy who had grown into his name. Bubba was a walking, talking Texas cliché, complete with a blinding white cowboy hat that had a dangling rattlesnake skin headband. He was also wearing a rodeo buckle the size of a watermelon.

It'd been years since Jana had had any dealings with Bubba or his family, but from what she remembered, the man wasn't a jackass. It was sad that her dealings with Dominick had swayed her to consider that about people she encountered.

"Say, is that a box of wiggling woodies on Judd's desk?" Bubba asked, hitching his thumb in that direction. He went scarlet though when he spotted Eileen and Jana. "Sorry, ladies. I didn't see you in here." He tipped his hat, causing the rattler headband to make nearly the same noise as the box.

"Personal pleasure devices," Kace supplied. "Someone left them on Eileen's property."

Bubba's face went sort of blank as if he were considering if that was a good thing or not. Jana didn't have to guess about that.

The answer was no, it was not.

This was obviously getting to her mother, which made Jana wonder if she should do some kind of public declaration that she was okay with the wedding. That would take her biting back some serious reservations about Peter, but it might help. Plus, a public declaration wouldn't have to be much. Just a mutter or two about her wishing her mom and Peter all the happiness they deserved and such.

"Are you okay with these folks being here while we discuss your delicate situation?" Bubba asked Kace. "And by delicate, I don't mean the date you have with Jana." He checked his watch. "Which you'll probably be getting ready for soon so I won't keep you too long."

Kace sighed and shook his head before turning to Eileen and Peter. "Could you excuse us?"

It was a polite way of telling them to get lost, but that dismissal obviously didn't apply to Callen or her because Kace motioned for them to stay put. *Good.*

Jana wanted to be involved, since this was a stink-storm that Dominick had created. And that meant she blamed herself for it.

"I want something done about those vicious pranks," Eileen insisted as she allowed Peter to lead her away. The moment they were outside Kace's office, he shut the door.

"That woman's sourer than spoilt nanny goat milk," Bubba said, giving his belt an adjustment. "Sorry," he added to Jana, but she just shrugged it off. Though she didn't have personal knowledge of spoiled goat milk, her mom did indeed have a sour disposition.

"Now, to this mess with Jana's ex," the mayor went on. "To get Dominick to drop his suit against Kace, I say the city council should offer him a settlement. We got about ten grand in what's called discretionary funds, and some folks will pony up more, I'm sure." He glanced at Callen for that, and while Callen didn't readily agree, Jana figured he would do pretty much anything to keep Kace out of hot water.

But it wouldn't be enough.

"Dominick would gladly take your money," Jana explained, "but he wants more. He wants a settlement from me. I can afford it."

Well, she could if she cut back on some of the improvements she'd need to make to Nico's place. Of course, that would in turn cut into her future profits, but she couldn't see another way to fix this.

"No payoffs," Kace said, and he didn't sound as if that was negotiable. "Dominick wants us to jump through hoops to settle this and make him richer than he already is. Let him file a lawsuit. That could drag on for years, and if it goes to trial, I have insurance for this sort of thing."

"Yeah, it could go on for years," the mayor agreed, "and this fool could drag your good name through the pig crap."

"So be it," Kace concluded. He looked Bubba straight in the eyes. "And if you need me to turn in my badge because of that, tell me now."

Jana sucked in a hard breath, her gaze snapping from Kace to Bubba. "No." She managed to eke out a reply.

"No," Bubba quickly answered. "You're keeping your badge," he told Kace. "This town has weathered storms from pissants before, and we'll weather this one. You're the sheriff, and it's staying that way."

Kace definitely didn't look convinced. "Thanks, but let's see how this shakes out. I won't let Dominick take down Coldwater because he's got a grudge against me."

"The grudge is against *me*," Jana insisted, and she groaned. No one was saying it, but this was all her fault.

Bubba stayed quiet a moment. Then, nodded. "All right, Kace. We'll try it your way and hold off for a while." Bubba tipped his hat in farewell, giving Jana an additional tip when he looked at her. "Enjoy your date."

As if. This was like a huge sack of manure hanging over their heads.

The mayor walked out, leaving Callen, Kace and her to volley glances at each other. Judging from Callen's expression, he, too, had that manure-sack feeling.

"We can cancel the date," Jana offered, figuring that Kace was about to say the same thing to her.

But he wasn't.

Jana soon discovered that when Kace walked over to her, hooked his arm around her waist and snapped her to him. "To hell with it. Let's get this date started right now."

And Kace kissed her.

CHAPTER SIXTEEN

KACE WONDERED IF his new attitude had to do with feeling totally screwed or if lust was the big player in this?

Maybe it didn't matter. After all, he had kissed Jana in front of Callen, but probably others had seen it, too. Others who had already spread the news about the lip-lock. It'd only been a couple of hours since that'd happened in his office, but Kace was certain that every living soul in Coldwater knew about it.

And he'd already heard from his brothers that they hadn't approved of what he'd done.

Welcome to the club.

Kace didn't exactly approve of it, either, but he highly suspected there'd be other kisses between Jana and him. Probably not tonight, though. Yes, he was going through with the prep for their date, but he also knew there was a high chance that Jana would cancel. After all, the events of the day didn't exactly stimulate a desire to roll around naked.

He sampled some of the red sauce he'd made for the pasta dish, added a bit more pepper and put it on the back burner. Kace hadn't thought to impress Jana with his culinary skills but rather had decided to cook since there weren't many places he could have taken her to eat in Coldwater. The diner and the café at the inn were about it, and they might as well have positioned themselves on a stage. Everybody would have been gawking and speculating. Serving her dinner here wouldn't stop the speculating, but it would nip the gawking in the bud.

He grabbed a beer and headed for the shower. Kace didn't wash with anything other than his usual soap, didn't do anything special with his clothes, either. He'd always been a jeans and boots kind of guy and stuck with that now.

Then, he waited.

Kace hated that he actually checked the time. Hated, too, that he felt the punch of dread and disappointment when he realized that Jana was officially late. Not by much. Only ten minutes, but she was probably debating and agonizing over calling him to tell him the date was off. Jana might even spare his feelings and tell him that she'd had trouble getting a sitter.

He was working his way through a second beer when he heard the sound of an approaching vehicle. Kace stayed put, figuring he'd already done enough fidgeting and pacing. Enough dreading. Besides, it might not even be Jana. It could be one of his brothers, coming to try to talk him out of this.

There was a knock at the door, but it opened before he could even take a step to answer it.

Jana.

There was sort of a wild look in her eyes, and she

seemed out of breath. Using the heel of her boot, she kicked the door shut, and in the same motion, she started toward him. Kace hadn't thought himself clueless when it came to judging a woman's mood, but he was having trouble figuring out what was going on with Jana.

He soon got a clue when she kissed him.

Her mouth landed on his. *Hard.* And she wrapped her arms around him while her body practically crashed into his. Unfortunately, the cold beer got trapped between them, but that didn't deter Jana. She parted his lips with her tongue and took the kiss from hard to deep in a heartbeat of a second.

Obviously, Jana had some kind of point to prove, and while Kace still wasn't clear what that point was, he quickly realized he had a vested interest in making sure this kiss led to a whole lot more.

Jana clearly wanted more, too. Jamming her hand between them, she took hold of his beer, worked it out of the tight fit of their bodies and set it on the end table. Or rather, that was likely what she had intended, but her aim was off. Probably because her eyes were closed. The bottle clanged onto the floor, and while the glass didn't break, the beer spewed around their feet and legs.

Kace remedied the possibility of them slipping and falling by moving them away from the spill. Of course, that wasn't an easy maneuver since Jana and he were still kissing, and her grip on him had tightened even more. It was as if she was making sure he didn't get away from her.

There was no chance whatsoever of that happening.

Kace was exactly where he wanted to be.

The urgency of her kiss let him know that Jana had very short foreplay in mind. He would have preferred that, too, but since he wasn't an asshole, he had to get something clear.

"Are you sure you're doing this for all the right reasons?" he asked—after he managed to tear his mouth from hers.

Her breath was gusting now. Hitting against his damp mouth to make it feel like a kissing blow job. Her eyes still had that wild look, but there was also plenty of heat in them, too. No surprise there since the kissing and body-to-body contact had produced a cauldron of heat inside him. Kace had the hard-on to prove it, too.

"The right reasons," she repeated. Her forehead bunched up as if she was trying to suss that out, and she shucked off her coat, letting it plop to the floor. "I'm on fire and want to have sex with you. Does that answer work for you?"

Hell yes, it did. And while he should have probably pressed to make sure the events of the day weren't playing into this, Kace was past the point of reason now. He took her mouth as if he had the right to do just that.

The taste of her was like coming home, Christmas and a couple of birthday parties all rolled into one. So familiar and yet as far from ordinary as it could get. Of course, it had always been that way with Jana, and apparently time hadn't changed a thing.

Well, not her taste anyway.

And the way she made him go scalding hot.

But there were certainly more curves. Something his hands greatly appreciated when he worked his palm down her throat and to her breasts. *Oh yeah. Curves, all right.* He'd never actually considered himself a breast man, but Kace thought he could learn to be.

She reacted when he skimmed his fingers over her nipples, which were hard against the front of her shirt. Jana made a little hitching sound in her throat, her head lolling to the side so that while he touched, he could also kiss her neck.

Jana liked that, too.

Another hitch of breath. More wiggling to do a bump and grind against the front of his jeans. Her hands pressed hard along his back muscles.

"Could we make this dirty?" she asked.

Oh, and he knew exactly what she wanted. That was the advantage of having been her first lover, but also because Jana and he had basically learned all about sex with each other's bodies.

And that advantage told him that she wanted hard and fast.

No frills. No more foreplay. Of course, she could want that speed and need simply so she didn't have to think about this, but Kace's erection thought that was a stellar idea. No thinking time meant he could be inside her as soon as he could rid her of her clothes. So Kace got started on that right away.

Jana started, too, with her hands fumbling between them to undo some buttons on his shirt. Kace also worked on her buttons, but he kept up the kissing. No frills didn't mean he couldn't torment that sensitive little spot on her neck. It was still a hot spot, he learned, when he gave her a little tongue.

"You need to be naked for our next date," she grumbled when the belt buckle gave her some trouble. *Next date, huh?* Did that mean she wasn't thinking of this as a onetime deal? Kace didn't want to read into that, though. Right now, anything she said or did was basically lust-induced insanity.

Jana was still reacting to the neck kisses with little moans and sighs, but she made another sound—one of triumph—when she finally opened the buckle and got him unzipped. The last was no easy task since he was as hard as a hammer and was straining against the front of his jeans.

Kace made his own sound when her hand dipped inside his boxers.

It wasn't a pretty sound. More of a grunting curse. Damn it all to hell, touching shouldn't feel *that* good. And when she gave him some squeezes and a well-placed flick of her thumb, the urgency to get her undressed soared.

Again, it wasn't easy because Jana obviously wasn't going to give up the strokes and those blasted thumb maneuvers over the tip of his throbbing penis. Nope. And he wasn't giving up tormenting her neck, though Kace did know that she was toying with the biggest hot spot that he had.

They scrambled to push off their boots, and Kace

went after her zipper. He practically gave them both a hand job before he finished, but he finally managed to get those Wranglers off her. The panties went next, and even though Jana had demanded dirty sex, Kace did a quick detour.

Maybe it was a little payback, too, but he gave her a tongue kiss right between her legs. In the center of all that heat. That gave him plenty of information, along with a jolt of pleasure. Jana tasted the same there as well, and she was already slick and ready for him.

Jana cursed him, calling him a bad name, which might have prompted him to do more tasting, but she caught onto his hair and yanked him back up.

"This time when I come, you'll be inside me," she insisted.

Kace had no problem whatsoever with that, but he did have to retrieve a condom from his jeans pocket. Jeans that she was hastily pushing off him. Both his jeans and boxers landed around his ankles. However, before he could even step out of them, she'd already wrangled them in the direction of the sofa. It wasn't exactly a big comfy space for sex, but it apparently would have to do.

He landed on top of her, and the moment he had the condom on, Kace pushed inside her. Or rather it would have been just a push if Jana hadn't caught onto his butt and made the thrust into a shove. It was too hard, too deep, too fast, and yet somehow it was still perfect.

Damn her.

In the back of his mind, he'd hoped this would be awful sex, and then that might bring them to their senses. But nope. Not awful. The label that Kace would put on it was Best Sex Ever. Hardly a deterrent to future nailing moments like this.

Still going with the urgency brought on by the scorching heat and her demand for dirty sex, Jana wrapped herself around him. Legs and arms. Her mouth and fingers tormenting any part of him she could reach. All of that was, well, a nice perk, but Kace didn't need it to send the pleasure to a spearhead peak. A peak that he knew neither of them could outlast for long.

And they didn't.

He felt her tight wet muscles begin to clamp around his erection. A silky, greedy fist that he had no intention of resisting. Kace just gave her the deep hard thrusts that she needed to fall completely over the edge. Then, he gave her more of those thrusts so she'd get all the ounces of pleasure she wanted. And when she was drained and shuddering beneath him, Kace let himself go.

Even though his heartbeat was drumming in his ears, it was possible they moaned out each other's names at the same time.

JANA TRIED TO hang on to the slack, pleasured feeling as long as she could. A raging fire had been sated in her body—thanks to Kace. But soon they'd have to talk about the sating. Talk about whether or not this had been a good idea. And that kind of talk could wait.

Kace shifted, obviously trying to keep his weight off her, but Jana didn't mind. Having him pressing down on her only added to the pleasure aftermath. So did the little aftershock of her climax. Kace certainly hadn't lost a step when it came to sex. In fact, he'd gained a leap or two. Of course, maybe she was feeling that way because it'd been so incredibly good.

"I thought it best if we just got this out of the way," she said. "You know, so we wouldn't be thinking about it all through dinner."

He lifted his head and looked at her. Then, nodded. "Now we'll just be thinking about what we did all through dinner," he pointed out.

"True, but this way will probably be better on the digestion." It wasn't a very good explanation, but a sated body wasn't clever at snappy comebacks.

Kace brushed a kiss on her mouth, a rather chaste one, and he got off her to head to the bathroom. She knew it was necessary to deal with the condom, but Jana figured what would follow next would be a mountain of awkwardness.

Maybe with some regret drizzled in.

At the moment though, there wasn't a trace of regret as far as she was concerned. Kace and she had been dancing around each other since she'd come back to town, and what had happened had seemed as necessary as the breaths she was taking.

Since that awkward feeling was moving in fast, Jana got up to dress so she wouldn't be sprawled out naked when Kace came back in. Unfortunately, her clothes weren't all in the same place. And not all items were wearable. She located her panties hanging from Kace's boot, but her bra was lying in the beer puddle. It was sopping wet, and she doubted the aroma of Lone Star complemented her own body's natural musky scent.

Dragging on the panties, then her jeans, Jana hurried to the adjoining kitchen to wring out her bra in the sink and get some paper towels to wipe up the rest of the beer on the floor. She was only partway done with that task and on her hands and knees when Kace came back in.

As naked as the day he was born.

If he was feeling any awkwardness, he certainly didn't show it, but he did show some interest in what she was doing. Kace had his attention nailed to her, and that's when Jana realized her breasts were jiggling while she cleaned the floor. Her completely bare breasts.

"No, don't pause because of me," he said. The corner of his mouth lifted just a little.

"Please don't tell me that you have a fantasy about watching a half-naked woman clean."

He shrugged. "I'm a guy. The fantasy is pretty much a half-naked woman doing anything."

Resting her weight back on her heels, Jana looked up at him. "I'm a woman. My fantasy is a naked cowboy in a Stetson. Think you can oblige me?"

Much to her surprise, he did. Kace went to the pegs by the door and put on his cowboy hat. She laughed, even though that hadn't been her first response. Actually, Jana hadn't known that this was indeed her fantasy, but seeing him like that was stirring a lot of heat inside her. Of course, Kace was the ultimate heat generator.

"I'll finish that," he said, tipping his head to the beer spill. "And then we can eat. Everything's cooked."

With all those muscles flexing and responding, he took the paper towels from her, wiped up the rest and carried both the wet towels and the beer into the kitchen to put them in the trash.

She watched.

Jana made sure she didn't blink because she didn't want to miss a moment of this. Dry eyes were a small price for getting to see his spectacular butt. Oh my. The man could certainly fan some fantasies. That only continued when he came back into the living room and dragged on his jeans.

Commando.

No way would she forget that anytime soon—especially since he didn't zip all the way. The flap of his jeans shifted and dangled when he walked as if giving her a peep show.

Mercy. She shouldn't be so worked up only minutes after an orgasm. Plus, this was her ex-husband so it wasn't as if she'd never had her fill of him. She had. But her body quickly reminded her that the "fill" had happened way too many years ago and was a suddenly recurring need.

With no shirt, no boots, and his butt filling out

his jeans in the best way possible, he returned to the kitchen. Jana stood there, still a little mesmerized by all his hotness as he began to plate the food.

It was only after she felt her nipples tighten that she remembered she was topless. Probably not the best way to eat this meal he'd prepared. It was going to be hard enough to concentrate on food because of all the other distractions Kace was giving her.

Since putting on her wet, beer-scented bra was out, Jana just tugged on her shirt. Glancing down at herself, she wished she'd done more exercises—as Kace clearly had—so she wouldn't have felt so jiggly. It felt foolish to fold her arms over her breasts, considering that Kace had seen her naked, but that's what she did as she made her way to the table.

He'd fixed penne with red sauce, bread sticks and a salad, and it all looked and smelled delicious. So did the wine he poured.

"You learned to cook," she said.

Kace nodded. "Out of necessity." He kept his gaze on her when she sat across the table from him. "You know, you'll have to take your arms off your breasts in order to eat."

He smiled. Something he so rarely did that it was like a special weapon in his already large, hot cowboy arsenal.

Jana didn't smile, though. "I don't have the same figure I did when we were together way back when. There's, uh, more of me."

"I noticed. This is a nice improvement."

Until he'd added that last part, Jana had been

about to scowl, but that sort of melted her. As if she needed more melting especially since he didn't seem to be nearly as heated up as she was.

Jana ate some of the pasta—delicious!—and considered a way to nudge up the heat for him, too, so they'd have an equal playing field.

"Do you still have a thing for ear kisses?" she asked. "You know, the ones that involve tongue?"

Ah, now she saw that fire spark in his eyes. "Yeah, I do. But if you're thinking about doing that, we should probably finish eating first."

Oh, there was definitely going to be a round of that particular form of kissing along with some more sex. *Good.* And Jana hoped that she didn't eat so fast that she started choking. Maybe she should have gotten a sitter for Marley for the entire night instead of just a few hours, but she immediately rethought that. Best for Kace and her to pace themselves, and besides she didn't want to be away from Marley for that long.

Jana had barely made it through a bite of one of the bread sticks when her phone dinged with a text message. It wasn't something she could ignore because maybe the sitter had had some kind of emergency. However, finding her phone was a challenge. Before the crazy-paced undressing for sex, it had been in her jeans pocket, but it wasn't there now.

"It's on the floor by the coffee table," Kace told her—just as his own phone dinged.

Both of them got up to search, and when Jana

found hers, she wanted to curse. It wasn't from the sitter but rather Dominick. The text read:

You'd better sign that settlement if you don't want your current boyfriend to be screwed six ways to Sunday.

It was ironic that Dominick had used that particular term since Jana had indeed been thinking of screwing Kace. Only not in the way that Dominick meant.

She turned to Kace, figuring he would want to know what had put the scowl on her face, but he was doing his own scowling. Along with some cursing and groaning. He showed her the screen, and she soon saw what had caused his reaction. His text wasn't from Dominick but rather from Eileen.

Someone left another box for Peter at the end of the road. Get over to my place now because this time we caught the person responsible.

CHAPTER SEVENTEEN

THIS WAS EXACTLY the kind of situation Kace had hoped to avoid. First, he'd had to leave a really great date with Jana to come here and face… Well, he wasn't sure what he was facing, but he knew he wasn't going to like it.

Even though the sun was setting, he had no trouble seeing Peter and Eileen at the end of the road near her place. Eileen was pointing what appeared to be a puke-green stick at DeeDee. Or maybe she was pointing it at DeeDee's car since that's where the woman was.

"It's about time you got here," Eileen snapped the moment Kace stepped from his truck. Jana pulled to a stop behind him in her SUV. Her headlights joined Kace's to give the scene plenty of illumination.

"You need to stop her," DeeDee demanded, easing open her car door just a crack. "She's batshit crazy. She grabbed my car keys and started accusing me of stuff I didn't do."

"That piece of fluff is the one who's crazy if she thinks she can get away with something like this," Eileen snarled. And she did indeed have some keys clutched in her hand.

Kace ignored Eileen's snarl, and gave a snarl of his own. "What the hell is that?" Kace asked Eileen. He tipped his head to whatever she was holding while he stepped in front of DeeDee as she got out of her car.

"It's the base of a whip for a circus ringmaster," Eileen said as if the answer were obvious.

"It's one of my art pieces," Peter supplied.

Well, it wasn't recognizable as such. "Why are you pointing a *piece of art* at DeeDee?" Kace amended.

Eileen likely would have answered a little sooner, but her mouth seemed to freeze when she shifted her attention to Jana. One glimpse of Jana, and Kace knew why. Jana did indeed look as if she'd just had sofa sex with him. Mussed hair, overly kissed mouth, complete with some bristle burn, rumpled clothes and no bra.

Despite all of that, she looked hot.

But Kace knew he was very biased about that and refocused on what he should be doing. He made a circling motion with his finger to prompt Eileen to start explaining. While he was waiting for her to get on with it, he glanced in the box.

And groaned.

Like the artwork, he wasn't exactly sure what he was looking at. They appeared to be some kind of suction devices. When he saw the label, he groaned again. Mighty Dick Penis Enlargers. Kace didn't have to guess that this was another prank or that it was aimed at Peter.

"Peter and I were going into town to have dinner at the inn, and we saw this woman here with that box," Eileen snarled.

"I didn't put it there," DeeDee howled. "I was driving here to see Peter, and the box was in the middle of the road so I stopped. I hadn't even had a chance to look inside before this lunatic came speeding up and started accusing me of harassing Peter. Then, before I could stop her, she grabbed the keys from my car and said she wasn't going to let me leave until you'd arrested me."

"I am not a lunatic," Eileen practically shouted, and she began to tussle with Jana, who tried to take the art-piece weapon from her. In that moment, Eileen did indeed look as if she'd gone off the deep end.

Jana finally managed to wrench it from Eileen's hand and she passed it off to Peter. Kace gave her a muttered thanks and turned to DeeDee.

"Why are you here?" he asked, and Kace made sure it sounded like the unfriendly demand that it was.

"Papers," DeeDee said, motioning to her car. "I had my lawyer draw up papers so that Peter would buy out my half of the business."

"What?" Peter snapped, and either he was faking the surprise or the man hadn't known DeeDee's intentions.

DeeDee definitely didn't seem friendly, either, when she turned her frosty gaze on Peter. "A buy-out. I invested in you and your *art*." *Art* was said in the same tone as *roadkill*. "But the only reason I did that was because we were lovers. Partners. Now that we're not, there's no reason for me to keep pumping my money into a business that stands no chance of succeeding because you suck at what you do."

"How dare you—" Eileen started, and she would have no doubt continued if Jana hadn't stepped in front of her.

"Mother, you should give Kace a chance to work this out," Jana suggested, but there was an edge of a warning to that suggestion.

That sent Eileen's gaze snapping to her daughter. "You're only saying that because you're…with him. You are with him, aren't you?" However, she directed that angry question at Kace.

Kace huffed, something he figured he'd be doing a lot of tonight. "Do you want to talk about Jana's personal life or get to the bottom of what's happening here?"

He gave Eileen a couple of seconds to consider that, and when she didn't say anything, he shifted to DeeDee. "Get the papers," Kace told her.

For one thing, he wanted to be sure she wasn't lying about the reason for this visit. Also, if the papers existed, Peter would almost certainly need to see them.

"That woman is just trying to disrupt the wedding because she still wants Peter," Eileen went on. "Well, it won't work." She hooked her arm pos-

sessively around her fiancé, who was scowling at
DeeDee. "I'll be Mrs. Peter Laramie, and this bimbo
isn't going to stop our happy day."

"It won't be so happy once you figure out that
you're marrying a jerk with zero talent," DeeDee
muttered. Of course, she said it loud enough for Eileen and Peter to hear. "But don't worry. I won't mess
up your day. I just want your man to sign these papers, and then I'll be on my way."

"I have no intentions of buying you out. We had
an agreement when we bought that business," Peter
declared at the same moment, Eileen added, "That
woman has no right to come here and criticize Peter's artistic skills. He's a genius."

Kace was reasonably sure that only Eileen believed that. Even Peter looked a little uncomfortable
with the compliment.

When DeeDee handed him the papers, Kace
scanned them, and yes, they did appear to be legal.
Something that would have justified DeeDee coming
here. Of course, it could still be a cover for deliver-
ing the Mighty Dicks. No reason DeeDee couldn't
have killed two birds with one stone.

"You're sure you didn't deliver those?" Kace
asked DeeDee after he tipped his head to the box.
He passed the papers to Peter.

The woman frantically shook her head. "No. I
swear I didn't."

"Don't believe her," Eileen snapped. "She's lying."

Maybe, but Kace doubted he'd find out the truth

right now. Not with DeeDee and Eileen both digging in their heels.

"I want to press charges against her," Eileen went on.

Of course, she did. "At best, I can charge her with trespassing," Kace informed Jana's mom, "but since you don't have a sign posted on this particular part of the property, DeeDee can fight it."

"Trespassing?" Eileen protested. "How about harassment? Threats? Mental anguish? Defamation of character?"

Clearly, Eileen had been watching too many cop shows on TV. "Can you give me absolute proof that she put that box here?" Kace asked. "*Absolute proof*," he emphasized. "Not gut feelings, not guesses, not accusations."

Eileen sputtered out a few sounds of protest before she found her words. "She was here with the box, which should be proof enough."

"It's not." Kace continued to talk over Eileen's howling protest. "If you want to file trespassing charges, go to the police station, and I'll meet you there after I'm done here with DeeDee."

"Why doesn't she have to go to the police station?" Eileen demanded. "Why don't you just arrest her?"

"Because an arrest isn't warranted. Go ahead and leave. Liberty will do the paperwork for the trespassing. DeeDee and I will be there shortly, and she can give her statement then."

Oh, Eileen wanted to keep arguing, but Peter took hold of her arm—nearly stabbing her with his artwork in the process—but he got his angry bride-to-be moving back into his car.

While they drove away, Kace went to the box so he could put it in his truck. That's when he saw the note that was inside.

Dick Tubes for dicks like Peter Laramie.

It was in the same vein as the other messages, but this one wasn't typed. It was handwritten, and seeing it caused Kace to freeze.

Obviously Jana caught his change in posture because she went closer to him. "What's wrong?"

"That," he said, pointing to the note. He looked at Jana. "I'm not positive, but I think I recognize the handwriting."

Well, hell.

If he was right, this was going to be one big-assed shitstorm.

JANA LOOKED OVER at the box she'd just packed to see that the contents—clothes from the dresser—were now strewn over the bedroom floor of her grandmother's house.

Apparently, a toddler helper hadn't been a good idea.

But it was still a fun one. Marley had put one of Jana's bras on her head as if it were a hat. Even though Marley was pulling and stretching at the sheer red lace, Jana didn't mind. It was one of the few pieces of sexy underwear she had, and it hadn't seen much action over the past couple of years what with her being pregnant and then having Marley. Even before that, there'd been a string of fertility treatments, which hadn't exactly put Jana in the mood for sexy undies.

Of course, Kace might be a reason to wear a red lace bra, and on their next date, there might actually be enough time for him to notice such things. The night before they'd certainly taken each other in a heated rush. Fast, but incredibly satisfying. Maybe if they were together again, they could slow down enough to savor each other.

If they were together again.

Jana knew there were no sexual guarantees where Kace was concerned. If he came to his senses, he might remember all the reasons why they shouldn't go another round with each other. Unfortunately, Jana was having a hard time recalling those reasons. That was the lingering side effect of incredibly satisfying sex.

She was so going to get a broken heart out of this. But with her body still on a slow simmer, she was convincing herself that it just might be worth it.

"Ook," Marley said, garnering Jana's attention again.

It was her daughter's way of saying *look*, and Marley pranced around the room with the bra still on her head and a pair of Jana's red panties looped around her arm like some kind of lace bracelet. No way could Jana resist that so she scooped her up and gave her some raspberry kisses that made Marley giggle.

There it was. That feeling of happiness and contentment that washed over her. A reminder for Jana that there were plenty of uncertainties and bumps in her life, but Marley could make all of that so much better. Their new house and ranch might not be her dream place. However, it would still be a happy one. Jana would work hard to make sure that happened.

Her phone dinged with a text message, and Jana automatically frowned when she saw Dominick's name on the screen. She also stood Marley back on the floor so she could read it.

Have you signed that new settlement yet? My lawyer's not going to wait on you much longer.

"*My lawyer's not going to wait on you much longer,*" Jana repeated in a snarky, mocking tone. One that made Marley laugh. And it made Jana remember that she shouldn't do that in front of a little pitcher, big ears.

As much as Jana despised Dominick, she didn't want that to bleed over to Marley. Despite Dominick acting like an ass, he was and always would be Marley's father. She would need to report this though to her own lawyer who could maybe do something to stop Dominick from harassing her with stupid texts like this one.

"Tace!" Marley squealed, causing Jana to swirl

in the direction that Marley was now toddling at a rather amazing speed.

Yes, it was Kace all right. He was in the bedroom doorway, Bessie by his side. Obviously, the woman had shown him in, but Jana had been so caught up in her thoughts, she hadn't heard them.

But she could certainly see Kace. And just like that, she got a fresh jolt of the sex memories they'd created the night before.

Marley latched onto Kace's leg, and Kace scooped her up. "Trying on new clothes?" he asked her, eyeing the red bra and panties. Marley must have thought it was a fine joke because she giggled and babbled off some words that would have taken a baby translator to decipher.

Jana quickly went to Kace and Marley, retrieving the undergarments and tossing them into the packing box. Of course, they were still in plain sight. So were the other bras and panties that Marley had scattered on the floor, but the partial embarrassment of that faded when Jana saw the serious look on Kace's face.

Uh-oh. Something was wrong. Obviously though, that shouldn't be much of a surprise what with everything that was going on. So Jana wasn't sure if that look was for the personal stuff between them or the rest of the mess in their lives.

Bessie clearly picked up Kace's vibe because she took Marley from him, immediately offering the baby a cookie so that she wouldn't protest being taken from Kace's arms. Soon, they were going to have to come up with a different bribe to make sure Marley didn't get a sugar addiction.

"You have bad news?" Jana asked the moment Bessie and Marley were out of earshot. She also crammed her hands into the pockets of her jeans because she was itching to touch Kace. Itching to kiss him, too. But there wasn't much she could do to harness her mouth.

Kace took a deep breath before he answered. "Nothing new on the dick enlargers," he said, and he managed it with a straight face, too. "The lab will run them for prints, and I've asked them to analyze the handwriting on the note."

Jana waited because she was almost positive there was something he wasn't saying about that, but Kace didn't add more. However, Jana went with a hunch. "Do you have any idea who wrote it?"

He lifted his shoulder. "Some. But I'll keep that to myself until I have proof. There's no hurry despite all the fuss Peter and your mom are making about it. I mean, the person hasn't done anything else to endanger Peter."

No, and that should probably give her a clue to the culprit's identity. Whoever was behind this didn't want to hurt the man, only embarrass him with really odd sexual objects.

"You've talked to your mom today?" he asked.

Jana shook her head. "I had a lot of packing to do. I'll be moving to Nico's place later this week." Which meant she'd be able to spend Christmas there with Marley. "In fact, I've already had some of my horses taken there." Obviously, that didn't mean she hadn't had time for a conversation with her mother so she added, "And I've been trying to avoid her."

Kace made a sound of understanding. He would no doubt like to avoid her as well, but that wasn't going to happen as long as the pranks continued.

"Eileen wouldn't back down on pressing charges against DeeDee for trespassing," Kace explained. "DeeDee won't back down, either, and she's hired a lawyer to fight the charges despite the legal fees being much higher than any fine would be. DeeDee's lawyer said she's pressing to file charges against Eileen for defamation of character and slander."

Well, crap. That sounded like a tit for tat that could go on indefinitely. "I wish I could say I could talk my mother out of this, but you and I both know how far I'd get with that. She's not exactly happy with me right now anyway."

Kace kept his eyes on her while he nodded. "Eileen's riled because she guessed that we'd had sex."

Bingo. Too bad *riled* wasn't an exaggeration. Jana had been able to feel the Arctic chill from her mom even in this Texas heat, and it was one of the reasons Jana had worked it out with Nico so that she could move in earlier than originally planned. For now, it was best not to occupy the same acreage as her mom.

Judging from the way Kace kept looking at her, he felt the same way about her.

Jana decided just to go ahead and deal with the huge elephant in the room. "You're here to tell me that we should back off from each other and allow things to cool down."

He gave a too-fast nod. One that sent her heart into a tailspin before Jana could practically feel it falling at her feet. *Oh mercy.* This was going to hurt. Or so she thought. But Kace stunned her when he leaned in and brushed his mouth over hers. The stunning continued when he pulled her to him and made it a real kiss.

A deep and an especially tasty one.

"I *should* be here to tell you that we need to back off," he said with his lips hovering right over hers. "But that's not going to happen so I believe we should move on to option B."

"If it involves more kisses, I'm all for it." Her voice sounded dreamy. No doubt a result of her light head and lust-filled body.

"Definitely. And more. I think we should just have an affair," he went on. "An ex with benefits or some stupid label like that. I never did get those ear kisses from you, and I didn't get to go down on you like I'd planned."

That totally robbed Jana of her breath. "You'd planned on doing that?" she managed to ask when she could speak.

"That and plenty more," he verified.

There was no dreaminess to his voice. It was a husky drawl. The kind of slow Texas twang that qualified as foreplay. It wasn't actually needed since Jana had hurdled past the foreplay mode, but it was a nice bonus. So was the kiss that followed. Kace tasted like coffee and sin, not a bad combination at all.

"Go on another date with me," he said after he broke for air. "I know you're moving this week, but how about Saturday?"

Jana didn't even have to think about her answer. "I'll call Piper and see if she can babysit." And if the girl couldn't, Jana would ask Bessie.

"Good." More of that smoky drawl, and this time his breath hit against her damp lips. It felt a little like one of those postquivers and -quakes that happened after an orgasm.

The quivering and quaking stopped, however, when his phone dinged with a text message. Pulling it from his pocket, Kace stepped back and muttered some profanity.

"It's from the mayor," Kace said, and there wasn't a trace of smoke or heat left in his voice. "Dominick's lawyer is filing a multimillion-dollar lawsuit against me for mental and bodily harm."

Oh God. No. She certainly hadn't forgotten about Dominick and the altercation he'd had with Kace, but with everything else going on, Jana had put it on the mental back burner.

Kace muttered more of that profanity and showed her the rest of the mayor's message.

Kace, you'd better hire a lawyer—fast.

CHAPTER EIGHTEEN

"THERE WASN'T A single print on any of the dicks," Judd told Kace the moment he stepped into the police station.

Kace was betting plenty of lawmen had never heard that comment, especially one in an official capacity.

"There was no postal info on the box so the person responsible must have dropped it off at Eileen's. And worn gloves," Judd pointed out. "By the way, the lab was able to tell us the name of that particular brand of vibrators." He looked at the note he was holding. "They're called Happy Rabbit G-spot Locators, and they'd been set to the jiggle and squirm setting."

If this had been anyone other than Judd, Kace might have accused him of making that up. Since this was no fabrication and because the subject would likely come up again during interviews, Kace jotted down the brand name in the note section of his phone.

"As for the handwritten message in the box with the penis extenders," Judd went on, "no prints there, either."

"What about any handwriting analysis?" Kace asked.

Judd shook his head. "Couldn't be done. The lab just doesn't have anyone on tap to do that, and they can't outsource unless it's a more serious crime. Right now, all we got is this might be the same person who planted the stink bomb in Peter's car, and if so, we could charge him or her with reckless endangerment. That's not enough to get the lab hopping, especially after they've already hopped so much for us."

Yeah, but Kace was betting the lab guys had had a little fun processing all those sex toys. Still, lab tests cost money, and their budget was stretched to the bone paying for all of this. Tests that had given them zilch.

But Kace had more than zilch.

He had a hunch that he'd seen that handwriting before, and now he was going to have to pay that person a visit.

"I'm having the companies who make all these products send me a list of their customers who recently bought the items in these quantities," Judd continued. "The person might have used a bogus name, but we could still get lucky, and the companies are cooperating, more or less. They won't hand over addresses, email or payment info, of course, but each agreed to give us a name if the exact quantities and timing of the purchases match."

Kace made a sound of approval. His brother had

obviously spent a lot of time on this, and the case might have broken because of penmanship.

"You okay?" Judd asked, causing Kace to shift his attention back to his brother.

Hell, that was concern and worry he saw in Judd's expression, and Kace didn't have to guess why it was there. It was a similar expression to nearly everyone else's in town. Folks seemed to be on his side when it came to Dominick's lawsuit against him. A lawsuit that now also included the town council who'd hired him.

"I've got Roy on retainer, and he's handling everything," Kace explained.

And he hoped it was true. He didn't especially want to devote any time thinking or worrying about this, but it was hard to dismiss it. After all, he had punched Dominick, and he deserved some kind of punishment. However, the town didn't, and Dominick certainly didn't deserve millions of dollars for it.

"I guess you know that Rosy set up a fund?" Judd added.

Kace wasn't surprised about that, but it was somewhat of a miracle that he hadn't heard that particular tidbit. He shook his head.

"She put a big jar in her store, and people are putting in donations for your legal fund or to pay off Dominick. Rosy said she thinks there's already a couple of hundred dollars in there."

Kace was thankful for the generosity. Coldwater might be filled with gossips and colorful sorts, but they were good people. But the money would leave him with a problem, too, because he wouldn't use it. He had insurance, and if it came down to it, that's where the money would come from. That and his personal accounts. He wasn't rich though, not by any stretch of the imagination, and he might even have to sell off some land if the lawyers worked out a settlement.

Since thinking of that didn't improve his mood, he took his Stetson and jacket from the peg on the wall. "I've got to head out for a while," he told Judd. "A personal errand."

Which definitely wouldn't improve his mood, either, but it had to be done.

"Going to see Jana?" Judd asked.

Now, that would have improved his mood considerably, but Kace had to shake his head. Between work and her moving, he hadn't seen her all week. However, he did intend to run by her new place to see if she needed any help. And no, it wouldn't be a booty call since Marley would be with her. Any booty would have to wait until their date on Saturday.

Kace didn't fill his brother in on the visit he had to make now, but he would if and when it produced any results. He almost hoped that it would be a bust because the alternative sucked.

"Take an umbrella," Ginger advised him when he opened the door. "Storm's moving in."

Well, that would be two of them. Both the weather-related one and the one he was about to stir up.

"Sorry to hear 'bout your legal problems," someone called out to Kace as he walked up Main Street.

Gopher. Thankfully, the man was fully clothed today so there'd be no need to threaten him with arrest.

Kace thanked him, got similar sentiments from seven other people, all vowing to contribute to his legal fund, and he made his way to the bank—where he got more commiserations and offers of money. He thanked them, too, and made a beeline to Belinda's office. Since she was a loan officer, she was often with clients, but today she was alone, working on her computer.

"Kace," she greeted on a rise of breath, and smiling, she got to her feet. Her smile widened even more when Kace shut the door behind him.

No way did Belinda believe he was there for anything but conversation, but she looked hopeful anyway. Kace was about to send those hopes flying right out the window. Before Belinda could voice any of those hopes or say anything, Kace whipped out his phone and showed her the photo he'd taken.

The one that showed the note that had been in the box with the Mighty Dick Penis Enlargers.

"What is that?" Belinda asked, moving closer to take a look at the screen.

Because Kace was watching her, he saw her blink. Not an ordinary one, either. This one had guilt written all over it and suddenly so did her face.

"I recognized the handwriting," Kace told her when she didn't say anything.

There was no way Belinda could deny he'd seen her handwriting since she'd sent him countless cards over the years. For his birthday, Christmas and even ones that said "thinking of you."

"Oh." That was all she said before she went back behind her desk and dropped down into her chair.

Again, he waited and nada. "I'm going to need more of an explanation than an *oh*," Kace insisted. And then he did something he never thought he'd have to do.

He read Belinda her rights.

With each word, she looked more and more horrified. "I got the stink bombs, the balloons, the strippers…everything," she blurted out when he'd finished. "And I did it for you."

Yeah, Kace had already figured that out. Plain and simple, he was Belinda's motive, and because of the relationship they'd once had, she wanted to get back at Peter.

"That horrible excuse for a man ran out on you and your brothers," Belinda went on, and apparently now that she was wound up, she wasn't going to stop. "He didn't have a right to come here and throw all those horrible memories back in your face. He should have gone anywhere but here so you didn't have to run into him day in and day out."

That last part was somewhat of an exaggeration. In a small town, there was always the possibility of Kace running into him, but it hadn't happened nearly as often as he'd thought it would.

"You hired someone, a man, to put in the order for the strippers?" Kace asked so he could tie up that particular loose end.

She nodded and swallowed hard. "A friend of a friend. I told him I was planning a surprise bachelor party and that I was uncomfortable going into a place like that. Uncomfortable using my real name, too."

So, Belinda had told him to use Peter's. "And what about Jeb's Party Favors? Who did you send to pick up that order?"

"The same guy. He had no idea what I was really going to do with all that stuff. He thought they were just funny party favors."

Well, nobody was laughing. "I want the guy's name so I can ask him a few questions," Kace insisted.

Belinda frantically shook her head. "You're not going to arrest him, are you?"

"Not if what you've told me is true. I'll just give him a lecture about not doing stupid favors for friends of friends."

"Are you going to arrest me?" Belinda pressed. At least she didn't look ready to fall apart. Just the opposite. There was plenty of defiance in the way she hiked up her chin like that.

Best not to sugarcoat this. "Yes. The Smelly Bob in his car was dangerous. He could have been hurt."

"I wanted him hurt," she snapped. "I wanted him to pay for what he'd done to you." However, that fit of temper drained her because she sighed, and her shoulders and chin dropped. "But I didn't think he would wreck. I swear that never occurred to me."

Kace believed her. Belinda didn't have criminal

intent in her, but she did have a warped sense of how to get back at someone.

"You have a clean record," he said. "You won't get jail time unless Peter pushes this hard."

Which he might do if Eileen in turn pushed him hard. Kace still didn't know a lot about the man who'd fathered him, but it was possible he was a gold-digging weenie. If so, he'd cave to Eileen just to hang on to his gold-digging future.

Belinda stayed quiet a moment. "How can you stand to be around him? How can you even look at him?"

Kace wanted to shrug, but it didn't seem right to dismiss it. Not when Belinda had done all of this crazy shit because of some misplaced sense of loyalty to him.

"It bothers me to see him," Kace admitted. "But the only way I can keep getting on with my life is to get past what he did. If I hang on to that, it drags me right down into the mud. I've been in the mud, and I don't want to be there again."

"Well, I can't forgive him." She was back to snapping again.

"I didn't say I forgave him," Kace corrected. "I'm just doing my best not to hang on to the past."

"Except when it comes to Jana." Belinda spat that out, adding some snap to it as well. "You're hanging on to her."

Kace didn't respond to that. He was still working out in his head what was going on between Jana and him, and for darn certain he wasn't going to discuss her with Belinda.

"I need to ask if anyone else helped you buy or distribute any of the things you sent to Peter?" Kace continued. He had to refer to a note on his phone to fill in the rest. "That includes the Smelly Bobs stink bombs, the dick balloons, the strippers from Tit for Tat, the Happy Rabbit G-spot Locators vibrators or Mighty Dick Penis Enlargers."

Amazingly, Belinda kept a straight face through that litany of pranks. "No one helped me, and yes, it was expensive. I haven't kept a running total, but I think I spent over three grand."

Yeah, that's what he'd guessed, and that wouldn't play in her favor if Peter sued her in civil court. All those purchases were proof of a pattern of behavior. A bad one. And unless Kace could defuse this, Belinda could be out a lot more money what with the damages she'd have to pay the man, and Kace wasn't sure folks would be setting up a legal fund for her.

"I did this for you," Belinda repeated.

Before Kace could remind her that he'd wanted no such retaliation, Belinda burst into tears.

Oh hell.

He was so not good with a crying woman, especially one who had a reason to cry if she'd sussed out just how bad this could get for her. But knowing he had to do something, Kace pulled a handful of tissues from the box that was on her desk, and he gave them to her. He also stooped down so they were eye to eye. With all those tears, she probably couldn't see him that well, but she'd get the gist of this.

"I don't want you to do anything else to try to get back at Peter," he said. "In fact, I want you to stay far away from him and Eileen. Also, go ahead and talk to Roy and tell him what you've done."

Belinda nodded through the sobs, and she caught onto his shoulders, pulling him to her. Not good because it threw him off balance, and Kace would have fallen against her if he hadn't caught onto her desk.

"There, there," he told her because he didn't have a clue what else to say.

He added some more sounds that he hoped were sympathetic, and not once did he say that this was of her own making. Or that she'd made her bed and now she had to lie in it. Nope. He just stood there, dried her cheeks with another tissue and tried not to look as if he wanted to be anywhere but here.

The crying jag seemed to last a month or two, but Kace was reasonably sure that it was less than fifteen minutes. Finally, Belinda blew her nose and looked up at him.

"Sorry," she muttered, then paused a very long time. "What happens next?"

He'd get to round two of things he didn't especially want to do, but that's not what he said to Belinda. "I'll go talk to Peter and see if I can explain things. I'll let you know what he says. In the meantime, why don't you see if you can take the rest of the day off. If you don't want to talk to Roy right now, then go home."

That would have a twofold effect. Folks wouldn't keep asking her what was wrong—which they would do when they saw her puffy red eyes. Also, going home might mean she could get some rest and put all of this in perspective.

Of course, perspective might cause her to cry again, so Kace made a mental note to text her later to check on her. He could even ask Shelby, Eden or Cleo to run by Belinda's place. Sometimes, having a sister-in-law and his brothers' significant others helped.

After Belinda had gone a full five minutes without tears, Kace told her goodbye and headed out so he could get in his truck and start the drive to Eileen's. He considered practicing what he should say but realized for him to be able to do that, he'd have to believe that his word choice actually mattered.

It wouldn't.

Eileen was seeing red over these stupid pranks, and she'd turn that red on Belinda. The only silver lining was that at least it wasn't DeeDee who was responsible because Eileen would have hounded the woman with her very last breath.

When Kace pulled into Eileen's driveway, he immediately saw Peter's car. So, he was there, which meant no reprieve on telling him the news. Just as well. Best to get it over and deal with the fallout.

His eyes automatically went in the direction of Jana's grandmother's house. Her SUV wasn't where it was usually parked so she was likely over at her new place. That was probably a good thing, too. He didn't want Marley around if Eileen's temper blew up like an eruption of Mount Vesuvius.

Kace hadn't thought the "artwork" in Eileen's house could get any worse, but he soon discovered he was wrong about that when the maid led him past the foyer and toward the back. There was more circus stuff, including animals that could scare the crap out of little kids, and the usual Christmas decorations were squeezed in between the scary junk. He hoped Marley didn't have to see this.

He found Peter and Eileen in one of the two sunrooms where they were sipping what appeared to be martinis. As Belinda had done, the moment Eileen spotted him, she sprang to her feet.

"I hope that woman's behind bars," Eileen immediately snarled.

Kace knew Eileen meant *that woman* to be DeeDee. "She's not." And he continued talking despite Eileen's growl—yes, growl—of protest. "DeeDee's not going to jail because she's not the one who's been playing these pranks on Peter. Belinda did them."

Peter and Eileen gave him the blankest stares in the history of blank stares. "Who?" Peter asked just as Eileen said, "No way possible."

"Way," Kace verified to Eileen before he shifted to Peter. "Belinda Darlington. She works at the bank, and she was someone I was seeing for a while."

"She wouldn't do this," Eileen insisted. "It was DeeDee, and she must have set up Belinda."

"Belinda confessed," Kace explained, his attention still on Peter. "And for the record, she's sorry about the car accident. She didn't mean for that to happen. She only wanted to, well, harass you."

Hopefully the long silence that followed meant they were processing this news. In a good way, too. Kace hated what Belinda had done, but he didn't want to see her locked up.

"For God's sake, why would Belinda do this?" Eileen blurted out.

Peter didn't have any trouble coming up with the answer. "Because I abandoned Kace and his brothers. If Belinda cares for Kace, she would have wanted to punish me for what I did."

Bingo. Kace confirmed it with a nod. "Clearly, she wasn't thinking straight. She screwed up, and like I said, she's sorry. I'm sure Belinda wishes she hadn't caused both of you so much trouble and aggravation."

Kace would have continued to plead the woman's case, but he heard footsteps behind him and turned to see Jana. She had a sacked-out Marley in her arms, and the baby's head was on Jana's shoulder.

"Belinda did all those pranks?" Jana asked. Obviously, she'd heard at least part of what Kace had just said.

Kace nodded, but it seemed as if Eileen was still mulling this over. There was nothing to mull. Well, except for trying to figure out what would happen to Belinda. Kace had some suggestions about that all lined up, but it took him a moment to refocus. Jana had a way of distracting him. That was stupid, considering they weren't starry-eyed kids. They had a long bumpy history together, but his body didn't seem to give a rat's ass about that.

He cleared his throat, cleared his mind and turned back to Peter. "I know you could have been hurt in the wreck. Plus, you had to pay for repairs. I haven't run this past Belinda yet—she was still too upset when I talked to her—but I believe I could convince her to reimburse you for those repairs and your medical bills. Reimburse you, too, for any cleanup costs you had for the stink bombs that she left on the property."

"That's not enough," Eileen said. Her eyes were narrowed. Her mouth, flat and hard. "I want her to pay for what she did, not just get a slap on the wrist."

Jana caught onto Kace's arm and turned him toward her. "Why would Belinda do—" But she stopped, the answer obviously coming to her. "Oh."

Yeah, *oh*. That about summed it up, and even though Kace knew in his gut that this wasn't his fault, part of him believed he should have recognized what was going on with Belinda. Though it was hard to appreciate what she'd done. Not only because it had a stalker component to it, but it was also completely unwarranted. Yes, Peter had abandoned his family, but this was not the way to make him pay for that. Kace figured karma would take care of it.

"Is Belinda okay?" Jana asked.

Kace had to shrug, but he was thankful for the

question and the concern. Concern that Eileen sure wasn't showing.

"Who cares if she's okay," Eileen declared. "I want her punished. Arrest her if you haven't already."

While Kace would indeed have to arrest her, he still hadn't given up on making Belinda pay less than Eileen obviously thought she should. And although he didn't like asking Peter for anything, Kace thought he might be able to reason with the man.

"Just consider having Belinda reimburse you for those things I mentioned," he said to Peter. "I can also make sure she does some community service that would include scouring the woods and roads to pick up every last one of the cock balloons. Maybe even require her to get some counseling. But I don't think stiff charges, jail time and a civil lawsuit are the way to go here."

"Really?" Eileen shot back. "That's all just slaps on the wrist. Have you forgotten that Belinda tried to set up Jana by putting a box of those smoke bombs in her SUV?"

Nope. He hadn't forgotten that at all, and it was the thing about this that pissed him off the most.

Even though Kace hadn't questioned Belinda about that—yet—he figured Belinda had tried to frame Jana because she was jealous. Kace would get his version of a pound of flesh from Belinda about that, and he would insist that the woman apologize to Jana as well as stay away from her and Marley. A restraining order probably wouldn't be necessary, but it might give Belinda a clear warning that she'd better not pull this sort of shit again. Plus, it would be another layer of punishment since it would give the gossips more fodder.

Not that they didn't have enough.

Nope. This would be the talk of the town for at least a year or two.

"I don't want Belinda arrested for what she did to me," Jana said.

That was generous of her, and Kace figured she was saying that because of him. Because of the guilt he was feeling over this.

"Go and arrest Belinda now," Eileen repeated, and she likely would have just kept up the mantra/demand if one of the housekeepers hadn't stepped into the doorway.

"Mrs. Parker, you've got a visitor," the woman said.

It probably wasn't unusual for guests to come to Eileen's house, but there was something about the housekeeper that snagged Kace's attention. The woman looked as if she'd just gotten a gut punch.

"Well, who is it?" Eileen snarled to the maid. "I'm not in the mood to see anyone."

The maid hesitated and did some nibbling on her bottom lip. Hell, Kace hoped Belinda hadn't come here to plead her case. But it wasn't a woman's voice that he heard.

"Eileen, it's me," the man said.

It took Kace a moment to place that voice. Not

Eileen and Jana, though. Eileen gasped, and Jana whirled around so fast that it woke up Marley.

"It's me," the man repeated, and then Kace knew exactly who he was.

Jana's father, Arnold Parker.

CHAPTER NINETEEN

JANA BLINKED HARD, certain that her eyes were deceiving her. But if they were, then her ears were in on the deception, too, because that was her father's voice.

Her father was here.

Here.

Right in front of her.

Arnold Parker wasn't dead. No. He was very much alive. And here in her mother's sunroom.

Of course, he'd changed since the last time she'd seen him twenty years ago. His hair was all gray and shaggy. Not at all the hairstyle of a businessman. Neither were his clothes. Jana remembered him wearing suits a lot, but today he was in khakis and a Rolling Stones T-shirt.

"Jana," he greeted. Definitely her father, and he was smiling.

She smiled, too, and hurried to him, his arm coming around both Marley and her in a hug. Marley, who was cranky from being startled awake, wasn't happy about that and began to fuss. At least she did until she saw Kace, then immediately reached for him. Kace took her from Jana.

"Tace," Marley muttered, dropping her head on his shoulder and sticking her thumb in her mouth.

Jana was thankful that her daughter was content because right now Jana was dealing with her own whirlwind of emotions.

"You're here," Jana said, repeating the stunned reaction that was going through her head.

God, it felt so good to be in his arms like this. Felt equally good to hear him whisper her name while he stroked her hair. For now, she just held on to that *good* feeling and let herself be a kid again.

"My little girl's all grown-up," he said still keeping his voice low. "And you've got a little girl of your own."

"Yes," she managed to say, and that's when Jana realized she was crying. Not just a little boo-hooing, either. These were big fat tears, and there were plenty of them rolling down her cheeks.

She continued to stand there in his embrace, trying to take it all in. Her father was alive and he'd come home. Just that thought alone kept her anchored and in place for what seemed an eternity, and then Jana heard something that broke the magical father-daughter spell.

"Why are you here?" Eileen asked.

Jana felt her father's muscles go stiff, and he shifted his position, keeping one of his arms around her while he turned to face her mother. Jana faced her, too, and she saw her mother's ghost-white face and her trembling mouth. Actually, Eileen was trembling all over, and that's probably why Peter pulled her into his arms.

"A PI Jana hired got in touch with me," her father said. "I'm living in Maui now, in a little out-of-the-way place so it took him a while to track me down. He told me Jana was looking for me and how much she missed me."

That answer sent a new spike of emotion through Jana. She hadn't been anywhere near certain that hiring the PI would work, but it obviously had, and she couldn't have been happier about that.

But not everyone in the room was in her giddy, gleeful mood.

Her mother was staring daggers, and some of them were aimed at Jana. Mostly though, the sharp venom was for the man who'd once been her husband. No, that wasn't right. For the man who was *still* her husband.

Jana glanced at Peter, and while he wasn't doling out venom, he did look shell-shocked. And stayed silent. Kace did as well, but his attention was on her, as if watching to make sure she was okay. Because of her giddiness, it took Jana a couple of moments to realize why Kace was so somber.

Oh.

It all came back to Jana then, and it didn't come back in an especially good way. It crashed into her, robbing her of her breath and tightening her stomach into a hard fist.

"You left me. Left us," she said to her father, and Jana heard the tremble in her voice. Heard the emotion, too. There'd be more tears, but she also felt something else. Confusion.

And some anger.

"You let me believe you were dead," Jana added, and it was definitely an anger-tinged accusation.

Part of her wanted her father to deny that. Maybe to have him come up with an explanation. Amnesia, perhaps. Or that he was on the run from the mob. But she could tell from his heavy sigh and expression that the explanation wasn't going to be one she liked.

"I won't ever be able to make you understand," he muttered. Yes, a mutter. It likely meant he was ashamed about something he didn't especially want to spell out. Tough. He *would* spell it out anyway.

"Why don't I take Marley somewhere else?" Kace suggested. Obviously, he had picked up on Jana's fast change in mood. This wasn't going to continue to be a happy reunion.

Kace waited for Jana's nod before he got moving, and he stopped right next to her. "I'll be nearby if you need to talk," he told her. "Or vent," he added, sliding a glare to her father. "And, Mr. Parker, when you're done here, I'll need to talk to you."

No one could have missed the official tone in that last part. It was the cop talking because Kace would indeed have questions to make sure no laws had been broken. Jana wasn't sure about the legal aspects of this, but her father had certainly broken her heart by leaving. Now his return was bringing those breaks right back to the surface.

Her father gave Kace a nod, and Kace left with

Marley. Thankfully, her daughter hadn't picked up on the suddenly ugly vibes in the room because she started to babble cheerfully to Kace.

"Kace," Jana called out to him. He stopped and looked back at her. "Some of the stuff in the foyer gives Marley the willies, so could you put your hand over her eyes if you go there? Sorry," she added to Peter, since she'd just dissed his so-called art pieces.

"Will do," Kace assured her.

"I don't expect you to understand," her father said once Kace and Marley were gone, "but I was in a very bad place—"

"So was I when you abandoned us," Jana snapped. She didn't even try to tamp down the fury. And the betrayal. God, the betrayal suddenly seemed the worst of all. She'd loved him to the moon and back, and he'd tossed away that love as if it were a paper plate at a picnic.

Her father nodded again, obviously not arguing with anything Jana had said. He dragged in a long breath and turned to Eileen. "You know how it was between us. We were hardly speaking to each other, and you refused a divorce. You said you'd rather see me dead before going through the shame of being a divorced woman."

Eileen didn't admit to that, but it was definitely something her mom would have said.

"I felt trapped," her father continued. "Suicidal even."

Okay, so Jana wasn't immune to that last part. She'd gone through her own deep depression after her dad had left so she understood what a dark place that could be. But it still didn't excuse what he'd done.

"At first I thought I'd just get away for a while," he went on. "Only a couple of days to clear my head. I took the boat to the Gulf, and that's when I knew I needed more than a couple of days." He paused, gave Jana a sorrowful look. "That's also when I knew I couldn't come back."

Oh mercy. That hurt so much. It cut her to the core, and she could tell that her father understood that. He reached for her, no doubt to pull her back into another hug, but she batted his hands away.

"You let us believe you were dead," she snapped. "I grieved for you!" Her mom probably had, too. In Eileen's own way, that is. "Just because your marriage was over, that didn't mean you could stop being my father."

But that's exactly what he'd done.

In the moment, Jana wished she'd never hired the PI. Knowing the truth was harder, and that was something she definitely hadn't expected.

"I know," Arnold—no, he was *Arnie* now—admitted. "I was wrong, and I know I can never make it up to you."

"Damn straight you can't." And because Jana wanted to kick or hit something a little too much, she whirled around, moving away from him to put some space between them. She went to her mother's side.

The silence came. It was long, awkward and dripping with a whole bunch of anger. Jana didn't think it was her imagination that Eileen wanted to kick or punch something, too. Thankfully, there was plenty of weird artwork in the room if it came down to it, though Jana couldn't see much satisfaction in ramming her boot into an ugly circus animal.

"How dare you do this to me," Eileen said to Arnold, and yep—plenty of anger. Jana wouldn't have been surprised if killer laser beams hadn't shot from her eyes.

"I don't expect you to forgive me," her father piped up.

"Good because I won't. You ripped our lives apart twenty years ago, and now you've come back to do it again."

Eileen hadn't exactly aimed any of the blame for that at Jana, but she could feel it. That's because she blamed herself. This was a whole *let sleeping dogs lie* kind of situation. Maybe later she could put this in perspective and try to see her dad's side, but for now, seeing red was about all she could manage.

"I've got to get out of here," Jana snarled, and without waiting to see if anyone had any objections to that, she stormed out of the sunroom. She didn't know exactly where she was heading, but she wouldn't manage to get air into her lungs until she put some distance between her father and her.

She needed Marley. Possibly Kace, too. But they were nowhere in sight, which was probably a good thing because every room in sight contained some of the god-awful circus pieces. However, Jana soon heard her daughter's babbling coming from a closed-in side porch. When she stepped in there, Jana spotted them in the pair of rockers. Kace in one. Marley in the other. Kace had hold of Marley's hand, but Marley was also throwing back her weight to make the chair rock.

The porch wasn't heated, but the temps outside were in the high fifties so it wasn't too cold. The air though, was thick and heavy, and the gunmetal-gray clouds had already moved in, covering the sun and most of the blue in the sky. It felt dark and brooding—just like a mood. Of course, her mood had a dash of lightning and thunder in it, something that the weather would soon mimic.

One look at Jana, and Kace sighed. He was also probably silently muttering some profanity. She certainly was.

"Mama," Marley greeted with a big grin, and what she rattled off next sounded as if it had something to do with the rocking chair.

Jana wanted to scoop her up, but Marley appeared to be having fun so Jana sank down on the arm of Kace's chair instead.

"There's a mutant-looking clown that appears to be eating globs of tumorous butter in the living room," Kace said.

All in all, it wasn't a bad attempt to lighten things up. And Jana knew which figure he meant. Totally spooky, blank eyes, and eating what she supposed was meant to be popcorn. If her mood hadn't been in the deepest part of the toilet, his description might have caused her to smile, but it was going to take a whole lot more than that to loosen the expression on her face.

Then, Marley farted.

It was a loud series of rumbles and thumps against her diaper, and it caused the baby's loony laughter. "I tooted," Marley announced. Jana could tell from her baby's expression that she was trying to re-create the gassy experience. Okay, so it was indeed hard to mope around baby laughter even when it was inappropriate humor.

Jana did pick her up. She kissed her and because she knew it was the only way to keep Marley from fussing, Jana began to rock. It didn't get out the pressure cooker anger as fast as kicking that zombie clown, but it definitely helped.

"My father didn't love me enough to stay," Jana whispered. She kissed the top of Marley's head and tried to blink back the blasted tears.

Kace leaned closer, brushing his hand over her arm. In her lap, Marley managed another fart, another laugh. If her daughter kept this up, it might lead to the need for a diaper change.

"No, Arnold loved you," Kace assured her. "He was just a selfish you-know-what who put himself first. His beef was with Eileen, not you." Considering just how angry Kace sounded, and looked, it had likely taken a lot of self-control to leave out the curse words. "Think of it like temporary insanity."

She tried seeing it from that angle, and later, after she'd moved on from the thoroughly pissed-off stage, it might actually help. Well, it would help her anyway. It likely wouldn't do much to soothe her mother.

"I couldn't stay in there with them," Jana said. "I couldn't listen to another word he had to say." She paused. "But I probably should have been there for my mom."

"No," Kace quickly disagreed. "They've got their own issues to work out, and it's best you not be part of that."

At that exact moment, Jana heard her mother shouting something that included "you spineless piece of shit." Kace was right. She didn't need to hear that, and neither did Marley. In case it got worse, Jana tried to put her hands over her daughter's ears.

"There'll be plenty of anger for a while," Kace went on. "Then, grief. Yes, grief," he said when Jana gave him a no-way stare. "This is like a death. The man you idolized and loved for so many years wasn't the man you thought he was. I went through something like that after Peter walked out on us."

Well, crud. Kace was right again. Grieving was just what she didn't need on top of all the other things she was dealing with. Ditto for her mother. Of course, the anger stage for Eileen might last so long that she'd never make it to the grief marker.

"You probably don't think I have the right to give you advice on dealing with your feelings about your father," he went on. "After all, I'm still coming to terms with the mental mess that Peter left behind."

He was still dealing with it. Jana didn't doubt that one bit, but the mental mess he'd gone through seemed worse than hers. She hadn't ended up in foster care the way he and his brothers had.

"I appreciate your advice," she let him know.

He nodded, paused. Smiled a little. "I think it's called irony that I believe you can get past what you're feeling but I can't do the same. And maybe it's just plain hope to think eventually they'll work all of this out." Kace's voice so soothing now. "Eventually, you'll work it out, too."

While part of her would have liked to wallow a little longer, Jana knew that Kace had just gone three for three in the right department. The question was though—how would she work it out?

She was just starting to mull that over when Peter came storming out. He didn't even pause. He went straight to the door that led to the yard, and he barreled down the steps so fast that he might not have even stopped if Jana hadn't called out his name.

Peter whirled around, his gaze clashing into hers. "Well, you got your wish," he spat out. "There'll be no wedding. Eileen is staying married to your father."

CHAPTER TWENTY

WHEN KACE WALKED into the police station, he knew it was going to be one of those days when he wished he'd just stuck with being a cowboy. Dealing with even the orneriest of steers had to be better than what he was facing now.

There were people milling around both inside and out, all of them likely hoping to get in on the gossip about Arnold's return. Yes, news had traveled that fast. Kace figured the moment after Eileen's maid had shown Arnold into the sunroom, she'd gotten on her phone and texted everyone in her contacts.

Kace would soon have to deal with Arnold since the man was already on his way to the police station, but first he was apparently going to have to chat with Belinda since the woman was waiting for him in his office. She wasn't seated, either. She was pacing and looked like a fuse that'd just been lit. Since Kace had just left two women, Eileen and Jana, who'd looked pretty much the same way, he doubted he was going to put off Belinda with a quick *whatever you've got to say will have to wait.*

"If Arnold gets here before I'm finished with Belinda," Kace told Ginger, "tell him to take a seat."

That wouldn't be a pleasant wait since Arnold would be gawked at and peppered with questions, but Kace had moved on to not caring squat what Jana's father had to endure. Arnold had crushed Jana's heart, and that put the man on Kace's shit list.

"Eileen's trying to have me thrown in jail," Belinda blurted out the moment Kace stepped inside his office.

Even though people would still be able to see Belinda and him through the glass, he shut the door. That wouldn't stop anyone with good ears or lipreading skills from being privy to this conversation, but it was the best he could do.

"Yes, she is," Kace admitted. "But Eileen might back off now that she's got other things on her mind."

"No, she won't. Her husband's return might make her even meaner than she already is. Her lawyer just called me and started talking about stuff like depositions and charges."

Kace sighed and moved a notepad and pen closer to her. "Give me his name, and I'll call him. Better yet, I'll have Roy call him." Of course, there was a solution even higher than "better yet" and that was having Belinda take this to Roy herself.

"If I go to jail, I'll lose my job," Belinda went on, and the tears came.

He wished he could tell her that wouldn't happen, but Kace didn't know for sure. Maybe her job as a loan officer required her to have a clean record.

Kace glanced up when the front door opened, and he saw Arnold walk in. His expression wasn't much better than Belinda's, but he still greeted Ginger with a smile and handshake. Ginger smiled back, and Kace figured she did that because she was anticipating all the juicy gossip she was about to hear.

"Do you think it would help if I tried again to apologize to Eileen and Peter?" Belinda asked.

"No. And don't try to apologize to Jana, either. Not yet anyway. Wait until things settle first."

Belinda gave him a blank stare. "Why would I need to apologize to Jana? She doesn't even like Peter."

Kace gave her a blank stare right back. "Because you put a case of stink bombs in Jana's SUV to try to set her up. That was a shitty thing to do."

"But I didn't." She frantically shook her head. "Is that what Jana told you? Because I didn't do that."

He looked for any signs that Belinda might be lying, and he didn't see any. Besides, after everything else she'd confessed to, why wouldn't she include that? Maybe because she thought it would rile Kace?

But that didn't seem right, either.

"You're positive you didn't put anything in Jana's vehicle?" Kace pressed.

"Absolutely, one million percent positive. Give me a lie detector test, or I'll swear to it in court. But I didn't do it. You believe me, right?"

That was a whole lot of denial. And Kace nodded because he did indeed believe her. But that left him with one big question—who had tried to set up Jana?

"God, Jana believes I did something like this," Belinda went on, causing another round of tears. "She must think I'm some kind of jealous witch."

"No." With all of Jana's other problems, she likely hadn't given Belinda more than a passing thought.

"Yes," Belinda disagreed. "She'll help Eileen put me in jail."

And sweet baby Jesus, Belinda had moved on to wailing now.

"Don't dwell on the worst-case scenario until we know what's going to happen," Kace told Belinda. "Once all the paperwork's done, I'll take this to the DA, and maybe we can work out some kind of deal. Any deal though is going to require some kind of punishment, but like I already told you, I'll push for community service."

"Thank you," she said, her voice soggy from the crying. "You're so good to me, and I know the timing sucks for you." Belinda looked up at him. "How much trouble is Jana's ex-husband causing for us... I mean for *you*?"

Kace nearly winced and truly hoped that was a slip of the tongue and not because Belinda still thought of them as a couple. "Everything will be fine." That was more wishful thinking than likely, but Kace didn't want to get into that with Belinda.

She nodded, but it was obvious she didn't quite buy what he'd said. "Well, if there's anything I can do to help, just let me know."

Kace assured her that he would, knowing there was no chance of him involving her in this, and he opened the door. When she spotted Arnold, Belinda said, "Oh," and headed out in a hurry. Obviously, she knew Kace had business with Jana's father.

Even though Ginger was chatting up Arnold, the man went straight back when Kace motioned for him. Unlike Jana, Eileen and Belinda, there was no lit-fuse look for Arnold. As somber as a preacher and as uncomfortable as a hooker in church. Since Kace was feeling plenty of discomfort himself, he could commiserate.

Once again, Kace shut his office door, and he was about to tell Arnold to take a seat so they could get started, but the man spoke first.

"I know who you are," Arnold said. "I mean, I kept up with Jana over the years, which means I know about you."

Intrigued, Kace asked, "How exactly did you keep up with Jana?"

"A private investigator and through social media," he readily answered. "I'm aware that's stalking of sorts, but I wanted to make sure she was okay."

Kace wished he could just be a cop and let that pass, but he owed this to Jana. "If you'd really wanted to make sure she was okay, you would have let her know you were alive."

Arnold nodded in agreement and had the decency to look disgusted with himself. *Good.* Because Kace was certainly disgusted with him.

"Take a seat," he told Arnold, and he continued before the man could say anything else. "I'm going to read you your rights. And no, I don't know if you've committed a crime or not. I've got to do some research on that. But I want all bases covered just in case."

Kace Mirandized him and then added, "You want a lawyer?"

"No," Arnold said on a weary breath. "I just want to finish this."

Kace wasn't sure that was going to happen. Not anytime soon anyway. "I'll need a statement as to where you've been for the last twenty years and why you walked away from your family. I also want to record this."

He gave Arnold a couple of seconds to argue with that, but when the man only nodded, Kace took out a recorder that before this week, hadn't seen much use. But what with his own statement over punching Dominick, Belinda's confession and now this, the machine was getting a workout.

"You didn't live here in Coldwater when I was still with Eileen," Arnold started. "So, you don't know what it was like to be with her."

Kace could guess, but it was best not to add his opinion of his ex-mother-in-law on an official record. "Your marriage was troubled?" he prompted.

A burst of air left Arnold's mouth. A sort of laugh without the humor. "Yes. Eileen was driving me crazy what with all her parties and putting on airs. She was also spending money like water, and while there was plenty to spend, we didn't see eye to eye on finances. On anything," he amended.

"Except for your daughter. You both loved Jana." Kace did want Arnold to admit that he loved his daughter on the record. Heck, Kace might even play it to her to get her out of this dark cloud of a mood.

"Yes, except for my daughter." Arnold's eyes lifted, and Kace couldn't help but notice just how much they were like Jana's. "I love her. Try to make her understand that."

He would do that—if it would help Jana. "You loved her, but you still left," Kace pointed out. It wasn't hard for him to sound like a cop now because he damn sure felt like one.

Arnold nodded. "I just couldn't live with Eileen anymore, and she refused to give me a divorce. She said she'd be a widow but that she'd never sign divorce papers."

Kace let that play around in his mind for a moment. "She threatened you?"

"Not really, but she made it clear that she'd do everything in her power to stall any kind of official breakup, including a legal separation."

Unfortunately, Kace could hear Eileen saying just that. Divorce was an embarrassment to her.

"So, I figured if Eileen wanted to be a widow, that's what I would give her," Arnold continued. "Even if it meant leaving my daughter behind."

Kace could have pointed out that it was too high a price to pay, but Arnold had perhaps already realized that.

"I took my boat to the Gulf of Mexico," Arnold added. "Then, I arranged for someone to come and get me. No one from here. No one you know. He was someone I went to college with way back when.

I wanted people to believe I'd fallen overboard and drowned."

Yep, people had believed that all right. Well, except for Jana. "Your daughter continued to look for you all this time."

Arnold nodded, and Kace thought he saw genuine sadness in the man's eyes. "I didn't plan to stay away this long," he explained. "I thought I just needed a break. Time to think. And that I'd come back to Coldwater in a year. But a year turned to two, then three…and then twenty. I probably wouldn't have come back, but when the PI showed up, I thought that maybe Jana loved me enough to forgive me."

"She probably does love you, but you'll need to give her plenty of time on the forgiveness part."

Arnold made a sound of agreement. "Are you going to arrest me?"

"To be determined." Kace glanced up again when the front door of the station opened. Not Jana as he'd hoped. But rather Peter. Arnold saw him, too.

"FYI, I offered to file for a divorce," Arnold said, "so that Peter and Eileen can get married, but Eileen refused again."

That both surprised Kace and it didn't. Eileen could dig in her heels, but he was pretty sure that she had truly wanted to marry Peter. And vice versa.

Kace couldn't hear whatever Peter said to Ginger, but judging from the way the woman looked back at him, Peter was there to see him. Kace didn't especially want to see him, either, but it might take a while to get the details of Arnold's statement, and he didn't want Peter lingering around, waiting for him.

"I'm turning the recorder off," Kace said, and he pressed the stop button. "Wait here while I get a deputy to finish this."

Kace stepped out of his office and looked around. Judd wasn't there because he'd had some parent-teacher deal at school with one of his foster sons. That left Liberty, so Kace filled her in on what he needed and then motioned for Peter to follow him to the break room in the back of the building. Not exactly a private place, but it was better than being in earshot of Ginger.

"I'm betting you're having even more regrets about me coming here to your town," Peter said when they stepped into the empty break room.

"Nope, just the same regrets I've always had. Besides, this latest stuff doesn't seem to be your fault. Unless, of course, you knew that Arnold was still alive."

"No, I didn't know," Peter insisted. He paused as if he might add something, but then he scrubbed his hand over his face. His weariness matched what Kace was feeling. "This'll cause plenty of talk that will only agitate Eileen even more than she already is."

"No way to prevent that." And while this would move any gossip about Kace to the town's back burner, it wasn't worth it. Because all of this wasn't just hurting Eileen. It was hurting Jana, too.

"There's no reason for you to believe this, but I

do love Eileen," Peter added a moment later. "I love her enough to walk away from her."

As a cop, Kace was often skeptical about things people said to him, but he heard the emotion in Peter's voice. Emotion that might be actual love. Of course, it could be that the man was just feeling sorry for himself because he was no longer going to get his hands on Eileen's money.

But Kace didn't believe that.

Well, hell. Best not to let his brothers know that he was giving their sperm donor the benefit of the doubt.

"You think Eileen will change her mind about staying married to Arnold?" Kace asked.

"No." Peter didn't hesitate, either, and there it was all over his face. More emotion. He seemed, well, heartbroken. That was something Kace had firsthand experience with after his breakup with Jana.

"Arnold said he wanted a divorce," Peter went on, "but Eileen insisted that she wouldn't sign it." Another pause, followed by a long exhale of breath. "She told me that she loved me but that she just couldn't be a divorced woman."

That was Eileen. Keeping up appearances had become her albatross, and it was going to cost her happiness. Though Kace hadn't truly believed Peter would have kept her happy for long.

Kace's phone dinged with a text message, and because he thought it might be from Liberty, he glanced at the screen. "Roy," he mumbled. He hadn't intended to say his lawyer's name aloud, but obviously Peter heard it.

"Roy?" Peter repeated. "This is about Dominick's lawsuit?"

Of course, Peter had heard about that, and while Kace didn't confirm it, it was indeed about the lawsuit. According to the text, Roy had gotten the paperwork from Dominick's attorney.

"Eileen's upset about Dominick, too," Peter continued. "Well, I guess her anger is more directed at the settlement for alimony that Dominick is pressuring Jana to sign. Actually, Eileen's *very* pissed off about that, but she's mad about what Dominick's doing to you, too. She's glad that you tried to defend Jana."

That was something at least. And it was also the first time that Eileen had ever been on Kace's side.

"Is there anything I can do to help you with Dominick?" Peter asked.

Kace's first instinct was to snap out a no, but he merely shook his head. Sometimes, hanging on to shit only created more shit, and he was tired of old baggage, old wounds and especially old shit.

"I can handle it," Kace told him.

Peter nodded. "Good. Because all of this is tearing up Jana, too. And now with her father's return… Well, she'll be going through an even tougher time."

Yeah, she would. And while Kace hadn't needed to hear Peter say that, it was an in-his-face reminder that he should check on her.

"I need to go," Kace told Peter while he fired off

a quick text to Roy to tell him that he'd come in later to review the lawsuit paperwork.

"One more thing," Peter said, stopping him. "Could you check on Eileen, too? She said it wasn't a good idea for me to go back to her place, but I'm worried about her. Worried that she'll do something reckless about Dominick."

Until Peter had added that last part, Kace had been about to walk out. "Reckless?"

Peter nodded. "Before you showed up to tell us about Belinda, Eileen was talking on the phone with someone, and I heard her say that she wanted Dominick to pay. That there was only one way to fight fire and that was with a bigger fire. I just don't want her to do something that would get her in trouble."

Shit. Neither did Kace. Apparently, he was going to have to put out some flames before they came back to burn all their asses.

JANA FIGURED IT wasn't a good idea to bring this much ire and negative energy into her new home, but she couldn't help herself. She was pissed, and the anger raged through her like a boatload of PMS on a mountain of steroids. But since his return yesterday, it was hard to hold back the anger now that she realized something.

Her father was an asshole.

That was the kindest of terms she could come up with for a man she'd once loved and adored in a way that only a child could. She'd been Daddy's little girl, and then "Daddy" had flushed that down the toilet because of the strain of his marriage.

"Well, boo-frickin'-hoo," Jana grumbled as she dragged another box into the house.

Her marriage had been strained, too, but she hadn't run out on her child. She'd divorced the lousy excuse for a husband and was trying to get on with her life. Despite the lousy excuse's continued attempts to drive her batshit.

Of course, her asshole father had been quick to point out that Eileen wouldn't give him a divorce, so that's why he'd left. Well, boo-hoo again. He should have just sucked it up, moved out and continued to be part of his only child's life. That's what non-asshole men did.

She yelped when she kicked the box she'd just set down, and Jana knew she had to do something to cool off. A throbbing toe wasn't going to help matters. Neither would damaged goods—especially since this one was marked Dishes/Fragile. Next time she needed to kick something, she should wear boots instead of shoes and find a box filled with towels.

Jana went to the porch and saw the first drops of rain on the steps. The storm had finally moved in. *Good.* Her mood didn't want sunshine and blue skies. It wanted the clumps of angry gray clouds and the sting of the chilly winter wind that the storm would bring with it.

Limping a little from the jammed toe, she dragged on her coat, went down the porch steps and straight out into the yard. The raindrops came at her like little pointy missiles. It was too warm for any sleet or ice, but it was plenty cold enough. That didn't stop her. She not only stayed put, she lifted her face to the bubbling dark skies and outstretched her arms.

And that's how Kace found her when he pulled his truck to a stop in front of her house.

"Is your shower broken?" he asked, and it was surprisingly the right thing to say. Of course, maybe that's because he said it with a quick smile.

Then, a not-so-quick look of appreciation.

It took Jana a moment to figure out the last one, but then she noticed her pose had caused her shirt to stretch over the outline of her breasts. Maybe this was turning into a habit of hers since she'd done the same thing when she was in the kiddie pool with Marley.

Thumbing back the brim of his hat just a little, he went to her, and in the same motion, he slid his arm around her waist, pulled her to him and kissed her.

"I'm in a rotten mood," she said. It came out though as a breathy purr because one kiss from Kace could hit multiple erogenous zones at once.

"So am I." He kissed her again, going from a mere lip-to-lip to using his tongue. Of course, he also knew how to use that well, and more erogenous zones fired to full alert.

"Is Marley inside?" he asked, easing back just a little.

She shook her head. "She's with the sitter. It wouldn't have been a good idea to have her here with all the boxes I'm moving. Plus, I've got anger oozing off me so I thought it best that she not be around me for a couple of hours."

"So, you're alone," he said, and Kace kissed her again.

With their mutual bad moods, they stood there, kissing, even doing a little body rubbing while the brim of his hat acted like a little umbrella for their heads. Not their bodies, though. They were getting even wetter, and Jana didn't care. Kace was wrangling some of her temper and making her feel a whole lot better.

She wasn't stupid though, and knew this wasn't curing anything. That once they'd finished, her problems would still be there, but this was like getting a double recess in fourth grade followed by a pizza party. This was a bonus treat that she wasn't going to refuse.

Jana felt herself moving, and only then did she realize Kace had scooped her up in his arms. All in all, that was an incredible place to be, especially since he was carrying her as if she weighed nothing and kissing her as if these were the last kisses he'd ever get.

Kace carried her inside, kicking the door shut—then he cursed when he bashed into a box. Since she didn't want Kace limping as she was, Jana slid out of his embrace, getting her feet back on the floor so she could maneuver them around the hazards of not only the boxes but also the out-of-place furniture.

Jana didn't manage to get them more than a few feet inside before the kissing started up again. Kissing, touching and more of the body grinding. The urgency had gone up darn fast, but then it also had the last time. Come to think of it, things had often been this way between Kace and her, and making it all the way to the bedroom had been a rare occasion.

They wouldn't make it there today, either, which was probably a good thing since she didn't have furniture yet in any of the bedrooms.

Cursing what exactly she didn't know—maybe this clawing need or lack of comfortable furnishings—Kace dragged her to the floor. Though it didn't take a whole lot of dragging since Jana had already decided that was a faster option than aiming for vertical sex.

Kace had a special skill set for undressing her. Or rather getting off all the necessary clothing fast. He shoved up her top. His, too, and she got the heated thrill of skin on skin. His chest muscles to her breasts. Even his erection to the V of her thighs. She didn't need that extra slippery slide to get her ready for him, but it was another recess along with dessert for that pizza party.

Jana, however, had no such undressing skills. She managed to get off his coat, then his Stetson, but that was more the result of an accidental bump and gravity than her own doing.

While Kace tormented her neck with his tongue, she continue to struggle with his belt buckle. And he didn't help her with it, either. He shimmied her out of her jeans, out of her panties, and then proceeded to kiss every interested place on her body.

Lots and lots of her places were interested.

She had to give up struggling with his belt buckle

when he went down on her. Heck, she had to give up breathing. Along with tangling her fingers in his hair, the only other thing she could manage was a moaning sound of pleasure.

He was true to his word about wanting to do this to her, and like everything else, he was good at it. So good. In the back of her mind, she supposed she should have insisted that they head to the orgasmic finish line together, but a couple of flicks of his tongue and the clever use of his teeth—mercy, his teeth!—and she was a goner.

The climax was as fierce as the kick of the raging storm outside. Lightning, thunder and a slam of pleasure that made her want to vow to praise Kace's orgasmic talents for the rest of her life.

He didn't let up despite the spasms and tremors in the place she should be spasming and tremoring. Kace kissed his way back up her body, and multitasking, he undid that chastity belt of a buckle. Despite the kisses and her hot hazy mind, Jana was also aware that he got his jeans unzipped. That happened a nanosecond before another amazing thing happened.

Kace pushed into her.

The sound he made was a low, hoarse groan, and she knew it was from pure pleasure. That's because Jana was experiencing a renewal of her own pleasure. His going down on her was incredible, but this was mind-blowing.

Kace didn't disappoint her. Of course, he didn't. He started those slow thrusts, deep inside her and hitting the right spot to rebuild that same tension and the same need that she'd had just minutes earlier. She quickly found herself right back on that knife edge of a point between pleasure and relief. It seemed too soon for her to shatter again, but Kace didn't give her a choice about that. Jana just held on and let him do what he did best.

A two-fer.

This orgasm quaked her to the core, which wasn't a bad place to quake, and she didn't have to guess it was the same for Kace. That's because he made another of those low sounds.

And then she heard him curse.

That brought her out of the haze enough to lift her head a fraction and look at him. "Don't worry, I didn't forget about the ear kisses," she muttered. She could add some teeth to that, too.

"I didn't use a condom," he said.

"Oh." And because Jana didn't know what else to say, she just repeated that a couple of times until she could think straight. Not easy, considering Kace was still inside her.

"Okay," she added, and she repeated that several times, too.

Kace pressed his forehead against hers and groaned. "I'm sorry. God, I'm sorry."

Considering the sex had been darn amazing, Jana hated that Kace sounded, well, the total opposite of amazed. She'd heard less serious tones at funerals. When he lifted his head and stared down at her, she saw the seriousness and regret in his eyes.

Great. Now he'd likely never touch her again, and even though that shouldn't be her prime concern right now, it was.

"My chances of getting pregnant are nil," she told him. "Trust me. It took in vitro for me to get pregnant with Marley."

All right, so that was one base covered, but since there was another, Jana continued, "I've been tested for STDs recently, and I'm clear."

Ironically, she could thank Dominick for her having taken that test. With Jana's concerns about his cheating on her, she hadn't wanted to take any chances.

"I'm clear, too," he said. "And the last time I had sex without a condom was when I was with you."

In other words, when he'd thought he had gotten her pregnant. No wonder Kace looked so shell-shocked. That pregnancy scare had led to him proposing to her.

"We'll be fine this time," she assured him. "I promise."

It was a heartfelt promise, too, which was why she was surprised when she heard Kace curse again. Not because of anything she'd said, though. But because someone was knocking on the door.

Crap on a cracker. "Maybe whoever it is will just go away," she whispered despite another knock.

Kace clearly had more functioning brain cells than she did because he got off her and moved her to the side of some boxes. Probably so that she'd be at least partially hidden if someone came in. He dragged his jeans back up over his hips.

"Uh, Jana, it's me," the knocker on the door called out.

Her father.

That automatically put her back in a bad mood, which was hard to do considering the second climax was still rippling through her.

"I just need to see you for a minute," her father continued. "I'm leaving, and I want to say goodbye. Just let me tell you goodbye, Jana, and then I swear you'll never have to see me again."

CHAPTER TWENTY-ONE

JANA DOUBTED HER father knew that this was the worst possible time for a visit. But she immediately amended that notion. As bad as her mood had been, before the orgasms would have been the worst possible time. However, this wasn't exactly a stellar circumstance, either.

"You should probably talk to him," Kace said. He helped her to her feet and even gathered up her clothes for her.

Even though chatting with her dad wasn't high on her wish list, Jana knew Kace was probably right. If Arnold was indeed leaving and saying things like she'd never have to see him again, then a talk was in order. A short one that would likely include some anger and confrontation since she was still feeling plenty of that. Though she wasn't sure how much a confrontation would actually accomplish. It wasn't as if they could go back in a time machine and undo the past twenty years.

"He needs to hear how you feel," Kace added.

"He might not want to hear that when I'm done with him," Jana countered.

"And that's the point. Holding all of this in isn't good for you."

Such wise words. Ones that made her think of Kace as well. Maybe she was holding in things about him, too, but that was another fish to fry on another day. Apparently for now, she had some venting to do so that maybe the knot in her stomach wouldn't end up giving her ulcers.

"I'll be there in a minute," Jana called out to her dad.

She took her time getting dressed. Not solely because she wanted to keep him waiting—though that was part of it. But it was also because Jana wanted to make sure all of her clothes were in the right place. This conversation was going to be awkward enough without her dad speculating about whether she'd just had sex with Kace.

Of course, it likely wouldn't take much speculation because Kace certainly looked wet, rumpled and rode, and Jana suspected she did as well. That was especially true since her clothes were still damp from the rain.

"You want me to stay with you while you talk to him?" Kace asked her.

Jana debated his offer. It never felt wrong to have Kace backing her up. Which was part of that "another fish to fry," but she shook her head. His being her backup would only end up with them both being pissed and both candidates for those future ulcers.

Jana brushed a kiss on his mouth as they headed for the door. "Thanks, but it's okay. I can do this."

After all, it wouldn't take much to open her mouth and give Arnold a verbal blast that would land him in the middle of next week. Her time with Dominick had given her prime skills in saying mean stuff.

She took hold of the doorknob, but Kace put his hand over hers. He also studied her and even smoothed down her wet hair. "You're sure?" he pressed.

No, she wasn't, but she didn't want Kace having to help her fight this particular battle. "I'll be fine. You can go."

After another few moments of studying her, he nodded. "I do need to see your mother and talk to her about Arnold's return."

Ouch. That wouldn't be pleasant. Kace definitely had the worse deal of the two of them. She could just scowl and snap at her father before sending him on his way, but it was going to be a dramafest with her mom. Tears, wailing and the mother of all pity parties. Of course, eventually Jana would have to see Eileen as well and deal with round two of all that drama, but she could put that off for a little while.

"I also need to talk to Eileen about Dominick," Kace added, getting her full attention. He took a deep breath as if what he was about to say would be hard for her to hear. "Peter told me that before I showed up to talk to them about Belinda, Eileen was on the phone, and he heard her talking about making Dominick pay."

"Great," Jana said with plenty of sarcasm. Maybe this mess with Arnold would distract Eileen from doing anything, but nothing good could come of her mother getting involved with Dominick. He already had enough ill will against Jana and didn't need any more of the fuel that Eileen would certainly add.

Kace gave her a quick kiss and moved so she could open the door. Her dad was right there, practically in her face, but that was maybe because the porch wasn't that deep, and the rain was slanting in at him. Big fat drops were splattering onto his shoes.

"Sheriff Laramie," her father said, as if surprised to see him there. And maybe he was. Arnold wouldn't have necessarily recognized Kace's truck. Also, he maybe wouldn't have expected to catch them at the tail end of a booty call.

If that's indeed what it was.

A quick fleeting question popped into her head. Was it truly just ex-sex with Kace? Was that all there was to it? Okay, that was two questions, not one, but Jana gave them a mental swipe like erasing a chalkboard. That didn't mean they wouldn't just pop back up again, but for now she had to deal with the weasel who'd run out on her when she was a teenager.

"I'll be at your mother's for a while if you need me," Kace told her, and he stepped around Arnold.

"Good. I'm glad you're going there," Arnold said, causing Kace to stop in his tracks. "I'm worried about Eileen."

That sounded genuine, and despite Arnold not having a right to voice anything about Eileen's welfare, it was warranted. Eileen would fall into a pit of despair over this, but since Arnold was the cause of that despair, Jana didn't want him doling out any comments or concerns about it.

Her father and she both watched Kace run out into the sheet of rain to get into his truck and drive away. The silence came, and Arnold was likely waiting for her to invite him inside, but Jana wasn't feeling a shred of hospitality right now.

"I, uh, finished my interview with the deputy," her father finally said. "I also spoke briefly with the lawyer. Roy," he added. "He doesn't think any laws were broken in my absence. In other words, no social security collected. Eileen didn't even cash in on the life insurance."

Jana hadn't known that, but then her mother hadn't needed the money since Eileen had her trust fund and investments. For that matter, so did her father.

"Roy said I could start paperwork to reclaim any of my own property and funds," Arnold went on, "but I don't want it back. Your mother can keep the money from my accounts."

"How righteous of you," she grumbled, and instantly hated her tone. It sounded so childish and petty. Which was exactly how she felt.

Arnold nodded, swallowed hard as if he not only expected the petty but also deserved it.

"What about yours and Mom's marriage?" she asked. "Will you get a divorce?"

"Yes. I'll try to convince your mom that it's for the best, but I doubt she'll talk to me."

"You're right. She won't want to talk to you."

However, Jana would definitely have to chat with her mom about it, and in doing so, would maybe give Eileen a clear path to marrying Peter. Or not. Eileen might be so shaken from all of this that she would swear off men completely, and besides she might not budge on the idea of a divorce—ever.

"Roy didn't come out and say it, but I got the feeling that he thought I should just continue to think of myself as dead and not try to have any part in your life," her father explained.

Talk about giving her a round of mixed feelings. It twisted at her to hear "dead." That's because she'd spent all these years grieving for him and wanting him to come back to her. But Arnold's return had stirred up things that Eileen almost certainly wished hadn't been stirred.

Jana was still trying to decide if she felt the same way.

"I know I don't have a right to say this to you, but I'm sorry for how this hurt you," he told her. "It was really never about you. It was about me and how I felt about your mother."

"Funny, it feels as if it's about me since you left me when you left Eileen," she fired back.

"I know, and I'm truly sorry."

Maybe. And maybe he was just sorry he was having to look at her face and see how much he'd hurt her. Of course, he had come back when the PI had found him so he must have known he'd be walking in front of a firing squad.

"Why'd you come back?" Jana demanded.

He stared at her a long time. "Because I love you, and when I found out you were looking for me, I wanted to see you. I knew you wouldn't be happy about what I'd done. I knew you'd hate me for the rest of your life, but I still had to see you."

Because I love you.

Well, if that wasn't a kick in the teeth, she didn't know what was, and it brought her nerves so close to the surface that she could feel them firing just beneath her skin. She could also feel the tears threaten, but Jana quickly blinked them back.

Maybe he did love her. *In his own way.* God, she hated that phrase, that qualifier of what was supposed to be the most important emotion for any living, breathing human being. I love you shouldn't come with qualifiers. Either you did or you didn't, and if you did, you needed to show that love.

Tucking tail and running *wasn't* showing it.

"I just wanted to make sure your mom and you are okay," he added several long moments later.

With her emotions still on a roller coaster, another wave of childishness raced through her, but Jana bit off the mean comment she nearly made. "We'll be fine," she insisted, and wasn't sure if that was a lie or wishful thinking. "But if you're waiting for me to say you can go with a clean conscience, that's not going to happen."

He nodded again, and for something that wasn't even verbal communication, it managed to convey a lot. Jana could practically feel the sadness coming off him in waves.

"You're going back to Hawaii?" she asked, conflicted again because she was letting that sadness add some sympathy to her tone. Well, maybe not sympathy exactly, but she hadn't growled that question and coupled it with a glare.

"Yes. I'll need to tie up a few things here first. Paperwork for Roy," he added. "But I have a business in Maui. A surf shop—though you might have figured that out from the clothes."

She nearly smiled. He was indeed wearing a cornea-searing flowered shirt. As a child she'd always seen him in suits while he ran his real estate and investment empire so the clothes were indeed a big clue that he no longer had the same lifestyle.

Or the same life.

"I am sorry," he said, his voice shaking a little. "I screwed up. I let my own weakness send me into a run."

Jana shook her head and cursed her burning eyes that wanted to let the tears fall. "I can't accept your apology.

"I'm sorry," she repeated. An apology that encompassed a whole lot. With every fiber of her being, Jana regretted and mourned what he'd done to her. To their family. She hated him for it. Hated herself because it still mattered and that she hadn't been able to let go of it.

But at the top of the list of mourning was that Marley hadn't had a grandfather in her life. Dominick's father had died when he was young, and his mother hadn't remarried. Marley had missed out on having that connection.

"I'll go," Arnold said, glancing over his shoulder at the streak of lightning that slashed through the sky. But he didn't budge. "You can tell me to mind my own business, but I know about what happened between Dominick and you. Is there anything I can do to help?"

"No." She couldn't say that fast enough. Even if Arnold could indeed help, she didn't want him using that to earn forgiveness points with her.

Another nod, and his eyes connected with hers. "Whatever happens, just don't hold any of this against your mother. Eileen's a tough woman, but she's been through enough."

Jana blinked, and it didn't have anything to do with the angry rumble of thunder. "Excuse me?"

Her father pulled back his shoulders, stared at her a moment and then made a dismissive wave before he turned. He would have no doubt left, not explaining that odd "don't hold any of this against your mother" remark if Jana hadn't caught onto his arm.

"What do you mean by that?" she demanded.

He shook his head, opened his mouth, closed it and then opened it again. "I thought you knew. I thought Eileen had told you."

She tried to go through some possibilities. Eileen could be keeping many things from her, but Jana didn't know of one that specifically related to her father.

"You're not leaving here until you explain that," Jana warned him.

Even though he gave her another nod, he sure took his time answering. This was despite the shift of the direction of the wind that caused the rain to start dousing his backside.

"Eileen knew I was alive," he said. "I emailed her shortly after I left and told her I hadn't died but that I didn't want to live the life I'd had here in Coldwater."

Jana was certain the sound she heard was more thunder, but it felt as if a Mack truck had just crashed into her chest. "No," she managed to say. That couldn't be. No way had her mother known this whole time.

"I'm sorry," Arnold repeated, and with that apology ringing in her ears, he stepped off the porch and hurried to his car.

Because her hands and legs were shaking, it took Jana a couple of minutes to go back inside and locate her phone. It must have fallen out of her pocket when Kace and she had had sex because it was between two boxes.

She pressed her mom's number as fast as her trembling finger could manage. Normally, it was hit or miss if her mom would actually answer, but it was a hit today. Her mother answered on the first ring.

"Jana," Eileen immediately said, and it sounded as if she was crying. "I need you here with me right now."

Jana would go there, but for now she had to get this straight. No way could Arnold be right about this.

"Did you know Dad was alive before he showed up today?" Jana came out and asked.

Silence. For a long time. *Oh God.* That in itself should have been the answer, but Jana wanted to hear it from Eileen's own lips.

"Did you know?" Jana snapped.

More silence, and then her mother cleared her throat before Eileen gave the one-word answer that felt like an entire fleet of Mack trucks coming right at her.

"Yes."

CHAPTER TWENTY-TWO

KACE READ THE text from Jana that popped up on
his phone.

Please come by the new house if you get a chance.

It was such a simple message. Polite, even. No urgency whatsoever. But Kace could practically feel
the emotions flying off each word.

Because it had only been a couple of hours since
he'd been with Jana—correction, since he'd had sex
with her and then left her to "chat" with her father—
there hadn't been much time for things to go further
to hell in a handbasket. Of course, it didn't take a lot
of minutes for her to fall deeper into a pit of despair
over the crappy turns that her life had taken.

It was possible he was one of those crappy turns.

He'd already lectured himself about having sex
with her, but it was forgetting the condom that made
him want to hit himself on the head with a huge
rock. Jana might want to do that as well, but rather
than demand he show up so she could verbally blast
him, maybe she'd sent that pleasant message instead.

Kace knew he would go, of course. He had apparently gone mindless and stupid when it came to Jana. But even if he'd had all his senses, he would have still wanted to see her. She was going through a lot, too much, and if he could help her in any way, he'd have to try.

Be there soon, Kace texted her back, and he glanced out into the squad room to see what obstacle he'd have to face before getting out the door.

Nothing.

No one other than Judd was working. Even Ginger and Liberty had already left for the day, which meant any emergency calls now would go through to Liberty's brother, Deputy Rusty Cassaine, who was pulling the nightshift.

Taking his hat from the peg, Kace slipped it on and went out to Judd's desk. "Going to see Jana?" Judd immediately asked.

Kace would have wondered if the age-old question applied here—am I wearing a sign or what?—but Judd hadn't even looked up when he'd said that. He took out his phone and showed his brother the text she'd sent.

Please come by the new house if you get a chance.

Judd frowned. "Is that code for sex?"

Possibly. But Kace doubted it. "I think it might be code for Jana's upset and wants a shoulder to cry on."

Now Judd finally looked up at him, and their gazes connected, held. "Just how deep are you in with her anyway?"

Kace thought of the condom he'd forgotten to use. And of the two and a half times they'd had sex since Jana had returned to Coldwater. He thought about how it'd felt to kiss her in the rain and this pull he had to make sure she was okay.

"Deeper than I should be," Kace verified, figuring that would earn him a *have you lost your mind?* lecture from Judd.

No lecture, though. Judd just made a sound of understanding, and as if it were some explanation for this softer, less judgmental side of him, he slid a card across his desk to Kace. When Kace picked it up, he saw that it was a wedding invitation for Judd and Cleo.

"Two and a half weeks from now," Judd said.

"That's Christmas," Kace quickly pointed out when he saw the date.

"Yeah. We'll have it at Buck and Rosy's. We figured that was a good time since all of us will be there anyway, and we'll make the ceremony short and sweet."

That was fitting since it was not only where Cleo and Judd had met but also where they'd fallen in love. Plus, they'd be living there together as a family with their three foster sons that they would soon be adopting.

"Are you scared?" Kace asked, joking.

"Scared that Cleo will come to her senses and realize she could do a whole lot better." Judd paused and smiled in his own way. A quick hitch of the right side of his mouth. "Cleo's good for me."

Yeah, she was and vice versa. That's why Kace smiled. Two and a half weeks wasn't that far off, but maybe it'd be enough time for the rest of Kace's life to have settled down so he could really enjoy his brother's wedding.

Kace tucked the card in his pocket, muttered an "I'm heading out" to Judd, and he went to his truck. The rain had finally stopped, and the storm had brought in some chillier temps. It still wasn't cold, considering it was winter, but it was in the low fifties.

He used the drive to Jana's to tamp down his worries and tried to convince himself that he hadn't made a huge mistake by not hanging around while Jana talked to her dad. However, it hadn't been lip service that Kace had really needed to speak to Eileen. Not that it'd been especially productive. Still, he'd done his lawman's duty by getting the woman's statement about Arnold's return. Even if that statement had been filled with venom and mean commentary about her hoping Arnold's manhood rotted and fell off.

Clearly, this was not an amicable separation.

Kace hadn't ever thought he would say this, but he was on Eileen's side. Arnold shouldn't have taken off like that, and he'd certainly understand if neither Eileen nor Jana ever forgave the man.

His tamped-down worries shot straight to the surface when Kace pulled to a stop in front of Jana's place. Wearing a coat with the hood up, she was in the porch swing, a box of tissues in her lap. There were more tissues in her hand, and while he couldn't see actual tears from this distance, he suspected they were there.

Hell.

Obviously, the chat hadn't gone well with her dad, and that gave Kace another poke of guilt. Yeah, he should have stayed with her.

Thankfully, the blue mood didn't extend to Marley. She, too, was wearing a hooded coat, pink boots and was doing a wobbly toddler version of splashing in puddles left on the porch. She squealed with glee when one particularly good splash sent drops flying into her face and hair. There were so many water blobs on her that she look like she had a severe case of chicken pox.

"Tace," Marley called out when she spotted him. She tried to come toward him, but she off-balanced and splatted on her butt into the puddle. That made her squeal in delight, too. Obviously, she was one happy kid.

Jana wasn't happy though, and her reaction was a tad different than Marley's. Jana frantically began to wipe her eyes and blow her nose as if she hadn't wanted him to catch her crying. Too late. He saw all right, and judging from the red puffiness, she'd been crying for quite a while.

"Tace," Marley repeated as he got closer. She managed to get up, and the moment she was on her feet, she toddled toward him.

"Wait, Marley. No," Jana called out. "You'll get water all over Kace."

That was also too late. Marley latched onto his legs, and since she was trying to crawl up him, he hauled her up into his arms. He got a wet cheek kiss greeting and some giggles when Kace gave the puddle a stomp with his boot.

"I'm so sorry." Jana scooped up a towel that she'd had next to her and hurried out into the yard to take Marley from him. Or rather that's what she tried to do, but Marley held on, batting Jana's hands away. Once again, Kace was surprised that the kid actually liked him, but that was fine with him because he liked her, too.

"It's okay," Kace assured Jana, who was still trying to take the toddler from him. "We can take her inside while we talk." After all, the kid's bottom was wet now, and he didn't want her to get cold.

Jana didn't put up nearly as good a fight as Marley had. In fact, Jana gave a weary sigh of resignation while Marley giggled as Kace went in the house with her.

Kace didn't even have to ask Jana what was wrong because she blurted it right out. "My mother's known all this time that my father was alive. She even knew where he was."

Well, hell in a big-assed handbasket.

Eileen had known about this and hadn't mentioned it to Jana? This despite Jana's grieving and missing her father for the past two decades? Added to that, Eileen had been on the verge of knowingly committing bigamy.

Okay. Kace could see why that had sent Jana into

an emotional spiral. He started to ask her if she was sure, but of course, she was. Jana would have verified that before she even shed a tear over it.

"My father told me," Jana went on as she peeled off Marley's wet clothes. "And when I confronted my mother, she admitted she'd known but then wouldn't say anything else to me. She hung up on me, and when I drove over to her house, she wasn't there."

That was a chickenshit thing for Eileen to do, but it was a blip compared to keeping something like this from Jana.

"I can talk to her about it," Kace offered.

Jana shook her head, wrapped the towel around Marley and headed toward one of the bedrooms. "There's no explanation she can give to make me forgive her. What she did is unforgivable."

Kace was with Jana on this, but that didn't mean he wasn't concerned about Eileen's state of mind. A returning husband, a broken engagement and now a possible permanent rift with her only child. While Eileen deserved the rift, Kace hoped the woman wasn't suicidal.

After she'd put a dry outfit on Marley, she joined Kace on the couch. He slid his arm around her and brushed a kiss on the top of her head. "What can I do to help?" Kace asked.

Jana lifted her head, looked up at him with those tear-filled eyes. "You're doing it," she said as she settled her head back on his shoulder. She didn't say anything else for several moments. "It's a bad case of irony, you know. I started searching for my father again because your father was marrying my mother. Do you think this was some kind of cosmic kick in the butt?"

"No." He didn't have to give that much thought. "Neither of us did anything to make our fathers leave. And in some ways us not having fathers brought us together."

She didn't hesitate, either. "True. We were sort of the misfits in a town with mainly two-parent families and a low divorce rate."

Yeah, birds of a feather. But it still hadn't stopped them from notching up the divorce rate.

"Remember that father-daughter dance at the rodeo our senior year of high school?" Jana went on, her voice sliced with Marley's squeals of delight as she found a toy horse to play with. "You defied tradition and danced with me."

Kace had indeed done that, but in part because it'd pissed him off. He hadn't liked something that had excluded his girlfriend. So, when the Lee Ann Womack song "I Hope You Dance" had started playing, Kace had done just that with Jana. They'd danced.

"You nailed me in the barn later that night," Jana added in a whisper, and she gave him a poke in the ribs with her elbow.

That caused him to smile. Not just because of the fond memory but because she no longer sounded as if she was crying. His smile quickly faded, though.

"I remembered to use a condom that night." He kept his voice low despite Marley being way too young to understand this conversation. "It's hard to believe I was smarter then about stuff like that than I am now."

She gave him another nudge. "Hey, I didn't remember to use one, either. The safe sex burden doesn't fall only on your shoulders."

No, but it certainly felt as if it did. Which led him to something else he needed to say to her. Something that might not go over too well. "Look, I know what I told you earlier about us hooking up, but I'm not good at casual sex." Well, not since Belinda anyway.

Jana lifted her right eyebrow. "I beg to differ. You were really good with me earlier." And then she smiled, winked at him.

"That wasn't casual," Kace said, and waited to see what Jana's reaction would be. He figured he wouldn't have to wait long.

Kace was bracing himself for a heart-to-heart that would make him even more uncomfortable than he already was. Or the conversation could go in another direction. An equally uncomfortable one where Jana might think he was fishing for a commitment.

"You're breaking up with me?" she blurted out.

All right, so that was a third direction he hadn't expected, and Kace frowned. It wasn't exactly easy to answer since there was an expectation in that question. One that made him think she believed them to be a couple. If so, then it clearly wasn't casual sex for her, either.

Kace got a reprieve from answering her when his phone rang. There was instant anger though when he saw Dominick's name pop up.

"What the heck does he want?" Jana snarled, obviously seeing what was on his phone screen.

"Don't have a clue." Kace hit the decline call button, figuring anything Dominick had to say to him should go through their lawyers.

Before they could get back on track with their conversation, his phone rang again. Belinda, this time. Yet someone else he didn't want to talk to so he gave the decline call button another hit.

Just as Jana's phone rang.

She pulled her cell from her pocket and muttered some profanity. "It's Dominick," she said.

WTF? and Kace mentally repeated that question when he got a third call. This one was from Peter. He hit the decline button again so he could ring back Belinda and find out what was going on. She was the lesser of the evils in this case. However, before he could even press in her number, his phone rang again, and this time Unknown Caller appeared on the screen.

Jana's phone wasn't exactly staying silent, either. She got a call from Peter as well, and Kace was about to tell her to answer it when he finally got a call from someone he actually wanted to talk to.

Judd.

"What the hell's going on?" Kace immediately asked his brother after he answered.

"I was hoping you'd know. Dominick just called the police station, and he's pissed. He said something about strippers and pictures. And according to him, it's all yours and Jana's fault."

Jana must have heard what Judd said because repeating some of Kace's muttered profanity, she pressed in Dominick's number.

"I'll have to call you back," Kace told Judd when he got a call-waiting alert that none other than Dominick was on the line.

"What the fuck are Jana and you trying to pull?" Dominick immediately greeted.

Yeah, he was pissed all right, and the man clearly thought Kace was the cause of that anger. "At the moment, I'm not trying to pull anything. Neither is Jana."

"Bullshit!" Dominick added a whole bunch more curse words, and that's the reason Kace didn't put the call on speaker. Instead, Jana moved closer, squishing herself against him and putting her ear right next to Kace's phone.

Since Kace didn't want to prolong this chat, he went with a direct question. "What is it you think we've done?"

Dominick made a sound, part hiss, part growl. "You damn well know."

Kace kept his voice calm but also added a cop attitude to it. "If I did know, I wouldn't have asked, and if you're not going to tell me, there's no reason to continue this call."

"Don't you hang up on me, you bastard!" Dominick shouted.

Which, of course, made Kace want to hang up, but he did want to know whatever the heck was going on. Something that according to Judd involved strippers and pictures. Kace also suspected Peter, Belinda and Unknown Caller had info that could contribute to this in some way. He doubted all those other calls he'd declined were a coincidence.

"Use your inside voice and tell me what happened," Kace insisted.

It was probably the *inside voice* crack that caused Dominick to rattle off some creative curse word combination that Kace was extremely glad Marley couldn't hear.

"Jana and you sent those strippers to my house," Dominick said after the latest round of cussing, "and there were photographers with them."

Okay, so they were getting somewhere, and since Belinda had done something like this to Peter, she might have tried the prank with Dominick. This was despite the warnings Kace had given Belinda.

"More strippers came after that first batch," Dominick went on. "More photographers, too. You sonofabitch, they put the pictures on the internet and emailed copies to Jana's lawyer."

That sent Jana into a search on her phone, and it didn't take her long to pull up a picture of Dominick with, yes, strippers. It looked like the same three women from Tit for Tat. In the background were penis balloons and another woman, a blonde who was clinging to Dominick in what appeared to be a doorway of a house.

Part of Kace wanted to laugh, but he could already see a bad side to this. It wasn't good to get Dominick this pissed, especially when the man thought Jana was in some way responsible.

"Do you know the blonde with Dominick?" Kace quietly asked her.

Jana nodded. "Kristy Madden. She used to work for me as a horse trainer."

Well, it appeared the woman had moved on to having a personal relationship with Dominick. Not that it mattered. After all, Jana was having a personal relationship with Kace.

"A third set of strippers came before the first two groups left," Dominick went on. His voice got louder with each word. "They brought vibrators and shit."

Kace figured that wasn't literal shit, but maybe it had been. Sometimes, pranks were not only stupid but smelly as well.

"Call off your dogs, Laramie," Dominick spat out.

"Even if I had dogs, I wouldn't know which ones to call off because I didn't have any part in this. Neither did Jana. In fact, she's been dealing with her own problems."

"Bullshit," Dominick repeated. "You're both plotting to get back at me. Well, it's not going to work. You tell your asshole father that if he goes through with this, then he'll be very sorry. You'll all be very sorry," he amended.

Kace figured he wasn't going to like the answer, but he had to ask. "What does my father have to do with this?"

"Everything, you shithead. Jana and you helped him set it up so you damn well know."

Kace didn't, but the little sound of surprise Jana made had Kace shifting his attention back to her phone. It was a video that someone had posted on YouTube. There were still strippers, balloons and such. No actual shit that Kace could see, but at the center were Dominick and Peter.

Specifically, Dominick plowing his fist into Peter's face.

Kace winced because the video had sound, and it was the unmistakable sound of Peter's nose being broken. With blood spurting, Peter stepped back, his hands lifted as if in surrender, and Dominick clocked him again.

"Your bastard father said he was going to file assault charges against me," Dominick went on, but his rant sort of faded to the background as Kace continued to watch the video.

Arnold moved into view, maybe trying to break up the fight, but Dominick punched him, too. Neither Peter nor Arnold made one move to retaliate. And Kace knew why.

This was a setup.

Shit. Shit. Shit. Kace wouldn't be thanking them anytime soon. Nor would he thank Belinda, who was filming this ordeal. Kace figured that out when Dominick charged at her, and the camera shifted enough for him to see Belinda's face. She howled in pain—either real or faked—as she tumbled to the ground. Kace suspected it was fake and well orchestrated because Arnold helped her to her feet, and with Peter and the strippers running interference, Belinda, Arnold and Peter hurried to the vehicle.

"You tell your shithead father and Jana's that they'd better not think of filing assault charges against me," Dominick continued to rage. "I'll countersue. I'll tie them up in court until their balls shrivel up."

Kace didn't think what he had to say was going to improve Dominick's mood. "Have you seen the video on the net?" Kace asked. "Because it clearly shows you assaulting three people."

And Kace was betting that the calls from those three were to fill him in on the charges they were already filing.

"Bullshit," Dominick shouted. Apparently, that was his favorite word today. "They're not going to get away with this, and neither are Jana and you. You'd better talk them out of doing something more stupid than they already have."

"And why would I do that?" Kace asked, and he was serious, too. Yeah, this was his rodeo and those were his bulls, sort of, but the assaults hadn't taken place in his jurisdiction. Nor did he feel compelled to seek justice for a man who'd been pretty much a bastard in every way that counted.

"Because this shit will come back on Marley," Dominick said without hesitation but with a whole lot of conviction.

Enough conviction that it caused everything inside Kace to go still. He had to get his teeth unclenched before he could ask, "What the heck do you mean by that?"

Now Dominick gave a snarky laugh. "Thought that would get your attention. Tell my bitch of an ex-wife that she'd better fix this problem or I'll take Marley from her."

"No," Jana said. She frantically shook her head and took the phone from Kace. "No," she repeated.

"Yes," Dominick taunted, and his voice was still so loud that Kace had no trouble hearing him. "Either get Kace to call off his dogs, or I'll file a motion to get full custody of Marley."

"You can't," Jana snapped.

"Oh, but I will," Dominick argued. "One way or another, I'll get Marley, and you'll never see her again."

CHAPTER TWENTY-THREE

JANA HAD SO many emotions hit her at once that she didn't know what to do. Yelling and cursing were at the top of her go-to responses, but since that would likely scare Marley, she discarded those.

However, she couldn't discard the anger.

No way in Hades could she tamp that down. Ditto for letting Dominick take Marley. Even if Jana had to run to the ends of the earth, she wouldn't let that snake get full custody of her baby. Dominick would only use Marley to try to get what he wanted.

"You should let go of the phone," she heard Kace say, and Jana looked down at the white-knuckle grip she had. She was squeezing so hard, there was a possibility that it might shatter.

Dominick had already ended the call so Kace pried the phone from her and fired off a text to someone. "I'll have Judd bring in Peter, Belinda and Arnold, and after I've talked to them, I'll go through Dominick's lawyer to request he come in as well. I'll see if we can work this out."

It was the bubbling anger that caused her to shake her head. "I'd rather castrate Dominick and put his balls in a meat grinder."

Kace flexed his eyebrows. "I'm thinking more of a negotiation with all parties," he said, giving her a quick kiss. She was surprised that it didn't bruise his mouth because she had her lips pinched tight.

"The meat grinder will be more effective," she snarled. God, she wanted to throttle him. Wanted to stomp him into dust. But most of all, she just wanted Dominick to quit acting like an ass.

Thankfully, the tears didn't threaten again. That's because she'd likely squeezed off her tear ducts what with every muscle in her face as hard as iron.

Kace stood, helped her to her feet. No easy feat since her legs were iron, too. However, she did soften considerably when Marley came toward her. Jana scooped her up, and Marley gave her a sloppy hug.

"Mama," Marley said. Then, "Tace." And Marley leaned over and gave Kace a hug, too.

Just having her baby in her arms helped. And hurt. Mercy, it hurt. Because it crushed her heart to think that Dominick might succeed in getting this precious child. He didn't deserve her, that was for sure, but plenty of times people got both good and bad things they didn't deserve.

"I want to be at the police station when you question them," Jana insisted, and she steeled herself for Kace to argue with her about that.

He didn't. After a long pause, Kace just gave a nod and a sigh. "You're not thinking about having Marley with you, are you?"

"No." That meant Jana needed to call Bessie. The woman was packing up things at Jana's grandmother's house, but she could maybe watch Marley. No way did Jana want her at the police station, where there'd likely be plenty of cursing and yelling.

But Jana immediately rethought that.

What if Dominick came to the house and took Marley? Bessie might not be able to stop him, but Jana certainly could and would. Plus, Dominick wouldn't pull a stunt like that if Kace and Judd were around.

Even though Jana had just put Marley in dry clothes a few minutes earlier, she shucked them off the little girl. Jana headed straight to the bathroom, turning on the shower. Something that Marley loved, and her daughter went straight under the spray of water. Marley giggled and splashed just as she'd done in the puddles on the porch.

Once Jana had her clean, she dried Marley, put on a diaper and brought her back into the bedroom to put her in some clothes. However, she looked down at her own wet clothes and knew she had to take care of that first. Trying to keep a grip on a wiggling Marley, Jana laid out the baby's clothes on the bed and started toward the closet.

"Here, let me do that," Kace said, taking Marley's hand.

Jana's mind was in full-throttle mode, but his offer still caused her a mental pause. "Do you know how to dress a toddler?"

"No, but I can wrestle a calf back into a pen. I think it's a similar skill set with a whole lot more gentleness."

It was indeed, and Jana didn't have high hopes for Kace's success, but since she was in a hurry, she let him try so she could get herself a clean top and jeans. She dressed in the closet, throwing the items on as fast as she could, and when she went back into the bedroom, she got a surprise.

Marley was dressed in pink overalls and a top and was babbling away at Kace as if telling him a fine story.

"Did you bribe her?" Jana asked.

Kace nodded without any hesitation or shame. "A cookie and a bedtime story."

Not a bad bribe. Jana had used variations of those herself. Considering her daughter's toddler vocabulary, Marley had no trouble deciphering if a bribe was worthy of her cooperation. However, Jana did wonder how many bribe choices Kace had offered her before she'd settled on those.

Since Marley would want an immediate pay-up on the cookie bribe, Jana took a vanilla wafer from her stash in the diaper bag and gave it to her. She'd make a mess with it, but that's what baby wipes were for.

They went outside, using her SUV because of the car seats, and while Jana drove to the police station, Kace got on the phone, making his first call to Judd and then following it up with one to Dominick's attorney. Kace had to leave a message for that one, and he told the lawyer to contact him ASAP. As for his conversation with Judd, it was short, with Kace telling his brother they were on the way.

The cookie definitely put Marley in a good mood,

but with each passing second, Jana's anger over Dominick's threat turned to serious concern. That concern only went up some notches when they went into the police station and saw Peter, Belinda and her father waiting in Kace's office. Judd wasn't with them. He was at his own desk and was sporting a scowl that matched Kace's.

"I figured you'd rather handle this yourself," Judd told his brother, "but my take is all three should be up for the idiot of the year award. I mentioned to them that this was a—" Judd stopped, eyeing Marley "—goat rope."

Obviously, that hadn't been Judd's first choice of words to describe things, but Jana was thankful he hadn't used profanity. The others had better adhere to that, too, or she would blast them with as many G-rated curse words as she could manage.

It helped, some, that this trio had done all of this to help Kace and her. And in Arnold's and Peter's cases, to get back at Dominick. Belinda likely had more personal motives. Probably because she was still in love with Kace, but after the trouble she'd gotten into over the pranks on Peter, it shocked Jana that Kace's former girlfriend hadn't learned her lesson.

"Anything yet from Dominick on when he'll be coming in?" Kace asked Judd.

Judd shook his head. "I'll keep you posted. Uh, you want me to hold Marley while you go in there?"

It was a generous offer, but Jana could tell it wouldn't be a comfortable one for Judd so she declined and thanked him. Besides, having Marley with her might help her tamp down her emotions. It was hard to vent or cry when holding a cute toddler that she just happened to love more than life itself.

By the time Kace and she made it into his office, all three culprits were on their feet, and the only one who appeared to be remorseful was Belinda. She'd been crying. Arnold just looked pissed off, and Peter, well, he had one of those big bandage things for a broken nose.

God, this was as bad as Jana had thought it would be.

"Boo-boo," Marley said, aiming her finger at Peter. "Ouchie."

Despite the bruising, Peter smiled at her. It was sort of creepy what with his injuries. "It's okay, baby. I'm fine."

Marley seemed to take that as gospel, and she wiped her cookie mouth on Jana's shoulder.

"Speak one at a time," Kace warned the trio, "and don't curse. You first," he said pointing to Arnold.

"I wasn't going to let that…you know what get away with what he was trying to do to Jana," her father said after a long breath. "The lady at the inn told me about what Belinda had done to Peter so I called her, and she gave me the names of the stripper and…party favors places that she'd used."

Kace shifted to Belinda. "And you decided to help him with more than just giving him information?"

Belinda blinked hard when she looked at Kace. "Dominick was trying to…screw you over."

Apparently, this was going to be a pause-filled

conversation with explanations that Jana was still trying to wrap her mind around. Jana understood Belinda trying to help Kace, but what was with her father trying to help her?

Kace turned to Peter next. "And how did you get involved in this plan?"

"It was my idea," Peter readily admitted. "Dominick was not only going after you with that lawsuit, he was trying to milk money from Jana and Eileen, too."

Jana wasn't surprised that her ex had gone after her mother in that way. Not surprised, either, that Eileen would have shared that news with Peter. But with their engagement over, it seemed odd that Peter would attempt to fight this battle for them. Of course, maybe his standing up for Kace was the main reason to spur him to action.

Stupid action.

"Are you okay?" Jana asked Peter.

"I've been better." He motioned toward his nose. "But this will look good in the lawsuit that I intend to file against Dominick. I'll give him a dose of his own medicine."

Kace groaned, causing Marley to giggle at the sound. "Did it occur to any of you that Dominick could rightfully claim this was a setup?" Kace asked. "After all, the three of you were on the scene when it happened."

"He wasn't supposed to see us," Belinda said. "I rented a van, and we were going to stay inside it while we got pictures and video of him with the *la-*

dies and such. But Dominick started yelling at one of the ladies, and he grabbed her by the wrist."

"I didn't want him to hurt her so I got out of the van." Arnold picked up the explanation. "I don't think Dominick even knew who I was, but he spotted the camera and came after me."

"That's when I got out," Peter piped in. "I told Belinda to stay put, but—"

"I wasn't going to let that weasel get away with punching Peter," Belinda interrupted. "But like Peter said, this will give Dominick a taste of his own medicine."

Marley attempted to say "yuck." It came out more like "uck," which must have sounded enough like the *F*-word that it caused everyone to look at her. Belinda even protested that she hadn't cursed, that none of them had used that word and Jana waved it off.

It took Kace a couple of moments to get back on point. "Dominick can and will cry that he was set up, and he'll have some proof. He could sue all of you for defamation of character. And while that'll line the lawyers' pockets, that's about the only positive thing that anyone will get out of it."

Sad but true.

"So, we might have made this worse?" Belinda asked as if she hadn't realized that before Kace had just spelled it out.

"You made it worse," Kace confirmed and then said to all three of them, "Now, here's what you're going to do. You'll leave, go home, or back to wherever you're currently staying, and you won't communicate with Dominick in any way. Wait to hear from me. I'll contact the district attorney and get some legal advice on this."

Belinda was the first to agree. Peter and Arnold mumbled barely audible agreements, but Jana could now see some regrets in her father's eyes. *Good.*

"Did the hospital take photographs of that injury?" Kace asked Peter.

He nodded. "I'd planned to use them for the lawsuit. But I'll put that on hold," Peter quickly added.

There were still thick layers of tension in the room, but Arnold turned toward Jana. Well, actually toward Marley, and he smiled at her. "Hello there, sweetheart," he said.

Marley studied him for a moment, but she wasn't buying his greeting. She whipped her head around, her curly hair slinging in Jana's face. "No, no," Marley declared, and then she reached for Kace. As he always did when she reached for him, Kace took her.

"If Dominick or his lawyer contact you," Kace went on, talking to the trio as if he weren't holding a cute toddler in his arms, "you don't speak to either one of them. Understand?" He waited until he got nods. "Now leave and hire attorneys because this could get messy fast."

"Does that mean I shouldn't leave town?" her father asked.

"Stay at least a day or two," Kace advised. "Same for you," he told Peter.

"I'm staying at the inn anyway," Peter said. "I've

still got to pack up my things from Eileen's guest-house."

Jana's phone rang, and when she saw Bessie's name on the screen, she stepped in the squad room while Kace continued to instruct the trio.

"You need to come to your mother's right away," Bessie blurted out the moment Jana answered.

Her heart went to her kneecaps. It didn't matter that she was still pissed off at Eileen for keeping Arnold's whereabouts a secret, this was still her mother. "What's wrong?"

"Plenty. Just get out here as fast as you can. I think your mom's gone crazy."

Jana had opened her mouth to ask "Crazy, how?" but Bessie had already ended the call. *Definitely not good*. Jana opened Kace's office door, and he must have known something was wrong from her expression.

"What happened?" Kace asked.

"It's my mother. Bessie said I need to get out there now."

Kace had already started walking to her before she finished. So had Peter and her father. Both of them followed Kace and her toward the door.

"No," Kace said. "Go take care of finding a lawyer. If Eileen wants to see you, I'll call you and let you know."

Good move because if her mom was truly having a breakdown, it might not be wise for her father to just show up. Even Peter might not be in her mother's safe zone right now. Still, that didn't stop Peter from following them.

"I'll stay back," Peter assured them, "but I have to make sure Eileen's okay."

They didn't argue with the man. No time for that. Plus, if their positions had been reversed, Jana would have insisted on going, too.

Peter went to his car, and Kace and Jana went to the SUV. After they got Marley in the car seat, Kace took Jana's keys so he could drive. She was thankful for it because she definitely wasn't feeling too steady at the moment. Hoping to tamp down her fears of a worst-case scenario, she phoned Bessie and put the call on speaker so that Kace could hear.

"Kace and I are on the way," Jana told the woman once she had her on the line. "What happened?"

Jana heard someone shouting. If she wasn't mistaken, it was angry, slurred shouts.

"Your mother's drunk," Bessie said. "She climbed one of the apple trees and is throwing twigs at anyone who tries to get her down. She's also got a bottle of tequila with her."

All right, that definitely wasn't worst-case. Jana had gone in a bad direction, thinking of a possible suicide attempt. Still, she couldn't ever remember seeing her mom drunk. Ditto for Eileen never having climbed a tree. Still, she'd managed it while holding a bottle of what was likely top-shelf tequila. Jana was surprised, worried and somewhat impressed.

When they reached the house, Kace got out and opened the back door of the SUV to get Marley from the car seat. "Go ahead and check on your mom. I'll be in the sunroom with Marley if you need me."

Apparently, her mother wasn't the only one who could surprise and impress her today, and this time there was no worry that Kace would indeed take care of her little girl. Unfortunately, he would have to manage that with Peter, since the man was right on Kace's heels.

"Thank you, Kace," Jana told him, giving both Marley and him quick cheek kisses before she ran to the backyard. She didn't have to guess which apple tree her mother had climbed. Jana just followed the sounds of the ramblings.

Which were indeed slurred.

If her mother's words hadn't given away her intoxicated state, her appearance certainly would have. Wearing her pink yoga outfit, a bathrobe and with her hair a tangled mess, Eileen was indeed in the tree. Not on the first branch, either. She'd gone up a couple and was sitting, her legs dangling a good ten feet off the ground. She had a bottle of Patrón Platinum in one hand, a small broken-off tree branch in the other.

Eileen likely wouldn't kill herself if she fell, but she could break a bone or two. If so, she likely wouldn't even feel it because it was obvious her mom was past the stage of a little buzz. This was sloppy drunk.

Bessie and the other household staff were there. All of them were looking baffled and worried.

Jana didn't want it to happen, but all the anger

she felt for her mother vanished. Well, most of it did anyway. Eileen was hurting. *She* was hurting. Peter was hurting. Heck, Arnold probably was, too. Staying pissed off wasn't going to do anything except fuel an emotion wildfire that already had way too much fuel.

"I told your ex-husband to go to *h-e-l-l*," Eileen said, and yes, she spelled the mild curse word. *Good.* It was possible that as loud as her mom's voice was that Marley might be able to hear.

"Kace or Dominick?" Jana calmly asked as she stepped around the small branches and twigs to go closer. She hoped the Patrón had affected her mom's aim and that she hadn't actually hit anyone.

"Dominick, of course. He's a *d-i-k*."

Yes, he was, even if Eileen had misspelled the word.

"What happened between Dominick and you?" Jana pressed. While she waited for her mom to answer, Jana motioned for the others to leave. Once Eileen sobered up, this was going to be humiliating enough without the added benefit of an audience.

"He called me and said he was going to take Marley." Even though a lot of those words were slurred, Jana figured enough of them out. "Sole custody, the *d-i-k* said, and that I'd never get to see her again."

Even in drunk-speak that reminder still packed a punch, and it robbed Jana of a couple of breaths along with giving her enough stomach acid to create multiple ulcers. It didn't matter that Dominick didn't have a leg to stand on when it came to getting anything more than shared custody. Just the possibility of him doing that hurt Jana all the way to the marrow.

"I'm going to fight Dominick," Jana assured her, and she went closer, keeping watch to make sure a twig missile didn't come her way.

"Good. Kick his *a-s-s*."

While Dominick did indeed need an ass kicking, Jana wouldn't get the pleasure of doing that. Unlike the stunt that Arnold, Peter and Belinda had pulled, Jana would have to keep this fight a legal one. Civil, too. Not for Dominick's sake but because of Marley. She didn't want her baby's memories peppered with bitterness between her mom and dad even if that bitterness was there in spades.

Eileen gave a hoarse sob. "The *d-i-k* wants to take our little girl."

The crying wasn't a good sign because eventually her mom was going to need to wipe her eyes. With both her hands occupied, Jana wasn't sure how Eileen would manage that, and Jana didn't want her trying to manage it.

"Mom, you need to come down so we can talk," Jana said.

"We can talk just fine from here." With that, Eileen took another swig of Patrón.

No, they couldn't. Not with Jana worried that her mother would splat on the ground. That left Jana with the possibility of doing her own splatting, and she caught onto the first branch and hoisted herself up.

Jana had never been much of a tree climber as a kid, and she quickly remembered why. Even this small amount of height made her a little light-headed. Going up the next branch didn't help, but she finally got close enough to her mother to grab onto her if she started to fall.

"My lawyer will deal with Dominick," she told her mother. "I could use your help on that, though. Maybe legal double-teaming him will get him to back off." It wouldn't, but Jana thought the quickest way to pull Eileen out of this drunk funk was to give her a course of action.

Eileen seemed to consider that, and while she did, Jana took the twig from her, tossed it—nearly off-balancing herself—and she wrapped her mom's now empty hand around the tree branch.

"Is it just Dominick that's got you this upset?" Jana asked.

Her mother sobbed again. "It's everything. My life's *s-h-i-t*. The garden guild told me that my services as social chairperson would no longer be needed."

In the grand scheme of things, that didn't seem important, but Jana knew it was to her mother. "Mom, can I have a drink of the tequila?"

Eileen passed the bottle down to her, and Jana immediately tossed it to the ground. "Aww, why'd you do that?" Her mom's voice was a sullen pout. "That's a waste of good tequila."

"And a way to avoid possible alcohol poisoning. Come down from that branch so we can talk," Jana tried again.

Her mother leaned over too far to watch the Patrón

spill onto the ground. She got a pensive look in her unfocused eyes. "Are you falling in love with Kace?"

The question threw Jana, and maybe that's why she blurted out her answer. "No, I'm already in love with him."

Eileen blinked like an owl, probably trying to figure out if Jana meant that. Jana was trying to do the same thing, and it wasn't much of a surprise when she realized that it was indeed true. Heck, maybe she'd never stopped being in love with him. She would certainly do a lot of thinking about that later, but for now it gave Jana a new angle to try to convince her mother to get down.

"I think you're in love with Peter," Jana threw out there.

Apparently, even a drunk person could make a wistful sigh, and it told Jana what she needed to know. "You should marry Peter," Jana insisted.

More of the owl eyes, followed by another of those sighs. "You believe he's a gold digger."

Jana lifted her shoulder. "Sometimes, I think the biggest mistake we can make is not doing something because it might be a mistake. Of course, I do have two divorces under my belt so what do I know?"

"You know not to let a good man like Kace get away a second time."

Wow, from the mouth of a drunk person to Jana's very sober ears. Who would have ever thought her mother would have given her the very advice that Jana wanted? Of course, this particular ball wasn't in her court. Despite the crap she'd gone through with Dominick, she'd risk her heart again—for Kace.

But Kace might not be willing to risk his.

That felt like a new vise around all the feeling parts of her body.

Her mother had a quick cure for that, though. As if she were a tree-climbing champion, Eileen scooted down on the branch next to Jana. Her mom still didn't hold on but rather hooked her arm around Jana. It was good to have her this close, to get that hug, but smelling her mother's breath was a reminder that sobriety was still a big issue. Plus, their feet still weren't on the ground.

"I miss the sex," Eileen said with a third of those sighs. "Peter was very good at sex."

"Mom, stop," Jana scolded. "I can't put my hands over my ears because I'll fall out of this tree so no more sex talk."

Eileen giggled, the sound of a woman who had indeed enjoyed some good sex that Jana didn't want to think about. Jana decided to turn the conversation in a different direction. It wouldn't necessarily be a more comfortable discussion, but it was something Jana needed to know.

"Do you still have feelings for Dad?" Jana asked.

"Feelings?" Her mother gave that less than a second of thought. "Oh yes. I despise him. And you despise me for not telling you he was alive."

Jana thought about it for much more than a second. They sat there, the flies now buzzing around them, and the heat causing the sweat to trickle down her back. "I hate what you did, and it was wrong. So very, very wrong. But I'm trying hard to understand it."

That's where Dominick helped. If he pulled a disappearing act with Marley and didn't want to see her, Jana might try to soften the blow by not mentioning where he was.

No, she wouldn't.

Even after everything Dominick had done, she couldn't lie to her daughter like that. Still, she wasn't Eileen and vice versa, so Jana would try hard to see this through her mom's socially important lenses. Maybe in a year or two, she could actually forgive her. And what the heck? Maybe she could forgive Arnold, too, though she wouldn't be sending him Father's Day cards anytime soon.

"Peter is here, by the way," Jana added. "He's very worried about you."

"He's here?" Her mother sounded instantly sober. And horrified. She actually fluffed at her hair and blew her breath against her palm as if testing for the odor of alcohol.

"Do you want to see him?" It was definitely a question, since last Jana heard, Eileen had broken the engagement and told Peter to leave the guesthouse.

"Maybe," Eileen said, but what Jana heard was a "yes."

Eileen's actions confirmed that yes, too, because using the spider monkey skills that Jana hadn't known she had, her mother scampered—yes, scampered—to the ground. "I need to freshen up before I see him," Eileen said before she disappeared into the house.

Jana sat there in part because she was shocked at her mother's quick-fire change in attitude but also because she hadn't inherited any spider monkey skills from her. She looked down at the ground, some queasiness rolling in with the light head, and she took the wimpy way out.

She called Kace.

"Uh, I need some help," Jana told him. Since she wanted a better grip on the tree branch, she sandwiched her phone between her shoulder and ear. "Not with Eileen," she quickly added. "That's taken care of. I just need your, uh, biceps."

Of course, he made a *huh* sound, but while he was still on the phone with her, he came. It only took a few seconds for him to get to the backyard. He was carrying Marley, who immediately squealed with delight when she saw Jana in the tree. Obviously, this was something her little girl wanted to give a try.

Like a cop studying a crime scene, Kace looked at the tequila bottle, the twigs and branches and then at the death grip Jana had on the tree.

"Everything's okay with Eileen?" he asked. He put his phone back in his jeans pocket.

"Okay enough." Her voice squeaked.

"You can't get down?" he added when she didn't say anything else.

"Nope."

The corner of his mouth lifted. Not a blinding smile, but it was enough to cause her stomach to flip-flop, and Jana didn't think it was doing that solely because of her fear of falling.

Kace stood Marley on the ground, something that pleased her immensely because Marley started picking up twigs and throwing them like boomerangs.

"Good thing you didn't have on a dress today," Kace remarked, looking up at her.

That caused more of the flip-flopping, and despite the terror she was feeling, Jana smiled, too. It got even better when Kace lifted his arms, complete with superior biceps. Of course, she couldn't actually see them because of his jacket, but she knew they were there.

"A leap of faith," he said. "You jump, and I'll catch you."

Jana knew it was silly to apply those instructions to anything other than this specific situation, but they warmed her from head to toe. Holding her breath, she jumped. Kace caught her.

And then he kissed her.

It wasn't French—his preferred type of kiss—but it still packed a wallop, and in that moment, Jana felt both rescued and loved. She didn't get to feel it for long though because Kace's phone rang. He let go of her, standing her on the ground, and he took out his phone.

"I need to answer this," Kace said, doing just that.

Jana was not only close enough to Kace to have seen Judd's name on the screen, she had no trouble hearing Judd's voice.

"Everything okay with Eileen?" Judd asked.

Kace repeated the answer she'd given him. "Okay enough."

"Good. I just got the sales records from those places that Belinda used for her prank purchases," he added without even pausing. Jana thought she heard, well, some gloating in Judd's tone. "You're not going to believe who else bought a case of Smelly Bobs stink bombs."

CHAPTER TWENTY-FOUR

THERE WERE SOME things that Kace hated about his job, but this wasn't one of them. Nope. This was one of those times that he could use the law to deliver some karma to a dickhead.

The dickhead, Dominick, came in the front door of the police station, a guy in a suit by his side. His lawyer, no doubt. Both men appeared smug and ready to draw blood.

Yeah, Kace would like his part in wiping those smug-assed looks off their faces. This was definitely something Jana would have liked to see, and she'd pressed for it, too, but no way had Kace wanted her and especially Marley here. He suspected there'd be some cursing, shouting and lying.

All from Dominick.

No need for Jana or Marley to witness that, and besides, Kace didn't want Dominick's lawyer to have any reason to object.

Judd, looking very much like the badass that he was, showed Dominick and the suit into Kace's office, and they'd barely gotten their feet through the door when the lawyer started.

"I'm Edwin Carmichael, Dominick's attorney, and

this is harassment," the lawyer declared. "You have no cause to demand my client come in. The incident with your *acquaintances* happened in San Antonio and is out of your jurisdiction."

Kace let Carmichael bellow on for a little while longer while he spouted legalities and such, and then Kace stopped him with two words. "Smelly Bobs."

The lawyer likely shut up because he was confused, but Kace saw the flicker in Dominick's eyes. Ah, just what he'd wanted to see. The flicker of someone as guilty as sin.

"Is that some kind of threat?" Carmichael asked.

Kace ignored him and read Dominick his rights, which had both the lawyer and Dominick howling in protest. Carmichael was adding questions about what any of this had to do with his client, but Dominick wasn't asking anything of the sort. Because he knew. However, he probably didn't know just how much of a legal stink this would cause.

"I'm charging your client with criminal trespassing, obstruction of justice and withholding evidence in the course of an investigation," Kace went on, talking right over them. "Perhaps you'd like a moment with your client so he can explain that he not only did those things, but he did it to frame his ex-wife for a crime."

Finally, there was silence. Carmichael turned his head toward Dominick so fast that Kace heard his neck pop. Dominick just glared at Kace.

"I didn't do anything of the sort," Dominick said through clenched teeth.

"Now, you see, that's another lie," Kace told him, enjoying this a whole lot more than he should be. "Don't make me keep adding more charges because it'll just cause more paperwork."

Carmichael started blustering again, but Kace kept his attention nailed to Dominick when he continued. "I have proof that you ordered a case of Smelly Bobs stink bombs. The very case that showed up in Jana's SUV. You did that to implicate her in a series of crimes."

All right, it was pranks. But *crimes* sounded more official, and there had been charges against Belinda, which made it criminal.

"Prove it," Dominick spat out, that smug look returning to his idiot face.

"I already have," Kace assured him. "The case number shipped to you matches the one found in Jana's vehicle."

Carmichael latched right onto that, saying that even if his client had ordered such devices, that he didn't plant them in his ex's vehicle. But Kace didn't blink. He kept his cop's stare on Dominick.

Since Kace was allowed to lie and fudge the truth during an interrogation, that's exactly what he did. "The box is at the lab and is being tested for your fingerprints."

"I wore gloves," Dominick blurted out, confirming that he was just as stupid as Kace had thought he was.

"Don't say anything else," Carmichael warned

his client, but he'd definitely gone a little pale. So had Dominick.

"I won't need fingerprints," Kace went on, "because there was a signed receipt for the box when it was delivered to you. *Your* signature, your address," he pointed out. "And the delivery person remembers you."

All right, that last part was a lie, too, but Kace didn't regret telling it one bit.

The silence came again, broken only when the lawyer finally said that he needed to have a word with his client. However, Dominick slung off his grip when Carmichael tried to lead him out of the office.

"None of this means shit," Dominick concluded.

"Well, actually it does," Kace said. "These are criminal charges, and it opens a door to a civil suit that Jana can and will file against you." That wasn't a lie. Jana had been pissed when she found out what Dominick had done. "You sullied her reputation when you tried to frame her for a crime."

"Bullshit," Dominick snapped out like a whip. "This isn't going to make me drop any of the charges against you, Peter, Arnold or your girlfriend."

Kace shrugged as if that didn't matter in the least. "When you planted that box in Jana's SUV, that's conspiracy, coupled with all those other charges I've named. In addition, you lied during a police investigation when you told me that someone had called you from a blocked number to warn you that Jana had planted a device to do bodily harm."

Kace hadn't known for certain that Dominick had

done that, but he saw the confirmation in Dominick's eyes. Clearly, this guy didn't have a poker face.

"Wonder how all of this will affect your challenging Jana for custody of Marley?" Kace asked. "Or the alimony settlement you're pressing her to sign? This could end up costing you big-time."

Oh, Dominick didn't like that much at all. Kace could have sworn he saw little puffs of steam spew out of his ears.

"I figured you set up Jana to torment her," Kace went on, "but you might have thought it had the extra benefit of running Peter off. That way, he wouldn't get his hands on any of Eileen's money. You were saving it for yourself."

Dominick made a low growling sound.

Ignoring it, Kace shifted his attention to Carmichael. "Here's the way I see this playing out for your client. He loses any chance of getting custody of his daughter. He gets no alimony. He gets sued by not only Jana but also Eileen since Dominick tried to extort money from her. Then, there's Peter Laramie who'll also be suing him—"

"That's bullshit," Dominick practically shouted. "Your dickwad of a father set me up."

Kace shrugged again because he knew it would get Dominick's goat. It did. He turned an ugly shade of rage red.

"You attacked Mr. Laramie," Kace pointed out, "and his injuries were serious enough for him to be hospitalized." Kace tapped his finger to one of the photos that Peter had given him. It showed the man's bruised, bloody face.

"He set me up!" Dominick repeated.

"The courts will decide that," Kace replied, "but there's not much of a decision to be made on the assault. SAPD will be informing you of those charges today."

"You're lying." And Dominick would have launched himself at Kace if Carmichael hadn't held him back.

Nope. Kace wasn't lying this time, and he was certain his smile confirmed that. "Let's see. Assault charges in that jurisdiction and that whole litany of others in my jurisdiction. It looks as if you've fucked yourself." And he waited.

Kace didn't have to wait long.

Cursing and shouting—just as Kace had predicted he would do—Dominick lunged at him again. This time, Carmichael wasn't fast or strong enough. Kace considered taking the punch as Peter had done, but he just didn't want to live with this piece of shit clocking him. Kace stepped to the side, letting Dominick's momentum send him crashing into the desk. Papers flew, and Kace's favorite coffee mug crashed to the floor.

"And I can add destruction of property to go along with that attempted assault of a police officer," Kace calmly added.

However, there was nothing calm about Dominick. "You sonofabitch," Dominick snarled. Carmichael finally got control of him and wrestled him away from Kace. That didn't stop Dominick from raging on. "You assaulted me first. I'm suing you."

Kace looked him right in the eye. "If you're going tit for tat, I think it's obvious that my tat is a whole lot bigger than yours."

"I need a word with my client," Carmichael repeated while trying to drag Dominick out the door.

"I don't want a fucking word with you." Dominick rammed his elbow into the lawyer's stomach, knocking him back.

Kace steeled himself up for Dominick to come after him again. Not that Dominick got the chance to do it. That's because Judd stepped in. He didn't put his hand on his weapon—he just gave Dominick that hard icy look that only Judd and serial killers could have managed.

Dominick stayed put. But the anger was coming off him in nearly visible waves.

"All right," Dominick finally said through clenched teeth. "You win. I'm done—not just with this bullshit town but with Jana."

That sounded like music to his ears, and Kace thought Jana would be happy about it, too. Except there was something else, something more than the rage in Dominick's eyes and voice.

"What about Marley?" Kace asked.

Dominick gave a dry smile. "I'm done with her, too. Congrats, Sheriff Laramie, this is all your fault. Because of you and this bullshit, Marley will never see her father again."

And with that, Dominick walked out.

JANA WAS SUDDENLY wishing that she'd kept Marley with her instead of taking her to Piper's. Holding her baby might have settled some of her raw nerves.

Of course, it was just as possible that she would have passed on those nerves to Marley, and neither of them needed that. What Jana did need was answers, and she wasn't getting any.

First and foremost, she wanted to know what was going on with Kace and Dominick at the police station. Whatever happened there could be huge, but her mom was a hot concern as well.

When Jana had left her mother's place, Eileen had been talking things out with Peter, but considering there were still the lingering effects of tequila, Jana wasn't holding out hope that all would go well there. Still, if things fell apart, Bessie had promised to call her. No news could be good news, but Jana wouldn't believe that until she heard from her mother.

At the sound of a car engine, Jana hurried to the door, threw it open and cursed. It wasn't anyone she wanted to see but rather the one person she didn't.

Dominick.

Great. Since he wasn't behind bars, that meant things hadn't gone well. Not for her anyway.

"What do you want?" she snarled at the same moment he snarled, "This won't take long. I just wanted to let you know that your cowboy lover really fucked up."

Oh mercy. No. Still, Jana managed to keep her chin high and her eyes mean and narrowed. They widened though when she saw Kace pull his truck to a stop behind Dominick's car.

"I'm washing my hands of you because of him." Dominick rammed a thumb at Kace, who was quickly approaching them. "I'm done with you and your drama. That includes dropping the suit I filed against Kace and the town council."

That had her relaxing a little. Because it sounded good. Rah-rah for *drama*. Who would have thought it'd turn out to be a Dominick repellant?

"He's sulky and isn't going to see Marley again because he's pissed off at me," Kace informed her.

"Oh," she said.

Oh. Both a blessing and a curse. One that Jana didn't have time to comment on because Dominick spoke first.

"Arnold's giving me the settlement so I got what I wanted," Dominick said.

Another *oh*. Jana looked at Kace to see if he'd known about that, but he only shook his head. So, her father had paid up, and Jana had no doubts, none, that the settlement meant lots and lots of money.

"Anyway, I've met someone," Dominick went on. "And I plan to start a new life with her."

"Kristy Madden," Jana supplied. "The horse trainer who used to work for me."

"Not her." Dominick made a face as if disgusted with the idea of that. "Kristy was, well, just someone I was seeing. No, I've met someone else, a real woman. She's amazing, and I'm in love with her."

Jana figured Miss Amazing was also rich. Possibly stupid, too, just as she'd been when she'd gotten involved with Dominick. Of course, he had played the charm game very well.

"I'll be moving to Montana," Dominick added. "So if you want to blame someone for Marley not having a father, just look in the mirror. Or look at him." He sent another thumb hike at Kace. "Good riddance, Jana. I hope you have the miserable life that you rightly deserve."

It sounded like something a bratty kid with a decent vocabulary would have said, and Dominick's stomping-away exit was juvenile as well. She didn't stop him. No way. But the realization of what this meant settled right in the pit of her stomach.

"I'm sorry," Kace said, making her understand that he, too, knew what this meant.

Dominick was walking out on Marley.

"I don't know if I should be worried that he'll do as he says or that he'll come back," Jana murmured.

On a heavy sigh, Kace pulled her into his arms, brushed a kiss on her temple. "I thought the threat of arrest would cause him to back off from everything else. I didn't know he'd use Marley like this."

A year ago, Jana wouldn't have thought it possible, but she'd lived for months now with Dominick's antics so it didn't surprise her. But it did hurt her. Kace and she both knew what it was like to be without a father—even a bad one.

"If I thought it would help, I'd ask you if you want to get drunk and climb a tree," he said.

Well, it had certainly seemed to help her mother

so Jana wouldn't rule it out. As long as it was a very low branch on a tree, that is.

"This isn't your fault," she told Kace because she figured that's what he was thinking.

Yep, he was. She got confirmation of that when she eased back to look him in the eyes. Guilt and regret in abundance. Jana pulled him back to her to console him, and she ended up consoling herself. Having Kace close to her seemed to be a cure for the worst of her fears. The ones that would make her crazy if she played a mom's favorite mental game of worst-case scenario.

If Dominick carried through on his threat not to see Marley, Jana didn't know what she'd tell her little girl. Of course, it wouldn't be a factor for a while. Marley was too young to know if her dad was around or not. Heck, even her toys were in an "out of sight, out of mind" realm for her. Still… Yes, still.

"Maybe I will get drunk and climb a tree," Jana grumbled.

It wasn't a stellar idea. Neither was another crying jag, pacing or any of the other coping mechanisms she'd tried. But when her mouth went to Kace's, Jana realized she'd found a temporary cure. A Kace kiss was guaranteed magic. A human fire starter. And this one didn't disappoint.

"This probably isn't a good idea," he said when they broke for air.

Considering the huskiness of his voice and grunt of discomfort he made, Kace had labeled it not good because kissing for them usually led to sex. This would be no different. And that's why Jana kissed him again.

She might as well have sent up a big "come and nail me" flag, and while the timing did suck, that, too, was the norm for Kace and her. Their reunion-sex encounters hadn't come at the best times nor at the best places, but they'd been mind-blowing and for at least a little while, they had chased away the demons.

Along with giving her some incredible orgasms.

It was a win-win, and right now she needed every inch of win that he could give her. Well, he would if he didn't let his conscience or doubts get in the way.

Kace pulled back again, keeping his hand around the back of her neck, letting his warm breath hit like butterfly kisses against her mouth. "This feels as if I'm taking advantage of you," he said.

Mercy, what a guy. Here she had thrown herself at him and was even gripping his butt to press his erection to her, and he was giving her an out. One that she didn't want.

"Do you think I'm taking advantage of you?" she asked.

His forehead bunched up. His mouth tightened. "That's the first time I've ever gotten that question from a woman whose nipples are pressed to my chest."

Jana smiled, didn't wait for the answer and went in for the home run of kisses. Full open mouth. Tongue. Complete with her running her hand down into the back of his jeans and boxers and over his bare butt.

Jana squeezed, shoved him even tighter against her and reminded him of those early days when they'd discovered the magic with the tacky name of dry humping.

If Kace had a response to that—other than a manly grunt—he didn't voice it. However, he did respond with actions. He lifted her off her feet, hooking his arms around her butt so that it anchored them sex to sex when he maneuvered them into the house.

"I have a bed," she managed to say.

Kace must have noticed that earlier when they'd cleaned up Marley because he headed that direction and dumped her onto the brand-new mattress. In the same motion, he reached behind him, caught onto his shirt and pulled it off. Jana thought it was an incredibly hot move. Not just because it got him partially naked and she could see all those tight pecs and such but because it seemed so, well, male.

He continued with the male thing by unzipping and pushing his jeans and boxers down his hips. *Oh my*. This was her best look at him in a while, and it'd been worth the wait. Good grief, the man was built everywhere.

Jana was sort of mesmerized with the sight of him, but thankfully Kace wasn't paralyzed from the gawking bug. He stripped off her shirt as fast as he'd done his own. Then, her boots before he dragged her jeans and panties off her. Being a hot busy bee, he did some kissing and licking while he fumbled through his pocket and came out with a condom.

Yes, he was a winner all right.

Jana figured that once he had the condom on, that there wouldn't be much foreplay, which was fine with her. She was ready. But she was also wrong. There was foreplay. Kace started some kisses at the neck that trailed all the way down to her stomach.

When he had her to the point of being a quivering, quaking ready-to-beg mess, only then did he plunge inside her. And she went from a hot, quivering mess to being on that knife edge, teetering between a screaming climax and trying to hang on for at least a few more moments of pleasure.

She couldn't.

Kace must have had some special G-spot detector because he tipped her right over the edge. And what a fall. Ripples and ripples of pleasure all the way down. Kace didn't wait, either. He made a couple more thrusts, and he buried his face against her neck when he jolted from the climax.

Jana lay there, his weight pressing on her, and she allowed herself to come back to earth. *Slowly* come back. Good sex had a way of making you stupid, and she knew that once the remnants of the orgasm cleared, then so would the stupidity.

Reality could be a mean witch.

It would be so easy to stay in Kace's arms. To let him soothe all of this away. And she could even remind herself that Marley really liked Kace and that maybe her little girl wouldn't miss having a father role model—

Jana cut off that thought as if it were the head of a poisonous snake ready to strike.

Sweet heaven, what was she doing?

Yes, this was reality all right. A really bad one that she didn't have a choice about facing. She couldn't let Kace cure anything. Couldn't let him be anything other than the great guy that he was. Maybe she'd finally learned something from her two divorces and that was she needed to stand on her own, that she didn't need a man to fix her, her situation or anything else.

Jana adjusted her body, a signal for Kace to roll off her, which he did. He landed in a sated flop on his back. To stop his hotness from making her wimp out, she brushed a kiss on his mouth. However, there must have been something in her expression that caused him to stare at her with those intense gray eyes.

"That felt a little like goodbye," he said.

"Because it was." And before Jana could change her mind, she got up, went into the bathroom and closed the door.

CHAPTER TWENTY-FIVE

Christmas Day

KACE, JUDD, CALLEN and Nico stared at the dead stuffed thing that Shelby had just set on the bed in one of the guest rooms at Buck and Rosy's. His brothers and he were all familiar with the armadillo that Rosy had affectionately named Billy.

Familiar and creeped out.

Kace would have an easier time viewing road-kill because those critters looked dead. Billy had a glassy-eyed zombie feel to him. Worse, Rosy had put him in a tiny Santa outfit.

"Rosy thought Billy would bring you good luck for the start of your married life," Shelby said, not sounding very convinced.

"She didn't want Cleo to get a chance at that *luck*?" Judd asked.

Shelby shook her head. "Cleo's downstairs in the den where there are kids, and when they saw Billy, it caused some of them to scream and cry."

That got Kace's attention, and he immediately thought of Marley. She might be in the den, and he definitely didn't want her upset. But going in there to check on her would likely mean seeing Jana, and she wouldn't want that.

When they'd parted ways two and a half weeks ago, Jana had made it clear to him that she needed some time to get her head together, and while he'd seen Marley around town with Eileen and even Piper and Bessie, Jana had made herself scarce. Kace had heard that she'd be breaking that scarceness today to attend the wedding.

"Maybe you could cover Billy with a hat or something," Shelby suggested, but she was no longer in the creeped-out, ick mode. Nope. She was making eyes at Callen, and Callen was moving in for a kiss. Shelby was doing her own share of moving. Fast, too, considering she was having to hurry in a floor-length emerald-colored bridesmaid's dress.

Newlyweds.

Of course, Callen and Shelby had been that way before their wedding, too, and the heat between them didn't seem to be cooling down despite Shelby being pregnant. The heat was also true for Judd and Cleo. For Nico and Eden as well even though they weren't ready to pull the "I do" plug just yet. Still, they were madly in love.

When Kace realized he was scowling at that, he knew it was time to get out of the makeshift dressing room and stroll downstairs. That way, if he heard Marley crying, he could ask someone to make sure she was okay.

Because Kace had lived here in foster care, he'd walked down these stairs too many times to count.

Had seen the huge living room decorated for Christmases past, just like it was now, for birthdays and any occasion Rosy and Buck had deemed worthy of celebrating. Once, they'd had a soup and ice cream party when Nico's wisdom teeth had been extracted.

The whole downstairs was buzzing with a mix of both Christmas and wedding preparations. Rosy definitely hadn't kept things simple as Judd and Cleo had wanted, and he was a little surprised that the dozen or so people he saw milling around had given up their Christmas afternoon to come here. Kace figured that Rosy had it all under control, but at the moment it looked as if it might be a couple of hours before everything was ready for the ceremony.

He spotted Judd and Cleo's foster kids. Beckham, Leo and Isaac. Kace didn't know their exact ages but Beckham was a teenager with the *been there, done that* surliness that only a teenager could pull off. Isaac was eleven or so, and Leo around five. All wore jeans with black suit jackets and white shirts. Texas tuxedos. Leo was carrying one of Rosy's taxidermic critters—a little rabbit that looked only marginally less creepy than the armadillo.

"We're gonna get to give Cleo away," Leo proudly announced. "But she won't really go away. It's just something we gotta do to make it right."

"Judd better not hurt her," Beckham grumbled.

"He won't. He loves her." That from Isaac.

That was their family dynamics in a nutshell. Yes, the boys would give Cleo away because they were important to her. Along with Judd, they were her family. Beckham knew that, but after the tough past he'd had, Judd apparently still had some convincing to do. That was okay. If anyone could convince a surly teen of anything, it was a badass former surly teenager.

"Judd does love Cleo," Kace said, causing Isaac to give Beckham an I-told-you-so look before Kace moved on and down the hall toward the den.

He didn't go in. He just stood at a distance and scanned the room. More chaos. Cleo was indeed in there, wearing a long flowing silver dress and looking like some beautiful woodland fairy with little white flowers threaded through her long brown hair.

The other bridesmaids were there, too. Eden. Cleo's best friend, Daisy Gunderson, and another of Buck's former foster kids, Lucy Garcia. Nico's foster sister, Piper, was there as well.

No Marley, though. And no Jana.

Even though it felt a little like stalking, Kace went into the kitchen, turned around and went straight back out. There was a heated argument going on about whether something called bratwurst balls should be sauced or cheesed, and Kace knew he wanted no input in such a decision.

He wound his way back through the house and went onto the porch to get some fresh air. Kace nearly smacked into Peter, who was leaning down by the front door. The man was either leaving a wrapped gift or stealing one. It was hard to tell what with Peter's suddenly flustered expression.

"Don't tell Judd that the wedding present is from me," Peter said. "He'll never accept it."

While Kace didn't want to be part of any secrets involving their father, he also didn't want to do anything to piss off Judd on his wedding day. He took the gift and tucked it under his arm. He'd just find a spot for it on the gift table, and when it came time to open it, everyone would assume the tag had fallen off.

"How's Jana doing?" Peter asked.

Kace answered the question with a question. "How was she doing the last time you saw her?"

Peter lifted his shoulder. "She hasn't been around much. She's still getting settled into the new place."

Yeah, that's what Kace had heard. He'd also heard that Peter had done some moving of his own. According to Ginger, Liberty, Rosy and about four dozen other people, Eileen had already filed for a divorce from Arnold. Peter had moved in with Eileen and they were now living together. Of course, Eileen had come up with a palimony prenup that Peter had gladly signed. So, maybe it was true love after all. Kace couldn't think of a single reason not to want anything but happiness for Jana's mom and his dad.

The jury was still out on Jana's dad, though.

Arnold had bought a house in Coldwater and said he'd be making monthly visits to see Jana and Marley. That didn't mean Jana was going to forgive him. Didn't mean she *should* forgive him, but at least Arnold wasn't washing his hands of his daughter and granddaughter the way that Dominick had.

Kace doubted anyone who actually knew Dominick thought that the man's absence was a bad thing. Kace despised him and always would. He despised him even more because of the shit he'd put Jana through. It was that shit that had caused her to take a step back from Kace.

Kace made his way to the gift table. Or rather tables that were against the walls of the great room. Some of Rosy's *creations* were scattered here, too, making Kace wonder for the umpteenth time how such a wonderful, loving woman could create such things. The critters were sitting on scatterings of Christmas confetti.

"So, what'd you get us?" Cleo asked from behind him.

Kace didn't exactly jump from the surprise and guilt, but it was close. He turned, saw the teasing grin on his soon-to-be sister-in-law's face. Kace was ready to lie, but then he realized it would only lead to another lie when Cleo and Judd opened the barbecue grill he'd gotten them. It was on the back porch with a big white bow on it.

"It's from Peter," he admitted. There was no need for him to tell her not to mention it to Judd. Cleo knew her surly badass man inside and out.

She nodded, and her smile faded some. "Judd will get past this someday. All of you will."

Kace was about to tell her that he believed her, but Cleo continued before he could say anything.

"Jana's been in one of the upstairs bathrooms for a while now." Cleo lowered her voice to a whisper and even checked over her shoulder to make sure no one was listening. "She seemed upset."

Hell. Being here at a wedding was likely too much for her. "Is Marley with her?"

Cleo shook her head. "She's with Buck, Nico and some of the other kids in the barn. Buck's showing off his new mare."

Marley would enjoy that, and Kace would have liked seeing her reaction, but right now his concern was for Jana.

"It's the bath in the bunkroom," Cleo added as Kace started up the stairs.

He passed a trail of guests along the way but kept the conversation short to the point of being rude, and he made his way to the bunkroom. At least there was no one in here, which was probably why Jana had chosen it.

Kace tapped on the bathroom door and tried the knob when he got no response. Locked. But he was pretty sure he heard someone crying inside.

"Jana?" he called out as quietly and calmly as he could manage. He didn't want to sound alarmed, especially since he might be the last person in Coldwater that she wanted to see.

There was some shuffling around, followed by someone blowing their nose. "I'm okay."

Kace knew that was a whopper of a lie. "Please open the door."

"Really, I'm okay," followed by more nose blowing.

"No, you're not. You're crying, and I'm not leaving until you open this door." Okay, not so quiet and calm that time, and he gave the knob a hard jiggle.

Thankfully, she didn't give him the I'm-okay lie again, but it seemed to take an eternity or two for the door to finally open. And yeah, he got visual confirmation that Jana had indeed been crying.

She was wearing her green bridesmaid's dress, but she obviously wasn't ready to walk down an aisle. Her hair was mussed. Her face, red and splotchy.

He stepped inside, shutting and locking the door behind him so they wouldn't be interrupted. Jana immediately turned away from him, heading to the rug that was in front of the shower stall. She sank down on it, and considering her purse and box of tissues was right there, that was likely where she'd been sitting before she let him in.

"What's wrong?" he asked, dropping down next to her.

Still not looking directly at him, she shook her head and gave him a dismissive wave of her hand. Since she wasn't going to fess up, Kace went with the twenty questions approach that he hoped wouldn't take him all the way to number twenty before she told him the problem.

"Is it Dominick?" he asked. "Did he do something?"

A head shake, followed by a sound he interpreted as "no, thank God." Kace was relieved since that was the first of the worst things that had popped into his mind.

"Is Eileen or your father giving you some grief?" Kace pressed.

Another head shake that was fast and firm. *Good.* Because those two were grief-giving experts even when they didn't mean to be.

Kace continued with the questions, combining them so he could speed this along. Once he knew the problem, he might be able to help her. "How about Marley? Is she all right? Are you having money troubles? Are there problems with the new house?"

Now she looked at him while giving a collective answer of, "No to all of that."

Kace released the breath he'd been holding. Thank God, nothing was wrong with Marley. All those other things were fixable. The next one might not be.

"Does the wedding bring on bad memories for you?" he asked, not adding the subtext of that. *Does it bring on bad memories of us?*

Jana's forehead bunched up, and he was relieved that the question and the possibility of that seemed to be a total surprise to her. "No," she verified. "I'm very happy for Judd and Cleo."

All right, they were getting somewhere, and Kace was quickly running out of questions. Of course, there was one, and it twisted at him to even have to ask it.

"Are you sick?" That wasn't totally out there since Cleo had said she didn't think Jana felt well.

Bingo.

Hell, bingo.

Jana didn't give him a denial that time. No head

shake. And tears started to fill her eyes again. Kace pulled her into his arms and brushed a kiss on the top of her head. He wasn't going to push her to tell him more. He'd just hold her and let her cry it out.

Kace reached for some tissues, his hand bumping into her purse so that it shifted a little and he saw what was inside.

Shit.

He wasn't an expert, but Kace knew a pregnancy test when he saw it. And there wasn't just one of them, there were three.

His eyes whipped toward her, but Jana was already staring at him. "They're positive," she said, her voice hoarse. "I took sixteen of them. I thought it'd be too early to take the test, but it wasn't. They're all positive."

Kace wanted to say something, anything, but it suddenly felt as if a team of mules had kicked him in the chest. No air. None. And the only thing he could manage was a very unmanly wheezing sound.

"It's your baby," she added, which was totally unnecessary. Of course, it was his.

His.

Baby.

The baby they'd made when he'd been too stupid to remember to use a condom nearly three weeks ago.

"Of course, everyone in town will know it's yours," Jana went on. "No way around that. Well, unless the gossips want to get dirty and say it's Dominick's, but I haven't been with him in over eight months."

Yeah, there'd be gossip, which seemed way too insignificant considering everything else. Jana was pregnant. With his baby.

"I never thought I could get pregnant the old-fashioned way," she went on. "Heck, I never thought I could get pregnant again, period. The doctors called Marley my miracle baby."

She was just that—a miracle. So was this baby.

"I wasn't going to tell you about it here," Jana added a moment later. "I wanted to repeat the tests a few more times to make sure. Then, I would have told you later, after the wedding."

More tests? Kace wanted to say that sixteen sure would have convinced him, that these others weren't necessary. But it was obvious that Jana was reacting out of shock and desperation.

"Say something," Jana practically snapped.

Hell. She probably thought his silent treatment was because he was pissed and not because of the lack of oxygen in his lungs. But he didn't need oxygen to kiss her. So that's what Kace did. He hauled her into his lap, pressed his mouth to hers and hoped it would be enough to reassure her that he wasn't angry. In fact, he didn't know what he was.

But he did.

The moment that Jana's taste made it to his brain and the rest of his body, he knew.

"I love you and Marley, and I love this baby," he said when he eased back from her. Thankfully, he got a surge of air just in time to make that sound crystal clear.

Jana had a strange reaction. She scrambled off his lap and hurried to the toilet as if she might throw up.

"Morning sickness," she muttered. "It was my first clue that I was pregnant."

Kace crawled to her, holding back her long hair in case there was indeed puking. No way could he have made anyone understand, but he was glad that he hadn't missed this.

After a few minutes, she waved him off. "The queasiness passed, thank goodness."

He helped her to her feet to lead her to the sink so he could get her a drink of water. When she'd had a few sips, Jana even washed her face. It messed up what was left of the rest of her makeup, but Kace still thought she'd be the prettiest woman in the house. Heck, the prettiest in the state of Texas.

Yeah, he'd gone all sappy that way.

But hey, he had a reason. He was in love and was going to be a father.

"This might be déjà vu for you, but don't you dare ask me to marry you," Jana blurted out, her gaze meeting his in the mirror.

Well, the déjà vu did apply. His other proposal had come on the heels of a pregnancy scare, but even after they'd found out it was a false alarm, Kace hadn't taken back the proposal. Jana hadn't taken back her yes, either, and they'd gone through with the wedding date/elopement they'd come up with in that barn.

"We tried being together and it didn't work out,"

she unnecessarily reminded him. "Then, I tried it again, and I failed at that one, too."

"We were too young when we got married," he pointed out. "Dominick was too stupid when you married him. The only thing you failed at was not seeing his stupidity sooner."

She stared at him, and it wasn't a good, welcoming stare, either. "Are you really asking me to marry you?"

Kace glanced around. It wasn't a stall with horseshit, but it was a bathroom, one that had seen plenty of wear over the years. Plus, like before, he didn't have a ring.

"Come with me," he said, taking hold of her hand.

"I don't want anyone to see me like this," she protested.

"You're drop-dead beautiful," he countered, but she wouldn't believe him.

Even though it wasn't exactly playing fair he kissed her in the hopes of getting her to cooperate. Kace wasn't cocky, but he knew the effects his kisses had on Jana and was fully aware that she had an equally heating effect on him. Being a little mindless right now could play in his favor.

It took a couple more kisses to get her out of the bathroom and moving toward the stairs. They were halfway down when Nico started up. He was carrying Marley, who immediately reached out for Kace, greeting him with "Tace" and a cheek kiss. A sticky one that smelled like icing.

"I was bringing her up here to clean her up,"

Nico said. "She got into the wedding cake. Grabbed a handful of it as I was walking by it. The kid's fast," he added with a chuckle. "Don't worry. She didn't eat too much, and Rosy fixed the cake by sticking a flower over the part Marley ate."

Kace ignored all of that. "I need a ring," he told Nico.

Nico's eyebrow came up, and he slid glances between Jana and Kace before he grinned. "You knocked up Jana, didn't you?" Nico said, putting his hands over Marley's ears.

Shit, if his least clued-in brother had figured that out with a couple of glances, then everyone else would know within the next ten minutes.

"Good," Nico declared, kissing Jana. "Finally, he did the smart thing because I figure that's the only way he'd ever get you to marry him again."

Jana didn't say a word, but if she was feeling what Kace was, she might want to throttle his youngest sibling, who clearly had no sense of appropriate conversational boundaries.

"I need a ring," Kace ground out, though it didn't exactly create a romantic moment to speak through clenched teeth.

Still grinning, Nico held out his hand where he wore a rodeo ring. And the small silver red-stoned one on his pinkie.

"I found out it's carnelian," Nico said pulling it off. "It belonged to our grandmother, and she's wearing it in every picture Peter gave us," he added to Jana. "It must have been important to her."

At the moment it could have belonged to Attila the Hun, and Kace still would have used it as a temporary holding place until he could get the real one. But there was something, well, emotional about using a ring that had belonged to and meant something to family.

"Thank you," Kace said. No clenched teeth this time, and if he hadn't been holding Marley, Jana's hand and the ring, he might have given Nico a punch on the arm—which was the most acceptable form of brotherly affection.

People stared and whispered as Kace came down the steps with Jana in tow, but Kace just ignored them. He helped Marley and Jana into their coats and led them out through the front door. He didn't stop. Kace kept walking away from the crowd, away from the house and he didn't stop until he reached a particularly pretty part of the fenced pasture. There were horses, yes, but there was no muck stench.

"You're really going to do this?" Jana asked.

She didn't sound at all convinced that this was the right thing to do so he kissed her again. Even with Marley bopping at their noses and giggling, it was still plenty effective. Not just in revving up the heat and dulling the senses but also somehow making everything crystal clear.

"Do you love me?" Kace asked Jana.

"Ess," Marley said, though she likely didn't have a clue what he'd just asked, or that he'd meant it for her mom. But the kid had the right idea. She loved him. And he loved her.

Jana gave a more grown-up response. One that caused Kace to smile. "Yes. Of course, I love you. I always have."

Even better. Jana hadn't just been his first lover and his wife, she'd also been his first and only love.

"I just don't want you to ask me to marry you." Jana went on, "Since you'd be doing it because of the baby. Give it some time. Think this through."

He knew she was serious, and that this was truly bothering her. That was his fault. He should have already come clean as to how he felt about her. He should have told her that the reason he'd never loved another woman was because all other women weren't her. He should have made her understand that there was no amount of her baggage that he couldn't carry. And he should have spelled out that he'd love her little girl as much as he loved the baby they'd made together.

Of course, Kace had just realized all of that right now.

"Okay, I've thought it through, and I want you to marry me," Kace said.

"O-tay," Marley attempted.

Kace kissed her on her cake-sticky cheek. The kid was definitely on his side.

Jana stood there, nibbling on her bottom lip, but she didn't stop him when he slid the ring on her finger. She looked at it, blinking back tears, and she was still blinking them when she looked at him.

"Okay," Jana said, "but I don't want the wedding

to be until after the baby comes. That will give you plenty of time to change your mind."

He wouldn't change his mind. Nope. As far as he was concerned his proposal and her answer were set in stone.

Kace grinned and kissed her with that grin still on his mouth. It made for an interesting lip-lock. "After the wedding, can I come to your place so we can make out?" he asked.

Jana pressed her mouth against his ear and tongue kissed him. Kace was going to take that as a yes.

* * * * *

Don't miss the previous books in
USA TODAY *bestselling author*
Delores Fossen's Coldwater Texas series:

Lone Star Christmas
Hot Texas Sunrise
Sweet Summer Sunset

Available now from HQN Books!

SPECIAL EXCERPT FROM

⊞ HARLEQUIN®

I N T R I G U E

*When her WITSEC location is compromised,
former profiler Gemma Hanson turns to the only man
who can keep her safe: Sheriff Kellan Slater. The only
problem is, they share a complicated past...and an
intense chemistry that has never cooled.*

Read on for a sneak peek of
Safety Breach,
part of Longview Ridge Ranch
by USA TODAY *bestselling author Delores Fossen.*

"Why did you say you owed me?" she asked.

The question came out of the blue and threw him, so much so that he gulped down too much coffee and nearly choked. Hardly the reaction for a tough-nosed cop. But his reaction to her hadn't exactly been all badge, either.

Kellan lifted his shoulder and wanted to kick himself for ever bringing it up in the first place. Bad timing, he thought, and wondered if there would ever be a good time for him to grovel.

"I didn't stop Eric from shooting you that night." He said that fast. Not a drop of sugarcoating. "You, my father and Dusty. I'm sorry for that."

Her silence and the shimmering look in her eyes made him stupid, and that was the only excuse he could come up with for why he kept talking.

"It's easier for me to toss some of the blame at you for not ID'ing a killer sooner," he added. And he still did blame her, in part, for that. "But it was my job to stop him before he killed two people and injured another while he was right under my nose."

The silence just kept on going. So much so that Kellan turned, ready to go back to his desk so that he wouldn't continue to prattle on. Gemma stopped him by putting her hand on his arm. It was like a trigger that sent his gaze searching for hers. Wasn't hard to find when she stood and met him eye to eye.

"It was easier for me to toss some of the blame at you, too." She made another of those sighs. "But there was no stopping Eric that night. The stopping should have happened prior to that. I should have seen the signs." When he started to speak, Gemma lifted her hand to silence him. "And please don't tell me that it's all right, that I'm not at fault. I don't think I could take that right now."

Unfortunately, Kellan understood just what she meant. They were both still hurting, and a mutual sympathyfest was only going to make it harder. They couldn't go back. Couldn't undo. And that left them with only one direction. Looking ahead and putting this son of a bitch in a hole where he belonged.

Don't miss Safety Breach *by Delores Fossen,*
available December 2019 wherever
Harlequin® Intrigue books and ebooks are sold.

Harlequin.com

USA TODAY bestselling author

DELORES FOSSEN

**returns with a new series, Lone Star Ridge,
featuring the ranching Jameson brothers who
are reunited with their childhood sweethearts.**

Their past never faded—and neither did their passion.

TANGLED UP
IN TEXAS

"Clear off space on your keeper shelf, Fossen has arrived."
—*New York Times* bestselling author Lori Wilde

Order your copy today!

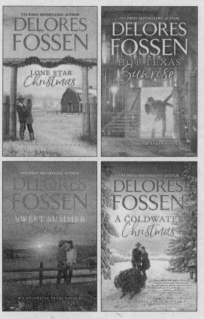

Don't miss the first book in the brand-new
Painted Pony Creek series by
#1 New York Times bestselling author

LINDA LAEL MILLER

COUNTRY STRONG

**A story about three best friends whose strength,
honor and independence exemplify the
Montana land they love.**

"Linda Lael Miller creates vibrant characters and stories
I defy you to forget."
—#1 *New York Times* bestselling author
Debbie Macomber

On sale January 28, 2020!

HQN™
www.HQNBooks.com

PHLLMCS0919

Get 4 FREE REWARDS!

We'll send you 2 FREE Books plus 2 FREE Mystery Gifts.

FREE Value Over **$20**

Both the **Romance** and **Suspense** collections feature compelling novels written by many of today's bestselling authors.

YES! Please send me 2 FREE novels from the Essential Romance or Essential Suspense Collection and my 2 FREE gifts (gifts are worth about $10 retail). After receiving them, if I don't wish to receive any more books, I can return the shipping statement marked "cancel." If I don't cancel, I will receive 4 brand-new novels every month and be billed just $6.99 each in the U.S. or $7.24 each in Canada. That's a savings of at least 13% off the cover price. It's quite a bargain! Shipping and handling is just 50¢ per book in the U.S. and $1.25 per book in Canada.* I understand that accepting the 2 free books and gifts places me under no obligation to buy anything. I can always return a shipment and cancel at any time. The free books and gifts are mine to keep no matter what I decide.

Choose one: ☐ **Essential Romance**   ☐ **Essential Suspense**
                  (194/304 MDN GNNP)   (191/391 MDN GNNP)

Name (please print)

Address   Apt. #

City   State/Province   Zip/Postal Code

Mail to the Reader Service:
IN U.S.A.: P.O. Box 1341, Buffalo, NY 14240-8531
IN CANADA: P.O. Box 603, Fort Erie, Ontario L2A 5X3

Want to try 2 free books from another series? Call 1-800-873-8635 or visit www.ReaderService.com.

---

*Terms and prices subject to change without notice. Prices do not include sales taxes, which will be charged (if applicable) based on your state or country of residence. Canadian residents will be charged applicable taxes. Offer not valid in Quebec. This offer is limited to one order per household. Books received may not be as shown. Not valid for current subscribers to the Essential Romance or Essential Suspense Collection. All orders subject to approval. Credit or debit balances in a customer's account(s) may be offset by any other outstanding balance owed by or to the customer. Please allow 4 to 6 weeks for delivery. Offer available while quantities last.

Your Privacy—The Reader Service is committed to protecting your privacy. Our Privacy Policy is available online at www.ReaderService.com or upon request from the Reader Service. We make a portion of our mailing list available to reputable third parties that offer products we believe may interest you. If you prefer that we not exchange your name with third parties, or if you wish to clarify or modify your communication preferences, please visit us at www.ReaderService.com/consumerschoice or write to us at Reader Service Preference Service, P.O. Box 9062, Buffalo, NY 14240-9062. Include your complete name and address.

STRS20